BY RACHEL JOYCE

The Homemade God

Maureen Fry and the Angel of the North

Miss Benson's Beetle

The Music Shop

A Snow Garden and Other Stories

The Love Song of Miss Queenie Hennessy

Perfect

The Unlikely Pilgrimage of Harold Fry

THE HOMEMADE GOD

THE HOMEMADE GOD

A Novel

Rachel Joyce

THE DIAL PRESS
NEW YORK

Published in the United States by The Dial Press, an imprint of Random House, a division of Penguin Random House LLC, 1745 Broadway, New York, NY 10019.

THE DIAL PRESS is a registered trademark and the colophon is a trademark of Penguin Random House LLC.

Originally published in the United Kingdom by Doubleday, an imprint of Transworld Publishers, a division of Penguin Random House UK.

Hardback ISBN 978-0-593-44829-8
Ebook ISBN 978-0-593-44830-4

Printed in the United States of America on acid-free paper

randomhousebooks.com
penguinrandomhouse.com

2 4 6 8 9 7 5 3 1

FIRST U.S. EDITION

BOOK TEAM: Production editor: Andy Lefkowitz • Managing editor: Rebecca Berlant • Production manager: Richard Elman • Proofreaders: Dan Goff, Becky Maines, Marcell Rosenblatt, and Barbara Stussy

Book design by Caroline Cunningham

Title page and part opener image of Lake Orta: marcovarro/Adobe Stock

The authorized representative in the EU for product safety and compliance is Penguin Random House Ireland, Morrison Chambers, 32 Nassau Street, Dublin D02 YH68, Ireland, https://eu-contact.penguin.ie.

For Paul, as always

A lake is earth's eye; looking into which the beholder measures the depths of his own nature.

—Henry David Thoreau on Walden Pond, *Walden*

THE HOMEMADE GOD

Prologue

That was the summer they wore flip-flops. Everywhere they went, they wore them. The bank, the *gelateria*, the hair salon and the bar, but also the undertaker and the police. Four pairs of rubber shoes on white-hot stone.

Slap slap, slap slap.

There was a heat wave all over Europe. No one could remember a summer like it. There were water shortages and wildfires. Warnings about too much sun and dehydration. Really the lake was the only place to be. Midday it shot forth tiny flints of light, but it could turn every color under the sun, and in the early mornings it was the best. There might be low-slung mists so that everything disappeared, including the reeds, and only the little island was left, floating in the middle on a bed of cloud. Or on a clear day the water was a piece of glass with a deep-blue sky inside it, fringed on all sides by hills, an upside-down island growing out of the one on top, and swallows skimming beneath the surface. At night the dark smelled of sweetened cypress, with all the lights across the mainland breaking out like low stars.

Slap slap they went, following each up and down. Whenever he hears flip-flops, Goose remembers that summer his father died on an Italian lake and he went with his three sisters to fetch him home. Sometimes, on the edge of sleep, he even finds himself back on the island in the middle, though in truth he hasn't been there for years. Like a ghost, he moves through the villa he knew so well—all those frescoed rooms, the glasshouse filled with lemon trees, the music salon with its ten harps that no one could play—until at last he finds Netta hunting for a phone signal in her giant straw hat, or Susan shining with sweat in the kitchen against a background of green majolica tiles, or Iris leaving food for the stray cat, and it's strange how content it makes him feel, how secure and happy. ("Iris!" Netta will roar. "Do not let that manky thing inside!" Too late. It is drinking milk on the table.) He goes over that summer in his mind, ransacking it for signs and clues, different ways of doing things from the terrible ways they got done. And yet it's also true he finds them howling with laughter, all four of them. He can't think how it was so funny, except it was. Until that summer, he had no idea you could laugh like that and still be sad.

They had to stick together, his sisters said. They were family. They shared the same beginning. They were woven into the same story. They'd spent birthdays together, Christmases together, all those summers on the lake. No one knew them the way they knew each other, so if they stuck together it would be all right. They would fetch their father's body and find his last painting. But his sisters had no idea what was coming, or what Bella-Mae might do next. They had no idea that trying to stay close would be the one thing that finally split them apart, as if she had crawled inside hairline fractures they could not see, and pushed them so far that one crack joined with another, then another, until everything broke, like a shattered pot. And yet it's strange. To this day, Goose is still not sure who she was, not really. An innocent, a grifter, worse? Even the hyphen in the middle of her name suggests not one person but two at the very least, holding hands. If only he had been different, strong and unbending like his father, he might have stopped things before it was too late. He could still be with his sisters now. But he isn't. He is a man in his mid-forties sending invites they'll say yes to, knowing full well they won't come.

Slap slap went their flip-flops, side by side on Lake Orta. *Slap slap, slap slap.*

PART ONE

Bella-Mae

London, 2015

1

Old Rogue

The first Netta heard about her was in a noodle bar on Greek Street. The Singing Wok was one of those new places in a basement that were opening all over Soho. You brought your own drink, and tables were long communal trestles with benches instead of chairs. The noise banged against the walls and was mind-blowing.

It was lunchtime, mid-March. Netta was perched at the end of a crowded table, not a wineglass in sight, let alone a bottle, just tin cups, as if everyone was on a camping holiday. If she'd known about the whole Bring Your Own, she would have Brought Some. As it was, she had tap water. Not so much as a cube of ice. Susan was rammed in beside her, then Goose, while their youngest sister, Iris, sat on the opposite side with their father.

Vic never went to noodle bars. He liked old-fashioned restaurants with furry wallpaper and starched white cloths, where he ate enough steak and ice-cream sundae to cause any normal person a cardiovascular attack. After that, he drank until he fell over. At which point, Netta or Susan, Goose or Iris—whoever's number he could pull into focus first—rescued him and got him home. It was a habit Netta was used to, reassuring in its way, if only because she knew where she stood. And as the eldest, she liked nothing more than knowing where she stood. As a child, she was always scrambling to the top of things for this exact reason, while the other three waited, admiring and grateful, below.

But here they were in a noodle bar. No alcohol. Vic using chopsticks—how had he learned to hold a chopstick?—while he drank a bowl of tea. When did he ever drink tea? He'd even brought his own Thermos. Then, just as Susan began a story about her stepsons, he banged the table and interrupted: "So, come on, kids. Who's guessed my news?"

Netta had turned forty. Susan was chasing her tail at thirty-nine. There wasn't a full year between them. Gustav, but they all called him Goose because as a boy he could never say his own name, was thirty-six, while Iris was seven years younger than Netta at thirty-three. Already they had lived more years than their mother. Yet Vic still called them kids and they called him Daddy.

He hit the table again. "Guess!" he said. "You'll never guess!"

He was right. Netta hadn't a clue. She shot a look at Susan, who shot one straight back: clearly she hadn't got a clue either. At the end of the bench, Goose began spiraling his noodles, while Iris placed all the bits of spinach and peppers from her vegetarian option to the side because she had a thing about not eating food that was green or red. No one knew why. Least of all Iris.

"Okay," said Netta. "I'll take a guess. You've finished the new painting."

"Nice try, Antoinetta. But you're wrong. For once, you're wrong. Goose? You guess."

Goose bowed his head so that he was hidden by dark-yellow hair. "I don't know. You know I don't. You're going to retire?"

"Retire? What would you do if I retired? You'd be on the streets. And when are you going to get a haircut? You look like a hippie. Before we know it, you'll be wearing a skirt."

"Please let's not spoil this," said Iris to her noodles, which were now immaculately separated from her green and red vegetables. "It's so nice being together."

Vic had summoned them by way of one of his infrequent group

texts. He'd sent the address of the Singing Wok and told them to get there early, then wait in the queue. He had news, he said.

"So why does he want to tell us in a noodle bar?" Netta had rung Susan to ask. "Do you think he's ill?"

Susan said she was worrying about the same thing, though why he would tell them bad news in a noodle bar she had no idea. Apparently she hadn't seen him for a few weeks, despite the fact that she always did his food shopping and cleaned his flat, but she just assumed he was at the studio over in King's Cross. After that, Netta got on the phone to Goose, then called Susan straight back, though it turned out Susan had done the exact same thing and also rung Goose, so mainly what they did was repeat what they already knew: namely that their father seemed not to have been at home but he'd barely crossed London to set foot in his studio either.

"Do you think he's having some kind of crisis?" said Susan. "A loss of confidence or something? He did seem low before Christmas. Or maybe his health is bothering him and he's too frightened to say. You know what he's like about doctors."

"I'll check with Iris," Netta said.

"Call me as soon as you've spoken," said Susan.

But not even Iris had seen their father and she only lived around the corner from his flat. "No, he's been too busy to meet up," she said, when Netta finally got hold of her. Iris still insisted on using her ancient Nokia phone, which was frequently out of charge and had the keypad strapped on with an elastic band. It would be quicker to communicate via a man on a horse, although she'd want to feed the horse and look after it, less so the man. "He said there were things he had to do," she told Netta. "I assumed it was the big new painting."

So Netta had arrived at midday, just as he said. Vic wasn't there, but that was no surprise. He wore a Rolex the size of a yo-yo but that didn't mean he ever checked the time. Susan was already with Iris in the queue, while Goose searched for a railing to chain up Iris's bike.

"You look well."

"No, *you* look well," they kept saying, like people who'd barely met, instead of siblings who rang each other all the time. It was only once Netta had got them a table downstairs, shared with a family of at least three generations, that their father finally arrived.

"I am late! I am late!" he roared, as if not only his children but the whole noodle bar had been on tenterhooks.

She couldn't stop staring. Because, whatever his news, he'd lost weight. Netta couldn't remember him so thin. Vic had always been good-looking—the shambles of his good looks only seemed to improve them, as if he were handsome by mistake—while years of too much drink and rich food had left him massive in every dimension. Now the skin hung from his neck in thick turkey folds and his face caved in beneath the cheekbones. But he didn't seem worried. He certainly didn't mention feeling ill, so she and Susan had been way off the mark about that. His white hair, always uncombed, was pulled into a ponytail, like a little fountain. His eyebrows that grew in every direction except sideways had been trimmed into neat arches. His face was clean and freshly shaved, except for a spiky thing on his chin that she realized, with a flicker of astonishment, was a goatee.

Even his clothes seemed to belong to a different man. On the whole, Vic walked a thin line between hung-over and actively drunk, and wore whatever item he happened to find on the end of his foot when he got up. But today he was in a smart collarless linen shirt she had never seen before, and a matching pair of white trousers. Not a spot of paint anywhere. He didn't smell of turps, but something altogether sweeter, like pine cones dipped in lemon. All in all, he looked more like a friendly hygienist than an artist. He was even tucking a paper napkin under his chin.

"Iris, my darling. Can you not guess?"

"I'm sorry, Daddy. I can't."

"Susan?"

"No, Daddy. I'd have said the same as Netta. I'd have guessed you've finished the new painting, but I know you want to take your time with this one so I don't even know why I said that. How's it going, by the way? We're all so excited."

When Susan was flustered, red spear shapes flared up and down her neck. Their father blew her a kiss. "Dear Suzie," he said. "One day you will mount my exhibition."

"You know how much I'd love that, Daddy."

"So are you going to tell us?" interrupted Netta, pricked by a distant jealousy, sharp as a pin. "Are you going to tell us your news or must we sit here making guesses all day?"

Vic had a temper, but she liked standing up to him and she knew he expected it. My second in command, he called her: She had been put into her mother's shoes as a child, without ever becoming maternal. It was Susan who was the natural. "I'm getting married," he said.

"I'm sorry, what?" said Netta. Somehow she had lost her place in the conversation.

"I've met the love of my life. Her name is Bella-Mae. And I'm going to marry her."

There was a pause. A hiatus that felt like reaching the edge of a cliff and not daring to move a muscle in case you went careering over the top. Netta could sense the other three looking at her, waiting for her to show them what to do, but he had completely stumped her. Then suddenly the people none of them knew farther along the table were laughing and holding up their tin tumblers, calling, "Congratulations!"

"My God," said Netta. "Really?"

Then Susan said the same. "My God. Really?"

"Wow," said Goose. "Wow, wow," until Iris threw her arms around Vic and said, "Congratulations, Daddy!" and that became the whole song. A mix of "Wow, My God, Congratulations." At this point, Netta still had no idea if he was serious. She was smiling, though. They were all smiling. But in more of a rictus kind of way.

Questions followed, questions that were confused and shocked, but also delivered at full volume because of the terrible background noise, so that they came out sounding somewhere in the middle between lost and aggressive. Who was Bella-Mae? When had their father met her? Was she another artist? Did she have adult children too? Grandchildren? Why had Vic never mentioned her before? Even Goose managed to say, "Bella-Mae? Has she been to the studio? I don't remember anyone called Bella-Mae." Netta still thought this had to be another of their father's jokes.

Only it didn't seem like joking. He answered them slowly and with a kind of awe, as if he had won the lottery without buying a ticket. Bella-Mae was an artist, he said. A true artist. He had met her online six weeks ago. No, she had no grandchildren. No children either. After a few days of constant online messaging they'd agreed to cut out the middleman and meet face-to-face. It had been like an explosion of two minds. They'd stayed up all night talking and all the next day, and they had so much still to talk about, they'd been talking here, there and everywhere, ever since. Only a few days ago, she had moved into his flat. "Wait—she's living with you now?" said Netta, but he sailed straight through that.

"She is twenty-seven," he said.

"Sorry, what did you just say?"

Months later, Netta would remember something else. A woman appearing, perhaps from the door, pressing past their table, a little too close. Brushing her hip against her father's shoulder. Their eyes appearing to meet. A smell, too, surprisingly masculine, with something sweet underneath. She was dressed, the same as Netta, top to toe in black. Had her father shaken his head? She couldn't say. There was so much going on.

"You're worrying about nothing." He laughed as they put forward the reasons he might pause a moment. The reasons he might, you know, think twice about marrying a woman he'd met only five minutes ago, who was also six years younger than his youngest daughter, let alone move her into his bachelor apartment overlooking Regent's Park. He'd had so many affairs since they were children that Netta couldn't remember half of the women, but he'd never talked about getting married. "Your mother was the only woman for me," he'd cry down the phone in his more drunken middle-of-the-night moments. And while this wasn't remotely true—he'd even slept with their au pairs—it had woven itself into the weft and warp of the family myth and acted as a form of security. Vic might fall in love at the drop of a hat, but his children were all he had. He would always provide for them.

"I am the happiest man in the world," he said, pouring more tea from his Thermos. "I've never felt so fit and young."

"But twenty-seven?" said Netta. She laughed, though she wasn't in the least bit joking. "Is she really only twenty-seven?"

"Goodness! That seems young!" said Susan. Also laughing and clearly not meaning it.

"Are you sure?" said Netta, daring to go further. "Are you sure she's not after your money?"

Susan gave her the smallest prod, warning her to be careful, but once again, their father did not explode. He gave a beaming smile, charm itself. "She's not that kind of person. She's not into material things. That's not the point for her. She doesn't even like my art."

A woman who didn't like his art? None of this was making sense. No one dared to criticize Vic's art. It was the center of everything. He rooted through his pockets and pulled out a photo-booth headshot, which he smoothed with his fingertips as if he expected it to break into a smile. Goose accepted the photo almost reverentially, cradling it in his big soft hands, while Susan and Netta craned forward, although Netta couldn't really see until he passed it to Susan and she gave it to Netta.

Close up, all she could make out of her father's bride-to-be was a sliver of nose and mouth, flanked by a wall of thick black hair. If it wasn't for that speck of nose, Netta would honestly have thought she was looking at the back of her head. She must have set the seat too low as well: half the picture was taken up by the background, so that even in a portrait photograph she seemed to be hiding.

"She has the daintiest hands," their father said with wonder to Iris, who said, "She's so beautiful, Daddy," as if they were speaking about something he had discovered on the pavement, like an ornamental bird.

"No, no. I'm sorry. I don't understand," Netta said, her voice straining to remain both light and audible. "You met this woman on your laptop?"

"I told you. Her name's Bella-Mae."

"Was it through a dating company?"

"Of course it wasn't a dating company."

"Facebook?"

He looked appalled. "I don't do Facebook. I never have."

Iris nodded and took another sip of her water, retiring from the conversation. Goose, who wasn't really anywhere near it, blinked again and smiled. Susan ran her fingers through her shoulder-length hair. It was flat as a veil.

"But you are seventy-six, Daddy." Somehow, in her shock, Netta was now telling her father things about himself he already knew.

"Age is only in the mind, Antoinetta. We're soulmates. We can't wait to tie the knot. She is the one. The love of my life."

All this would explain, of course, why he'd been so quiet recently, and perhaps why he looked so clean, though it wouldn't account for the drastic weight loss.

"She gives me herbs," he said.

"Herbs?" said Susan.

"I take them for my health. I drink them as tea. She makes them for me especially."

"She gives you herbs? And you drink them? Is this what you're having now?"

"Susan!" laughed their father. "You were always such a prude." He paused and took another sip of his tea.

"I'm just asking how much you know about someone you're talking about marrying. That doesn't seem prudish, Daddy. And what are these herbs exactly?"

But Vic never got to tell them. Iris swallowed something the wrong way and began to cough so much she couldn't stop. Susan went scrabbling through Iris's rucksack for her puffer, while Netta yelled at the waiter to fetch more water. Then the little fit passed and she was calm again. "I think it's excitement," she said. "Sorry, everyone. It's such lovely news, Daddy."

Vic threw his arm around her and she folded her body into his, as if to make the smallest possible gift of herself.

Netta was the spitting image of her father, but in female form. She had his wild hair, though hers was still dark and pulled into a semi-messy topknot on the back of her head, and she had his green eyes, too, his sharp nose, the slightly pugilistic set of his jaw. She'd learned early in life that, while she wasn't pretty in the conventional sense, like Susan, she was striking and that was even more powerful because she looked so unapologetically like herself. The only thing she hadn't inherited was Vic's height and it still shocked her that she was the shortest of the family—somehow, as the baby, she had expected Iris to be that. Susan was a fraction taller than Netta, her face softened by their mother's extraordinary pale eyes, though she hated her hair and was always straightening it, while Goose was as tall and broad as Vic, except he lacked the puff to fill it. Even his hands seemed too big. He was always lacing them behind his back, or swinging them out of the way. But the point was, you had only to glance at the three of them to see they'd pooled the same genes. Iris, though, with her long limbs and pale-gold bob, her sweet dolly face, was like a child from a different family. No one wanted to hurt Iris. It would be like taking a kick at Bambi.

"You okay, Iris?" Netta said.

"Yes, I'm all good."

"It's because she works too hard," said Vic.

"I'm only a waitress, Daddy."

"You'll never find a man if you don't look after yourself."

"I'm not looking for a man. I like my life as it is."

Netta said could they get back to Bella-Mae for one more second? "I still don't understand why you need to get married. If she's only just moved in, why don't you take your time? Get to know one another? You don't have to rush."

"I already know her. I want to marry her. Bella-Mae has bought her dress."

"But I thought that wasn't the point for her? I thought she wasn't into material things?"

Vic ignored Netta, or perhaps he was so happy he failed to hear. "After the wedding, we're going to the island. I want you to come, all four of you."

"But the wedding, Daddy?" said Iris. "What about the wedding? When is that?"

"It's going to be different. Bella-Mae wants it to be small. She doesn't want any press. She's a very private person—"

"But we'll be there, Daddy? You can't get married without us."

Vic ducked, as if the question was something difficult making its way toward him that he could avoid simply by repositioning his head. The answer was clear. Even Iris looked shocked. "The wedding is a formality, Little Fish. It's a piece of paper. The real celebration will happen at Lake Orta when we're together, like the old days. Bella-Mae asks about you all the time. I've never met anyone like her. She's made an honest man of me at last. And yet—I don't know—" He broke off, clutching at their hands and bundling them inside his own.

"Daddy, are you okay?" said Iris. "What is it?"

His mood had shifted again. He lifted his eyes toward the door, and Netta was appalled to see the light reflect a sudden tear. If only he would take off that paper napkin: He looked like a child. She couldn't bear to see her father so strange and small, as though all the greatness in his life had never happened and his whole existence had contracted to this tiny point in time. She didn't want him in a clean shirt with a funny goatee, drinking tea for his health; she wanted him covered with paint, so much paint it was in his ears, barking out insults and pouring too much red wine. She held his hand tight, really tight, willing him to come back.

"And yet I do not know," he said again, "what I have done to deserve her. Of all the people in the world she could have married, why would she choose an old rogue like me?"

2

Same Again, Please

They hugged their father at the end of the meal. You could say what you liked about Vic Kemp. You could say he was difficult, an alcoholic, a womanizer. You would be right on all counts. But he was also the best hugger in the world. It was like being held by a hill. When they were little, he could carry all three girls, squealing in delight, on his back, with Goose balanced on his shoes and clinging for dear life to his knees. He paid the bill and made more apologies about the wedding, promising how much fun they would have on the lake. There would be card games and swimming races, like the old days—they were all excellent swimmers. There would be lunches at the Venus restaurant that went on so long they became dinner, and hurricane lamps at night, their light spilling through the black water. They followed him up into the soft March sunshine, and then he was off, waving his goodbyes so extravagantly—"*Ciao* for now! Love you! See you soon!"—that he stepped into the traffic without looking and almost orphaned them on the spot.

Susan linked arms with Netta and pulled her close. Iris and Goose came alongside, him wheeling her bike. "You okay, sis?" said Susan.

"Fuck, no," said Netta. "That was too weird. Let's keep walking, can we?"

Susan adored Netta. As a child, she'd worn the same clothes and her hair in the same ponytail. She'd even thought the same thoughts, if not at the same moment then only a fraction of a second behind. They'd both entered a beauty pageant when they were girls, which Netta won because Netta always did, but Susan had happily spent the afternoon in a silky pink sash that said *Runner-up*. When Netta left home for university, she'd left a Netta-shaped hole in Susan too. For a while Susan slept in her sister's old room because it was the only place that smelled of Netta's patchouli oil and matched the emptiness inside her.

"I know it sounds odd, but I think Daddy's happy," said Iris. "He's been so lonely recently. I think he's really in love."

"Seriously?" said Netta. "I mean, seriously? He's known her six weeks. Besides, if he's so lonely he could get a cat. Apart from the fact he'd kill it, of course."

"And how can you say he's lonely?" said Susan. "He has us."

"This isn't love. I'm sorry, Iris. It's no wonder Daddy's been avoiding us. He's been shacked up with a twenty-seven-year-old."

But Iris stood her ground. She actually stopped walking for a moment. "Daddy wasn't drunk today. You saw that. He had tea."

"Yes, the tea," said Susan. "What is that exactly?"

"It's for his health. He told us. And it's working. He looks really well, with his smart hair and new clothes and everything. I didn't recognize him at first. I think Bella-Mae is good for him. And it would be lovely to be together on the lake. I miss the island so much."

"Oh, *Iris*," said Netta, without a hint of irony. "Why isn't the rest of the world as nice as you?"

They bought sweets to share and kept walking. Leaf buds were tiny green knots, waiting to crack, while the windows of the cafés and bars of Soho were folded open, releasing all the noise and smells from inside. It was a lovely day for mid-March, the promise of spring after a long winter, yet their father's news had left Susan feeling cut adrift, as if the blue sky and the tight little buds, the people taking first picnics in Soho Square and drinking at pavement tables, even the bossa nova coming from a rooftop, belonged to a world she had no part of. It had been like this when they were children and Vic started a new painting. His obsession would leave them abandoned in a place that seemed to have no bottom, no top, and no walls either. The only thing they could do was stick together.

Every summer on the island, they'd leave whichever au pair it was that year flat out on a sun-lounger and take the passenger boat to the mainland. They knew everyone in Orta San Giulio. The waiters from the lakeside bars, the one-eyed woman in the deli, the men dressed as navy captains selling tickets for water taxis from the jetty. They'd play brilliant games invented by Netta where they were secret agents following day-trippers she said were really Russian spies, or they'd pretend to be film stars. (Susan was Olivia Newton-John, Netta was Sigourney Weaver, Goose was never quite sure who he should be, while Iris always wanted to be a dog or a pony. "Okay. Lassie is a famous film dog," Netta would say. "You can be Lassie. And, Goose, you're Paul Newman.")

They did their first everything in Orta. Their first mopeds, their first cigarettes, their first vodka. They even went on Netta's first date, though Susan had to sit at another table with the little ones. At the end of each day they'd ferry back to the island sunburnt, often having lost at least one item of clothing between them, and their father didn't know they'd been gone.

They kept going, heading nowhere, but safe so long as they stayed together, until Netta said, "Does anyone fancy a drink at Kettner's? I could phone in sick." She said it with an air of defeat, as if they had agreed to walk forever.

"I can't afford Kettner's," said Goose.

Iris said she couldn't either and, anyway, she was wearing her old coat. Susan said Warwick would be waiting for her at home, so she'd better get a move on.

But none of that made any difference. They still went.

Susan drank too fast, like the old days when she was nineteen, working on the cookery page for a women's magazine around the corner. That had been when Kettner's was part pizza restaurant with tiny white mosaic tiles on the floor, and part champagne bar with bistro-style round tables and lamps made of colored glass. She would trail after the other women from the magazine and they would talk about restaurants Susan had never heard of and food she'd never tried, like Greek mezze and Middle Eastern kofta. Aside from the villa on the lake, Susan had thought Kettner's was the most exotic place in the world.

It was still lovely. A woman in a green dress was singing at the piano. Susan was there with her siblings. Why, then, did it not seem enough? It had to be shock. The thought that their father was planning to remarry was so startling and unexpected, Susan had no idea how to take it in. She didn't even know how to make a general approach. What would happen to her if he had a new wife? It was her role to look after Vic. Netta might be the oldest and his second in command, but Susan was a close third. She had made herself just as irreplaceable over the years, doing all the domestic tasks that Netta didn't understand but Susan was so good at, and without which everything would fall apart. Like keeping his flat clean, for instance, and stocking up the fridge with homemade meals. Putting fresh fruit in the bowl because otherwise he'd get no vitamin C, though she'd have to throw most of it out at the end of the week.

Netta had her brilliant career in litigation, but looking after Vic was one of the few things that brought real color to Susan's life. ("Such an amazing man," her friends at book club would say. "What an amazing childhood you had." It made her feel ever so slightly above them, but in a good way, because she'd never gone to university like Netta and the books they chose made her feel stupid.) And what about Bella-Mae's age? Did she really need to be only twenty-seven? Of course there was the gap between Susan and Warwick, but it was twenty-one years, not nearly fifty, and at least when they first dated everyone knew who he was—he lived down the road. Anyway, why did her father need to get married? Apart from their mother, he'd always been dead set against it. When Warwick asked him for Susan's hand, Vic was so horrified he walked out of the room. It had been almost too much for Susan, holding her nerve. So what could have made him change his mind? It had to be Bella-Mae. She must be pushing him.

"Well, of course she is," said Netta. "He's a rich man."

"But Daddy told us she's not into his money," said Iris. "He said she's an artist."

"Oh, Iris," sang Netta. Then she said, "She probably has a sketch-pad, and thinks that's the same thing."

"That's right," said Susan.

"Look, I'm a lawyer. There's no way I am going to let this girl ruin Daddy's life. And she's not going to ruin my drink with you three either." Netta told them about a case at work where a family had sued one another over their mother's ashes. "In the end they split them into five canisters and scattered them in separate places. Can you imagine?"

Then Iris chipped in and told them about her job at the burger restaurant where the smell of meat fat got into everything, including her hair, so she had to shower as soon as she got home. Susan had no idea why her youngest sister insisted on doing these horrible jobs when their father had paid outright for her maisonette, just as she didn't know why Iris's whole wardrobe came from charity shops. Inside that shabby dress, she had a figure to die for. But still. She listened carefully until Iris—who'd barely spoken, and whispered most of it: really, you had to be expecting her voice to hear it—said, "I'm talking too much. How are the twins?"

Susan gave a fast Christmas-card kind of update of what her stepsons were up to, though she left out how tricky it still was to have a conversation with them, and concentrated more on how brilliantly they were doing in the City. Then Netta said she'd been a saint with those kids, and Susan said, "Well, I do my best," even though having them to stay when they were little had been so hard she used to phone Netta from inside the airing cupboard, just to stop crying.

"I know you're not supposed to say this about children," said Netta, "but I could happily have killed those twins when they were small. Now who wants another?"

More drinks came and more drinks were drunk. Finally Susan felt the alcohol unbuckling her and she began to relax.

"Fair play to Daddy, though," said Netta. "I had no idea he was still doing it. I thought he was way past all that."

"Oh, God, please stop right there," said Susan. "This is one thing I do not want to think about."

"The tea she gives him, Iris?"

"What about it?"

"I bet it's Viagra."

"Oh, God, oh, God," said Susan. "No, Netta. No."

It was funny, though, and she couldn't help it: she began to laugh. Then they all cracked up, even Iris, because suddenly everything was hilarious. Their father's terrible goatee and his paint-free clothes, as well as his new health plan, and insisting they all meet in the loudest noodle bar in central London. By now, Netta's topknot was slipping to one side, Iris was so flushed she looked verging on healthy, and Goose was laughing to the point where he was hanging over his chair, with happy lines all over his face as if someone had been at him with a Sharpie pen.

"Remember Microwave Laura?" said Netta. "Remember the time she almost set fire to Iris?"

"Stop, Netta! Stop!" screeched Susan. "She was the worst au pair in the world. How did we get to be adults?"

It dawned on her that the room had begun to slide around at the edges. She had gone from stone-cold sober to full-on slaughtered without the sweetly drunk bit in the middle. Now she could swear there were two ladies in green dresses at the piano, kind of bobbing up and down, and her skirt felt too tight. ("Is that new?" Warwick had asked this morning, and Susan had lied and told him it wasn't. There wasn't even anything accusing in the way he said it—Warwick didn't have an accusing bone in his body—but she didn't want him thinking she needed a new suit to meet up with her family, just as she didn't want him thinking she'd had her hair especially straightened.) She went to stand, but the ground was a seesaw so she sat again and undid her zip at the back, where no one could see. Still, she'd meant what she'd said. It seemed so alive, so essential and good, this love for Netta and Goose and Iris. Imagine! Imagine being an only child, like Warwick. Brought up with no one except yourself. "You don't marry one of them, you marry the whole family," he'd said once, to Netta's fiancé. But since her marriage had lasted only a short while, that was water under the bridge.

"No one understands me like you three," Susan said. "Can you believe it? I've been married seventeen years. But cut me open and you know what you'd find? *Kemp.* Stamped in a pink circle, all the way through me. I'm like a stick of rock. We are all. We're sticks of rock with Kemp stamped inside us. We should get tattoos. It would be like a family thing. We'd all be matching."

"What would Warwick say if you got a tattoo?" said Netta.

"I don't know. I could get it somewhere he never looks. My arms. Or, better still, my bottom."

"He never looks there? Seriously? Where does he look?"

Susan laughed. "Well, just kind of my face. He hasn't looked at the rest of me in years."

"I'd get a tattoo," said Goose, "if you three did."

Iris said why not get "Kemp" but in Chinese characters? Goose said what about birds, and Susan said they could all get little circles.

"Why would we get those?" said Netta.

"Remember how Iris wanted to be a saint when she grew up? We could get little circles like halos. Like we were all the same."

"It's true. I did used to want to be a saint. I put that in my school book. The teacher called Daddy in because she thought I had issues."

Susan said she'd wanted to be a cleaning lady, and she wasn't even joking. That was before she'd wanted to be a TV chef. "Look at me now," she said. She laughed, but suddenly it felt empty again.

"Or what about a tattoo of the house?" said Iris. She was getting really into this whole idea. "Like at the lake?"

"Oh my God!" said Susan. "Imagine if all four of us got the house on the lake."

"I'd do it," said Goose.

"I'd so do it," said Iris. "We could do it right now. We're in Soho."

"Are you all crazy?" said Netta. "I'm not getting a fucking house tattooed on my arse. Now who wants another drink?"

Iris said, "I'm just saying I know what Suz means. I don't have anyone like you. I don't even know the other people where I live. It's like the real stuff is missing."

"At least you have friends," said Goose. "I'm in the studio all day."

That set them off yet again, far more than the joke deserved, because otherwise it was too sad, and anyway—after all he'd been through—you had to love it when he said something funny.

Susan wanted to say more. She wanted more words. Better ones. She wanted everything to stay exactly like this forever. She had her friends from book club and her neighbors, the parents she'd met on weekends when the twins were growing up, but none of them came close to her siblings. Even as a child, she'd felt they were separate from other people, as if being Vic Kemp's children gave them an extra glow of specialness. The only thing she'd never understood was why her parents had given her such a plain name when the other three were so original.

She took another swallow of cocktail, feeling the smudge of it. They never drank like this at home. She made a note in her head to buy mint imperials for the train.

"I wish we could go on all night," she said.

"Me, too," said Iris.

"Like the old days. Don't you miss the old days? All those summers when we were kids?"

"Remember that time we stole Laura's happy pills?"

"Oh, God," said Susan. "That was the best day of my life."

"I miss the island so much," said Iris, all over again.

Then Goose raked back his hair and spoke in his slow, careful way as if he were coming up with the words for the first time. "I really don't think Daddy can be serious about the wedding. But this is what he does when he's working. He gets these obsessions. And the new painting's going to be his most important yet, remember? He's even using a big canvas."

"He's never done that before," said Susan, in case anyone had forgotten she knew these things too.

"Has he told you yet what it's going to be?" said Netta.

"No," said Goose. "But he's excited. I can tell. He's really excited.

He says it's going to show the art world who he really is." A waiter came past and Goose apologized, pulling his legs back under the table and smiling shyly. "As soon as it's finished, he'll move on from Bella-Mae. He may not even stay with her that long. I guess a lot of artists are the same. They'll do whatever it takes to make the work happen. To keep the little flame alight. And for him, it's falling in love. But the canvases are primed. He's ready to go."

Netta brought her head to rest on Goose's shoulder. "You're right. Look at us. We're behaving like Daddy. We're completely overreacting. He'll drop Bella-Mae. She's a passing fad, like all the others. But he could have saved us the god-awful noodle bar. I bet he hasn't told Harry about her."

At the mention of their father's dealer, Goose nodded. "It's true. He's been avoiding Harry for weeks."

"Poor Daddy," said Iris. "He works so hard. And now I feel sorry for Bella-Mae too. What will she do with her wedding dress?"

"Well, I know this might seem harsh, but one of us has to say it . . ." Susan was aware she wasn't saying anything very much because her words were sliding all over the place, but her siblings looked so joined up she felt the need to have some kind of stake in the conversation. "At least this means he'll start the new painting."

Halfway home, Susan rang Netta from the train and said she loved her. "I love you, too," said Netta.

But Susan said no, no, she really loved her. "You are the best," she said. "Truly the best. I don't know what I'd do without you." Then she began to cry because Iris was the best, and Goose was the best, but Iris lived all by herself, and so did Goose for that matter, and it was so sad what had happened to Netta with her ex, until Netta said, "Suz, hang on. What's going on here? Are you sure you're okay?"

Susan stared at her reflection in the train window—her hair had begun to frizz and somehow her face looked very bare. As a child, she'd been skinny like Iris and full of cartwheels, but she'd put on weight in her thirties that nothing would shift. She said she wasn't drunk, in case that was what Netta was thinking, and this wasn't sad crying either, but she really did love her family so much. It was just that her life was easier than theirs because she had Warwick to go home to and they had no one.

"Of course, for some of us, not having Warwick to go home to is a blessing," said Netta.

Susan laughed so much she had to cover her mouth. She said, "Will you stay on the phone with me all the way back?" Netta said yes and offered to do her entire Donna Summer medley to pass the time until Tunbridge Wells. "It's because of Daddy," Susan said, as Netta warbled "I Feel Love." She was a brilliant everything, except a singer. "No one else can come close."

Susan shut her eyes so that it was only her and Netta, and also because the window was beginning to swing, until suddenly Netta was saying, "Suz? Suz? Wake up. Can you hear me, darling? It sounds like this is your station."

3

Portrait of the Artist

Vic Kemp was a self-taught artist. "Homemade" was how he put it. Everything he knew about art he had learned from copying. He wasn't a household name, and his work had never been shown in public galleries, but you knew it without actively knowing who had done it, because it was everywhere, both online and on the high street. Posters, signed prints, greeting cards and notebooks. Even mugs, keyrings, T-shirts and coasters. His pictures told semi-erotic stories in which women in heels and red lipstick met men in pinstripe suits and trilby hats late at night when the rest of the world was asleep. They were the lonely. The lost. People caught in a time that didn't look fully real but was not strange enough to be made up. They waltzed on empty streets, smoked in late-night diners, drank in down-at-heel bars. Sometimes they checked into hotels and got out whips and gloves. "Would you say your work is really about your own sexual fantasy?" he was asked by the only journalist who ever interviewed him. Vic laughed. His art was harmless, he told her. If people couldn't face a little bit of fun between consenting adults they were fools.

"Do you feel you've been deliberately overlooked?" she persisted, holding out her Dictaphone. Vic said he didn't mind either way—but wouldn't it be nice to go for a cocktail?

It wasn't true that he didn't mind. His work was in several private galleries, but he would have given anything to be somewhere mainstream, such as the Tate. To be taken seriously as an artist. And the status, too, like being part of an elite club. But it went to prove what he'd known all along—that the art world was not for the likes of him. After all, he'd never been to art college. As a boy, he went to the kind of school where anyone who liked art was called a bender, then got their head kicked in. Vic wouldn't have known an Old Master back then if it had jumped off a wall and introduced itself. But at least his paintings weren't forgotten in vaults. At least he made money: these days, an original could sell at auction for six figures, after which there'd be all the limited prints. Besides, he'd been on the outside of things from the moment his mother realized she was pregnant. She was a barmaid and seventeen. When she broke the news to the father, he ran straight for the hills. Vic's childhood was spent hanging out in a pub with women off the street and wounded war veterans when other boys were tucked up in bed with a glass of milk and a story.

That was the reason Vic so loved the villa on the island. It was the biggest house he had ever been in. Right up there, he thought, with a fancy palace. With its brightly painted stripes of yellow and pink stucco, its windows overlooking the water, it was the kind of house where a famous artist might live, its charm only increased because it was damp and falling apart. These days, most of the villas were owned by merchant bankers and stood empty from one summer to the next, but back in the mid-eighties when he'd bought Villa Carlotta no one was interested. They'd pay you just to take it off their hands. There wasn't gas or running water. In a storm, you lost electricity, and don't even think about air-con. But who cared? Never before had he seen a whole room whose sole purpose was housing harps. Harps! Who played a harp anymore? Or a glasshouse made with actual panes of glass, and not patched-up MDF, where the smell of citrus was so beautiful it was like walking into a gigantic lemon. There was even a garret room at the top for a studio. The garden met the water's edge, in a perfect shade of fig, cypress and palm, as well as dark-pink bougainvillea and a camellia tree. But it was the fading seventeenth-century frescos he loved most. All over the villa, the walls were painted with groves of trees, forested mountains and blue-green water. There were tropical fruits and ornate flowers, birds and monkeys, and between them the dragons and serpents that, according to legend, had once inhabited the island. Every year, damp infiltrated the walls a little more. Black spores appeared where there had once been a painted lily. Blue plaster collected on the floor where a patch of sky had chipped and fallen off. Turn your back for five minutes and another crack appeared. The housekeeper complained it was a wreck. You should whitewash the whole thing, she said. *"Vecchio posto orribile e umido. Meglio ancora, abbattetelo."* Horrible, damp old place. Better still, knock it down.

Each night Vic strolled along the Via del Silenzio, the one cobbled lane that followed the shape of the island, thinking how perfect the world was when everything stayed the same. The walk took less than ten minutes. There were no cars on Isola San Giulio. There wasn't even a shop, unless you counted the little one selling postcards to day-trippers. The ancient basilica stood at one end, with the Bishop's Palace and the abbey like a pale stone fortress in the middle, a trail of smoke drifting from the chimney all winter long. Vic loved having the nuns close by, even though he was not religious. He treated his proximity to them as a kind of insurance policy. He loved the one trattoria, too, Ristoro San Giulio, where he spent most afternoons, drinking with whoever turned up. Then there was the radius of thirteen ochre, pink and white villas that had once been canonical houses for the abbey, each one different from the last, like little baroque palaces looking out from the shores, so that on the mainland you saw a jigsaw pattern of ancient rooftops, boathouses, loggias, balustrades and balconies, with cypress and palm trees growing in between. A boatman once told Vic that the villas were painted those bright colors so that you could find the island even when the mist fell. It wasn't entirely true: when the mist came, everything disappeared and you had no clue what was east or west, but he loved the idea that when the world was lost to cloud, Villa Carlotta would still be there for him, its happy stripes of pink and sherbet seeping in and out of white air.

And all this owned by a man who'd made himself out of nothing.

Vic had left school with no qualifications and without venturing anywhere near a paintbrush. At sixteen he went to London and got a job in a meat-packing factory. His nights were spent hauling dead pigs onto hooks, every part of him reeking of blood and raw flesh. Then, walking home in the early hours, he met a woman in a fur coat beneath which her dress was doing its best to contain her significant cleavage and failing.

She said, "Where are you going, little boy?"

No one had ever called Vic a little boy, not even when he'd actually been one. He assumed she must be in some kind of trouble—he'd met plenty of women in trouble at the pub—though it turned out she was more specifically looking for it. Vic learned over the next few months everything he had not known about sex and it turned out to be considerable. Veronica was in her mid-thirties, which he came to realize was somewhere in the general camp of forty-five, and estranged from her husband, though not far enough to get a divorce; she called Vic her sweet bit on the side. He wasn't allowed in her Belgravia house; mainly she required sex in toilets or the back of her chauffeur-driven car. She flew into a fit if she saw him talking to another woman, she slapped him on occasion, but she was also a sucker for a nice painting, and for that Vic would always love her. Veronica had been half crazy about her art teacher at school and still had this romantic notion that it was her missed opportunity for a better life. If only she had married an artist, not a CEO, she would have been impoverished but happy. She took Vic to the National Gallery, the Tate, exhibitions at the Serpentine. She showed him artists like Van Gogh, Turner, Rembrandt, Cézanne. "Don't you just *love* this?" she would say, pointing to a great masterpiece with her pink dagger nails.

In the frozen bedsit where she'd now installed him, Vic decided he, too, would be an artist. He got a box of paints and books of *Great Artists* on a permanent basis from the library and copied everything. Sunflowers and big blue skies and beautiful women in hats. He taught himself the bare rudiments of line, perspective and shading. He learned about vanishing points and how to work out where the horizon would be. He learned that if he primed a canvas with deep orange, like Monet, it gave the picture a warmer glow. He learned to block out the basic shapes of a scene, then add light and shade, like Van Gogh. He found that if he kept the canvas small, it was easier to hide his mistakes, and that watercolors were too difficult, but if you went wrong with oil paints you could wipe the whole thing clean with turps and start again.

His affair with Veronica continued on and off for ten years until she left him for someone new—a younger version of Vic, sweeter and rougher. His world fell apart. And this was how he learned a new truth about love. You can be overmastered by the most powerful feelings for a person, and yet they can happily exist without so much as giving you a second thought.

Vic threw away his paints. Took work on building sites. Got wasted every payday. He had affairs that went nowhere—it still surprised him, the effect he had on women. And he might have continued in the same vein, not unhappy but on hold, just thinking this was how his life would be, until the death of his mother unhooked him in ways he didn't expect, and he realized in his mid-thirties that he wanted change. On a bus one day he overheard a young woman talking to her friend, her voice so cut-glass she sounded like the queen. He turned around and there she was, an insanely neat, small woman, her voice by far the biggest thing about her, with a face that was lit by two starry eyes, and her hair in a plait she'd pinned around her head in a cartwheel. He fell in love right there on the number 68.

He persuaded her to give him a phone number and from there they began an old-fashioned courtship: Vic waiting for her after work, and carrying her bag as he took her to a film. Martha was twenty-three but going on forty, so a bit like Veronica but in the opposite direction. She was an only child, the same as Vic, and had also lost her parents. She called perfume "scent." She called the couch a "sofa." When she ate a pear, she didn't tear into it with her teeth, but cut it into slices that she ate with a knife and fork. And even though there were parts of Vic's life she clearly didn't care for—such as the way he behaved with a drink inside him, or how other women sidled up to him at the bar, all dewy-eyed and he'd only said hello—there were other parts she loved. She took him window-shopping on Sundays, arm in arm, and asked whether he preferred a sofa that was brown or blue and what did he think of that curtain fabric? Was it too plain or too fussy? She wanted children, she said, lots of children, and, yes! he said, so did he. He wanted a tribe of them, lots of little Marthas and Vics, charging up and down. Why wouldn't two adults with no family want a whole ready-made houseful?

They married and used her inheritance to buy an Edwardian house in a not very nice part of southeast London, and for a while Martha was right. Vic found he magically transitioned into the kind of man who said no to a lock-in at the pub and came home for dinner, falling asleep on the new blue sofa. Netta arrived a year later. Susan was swift on her heels. The neighborhood, which had once been a place to leave as soon as there was money, became up-and-coming, then fully arrived. But Vic's old ways weren't so easy to leave behind. He was drinking again, he was gambling on the side, and women seemed to find him even more irresistible now that he had a wedding ring on his finger and two little girls, their black hair in ponytails and dressed in matching red capes. Goose was born—the son he'd always wanted!—but he was his mother's child. He followed Martha everywhere, wept if she left the room, and soon the couple were arguing about almost everything. By some miracle, Iris came three years later—no love left between them, yet they produced an angel of a child—but after a few months a tumor was found in Martha's ovaries. She was given half a year, though in the end she lived barely a quarter.

So there he was. A forty-three-year-old man with four children, one in a pram, the oldest just seven, and not one kindly grandparent anywhere on the horizon. It wasn't that he didn't love his children. When they were pressed against their little pillows, thick with sleep, Vic felt so much love he wanted to inhale them. But then they woke up. That was the problem. And not even at the kind of hour most people wake up, but so early it was technically the middle of the night. Netta and Susan would fling themselves onto his bed and bounce up and down, Netta already wanting to communicate the hundreds of things that had occurred to her in the full ten minutes she'd been awake.

The day went from there. It was bedlam. And there were so many essential accessories that seemed to come with children as they scampered from room to room and hurtled with lemming-like prescience toward anything that was vaguely dangerous. There were also piles of laundry, both washed and not, but mostly not; there were at least three meals a day and apparently those couldn't all be cornflakes, along with clothes that only just fitted. ("This is not mine," Netta would say. "Daddy, do you not remember? I gave this skirt to Susan." Remember? Sometimes he looked out of the window and had no idea what season they were in.) How was he supposed to be a father when he had no road map to follow? And how had Martha managed all these things and stayed human? He found, after she died, a letter that was not so much a fond farewell as a brief set of instructions. (*Netta can fend for herself but do not let her take over. Susan wants to be Netta. Take care of Goose. Do not be fooled by Iris. Deep down, she is a baby with a will of iron.*)

It was Netta who came up with the suggestion of an au pair. Or, rather, a nanny—they had just been watching the video of *Mary Poppins* on a loop. "Susan and me have an idea!" she loud-whispered in his ear at four a.m. Susan bounced on his head, singing "Feed the Birds," or at least a remnant of it, while also scattering the room with breadcrumbs she had torn all by herself, which Goose then proceeded to eat quietly, one by one, off the floor.

Netta was right, of course. She was always right, even at seven. If he kept going like this, someone would ring social services. Probably Netta. Vic engaged an au pair—Meike from Stockholm—because there was no way he could afford a nanny, and went back to work. At night, he came home, shut himself into his room and began to paint again. He escaped into X-rated fantasies in which people dressed like old-fashioned film stars went out drinking without any small children in tow and did whatever came next. But Meike from Stockholm was so tall and lovely she should have been in an advert for hair products and he wanted to put her in the painting as well, so he did—it turned out she was more than happy to model—but then she stopped being so interested in children and followed him like a shadow, mostly not wearing very much, so that now he was being woken every morning by four children and a woman in a thong.

By the time Iris was talking, it seemed as if they had gone through more au pairs than there were months in a year. He had slept with all of them. They were all in love with him. But he had also produced a wealth of paintings.

A drinking friend, Harry Lucas, asked why he didn't try selling a few. Harry was fifteen years younger than Vic and ran a market stall selling cheap prints. He didn't know a lot about art but he had a hunch people might go mad for the kind of thing Vic painted. ("The common touch," he called it.) His hunch was right: the pictures sold, every single one. Vic couldn't believe his luck. Because he could do them, no problem. He could do them in a day. He had only to close his eyes and there they were, another lonely couple meeting under the halo of light from a lamppost, another woman opening her coat to reveal not very much underneath. Harry set himself up as his full-time agent and dealer. The paintings kept selling, but for more and more money. Then one was used in an advertising campaign for Mercedes-Benz, and that was it: Vic Kemp was everywhere. Even film stars were buying them.

There was *Serenade*, in which a waiter on a ladder played the violin to a woman in a red slip on a balcony, the profile of her ugly sleeping husband reflected in the open window. *Love Is Real*—a gangster carrying roses through snowfall. *She Comes in the Night*, in which a woman stood in a pool of moonlight touching herself, watched by a gondolier. It had been reproduced time and time again—it was almost as famous as *Childsplay*, the later painting of Iris. And while it was true that his style was described by some as amateurish and that he still borrowed freely from the artists who had first inspired him, and while it was also true that he photographed his models, then copied the photographs because he still lacked the confidence to paint from life, no one buying his work seemed to object. Vic thought he might get a proper studio in King's Cross. Harry thought he might get a house the size of a cowboy ranch in Watford. Then, when Netta was twelve, Vic heard about a villa on an Italian lake that had been owned by a harpist, with seventeenth-century frescos in every room, and thought, Why the hell not get that too?

The drinking continued through the children's teens and adult years. Vic got so extremely drunk before Netta's graduation he didn't even make it as far as the ceremony. The same with Susan's wedding. He and Harry could go on benders that lasted a whole weekend; Harry in shades and a blue leather jacket that made him look like some kind of sleazy seventies DJ, Vic in an old trench coat with the collar turned up, though in the end Harry would always limp back to his wife. Harry eventually cleaned up his act because of a health scare, but Vic was still doing it. Only it wasn't like the old times. Now his drinking bouts could leave him sick and shaking for days. And there was something else.

Six months had passed since Vic's last picture. In all that time, he hadn't touched a paintbrush once. It was as if, after thirty years, someone had walked into his head and turned off the tap. He had no ideas. He couldn't think up a single title. He got Goose to move his easel to the other end of the studio, then he got him to move it to the center. It made no difference. He bought a book, *How to Paint*, by some crap artist he'd never heard of. He went to a hypnotist and a tarot-card reader and both told him he was experiencing a block and used their skills to shift it. But they made no difference either. In fact, they made it worse because they confirmed the one thing he was most afraid of. He was stuck. A crack of doubt appeared that had been inside him right from the beginning, when he first opened a box of paints and asked himself what right he had to use them; only now the crack yawned wider, and, before he knew it, it was a crater. The emptiness of the canvas that had always excited him because it was so full of promise and possibility was now terrifying. For the first time, he began to think about dying.

"You okay?" Goose had asked before Christmas, coming across him in the studio. Vic was sitting there, doing nothing, not even staring at the wall. His heart felt thick and heavy. But he had looked up at his son—tall and worn as beached driftwood, with tangled hair hanging over his face, and his soft, troubled eyes squinting down at him with an air of confused pain—and it was as if Goose was seeing everything, as if he were looking right into Vic's soul and seeing the failure that lay like bilge water at the bottom. So he'd lied that he was fine. Taking a rest because he'd had this amazing idea for a painting. "I'm going in a whole new direction." The relief that fell through Goose's face was pitiful. He said the same thing to Susan, then Netta and Iris. The more he said it, the happier they looked, and he found himself elaborating. The picture was going to be his best yet. A true original. As big as a French window. Once and for all, it would prove those people wrong who dismissed his work as amateurish and copying.

"Don't ask me what it's of, because it's in here." (Tapping his head.) "But the galleries will be fighting over this one."

It was the loneliest thing, the lying. Lonelier even than his childhood. Goose could prime as many canvases as he liked, the girls could keep asking how it was going, Harry could even talk about rounding up buyers, but there would never be a new painting because his head had nothing inside it. Vic looked at the world and the world sneered at him. He told Goose that he was searching for ideas every day, knowing full well he'd be roaming bars, morning till night, doing his best to obliterate himself.

Face it. He was a fraud, a cheat. A copycat with a porno twist, when the only thing worth being was the solitary and unseen artist who existed from first breath and stayed true to their vision. What, then, was great art? Vic had no idea, but he was pretty sure someone else did. He began to avoid the studio altogether. He couldn't even bear to see Iris. He was alone, just as he'd been as a boy, only this was worse than being a boy because he had tried to lift himself out of the mire—he had dared to pretend to be an artist—and failed. He drank, he went online, he drank. If only for some peace of mind.

And that was how he met Bella-Mae.

4

Porn Star

"So porn," said Netta. "Online porn."

"Porn?" said Susan. "Oh, no. Please."

"How else does a man in his seventies meet a twenty-seven-year-old woman on his laptop? It wasn't a dating site. He said it himself. So it's got to be porn. That's why he's being so secretive. And, anyway, her name? Bella-Mae? That's a porn-star name."

"Oh, no," said Susan again. "Come on now. No."

They were in a café, Netta, Susan, Goose and Iris. It was two weeks since the noodle bar and Netta had called for another family discussion. Sadly, it looked as if Goose had been wrong about Bella-Mae. She wasn't a passing fad and neither was she a muse to help Vic finish the painting—he still hadn't touched it. If anything, he'd become more obsessed by her. He'd joined a gym, he was on some crazy new health plan, and suddenly he was ringing them all the time just to talk about her. Did they know how smart she was? How beautiful? How unusual, talented and sexy? She was so many wonderful things she sounded less of a person and more of a wish list. Did they know she was a quarter Italian from her mother's side and had a passion for spicy chicken wings? Or that she'd fallen from a window when she was young and had the sweetest little gap between her front teeth? No, they didn't. They didn't know any of those things because, excuse me, how could they? They hadn't met her. Yet a meeting was the one thing she was clearly in no hurry to make happen. If they suggested a visit to the flat, Vic repeated all kinds of excuses to put them off. Either Bella-Mae had suffered a bad night and now she was asleep, or she'd gone to see the work of some new artist in a new gallery no one had heard of and he didn't know when she'd be back. They'd even agreed to meet for dinner once, but Vic sent a group text and canceled at the last minute. Clearly something had to be done.

Susan was going from Tunbridge Wells to London for the day—she still called it Going to Town—and had texted Iris, who was accompanying Goose to the dentist for moral support. *HE is haVing anishtitiK 4 a fillling*, she wrote back. Iris had always enjoyed an erratic relationship with spelling, partly because she rushed to get through it, but mainly because she'd missed so much school and her dyslexia had gone undiagnosed. As a child, she had only had to mention a tummy-ache and that was it. She got the day off. Sometimes she didn't even have to mention the tummy-ache. She had only to look a bit pale, which was very easy for Iris since translucent was her natural coloring, and Vic would be telling her she must stay at home. "Who needs maths," he used to say, "when they can swim a hundred lengths?"

The siblings had agreed to meet after Goose's appointment. He was still woozy and only half his face worked. The thing was, Susan told them as she tore open a sachet of sugar—"I know," she said, "I shouldn't"—Vic was not behaving in a rational manner.

"Too right," said Netta.

"He's got this girl living with him and he barely knows her. Of course Daddy always did his own thing, but this is on a whole new level. He's acting like a teenager."

"He's in complete denial."

"And now he's giving in to whatever she says. He called last week to say she doesn't want me going round to clean the flat. She doesn't even want me to do the shopping. I asked in a really nice way if they fancied coming for Sunday lunch. He told me straight off that Bella-Mae had plans of her own. 'What kind of plans?' I said. 'Plan plans,' he said.

He'd promised to take her shopping for the wedding. He couldn't wait to get rid of me."

"That means underwear," said Netta. "What else could it mean? Bathroom towels? Anyway, I thought she wasn't into material things."

"He sounded drunk. It was ten in the morning."

"Why are you surprised? They were probably both drunk. God knows what state the flat is in."

"I said, 'Daddy, why don't you tell me about Bella-Mae? We don't know anything about her. We don't know where she's from. We don't know how you met.' Do you know what he said?"

Netta shook her head, as if she knew this was going to be terrible.

"He laughed at me. He actually laughed. Then he said, 'What does it matter where she's from? What does it matter how we met?' "

"Porn star," said Netta. "I rest my case."

"She could be from anywhere. We don't even know her surname. The only concrete thing we know is that she has long black hair. You hear stories about women like her all the time. Gold-diggers and grifters. And now he won't answer his phone. I swear he sees it's me and he turns it off. Or most likely she turns it off. It's as if she's cast a spell on him. He's besotted."

Iris listened to her two older sisters—they could talk for England. As a child, she'd fall asleep to the sound of them in the bedroom they once shared at the house on the lake, Susan chattering nineteen to the dozen, then screeching with laughter when Netta said something outrageous. But she couldn't help it: her mind had unhooked itself from the conversation and drifted. Iris loved her siblings more than anyone, but somewhere along the line, maybe as far back as when she was born, she'd looked at the family cast list and realized that in terms of parts, they hadn't left her very much. Netta had bagged the brains. Iris could still picture her dressed top to toe in black, with a French beret on her head, Dr. Martens on her feet, charging out of the house with a pile of books. ("Netta, you sound like a herd of elephants," Vic would shout. She still did. She clomped everywhere. Even in flip-flops.) But only Netta could come top in every subject, including the ones she didn't like, get four A's at A level, then follow that with a first-class law degree.

She could have done anything, that's how brilliant she was. Going to school as her youngest sister had felt like being a dull gray day after a fantastically stormy one. Susan was amazing, too, but in the opposite direction. She was as pretty as a picture, and sensible. There was nothing she couldn't sort out with a list. "What's the problem here?" she'd say, and with Susan on board, it was halfway to being resolved. Susan was the one who'd explained to Iris about periods, though Iris was so appalled when the first came that Susan had lied and told her it only happened once. It was Susan who tried to take Iris shopping for clothes that hadn't previously been worn by other people, and to teach her how to drive. ("Much as we love it, we can't stay on the pavement, Iris.") When Iris got her flat, Susan came around with her color charts and a box of tools to create IKEA furniture where there had previously been flatpacks, and provided geraniums for the window boxes. She was also the best cook—which was a small wonder in itself because no one except Harry's wife had shown any interest in feeding them after their mother died. Unless Susan cooked, it was toast, Pot Noodle or the microwave.

As for Goose, he was the boy and Iris didn't want to be that, and while he had the biggest heart in the world and was never jealous or angry or demanding in any way whatsoever, he'd also become troubled, which she didn't want either. All that remained was for her to be quiet. The little one. Which she could do. Iris could do Quiet and Little really well. What she hadn't figured on was growing so tall. The day she realized she'd outgrown Netta, she felt like a traitor.

Iris had woken that morning convinced she was going to the house on the lake—it was as if she was physically traveling there in her sleep. She'd seen Isola San Giulio as you might first view it, like a small lit-up palace that had broken free of the mainland and set sail across the water by itself. In her mind, she'd got on board the passenger boat, then traveled the five-minute distance to the middle of the lake. On the island, she'd followed the curve of the cobbled path, the Via del Silenzio. Above, she saw the carved gray signs, encouraging visitors—in several languages—to be silent, though there was not much of that when the summer day-trippers came. She passed the high walls of the monastery to her left, the villas on her right, with little gaps between and a spike of blue where a narrow alleyway met the lake's edge. She heard the lapping of water, the creak of a boat she couldn't see, the *clink clink* of rigging. She was in the safest place in the world, the lake all around her and beyond that the hills and mountains. And even though, from the front, none of the houses were much to look at—they saved their extrovert side for the lake—when you entered Villa Carlotta, it was like walking into a spell. With its heavy wooden front doors pulled wide open, and those of the music salon beyond open, too, you could look right across the beautiful colored mosaic tiles of the floor, past the walls painted with dragons and butterflies, to the garden and full expanse of the lake. The water was so blue and sparkling that, as a child, she once told her father she wanted to be a little fish and swim in it forever. She was thinking how, now that it was early April, the camellia tree in the garden would still be in bloom, but not the wisteria; the hostas would be tight green pencils, just beginning to uncurl, and new pine cones would be the size of a child's finger, with a covering of snow up on Monte Rosa in the far distance. In Orta San Giulio, bars and restaurants would be opening for the summer season, sparrows hopping over the white tablecloths in search of crumbs, and ducks waddling up from the lake; the first day-trippers and groups of schoolchildren would be arriving in Piazza Motta, the main square; a workman might be touching up paintwork on a balustrade. She was thinking about how her father still called her Little Fish and she did not believe he could be marrying a porn star. Besides, she thought Bella-Mae was a nice name. A Disney-princess name. Romantic.

"What about you?" said Netta. "Surely he's spoken to you."

Iris was suddenly aware of them all staring at her. It was like being under three separate spotlights, a rare experience for Iris, who did her best to avoid that kind of attention. "Yes. We've spoken a bit. He always says how happy he is. I've stopped at his flat a few times after work. But there's no sign of them. Not even the lights are on."

"She probably has him in bed by seven. He's probably shagged out."

"Are you eating this?" Susan said, reaching for Netta's wafer biscuit and eating it.

"So he's still set on marrying her?"

"And he's still set on us going to the lake."

"Well, I won't be going," said Netta. "Some of us have work to do."

"Warwick won't go either. You know how he is with the heat. Besides, he says the house isn't safe anymore."

Goose nodded, agreeing, and so did Iris. But she was only agreeing because that was her habit and the easiest path—if you appeared to agree, people left you alone to think your thoughts, and nothing had to change. Besides, she wasn't like Netta. She hated her work. She only did it because otherwise she would be one of those privileged people who lived hand to mouth off their father. The problem was that, without any real qualifications, waitressing was her best option while also remaining fully dressed, and if there was one thing Iris was definite about it was that. But she wasn't like Warwick either. Warwick spent every summer by the lake smothered in so much sun cream it stopped infiltrating his skin and sat there in splotches, while Iris loved the heat. She loved swimming in the lake. It was a part of her, even when she wasn't there. More like a person than a place. Surrounded by wooded hills, peaked mountains and little towns that hugged the shoreline, Lake Orta was one of the smallest Italian lakes. About eight miles in length and a mile and a half wide; you could stand on one side and see right across to the other, with the island in the middle. But it was also a lake with a rebellious spirit, sending its waters north instead of south, and the one that day-trippers found only by accident. Locals called it La Cenerentola: Cinderella. Their best-kept secret. Like me, Iris thought. I am Lake Orta.

She turned now to her siblings and smiled helpfully. "I think Bella-Mae might be an influencer."

"I'm sorry. She's a what?" said Netta.

"Is that even a thing?" said Susan.

"It's what Daddy told me. She influences things. Or maybe she's something else and she influences on the side."

"I can't imagine being an influencer," said Goose.

No one replied, because there was nothing to be said. No one could imagine Goose as an influencer, not even on the side.

"He said she has a gift for interior design as well."

Netta rolled her eyes. "Basically that means she chose some paint once, and a matching lampshade."

Susan gave a tight little shrug until Netta gripped her hand. "I don't mean like you, Suz. You really do have a gift." Susan breathed out again.

Iris said, "But then he did also say to us she was an artist. So maybe Daddy's getting his words mixed up."

"And he really hasn't been to the studio?" asked Susan.

Goose shook his head, saying no.

"He's saying no," said Iris.

"Yes, darling, we got that," said Netta.

"So what's he doing about the new painting?" said Susan. "He was so full of it before. He talked about it all the time."

"Maybe she's drugged him," said Goose, or at least that was what it sounded like. His mouth was slurpy because of all the anesthetic.

Susan said that kind of thing didn't happen, and Iris, who was drawn to suffering because she couldn't help it, gripped tight on to her rucksack for courage and said actually it did, it happened all the time. Children got abducted against their will, women got date-raped, and what about all the trillions of trees that were being cut down, until Goose apologized and said he didn't really mean he thought Bella-Mae could be drugging their father. Besides, Vic's idea of a good night meant vodka and enough pills to knock out a horse.

"What about the herbal tea?" said Susan. "Is he still drinking that?"

"I don't see what's wrong with a cup of tea. It's just a cup of tea. That's a nice thing."

"So what are we going to do? Do we confront her? Try to stop her? Or do we go to Daddy? Warn him off?"

"If we do that," said Netta, "we're falling into her trap. Besides, Daddy never listens to anyone. The more we object, the more he'll want to go ahead."

"So the plan of action," said Susan slowly, "is that there is no plan?"

"The plan of action is that we leave him to it. You know what he's like. He loves a drama. But if we don't play along, this has no oxygen. It will burn itself out and she'll be gone. I give it a month. Tops. He won't even remember her name."

On the way home, Iris got off her bike and texted her father's dealer, Harry. *Iris?* he replied. *Are you okay?* All she wanted was a firm, soft shoulder to lean against, a capable hand setting her right. When she was a child, she would spend the time when her father was at the studio waiting for him at the window. She would breathe on the glass, fogging it, because she didn't want to look at the street without him in it. Iris was the only one who had no memory of their mother. She even wondered if Martha's cancer was somehow linked to her birth, though of course no one had ever told her that. It left her feeling she would always be the odd one out, that she belonged to the family ever so slightly less than the other three. So, when it came to her father, she must be vigilant at all times. Without him, she would disappear.

She bent down and stroked a passing cat. At her touch, it collapsed sideways, then wriggled on its back, purring like a piece of heavy machinery. She laughed. Then she sent Harry a new message, but she had to run some of the words together because the space bar kept getting stuck. *We r worid abotdady. imworieid.*

He replied straightaway: *Darling girl, don't worry. Your father has the constitution of an ox. He will be working on the new painting soon.*

So Harry didn't know about Bella-Mae, and yet Harry was Vic's best friend—you could reasonably say his only friend—and knew everything about her father. Iris was trying to decide how to reply but actually her phone got there first. It was him again.

Would you like to meet?

ne its ok, she wrote. Then she switched it off.

But Netta's plan to save their father worked, because Netta's plans always did. Over the next few weeks he barely mentioned Bella-Mae. If they rang and asked how she was, he said something vague, like, "Thank you, she's fine," then changed the subject. He went over to Susan's by himself for Sunday lunch and, even though he was still drinking his Thermos of tea, there was no mention of the wedding. Susan told the others he seemed subdued and stayed only a few hours. He didn't even have a glass of wine. "I honestly think Bella-Mae's gone," she said. "And now he's embarrassed about the whole thing."

Another time, he rang Iris and asked if she might like a walk in the park before her shift at the burger restaurant. It was a blue-sky day at the end of April: Out of nowhere, the weather had got really hot. People were stripped off on the grass while children splashed in and out of the pond. Vic looped his arm through Iris's and said, "Let's get ice cream." He bought two Mr. Whippy 99s, each the size of a bird feeder, with a Cadbury Flake on top and squiggles of chocolate sauce.

As they walked around the pond, he told her how much he missed swimming in the lake. There was nothing like it, he said, that feeling of being out in the deep and surrounded by hills, the springs rising in the water beneath you. And everything was different when you saw it from that perspective, even the mountains, as if it was only in the lake that you saw life for what it truly was. "Being there reminds me of how much I love life. I really think I love it most of all when I'm in the lake. I wish I could paint it."

"You should, Daddy."

"I don't think I'm good enough to paint a lake."

"Of course you're good enough. You painted me, remember."

There was a little frisson in her voice that she hadn't meant to be there and he stopped walking and swung around to look at her, the light catching his eyes, making them very green in the same way those of other people could be very blue. Just as sharp and luminous. No one had eyes like his, not even when he was drunk, and today he wasn't. He was stone-cold sober, she was sure of it. "Little Fish? Tell me the truth. Do you think I've been a fool?"

She said, "No, Daddy, no." She couldn't bear him to think that, just as she couldn't bear him to think he couldn't paint the lake.

When she called Netta later, her sister went quiet. Iris said, in a wobbling voice, "No matter what anyone says, Daddy can be wonderful."

"When Daddy's nice, he's great. He's like no other person. But please tell me he's shaved off the goatee."

"Sorry, Netta. The goatee stayed."

They laughed. In their different ways they wanted to gather their father and the whole sorry business into their arms, Iris pretending it had never happened, her sister declaring it done and dusted. Netta said, "So Bella-Mae was a passing fad. Goose was right all along. The wedding was a fantasy."

Except, as they would soon discover, with Bella-Mae it was not that simple.

5

Waiting in a Cab

So who was she, and where did she come from? Was she his latest model? Some kind of muse? Was she a grifter, like Susan said? Or was Netta right and she was a porn star? "A true artist," their father had told them in the noodle bar, but that could mean anything. It didn't necessarily mean she was a painter. Or was she actually an influencer, whatever that meant? And anyway, weren't all artists influencers in some way? As Susan said, the only concrete thing they knew was that Bella-Mae had thick black hair. They didn't even know her surname. Goose didn't mind who she was. He just wished his father would come back to the studio and start work.

Twelve years ago, Goose had tried to mount an exhibition of his own still-life paintings. Vic had hired a gallery and enlisted Harry's help. He'd splashed out for a champagne reception. Then at the last minute, Goose realized the truth. His art was terrible. It was shameful how bad it was. Just because his father was an artist didn't make Goose one too. He looked at each of his pictures hanging on the walls and, honest to God, he felt physically sick. Ever since he could remember, something had felt loose inside him, but now it uncoiled, like a snagged bit of wool on a sweater. He took the pictures down while no one was looking and, behind the gallery, made a pile of them, then doused it with lighter fuel and put a match to the whole lot. His sisters hadn't yet arrived, the champagne wasn't open, and the paintings were an incinerated mess in the backyard. It was Vic who paid off the gallery. They even charged him for damages. A few weeks later, Goose had a nervous breakdown.

Netta took him in for a while, then Susan, and in the end his father lent him the basement bedsit beneath his studio over in King's Cross as a kind of halfway house, though it was less of a bedsit and more of a storeroom, filled with all his father's junk. Somehow Vic never chucked him out, and Goose never got around to moving on. Instead he gave up his job painting sets for a theatre company and made himself useful to his father, doing the menial tasks Vic had no time for. The cleaning, the preparation of a canvas, the mixing of colors, the general maintenance of the studio. The only rule was that he gave up on serious art.

"Otherwise you'll end up in the loony bin," his father said. "And I love you, kid. No one's watching you go through that a second time."

This was all fine with Goose. He knew what art could do. How it could hold you in its claws until the work was finished, then lash back at you so viciously when you got it wrong that you couldn't get up in the morning, let alone look at your face in the mirror. His clothes were covered with paint—he smelled of turps even after a wash—but the painting was never his. It was his father's. The family joke was that everything that went into Vic's studio came out as a paint rag. Including his son. But it was enough for him to help his father, to know that when a painting was finished it was Goose who had enabled Vic to get there, if only in the most basic way.

Now turning the corner, he felt a flare of panic. He'd only gone to buy a tub of emulsion to smarten up the outside wall, but when he reached the square with its tall wedding-cake white houses, a communal garden in the middle, there it was on the opposite side. The front door, wide open. Anyone could be in the studio. They could be ransacking it right this minute. A cab had stopped a few doors down, the engine still turning over.

Goose pressed the tin of paint close to his chest as if it were a ball, though he'd hated sports at school—his size had promised a prowess that his clumsiness and general good manners failed to deliver—and ran the last few paces. From the door, he scanned the studio in a hurry, but everything was the same; it looked as if it had been ransacked even though it hadn't. Vic's workplace was a vast single room on the ground floor with windows overlooking the square and painting supplies everywhere. In winter, it was lit by bright electric lamps attached to long wires hanging from the ceiling, but in summer the light from the windows landed like luminous paving stones, crossed with lines from the security bars. The floorboards were bare, a hazardous mix of splinters and paint, and the walls were covered with photographs of all the women who'd modeled for him over the years. At the back, Goose had put up a dividing wall that separated the studio from a kitchenette where he made coffee for his father every day and set out vodka and slimline tonic, with Ritz crackers and little pieces of cheese. When Vic was in the thick of work, he survived on French cigars, vodka and bite-sized snacks.

"It's shit, it's shit," he would say. "I'm going to get rid of the whole thing. Pass me the turps."

"No, it's great," Goose would say, over and over. "I can really see it. Don't give up." But he would hide the turps, just in case.

Goose came to a halt so fast the rest of his body remained buzzing, charged with adrenaline that had nowhere to go. Someone was stooped in the far corner, one hand on the wall and the other to his chest, as if he'd run a long distance. He was dressed in smart linen, his hair in a ponytail—

"Daddy?" Suddenly Goose was thinking of the time before Christmas when he'd found Vic staring at an empty wall. For one terrifying moment, he'd been sure it was a heart attack. "What's wrong?"

Vic turned. He seemed surprised. Or maybe caught out. So that made two of them.

"Nothing's wrong. I'm hunky-dory." He took a few deep breaths, then steadied himself. His skin was sheened in sweat. "I thought you were out. I've come to fetch a few things. Bella-Mae's waiting in a cab."

"You mean she's here?" Goose felt a sudden inner *clang*, an instinctive certainty that wariness was called for. So Bella-Mae was back? His sisters had been wrong. Or had she not gone in the first place? "Does she want to come in?"

"No. She wants to wait in the cab."

Vic pointed at some tubes of paint and a huge canvas that Goose had prepared at the end of last year, back when Vic had begun talking about the new painting. It was stretched, primed with gesso and sanded, then reprimed several times more. All it needed was for Vic to start work on it. "But now you're here, you can do the job for me. Box up the small things, and I'll send a van over later to fetch the rest."

"Does this mean you're beginning the new painting?"

"Well, kid, I'm not planting a garden. Bella-Mae says I need a change of scene. It's time to shake things up, she says."

"I see," said Goose. He tried again and said, "Great! Good idea!"

His father never wanted a change of scene. He could never paint at home. Too much got in the way. But why was it that even when Goose wanted to agree with his father it came out sounding as if he didn't? "You shouldn't try so hard," Netta was always saying. But it was easy for her. She was as tough as Vic. They were practically partners. Yet Goose couldn't seem to indulge him like Susan, let alone charm him like Iris. As a boy, he'd found it hard just to look his father in the eye. "You need toughening up," Vic had said, when Goose came home from school once with a bleeding face. He'd taken to punching Goose lightly on his shoulder without warning. "It's only play!" he used to say. "Hit me back! Hit me back!" Only it didn't feel playful, and Goose didn't know how to begin to hit his father: he would rather be kicked and dragged through mud, which was arguably what had got him into all this mess in the first place. It meant he was being bullied at school—called names because he was arty, kicked in games, tripped up with his lunch plate—and also when he got back, and actually it was this that upset him most. But at the same time, Vic's fearsomeness had been reassuring when Goose lay awake at night, thinking about the many terrifying things that might kill him in his sleep, like robbers or ghosts or nuclear bombs. His father was so big he frightened away everything else. Except, of course, nightmares.

Vic asked for a chair, then took his Thermos from his pocket. He poured a helping of dark liquid—it looked like the dregs of a pond and smelled worse—while he continued naming the colors he would need. "It's all in here," he said, pointing at his head. "Every brushstroke. I've never seen a picture so clearly. I'm not even using photographs this time. I'm doing it from life. I'll be honest with you, kid. It hasn't been easy. There've been times over the last few months when I thought I'd lost my way. Thought it was over. But I was wrong. Bella-Mae says that's how it goes. You have to lose everything to find your true path. And now I'm there. I'm on the true path. I've got to trust the artist in myself. See what happens when it's just me and the canvas. It's fucking exciting."

Everything about this conversation was an about-turn for Vic. Not just working without photographs, and the massive scale of the picture, but such an abundance of color. It sounded beautiful. And Vic had never opened up before about feeling lost in his work, or vulnerable, though admittedly he was doing that in the past tense. But all in all, it seemed wrong to stand when his father was sitting, like being too big and powerful. Goose had no idea what to do with that feeling. It was the same way he often felt about his body: there seemed to be too much of it for the man inside.

He said, "Harry will be pleased. He keeps ringing to ask how you're getting on. He's already got private buyers lined up."

"Harry can think again. This is art we're talking about. Not the commercial shit he sells. I'm going in a whole new direction. That's been my problem, you know."

Goose didn't know, but nodded enthusiastically, as if he did.

"The fact is Harry's been holding me back. Bella-Mae can see it because she's coming to the whole thing with fresh eyes. But you couldn't see it. Neither could I."

"What couldn't we see?"

"Harry wants me to be commercial. He wants me to keep churning out the same old shit. But I'm an artist. I have to keep changing. That's what Bella-Mae says, and she's right. It's time to move on."

"Move on in your work?"

"Move on from Harry. I want Bella-Mae to be my dealer now."

Goose almost fell. It was like pieces of himself breaking off in chunks. Was his father serious? How could he drop Harry? Harry had believed in his father's work long before anyone else. Not only that, they'd been drinking and gambling partners for years. Harry and his wife had spent all those summers with them at the house on the lake. He was practically an uncle. Closer. A father in reserve, who was more paternal than the real one. It was Harry who once turned up on Christmas Day with a great carload of presents to put under the tree, and actually the tree as well, because Vic had forgotten both. You plugged it in and there it was, Christmas in a box, pulsing with so many colored lanterns Goose never wanted to look at a standard lamp again. Meanwhile his wife had gone to the kitchen with bags of groceries and cooked the only blow-out meal anyone had eaten all winter. ("Call me Shirley," she would say, but that was like calling your teachers by their first name in sixth form. Goose tended to call her nothing at all, except when he said "Mrs. Lucas" by mistake.) He could still remember lying under the tree after that lunch, his belly full to popping, gazing up through the miraculous branches with so much happiness he thought he might hear angels.

Besides, Goose was under the distinct impression Bella-Mae didn't like his father's art. Wasn't that what he'd told them in the noodle bar? He said, "Have you told Harry?"

"Not yet. There's plenty of time. We'll finish the painting first."

For one moment, Goose thought his father was referring to him. Among the chaos of everything else, there was this. This nugget of joy. He forgot about Harry or, rather, he left the idea of Harry for one moment, flayed in the corner. He even forgot about Bella-Mae. His father wanted his help. He couldn't wait to call his sisters. Goose had barely rushed to the end of the thought when he realized his mistake. Of course. His father wasn't talking about him. It was Bella-Mae. She'd taken Harry's job, and now she was going to take his too.

He found himself saying, "Well, yes, of course. Of course. And how is Bella-Mae?" An insane question since he'd never met her. She seemed so busy taking over Vic's life she had no time for meeting his children, but Goose was doing whatever the hell he could to sound like someone who wasn't turning somersaults inside himself. And yet the fact that Bella-Mae was so close, closer than she'd ever been before, meant that even though she was waiting outside in the cab, she also seemed to be very much inside the studio, not so much a person as a vast question mark hidden by thick black hair. "How are the wedding plans?"

"We're not in any hurry. Bella-Mae's been visiting a cousin. I mean, who am I? I'm just the *fiancé*."

His father passed his empty cup—or rather, he held it out, as if he believed there was a table next to him and Goose leaped forward to take it. He was half crazy for a spliff but he carried the cup to the kitchenette and washed it, keeping his hands under a stream of cold water in an effort to steady them. If Bella-Mae was now his father's art dealer and also his assistant, where did that leave Goose? He was devastated for Harry, but he couldn't help it, he was appalled for himself. Without the studio, he would be nothing.

When he left the kitchenette, his father was prowling around the room, sniffing the air like a pantomime villain. "It smells of turps in here."

"It always smells of turps. We get through turps on a level with vodka."

Vic caught hold of Goose's arm and pulled him close. There was a look in his eye. Suspicious, accusing. "Don't be smart with me. Have you been painting?"

"Of course I haven't."

"You sure?" He gave a little twist of Goose's wrist.

"Of course I'm sure. Anyway, I'm surprised you can smell anything. That stuff in your flask stinks."

At last Vic relaxed his hold a little and laughed. "I've stopped noticing."

"What is it? Is it for your health?"

"I've no idea. Bella-Mae makes it. She brews it up every morning. I feel like a new man. You should try it some time."

"Thanks, but I'll stick to plain old teabags."

At last Vic let him go and Goose got to work fetching the other things his father would need. Pencils, a bottle of turpentine, linseed oil, his favorite brushes, palette knives and rags. He boxed them all up carefully. Vic clicked his fingers and glanced at the door, getting impatient, but when Goose said he was sorry, he opened his arms wide, like a man who had everything. "Hey, kid. I'm marrying a woman I'm crazy for and I'm going to paint a fucking masterpiece. Life's never been so good."

He took the box of supplies and lumbered through the door. Goose called, "Hey! I'll get a haircut!"

"You do that, kid! Thanks for the loot!"

Minutes later there was the sound of a car door closing, the cab moving away, and by the time Goose had run outside to wave goodbye all he saw was the vehicle leaving the square—two head shapes in the rear window, one lower than the other and turning last minute to look back at him. There was a Sunday-morning silence.

But this was not the kind of expansive silence Goose experienced sometimes when he was alone in the studio and strange shapes began to fill his head, like ballooning fruits and corkscrew tendrils. This was the kind of silence that felt as if it had come about only because something had been snatched away, taking other things with it. Clearly the reason his father had chosen Bella-Mae to help him was because she was a true artist and could see things Goose couldn't. But suppose her ideas weren't good ones? Goose could watch his father block new shapes onto a primed canvas and had no idea how Vic kept his nerve. How you might dare to lift a whole world with all its chaos into the confines of one small square and keep it breathing. He took sandpaper and a bowl of sugar-water to prepare the outside wall and set to work, making thick strokes backward and forward, smothering his worries in a layer of bright and opaque whiteness.

Goose had no idea that he'd seen his father for the last time. Why would he? After all, it was a beautiful day. The first of May. After the surprise mini heat wave in April, the trees were in full leaf. Across the square, a man was pushing a buggy, while a little girl skipped behind him. Everything was full of new life: the only person who seemed to have lost a future was Goose. When he broke it to his sisters that Bella-Mae was still on the scene, he avoided mentioning that she'd taken his job and Harry's too. He only told them the good news about the painting and said Vic was trying a few ideas at home. Goose still hoped that if he stayed loyal to his father, he would return to the studio, and life would go back to the way it had been before Bella-Mae. Besides, he would have given anything to see the big new painting.

"Wait," said Netta. "You mean she's back? She was sitting outside in a cab? And you didn't go and meet her?"

"He said she didn't want to. Besides, I'm not sure she actually *went* in the first place. I think she was just visiting a cousin."

"A cousin? What cousin?"

"I don't know. He didn't say."

"Another porn star?"

"We don't know Bella-Mae is a porn star, Net. She could be a primary-school teacher for all we know."

Netta made a noise that sounded like *piff*. "Pull the other one," she said.

Susan was the same as Netta, only slightly less extreme, but relieved to hear that at least the wedding was on hold and the painting wasn't, while Iris said, "Well, at least Daddy's happy. That's the main thing."

A van driver came to collect the canvas and Vic went quiet again. Goose tried calling, but there was never any answer and his sisters said it was the same for them: he had gone into hiding with his work, just like when they were children, and didn't want to be disturbed. In the end, there was no time for Goose to get a haircut. Instead he did his regular shifts at the local charity shop, sorting through the bags of new donations (he put aside a few things for Iris), and helped out at the food bank. The rest of the time he spent deep-cleaning the studio and sanding down the woodwork, repainting the whole inside so that his father would feel inspired when he came back.

But Vic never did. A week after the visit to the studio, he sent a group text to say he and Bella-Mae had left London on the spur of the moment for the lake. He added a box of kisses and a PS: *Off to finish the big new painting!*

6

Wedding Photo

The picture wasn't the only thing Vic did out there. He also got married. So Iris needn't have worried about Bella-Mae's wedding dress. She got to wear it, after all. The first Netta knew about it was when Susan rang her landline and said straight off, "Well, can you believe it?"

It was a Friday night, late May now. The initial outrage they had all experienced about Vic taking Bella-Mae to Orta had been replaced by a deep hurt. ("Fuck him," said Netta.) She was watching a DVD with her closest friend, Robert, who spent so much time at hers he might as well have stopped pretending he had a place of his own and moved in. Netta's house was a narrow Georgian building close to the British Museum. Each floor was a single room stacked at an ever so slightly lopsided angle on top of another, with windows that didn't fully fit the frames, and plumbing that was so old it made gasping noises at night, as if it was being attacked with a sledgehammer. Netta said, "Suz? What's happened?"

"Haven't you seen his text?"

"What text? What are we talking about?"

"Daddy's new text!" Susan was shrill and a little breathless, the way she could get when she was emotional, as if she was standing on one leg. "Find your phone."

"Suz, this is my phone."

"I mean your other phone. Your phone phone. Your mobile."

"I have no idea where my mobile is. Just tell me what the text says."

"Netta, get up. Find your mobile. Is Robert there? Can't he help? You need to find your mobile."

So Netta moved up and down the house, throwing kilim cushions off chairs, flapping antique French throws, lifting empty wineglasses, shifting some already-dead house plants, knowing full well she wasn't going to find her phone because (a) it wasn't there, (b) she wasn't looking properly and (c) she was always losing things, like her wallet and keys, then discovering she hadn't lost them at all: they were right there in her handbag. She had read once that it was an actual condition caused by childhood trauma: Because she'd lost her mother when she was only seven, she was caught in a permanent holding pattern of loss. It was as if her head just expected things to go missing, so they did. Robert said that might be true, but it was also true that she moved through life like a hurricane. If only she slowed down, she might see what was staring her in the face. He waited now in his patient way, with those soft dark eyes that would make a gazelle feel envious, until finally he got up and lifted her coat—slung like a dead thing on the back of the sofa—and produced her mobile from the pocket, as she knew all along that he would, if she just kept going with her ridiculous pantomime of searching.

Netta was in love with Robert, though it hadn't always been that way. When they met, he was her husband's best friend. He was also a psychotherapist, and Netta was suspicious of anyone who dealt with the mind, convinced they would find her worst faults by subterfuge. Then, just three years into her marriage, the two men confessed they were lovers. At that point, Netta had honestly not realized her husband was gay. She didn't know which was worse. The scorching fury she felt at making such a disastrous mistake, or the darker humiliation—like tar moving through her—of her father's casual suggestion that she could not make a gay man straight. Unlike Susan, he seemed to be saying, Netta was unable to succeed in marriage. She'd dealt with the pain the way she dealt with most things, by annihilating everything to do with Philip—she used the same principle with weeds and Roundup, which was why she had no back garden, only paving stones. She dumped his clothes, books and CDs outside the house and divorced him so fast it took little over three months. After that the two men moved in together and she never spoke to either of them, though they lived in a modest flat only a few streets away.

Eighteen months later she received a card from Robert, informing her that his partner—she stumbled over the word at first, as if it were foreign—had died of an AIDS-related illness. It was an elegant note, even Netta had to admit that, well worded, generous about her feelings and the shock she might be experiencing. He asked for a meeting, but she never turned up. She didn't go to the funeral either, though Goose and Susan did. A fortnight later, Robert came to her house with two bottles of very good wine. "Netta, there is no easy way to say this," he said. "You need to be tested for AIDS." She could have died. Right there on her own doorstep, while he held out his two bottles of wine. She did not know how she would bear it.

It was Robert who accompanied her to the tests. It was Robert who sat with her as she waited for the results, so furious and frightened she shredded an entire toilet roll in her handbag. It was Robert, too, who offered to buy champagne when she found out she was clear. And it was Robert who told her that, sadly, the prognosis was not so good for himself. "But I am managing it," he said to her, that night. He had looked at her then with real kindness on his face. "And I'm lucky. I had love."

"What the fuck?" said Netta.

It wasn't Robert she was now speaking to. It was her mobile. There was a group text from her father with a photo of him and a young woman who must be Bella-Mae. This was the second time Netta had seen her picture and it was only fractionally more illuminating than the first. She was wearing a plain white dress, but there were still no actual details of her face because it was hidden by a veil that stopped just short of her chin. Vic was in some kind of shift and stooping because of the crazy height difference. He had also lost more weight. To Netta's mind, he still looked like a hygienist, but now a really hungry one. They were standing in the main square, Piazza Motta, in front of one of the arches of the Palazzotto, Orta's tiny medieval town hall, holding a wedding certificate, one corner each. Vic was laughing as if he couldn't believe his luck. He had written: *Married two days ago! Happiest day of my life! Come to the lake!*

By her bed upstairs, Netta kept a framed photograph of herself at twelve years old, laughing with him in the exact same spot, his arm around her. Behind them, the Palazzotto was borne high on stone columns, painted the color of an apricot, its crest and sundial faded over the years. The sky was a deep lapis blue, and beyond the Palazzotto were the horse-chestnut trees, the lake, a thousand winks of light bouncing off the surface. It was the first time she had drunk a full glass of wine and she still remembered that half-wild feeling of being cut loose from herself. Netta went to sit and realized she already was.

Vic had done it. He had got married behind her back. She tried to take it in, but the betrayal was a wall she couldn't see past. And to marry someone so young as well. It was the kind of thing you might have expected from Harry, except deep down he was loyal to his wife and always went home with his tail between his legs. But not Vic. And that was the thing that hurt most of all. That her father, whom she loved more than anyone, could drop her not for a woman who was smarter than she was, or even more obviously beautiful, but a girl from his laptop.

Susan was saying, "Two days ago! Two days! What—she seriously thought we'd stop the wedding? So she got him to Orta, then married him on the sly? I thought he was supposed to be finishing the new painting! And then for him to tell us, not even in a phone call, but casually in a group text, a couple of days later! I feel as if he's died. I really do. We don't even know Bella-Mae. We know absolutely nothing about her. And neither can he, if they've only been together—what?—four months? I'm not talking to him. Seriously, Net. I'm not."

Netta didn't point out that technically their father had got there first in the not-talking department. But Susan was still ranting. Netta liked it when her sister got angry. It took the pressure off Netta. In fact, she sounded indignant enough for all four of them. Besides, Netta was still so shaken, she felt winded. "I mean, if this is all about sex," Susan said, "then it's disgusting. I'm so ashamed, I can hardly bear to tell Warwick. And you know what this means? This means we could get nothing. Nothing, Net! I know that might sound shocking, but someone has to say it. Daddy always promised we would be okay. He always said he would look out for us, but now he's thrown everything away and married this girl on a whim. Do we need a lawyer?"

"Suz, I am a lawyer."

"A different kind of lawyer. A QC or someone. Maybe a private detective."

"To do what?"

"To find out who she is. It's the paintings I'm thinking about. And what about the big new one? Do you think Goose was right?"

"About what?"

"Is she drugging him?"

"Suz," said Netta, "I know you're upset. I'm upset. And I love Goose with all my heart, but you know what he's like. His head's in the clouds. There is no way anyone is drugging Daddy. That man creates chaos all by himself."

"Do we go to Lake Orta? What do we do? I could just about bear her living in the London flat. But this is too much. Shall I google flights?"

"Susan, stop. I thought you weren't talking to him."

"I'm not!"

"If we go out to the lake now, we'll be playing into his hands. Daddy wants us chasing after him. That is exactly what he wants. To have his cake and eat it. He's probably bored already and wants a big party. But we've spent our lives running after him. This time we have to stop. We can't drop everything just because he decided to get married without telling us. And we do not need a private detective, Susan. We know exactly what that woman is."

She hung up fast. Then she picked up the phone again. "Suz?" she said, but Susan had hung up too.

"What's happened?" said Robert.

All Netta could say was, "I don't get it, I don't get it, I don't get it."

Vic had always asked her opinion. Even Harry deferred to Netta. She was the one Vic had taken to Orta when the villa came on the market, while Susan and the others stayed at home. It was Netta he went to for advice about his affairs, even when she'd been too young to have boyfriends.

("I don't think this one is going anywhere, but Estelle has the loveliest legs and she does seem to like me. What shall I do, Antoinetta?"

"Dump her, Daddy. Dump her.")

Back then, she knew that boys called her snooty and frigid, but she didn't care: Netta cut like a blade through their foolishness. Besides, by fifteen she was drinking in a different way from them and teenage parties struck her as lightweight. At university, she'd phone Vic every night to rant about the latest story in the news. No one else rang home to talk politics: if they did it anywhere, it was with their friends in the student union. When Susan got engaged to Warwick, it was Netta Vic took aside. "See if you can talk her out of it. She'll listen to you. He's a drip and a bore." And even though she hadn't managed to pull it off, Netta had kept trying, right until the very last minute. These days, everyone at work knew that if Vic called, she should be interrupted, no matter what.

Robert went to buy the papers and came back with everything, including the tabloids and the *Financial Times*, but there was no mention of the wedding. If Bella-Mae was concerned about it hitting the press, that was another thing she'd got away with. Netta zoomed in and out of the image of her on her phone, as if her persistence alone would force her to lift her veil and reveal herself, but it didn't. Then she zoomed in and out of the wedding certificate, and had more luck. She got back on the phone.

"Gonzales," said Netta.

"Gonzales?" said Susan.

"That's her name. Bella-Mae Gonzales. She calls herself an artist, though I can't find any evidence of her paintings. Her father is an accountant."

Five minutes later, Susan rang back and said, "I googled him. He worked for a small finance company. Retired now."

Beyond that, there was nothing else to tell one another, but it sometimes seemed with Susan as if there might be—as if there was something between them, some small nebulous thing they had never found the words for or even chosen to acknowledge. Susan repeated how furious she was. "I am seriously wondering, Netta, if this is the start of Alzheimer's? Do we force Daddy to see a doctor?" Netta said they would be hard pushed to force him to a doctor, especially now that he was in Italy. You could barely get him to an English one. She repeated that they really must not give in to him. She was speaking to herself, as much as Susan.

"I can't believe it," Iris said, when she rang Netta later. Iris was crying so much she couldn't speak in full sentences. "I can't believe—he would. Do that to us. He doesn't even know this woman. And we would never have. Told the papers. Why couldn't he trust us? And why has he taken her? To the house? On the lake? It's ours!"

"He is a crazy old man," Netta said. "He is deluded, Iris. That's what he is. Give it a few weeks. He'll phone soon, expecting us to rescue him from another mess. Just leave him to it. Get on with your life. I am here. Susan is here. Goose too. I doubt this marriage will last five minutes."

And once again, this was something she was saying as much to herself as to her sister.

They all followed Netta's rule, though. The siblings held out. They didn't get in touch with Vic or go to Orta. They left him to get on with his new life and spoke to each other at least four or five times a day for moral support. Between them, they could spend hours on the phone. ("I don't know why you don't just meet up," said Robert. "Or at least buy shares in BT.")

"Listen to me," Netta said, as if they didn't always listen to her. "Do not get in touch with him." She said it over and over, but especially to Iris. She could sense her youngest sister wavering and everyone knew how much she loved Lake Orta. She had tried to live there one winter and only came back because she was so lonely. "Honestly. I will kill you, Iris, if you give in. You're doing this for Daddy."

"I'm not going to give in," said Iris. "Trust me, Net. I haven't even sent a message."

They agreed: there must be no weak link. After all, their father had done things that might split them in the past. He'd send a lavish check to the sisters, then forget about Goose. He painted Iris when she was a child—with her little face that was so sweet you just wanted to bite it—but he never once painted the others. And he was always telling Susan she would be the one to mount his exhibition, even though Goose had been his dogsbody, running the studio for all those years. Or what about the first time Netta broke the eleven o'clock curfew and he'd forbidden anyone to let her inside, so that she was left sobbing on the doorstep until she howled her apology? This time they had to stick together. It was the only way their father was going to realize they were adults now with minds of their own.

Yet all this resolve appeared to have no effect. June came and he still hadn't called. Susan said she kept picking up her phone, even in the middle of the night, just to check it wasn't on silent by mistake, but no, there was nothing. Now that he was married to Bella-Mae, he had forgotten them. How could he do that? Susan asked. What kind of father drops his own children? "After everything we've done!"

Somewhere deep down, Netta believed her mother was to blame, catering to Vic's whims and inflexible demands when they were children so that he had gone unchecked as a father, but really she couldn't remember. Vic had always been the colorful one, and Martha had died before Netta could get any real sense of her. To her shame, she couldn't even recall her face—and, as the oldest, she felt she should. Sometimes her memory got mixed up and she confused her with Shirley Lucas. She knew that Martha had been strict and the house was always clean. She remembered her baking, and the apron she wore in the kitchen with crisscross straps at the back. She had one memory of Martha taking her to buy a pair of school shoes and afterward for tea, though she had no idea why she remembered it. She had another of Martha in her bedroom in her last few weeks, a smell of disinfectant, or worse, that repulsed Netta, and a feeling she'd had that if only she could find the right way to be good, her mother would get better.

Then there was Harry. He was another who'd always given in to Vic, just for the quiet life. If the siblings didn't show a united front, Vic would never change. Only once Iris said, "Are you sure about this, Netta? Are you sure this is the best way to make Daddy see sense? Suppose something is wrong. There's something I maybe should have told you—"

But before she could reveal what that was, Netta interrupted. When she was in full flow, the only thing she heard was the sentence she was about to say: at university she'd discovered she was cleverer than most people and the conviction had never quite left her. "Iris. Stop right there. When has Daddy ever not said if he wanted something?"

Netta did some more detective work. Her assistant contacted Francesca, the housekeeper for the villa, and asked via Google Translate if everything was all right for the newlyweds? Francesca emailed straight back to say it was wonderful. *"Gli sposi sono molto felici!"* The newlyweds are so happy. Then Netta spent a whole morning trying to find Bella-Mae online and came up with nothing, not even a Facebook page, which struck her as a clear disadvantage for someone who was supposed to be an influencer. She tried hashtags for Vic Kemp, Orta weddings, a few porn sites. Still nothing. These days, you expected to find traces of young people all over the internet, but Bella-Mae was invisible. As if she were deliberately keeping herself beyond reach.

It was a hot afternoon in mid-June when Susan rang from outside their father's flat. She told Netta she was standing with Iris, right there on the pavement. Iris was the only one with keys; when Susan cleaned, Vic always left his own set under the mat. In a rush she admitted she'd driven over because the two of them had cooked up a plan to search for evidence that he was on some kind of medication that might explain his behavior. "Alzheimer's or whatever," she said. If Netta experienced a moment of outrage that her sisters had done something without her for once, it was gone so quickly she barely knew it had been there. Susan told her in a shocked voice that Iris's keys no longer worked. The locks had been changed.

"Iris is devastated," said Susan. "Why would he let Bella-Mae lock us out?"

"What did I do?" she heard Iris wailing in the background. "What did I do?"

"It's to keep us away," Netta said to Susan.

"But why? What have we done?"

"We haven't done anything. Don't you ever wonder what our lives would be like if he wasn't our father? If we had someone normal, like everyone else?"

"But he is our father," said Susan. She put the phone closer to her mouth, installing herself inside Netta's ear. "Iris is beside herself. She was always thin, but now she looks awful. And Goose isn't much better. He stays in the studio, waiting for Daddy to come back. But at least he can talk to Harry. I have Warwick, and Robert is there for you. It's different for Iris. She has no one. I asked her to come home with me, but she won't. She says she has to keep working or she'll lose her mind. It's unforgivable what Daddy's doing and it's all Bella-Mae's fault. I swear she's poisoning him against us."

But a few days later, Iris surprised everyone. She told Netta that, in allowing Bella-Mae to change the locks, their father had made it clear he was turning his back on her. This was personal. "I'm putting myself first from now on," she said. "To start with, I'm getting a new job."

The heat wave was serious. People said it had to break soon, but it didn't. It got hotter and hotter. Every day the sky was a sheet of white heat and London was a stew. It was exhausting just to step outside. There was talk of a water shortage, air pollution, a hosepipe ban, forest fires in Europe. At the office, Netta worked with her feet in a bucket of cold water to supplement the air-con. A new case came in involving a high-profile celebrity and suddenly she was working until midnight with barely time to eat a sandwich before she crawled into bed. Every morning she and Robert walked along the river at six a.m. because London was at its coolest then, and drank coffee outside her office before he jogged back to see clients. It was a novelty, she told him once, seeing the world without a colossal hangover, as if a curtain had been briefly opened and she saw another version of her life, clean and dazzling.

Susan and Warwick took a driving holiday to Scotland but came home early because of the insects. She'd noticed how exhausted he seemed since his retirement from the surgery: all he really wanted was to read the papers and admire the view from the guesthouse. But now they were back at home, he was much happier and she was free to think about redecorating the twins' bedrooms, which still had their posters from when they were teenagers. Then one night she ended up hosting the book club because she had the biggest garden, and even though she hadn't liked the novel that month and found herself stammering when it was her turn to talk about it, she served rounds of homemade canapés that disappeared the moment she set them on the table.

One of the women said, "Seriously, Susan. These are to die for."

And another said, "Oh my God, Susan. What have you put in these things? They're like cocaine in biscuit form." So instead of talking about the book, they listened as she told them how she'd done her best to cook for her family as a child, and got a job after her O levels working on the cookery page at a women's magazine, and how she'd always had this funny thing about being a TV chef.

"But you never trained?" one said.

"I mean, you have talent," added another. "Real talent, Susan. You shouldn't squander it."

As a result, Susan put away her paint charts and wallpaper samples, and began looking into professional cookery courses on her laptop. It was idle, of course. She wouldn't leave Warwick to fend for himself and, anyway, she could never hold her nerve with all those other cooks, who would be younger than she was and so much more accomplished. But still. She found her heart started to beat really hard as she watched online videos of the courses, and sometimes tried the recipes they talked about while Warwick took his afternoon nap. Two hours could pass and they felt like minutes. Maybe those book-club women were right. Maybe it was time to reconnect with something she felt passionate about.

There was change, too, for Iris. She got a new job running a cheese counter at an expensive supermarket—the hourly rate was much better than it had been at the burger restaurant and she got to wear a netted hat and white lab coat like a scientist. You could laugh all you liked, but the uniform made Iris feel like someone clever for once. Besides, she was stationed in the chilled-foods section, which at that point was the coolest place in the whole world, short of Alaska: Iris loved it so much she said she was thinking of moving in. And even though she'd lied about her qualifications to get the job, she made sure she quickly became a fount of knowledge in terms of dairy produce. She described the different textures and tastes to her customers, and how strong or ripe they were. Within no time, she had people who came back to her regularly, even if they just wanted to talk about the heat, and she always offered them something new to try. The manager took her aside and said she was so impressed with Iris's customer skills she was thinking of promoting her.

Then a quite nice couple in the maisonette block where she lived set up a screen in the communal gardens and invited everyone to bring their own drinks for a Saturday showing of *Cinema Paradiso*. Iris was barely on speaking terms with most of her neighbors and had never gone inside any of their flats, but because she couldn't visit her father, she found herself pitching up for the film at the last minute. She hovered at the back where no one would notice her, and sobbed so much she went back to her flat afterward feeling deliciously purged, but also having promised the quite nice couple that she would go to their place some time for dinner and attend another garden screening in a few weekends' time.

~

As for Goose, he was doing odd jobs for neighbors on the square and saving up for a mountain bike. A new volunteer called Steve started at the charity shop and the manager asked Goose to show him the ropes. After that, if they were sharing a shift, Steve always seemed to manage it so that the two of them worked on the same sorting table. When a framed print turned up of *Childsplay*, Vic's famous painting of Iris, Steve said, "To be honest with you, I never got the appeal of this. It's a bit sentimental, if you ask me. I don't think I'd even put it in the shop." Goose found himself looking at the painting of his sister and agreeing with Steve, or at least realizing that something about it made him want to put it out of the way. He certainly didn't mention it had been done by his father. "Maybe we could go for a beer some time," Steve said. Goose bit the inside of his mouth and said he would really like that.

He went for a haircut. Yes, Goose finally went to a barber. The young man said he had this great idea for a style that he thought would really suit Goose. And like anyone who goes for a haircut, Goose said, "Go ahead!," seized by a searing conviction that the young man knew what he was doing and would leave Goose not simply with better hair but a better personality as well. He noticed that a lot of hair was coming off his head and landing at his feet in straggles—but this was a good thing, surely, and proof of value for money. Then the young man reached for the clippers. The hair cutting, it turned out, was not the actual haircut but simply a preparation for the more radical style that followed. Before Goose could shout (and when had he ever shouted?), he barely had any hair at all. More of a fuzz. As if he had exchanged his hair for a microphone cover.

"No, it doesn't look funny," said Steve, the way people do when they think something looks funny. "But at least you work in the right place to buy a hat."

All in all, it was a new experience—exhilarating—for the siblings to stand up for themselves and discover they could survive. Even if it felt like play-acting at times, it suggested that other things might be possible. A way of being that might allow them to go into the world and function as separate individuals, leading normal lives.

Then, at the very beginning of July, Vic became the focus all over again, like a furnace that consumed whatever you threw at it and required still more. They were back with what they knew. They were back in the same intense drama that had always cut them away from ordinary life and made them feel a little different from everyone else—and, in a strange way, it was a relief. Because six weeks after he'd got married, Vic finally got in touch.

Iris woke Netta with a phone call. "Have you seen his texts?"

Netta got up. She found her reading glasses and her mobile, though not in that order. Seeing the word "Daddy" printed in blue letters across the screen gave her a flickering feeling, like being hungry. It was close to excitement. There were five messages. The first had been sent at three a.m., the second half an hour later.

Kids, why aren't you here?

What are you playing at?

Three more followed that were just question marks. Netta felt as if she'd been shaken into a jelly and had no idea how to put herself back together. Even her hands were shaking. All those weeks their father had ignored them, it had been relatively easy standing up to him, like fighting something that wasn't fully there—she had been driven by the same passion that made her a brilliant litigation lawyer, her argument so watertight the opposition could only stand back and admire it. Yet now that Vic had reached out to them, everything seemed to shift.

"Oh, Iris, I don't know what this means," she said, and her voice sounded strange, even to herself.

But just at the point when Netta faltered, Iris became belligerent. Out of nowhere, Netta had a picture of Iris as a child, always dressing up in other people's shoes that were too big for her—she had slushed around in their father's boots as if wading through mud. It was the same now. Iris seemed to step into Netta's shoes and become the one with a will of her own, while Netta felt lost and small.

She shouted into the phone, her voice uncharacteristically shrill: "Netta! Look at them! Those texts were sent in the middle of the night! He's drunk, Net! He ignores us completely, and the first time he gets in touch, he's shouting at us! You were right, Netta. We can't give in!"

There were more messages over the next two days, all short and sent in the early hours of the morning. A couple complained about the heat wave: *Hot hot hot!* And *So hot!*

Others referred to the painting: *I've seen the light!* and *It's all making sense!* But on the whole they asked the same questions:

What's happened?

What are you playing at?

Where are you?

Iris still insisted that Vic was bullying them and they mustn't give in. ("He locked us out of the flat, remember?") But Netta didn't know anymore. She had met with a fair amount of bullying in her life—and some had admittedly been dished out by her—and this didn't seem as straightforward. So many things seemed to have changed that she found herself stumbling over every single one.

Only Netta did not do stumbling. She had not stumbled when her father sent her to private school once he had money and the other girls refused to speak to her because she was new and flattened her vowels just like him: she had sat on her own at the front of the class, where she beat them hands down in every subject, though in fairness she did pick up her vowels. She had not stumbled at university when she was told a certain drinking club was for male students only, most of them with titles. She had stood outside with a placard until they acknowledged they had to join the twentieth century and change the rules. Neither had she stumbled, years later, when her boss took early retirement and she put herself up for his job, seriously upsetting at least ten men who were more senior, just as she had not stumbled when a case came up in litigation that no one would touch with a barge pole. She had won against the odds. She did not stumble, aged twenty-nine, after several affairs that had gone nowhere, when she saw a man across the room at a party who made the gates of her heart swing wide open. Leonine and flamboyant, surrounded by a crowd of people laughing, he was vastly overweight and as tall as her father, dressed in a midnight-blue velvet suit that took her mind straight to Lake Orta. A drinker like her—she could spot them a mile off—but blessed with a charm that she lacked. It was as though wherever he went, the party followed. "You and I need to meet," she told him, producing champagne and two glasses.

"What a pleasure!" he said. "Philip Hanrahan. Are you my prince in disguise?"

She'd decided right there and then that she would marry him. And six months later, she did, dressed in a sharp pinstripe suit and heels like icicles. Iris played "Where'er You Walk" very quietly on her recorder and had the whole register office in tears.

So what was this new thing Netta was feeling? This hovering dark pall she could neither name nor shake off and which, for once in her life, left her unable to do a single thing.

"What do you think is going on, Robert?" she asked, as he cooked supper. She was scrolling backward and forward through Vic's texts. She couldn't leave them alone. "Am I wrong about Daddy? Should we give in and go to the lake?"

"Netta," he said. He turned to her, his face full of tenderness. "Let's not pretend. You're going out there sooner or later. It's brave, what you've tried to do, but the four of you are tied up in something you can't even see."

Netta burst into tears. She hadn't known the tears were there. She said, "Robert, why can't you love me?" She hadn't known those words were there either.

He smiled and gave her his handkerchief. "Oh, Netta," he said. "I do."

Why? she wanted to say. Why would you love me, Robert? Sometimes she passed her reflection and, despite the firm set of her jaw, her fierce reputation as a lawyer, even her top position in the family, she had no idea who the person looking back at her was, let alone how they were lovable.

She took his handkerchief, but kept crying. She cried because she couldn't understand what her father was doing, and because Robert would never love her, at least not in the way she meant. She cried because his handkerchiefs smelled of fresh green meadows, or whatever the hell it was, and the man even ironed them.

But he was right. In his quiet, steadfast way he was always right. If Philip had been the life and soul of the party, then Robert was the one who cleared up afterward. Netta needed to go to the house on the lake. It was no use fighting her father, at least not in this way. She had tried to split from him long ago and failed—her body still bore the scars, but in secret places no one could see. She began shifting things in her diary and looking into flights. There was no need to tell the others. It would only alarm them. She wouldn't tell Vic either. So this was no betrayal or about-turn. It was just Netta testing her facts. Any lawyer worth her salt would do the same.

But she got no further. The news came the next day, and within hours they would be rushing toward Lake Orta, all four of them, too late to save their father, too late to do anything except try to find his new painting. Vic had known Bella-Mae five and a half months and been married forty-six days. When his body was discovered, he weighed less than one hundred twenty-five pounds.

There was a heat wave all over Europe. No one could remember a summer like it. The lake was the only place to be.

PART TWO

Lake Orta

Italy, 2015

7

Most Grave News

Death does not come in our own time. It does not check our diaries for a free window, or ask if this is a good moment. A woman was screaming down the line, "Gone! Gone! Gone!," her voice high and thin, like a piece of wire pulled too tight.

It was Vic's number. Susan had answered the moment she saw it. "I'm sorry," she said. "Who's this? Where's Daddy?"

Saturday morning, and she was in Clarks, trying to buy a pair of light sandals, but the place was packed. Everyone in Tunbridge Wells had decided to go shoe shopping—and even with the doors wide open, it was too hot. Worse, her ticket said she was customer number 176, and the two assistants who looked fresh out of school, if not still at it, were on customers 144 and 145. But Susan had spent so long waiting with the ticket in one hand and the shoe she wanted in the other—it was a jeweled flip-flop, casual but a little dressy, Netta would love it—that to leave would mean the whole morning had been a waste of time. Warwick was waiting in the car with the air-conditioning on.

"Uch. Uch. Uch," said the strange female voice.

"Daddy?" said Susan.

"No! No! Gone!"

"I'm sorry. This is a terrible line. What are you saying?"

The woman at the other end of the line began a wail that came in stops and starts. At this point another voice took over, crooning into Susan's ear, an extraordinary deep and unfamiliar foreign male voice. But since she didn't know this man, and she was in Clarks, and she had no idea when she would come out again, if ever, because she was customer number 176, it took an unconscionably long time for the words he was saying to take root in her head, grow shoots and mean anything beyond noise. Her stomach gave a twist, understanding already what her brain could not.

"Your. Father. So sorry. For this. Most grave news. So very sorry. Please. He die."

The air turned to glue. Susan slotted the flip-flop back on the correct shelf and excused herself to the shop assistants. Outside everything seemed to be in very bright colors but also strangely static. A pillar box was too red, the pavement too white, even the sky was a kind of blue that hurt. She felt a bite of sick in the back of her throat and vomited into the gutter, arching her back like a cat. Then she cleaned her mouth with a wet wipe and walked back to the car. "Why am I holding this?" she said, showing Warwick the flip-flop. "I swear I put it back."

"Susan?" he said. "What is going on?"

She told him in a calm voice that she'd just been sick because her father was dead. It was the first time she'd said the words and they didn't sound right. In fact she thought she must be lying. She held out her mobile and saw it was shaking in her hand. "Someone rang me," she said. "I don't know who."

Warwick redialed Vic's number. His tone was suspicious at first, then cordial, then soft and respectful: Even from the passenger seat, she could hear the same deep voice she'd spoken to in the shoe shop. The man said he was a friend of Bella-Mae. He repeated that he was terribly sorry, but Vic was dead. He had gone into the lake very early that morning for a swim and been found in the reeds a few hours later on the other side of the lake, on a small beach at Pella. An abnormally strong current must have dragged him there. Susan was aware of thinking as she listened that all this still sounded very much like something that couldn't be true, or at least happened to other people. That, sooner or later, there would be a punchline. The stranger's accent was thick Italian but she didn't know him. He told Warwick that Bella-Mae was in deep shock and the doctor had given her drugs to calm her down. Then the call ended. Just like that. No punchline.

Susan turned to the window. She couldn't look at Warwick. Not yet. To look at Warwick would be to see the concern on his face and she would have to concede that something seismic had happened. But for this moment she was safe. She was still in the ordinary world, alongside everyone else. A woman went past with her umbrella up and Susan wondered if it was somehow raining until she realized that the woman must be sheltering from the sun. She thought of the shoe shop and how none of this added up, as if she had missed an essential link between the time she'd been waiting with her ticket in Clarks and this one in the car.

"Warwick," she said. "I want the flip-flops."

He was a kind man. It made her ache sometimes, how kind to her he was. He didn't ask why a woman who'd lost her father would need flip-flops with a rhinestone trim. He started the car, but on the way home he stopped outside Clarks. He told her to wait and she did. She tried to think in a straight line, but something like a bomb had opened a crater in the middle of her head and everything she knew was falling through the middle. She called her father's mobile so that she could speak to Bella-Mae's friend again, but this time it went straight to voicemail. It was only when a traffic warden knocked on the window and told her she was parked illegally that Susan shouted, "My father has just died!"

This was the second time she'd voiced it, and it still felt untrue, but the traffic warden backed away and said, in a polite voice, "Yes, of course. You go ahead." It was in that moment Susan remembered how grief cuts you away from other people, while slightly elevating you at the same time, though she had been too little to find those words when her mother died. She was only six then. But she remembered how the head teacher had appeared at the door of the classroom with the look on her face that adults get when they can barely cope with what they have to tell you. Later, the school secretary had given her a bag of sweets while she waited to be fetched and Susan had eaten the whole lot, slotting them into her mouth one by one, like pennies into a meter. She reached for her mobile.

"Netta!"

"Oh, hi, Suz."

Netta complained about how boiling hot it was and how she couldn't think straight, until Susan said, "Oh my God, Net. Oh my God, no one has rung you. You don't know."

That was when it dawned on her that the first voice she'd heard in the shoe shop, screaming from her father's phone, must have been Bella-Mae's. And she was not from absolutely anywhere. She was English. She was the same as Susan.

Susan and Warwick lived in a crescent of Tudor-style mansions, with electric gates and streetlights like old-fashioned gas lamps, that they'd bought with Vic's help soon after they got married. The interior she'd decorated in neutral shades of almond and cream, with matching carpets and curtains. "Our dad lives in a house that looks like a Rich Tea biscuit," she'd overheard one of the twins laugh with a friend. Susan was appalled; it hurt like the stroke of a whip. All she'd ever tried to do, ever since the boys were small, was make sure their weekend visits were safe and hygienic—the things their mother failed to give them, and the same ones Susan had missed out on as a child. The driveway she'd had surfaced in a resin-bound gravel that looked like tiny beige stones but wasn't. It was solid, as if covered with shiny clear varnish, and incredibly expensive; the only way those tiny stones would move was if Susan took a hammer drill to them. Then Netta had come to visit in her old car that she didn't have anymore, and left an oily deposit nothing would clean up. One day she would get it redone. She would have the garden re-landscaped, and an alteration to the front porch, which didn't look as Tudor as the rest of the house, but more seventies. Susan spent her life replacing things with new ones that were the same but updated. Apart from Warwick, of course.

"I'm concerned about you," he said, as they walked to the car. It was midafternoon, but still very hot. The lawn was yellow and dried-up, and because of the heat wave the annuals had all flowered at the same time and were now sprawled over the beds, spent, while the sky was a cast-open blue, the sun radiating white heat from the middle. Warwick mopped his forehead and lifted her suitcase into the trunk. Netta said his SUV was the nearest you could get to a tank without firing missiles at people, but that was Netta: inside it smelled of his Pears soap and upholstery polish and Susan found it incredibly comforting. "You're in shock, Susan. Do you want me to come? I should come. You haven't stopped."

He was right. She hadn't stopped. It was only a matter of hours since the call from Italy, yet it seemed days. A new speeded-up Susan had installed herself inside her, a Super Susan who refused to allow Sad Susan to think any of the thoughts that were in danger of smashing her mind into fragments. After the shoe shop, she'd rung the others, Netta first, then Goose, followed by Iris at the supermarket. None of them knew. It knocked her for six. No one had told them about their father, so it was up to her to deliver the news. It was like standing several feet above them, at the exact moment she should have been howling with them in a gutter.

Netta was quiet and distant. Oddly formal. "I see," she said, when Susan explained about Warwick speaking to the male friend of Bella-Mae. "I see. Well. Thank you for letting me know."

Goose asked questions Susan couldn't answer, not least because he kept stopping for breath so his words were half finished and confused.

Only Iris cried openly. "No! No! No! What have I done? What have I done?"

Susan wanted there to be more to say, or at least a different voice in which to say it, but she'd never been the clever one.

Instead she'd made a list of the people they should contact. Harry and his wife, some commercial galleries, the people Vic drank with who were still alive, plus the few models he'd remained loyal to over the years. She split the list into four and got in touch with the others again. She told each of them who to ring and supplied an up-to-date number. She was only being helpful.

"Susan, don't tell people!" Iris almost screamed. "If you tell them that will make it real!" She could barely get the words out, she was crying so much. Susan felt like a disrupter of the natural order.

Netta said she'd been repeat dialing Vic's number and no one was answering. She was also trying to get through to the police in Orta and track down their father's solicitor, but the Italian police kept putting her on hold and the solicitor was on a golfing weekend. She had no time for phoning a list of people their father wouldn't remember if he fell over them. Besides, they needed to think about a public statement and getting to the lake. Someone would have to identify Vic's body. "Won't they ask Bella-Mae to do that?" said Susan.

"Are you kidding? She's known him five minutes." Susan had been right. There was definitely something sharp about the way Netta said that. She felt a little flicker of hurt.

Meanwhile Goose said he'd already told Harry and it had been one of the worst things he'd ever done. He was really sorry, Susan, but he couldn't face it again.

She told them in her brightest voice not to worry. She would do it. She'd made all the calls, the ones on the lists for her siblings as well as her own. She ticked off the names, one by one. Everyone said the same thing. They couldn't believe Vic was dead, and since Susan couldn't believe it either, this only compounded her conviction that she was not telling the truth. Besides, hearing the shock in other people's voices, the distress, somehow inured her to experiencing those things herself. What was most surprising, though, was that none of them knew a single thing about Bella-Mae, let alone the wedding. She rang several funeral companies, asking them to explain the protocol if your father died in a foreign country, and was told that to repatriate his body a translated death certificate would be required, stating the cause. She tried Vic's mobile again, but it went straight to an uninterrupted beep like a long road with no end point. To her shock, it had already been disconnected.

"I'll be two days, Warwick. Three at the most. I just need to identify Daddy's body and make arrangements to bring him home. Besides, you hate the heat."

"What of Goose? And your sisters? Where are they in all this?" Warwick had a slightly old-fashioned way of saying things. His bedside manner, she called it. "Don't they wish to come too?"

This was a question Susan neatly sidestepped. She was aware she was breaking rank but she wasn't prepared to give a name to it. She double-checked her new flip-flops were in her handbag, along with a bottle of water. A bead of perspiration slipped from her hairline all the way down her spine.

"I've told you," she said airily, knowing full well she hadn't. "Netta has to sort through paperwork, Goose will be at the studio, and Iris is too shocked. Anyway, you know me. This is what I'm good at. Organizing things. It's better that I go to Orta by myself. I'll explain it to the others once I'm there."

Years later, Susan would remember the drive to the lake as one of the purest of her life. As if she knew she would never return home, even then. It took just over fifteen hours and yet it also seemed instantaneous, as though the world had simply reordered itself before her eyes. One moment she was in Tunbridge Wells, ripples of heat rising from the tarmac and watering the horizon, sunlight reflecting so brightly off all the other cars that every color became silver; the next she was taking the Eurotunnel, then driving through France, the land increasingly scorched. The Rhône became the Alps, covered with pine and larch, and rose in harsh gray peaks. The sun dipped. The day dimmed and became secretive, then pitch black. Without her touching any buttons, the car turned its headlamps on full beam. For miles there was only Susan and two long yellow tracks of light on the road ahead. Somewhere past the Italian border, she stopped and briefly slept, bought more water and an old Coldplay CD, then kept going.

It wasn't yet six on Sunday morning when she approached the lake and the small town of Orta, making the final descent with the trees above her a weave of shadows. She parked the car and walked down to Piazza Motta. Already the dark had given way to palest morning. The lake was a soft gray pearl at the edges, still as glass, and the hills on the other side made jigsaw-cuts against the sky. In the middle, the island was peaceful, closed off, sharing its reflection with the water, the trees an inky green. Lights still dotted the mainland, the farthest trembling with the distance, those on the shoreline spilling into the lake. There was the clean, sweet smell of a day that is yet to begin. But even as she watched, silver took hold of the sky, followed by a humming gold, a hint of peach, streaks of pink, color also returning to the painted villas on the island, bright and refreshed. All around the lake, other things came to life: the Venetian-style palazzi, the houses like Swiss chalets because the border was so close. The faraway peaks of Monte Rosa flashed scarlet as the sun's light found them. Outside a café in the square, a woman was setting out tables and chairs. A man was delivering a trolley of beers. The woman looked up at the sky and smiled at Susan as if they knew a secret no one else did.

Susan made her way to the bar where some of the private boatmen would be playing cards. As soon as they saw her, they stared a moment, shocked, then scrambled to their feet and embraced her. *"Che tragedia! Che doloroso!"* What a tragedy. How painful. They offered her grappa, fetched a seat. It struck her again how grief makes an invalid of you and at the same time a kind of celebrity, so that the new world in which you find yourself remains unreal.

"*Grazie, grazie mille*," she said. They'd all heard about Vic, but no one could believe it. Such a great man, they kept saying, and only just married. His wife so beautiful and young! She asked if someone might take her to the island and within no time there she was, crossing the water in a rowing boat toward Villa Carlotta, everything still and quiet. Far away a dog barked. The bell tower chimed six thirty. The lake was like silk breathing.

The boatman wouldn't dream of allowing her to pay. He helped her up to the jetty and passed her suitcase. He didn't want to leave until she turned and waved goodbye. Then she pulled her luggage up the steps that led toward the basilica and took the single cobbled lane to the right, but the little wheels on the case rattled so loudly in the silence it sounded as if she were dragging a wooden cart to market. In the end, she picked it up.

Outside the villa, she pulled at the old bell and heard its clang inside. She waited, polite, her heart in her mouth, but no one came. She tried again. Still no answer. She went to tap the numbers into the security pad and found she couldn't remember them. It was the same as Vic's PIN code, but what was it? His birthday, or had he changed it to Iris's? What was Iris's birthday, though, and why was her head doing this? Why had it suddenly abandoned everything it knew and become a vacant space? She tapped in one number, she tapped in another. No luck. She shook the door. She pushed it. She told herself to be calm and think logically. She took a calming breath and thought logically, but she still didn't know the code. In fact, the only number she could remember was the twins' birthday, so she rattled the door handle, she thumped it, and then, to her surprise, it neatly slipped free of the catch, just like that, and gave way. The door was not locked. It had been open all along.

A slice of early-morning light fell into the large square entrance hall. The many-colored mosaic tiles at her feet glinted like fish scales. On a section of wall, the painted frescos sprang to life. A dragon with a blue tail was breathing out a flame of butterflies that a little boy in a pointed hat tried to catch in his net. A flock of yellow birds flew toward a tree covered with white tulip flowers. The doors to the music room were closed, so there was no view through to the lake, but she could smell the sweet, resiny tang she'd known since her childhood: pine mixed with damp. There was something else, too, another smell, almost sour, that she couldn't put a name to. She stepped inside, closed the door. Everything went dark again.

"Hello?" she called. "Hello?"

The house was inhumanly silent. She felt a shimmer of fear.

But, no, she was wrong. Her father was here. From downstairs, she heard him moving around in the kitchen. He would be taking his first brandy after his early-morning swim. "Hello?" she called. Louder this time.

There was the shuffle of his old sandals on the steps that led up from the kitchen to the hallway. The fear she'd felt was replaced by a surge of relief. Because this was the real reason she'd come. She saw it now. Not to identify his body or make arrangements to take him home, but because deep down she still believed he was alive—if not in England, then at the very least here by the lake. She had rushed all this way to Orta, ahead of her siblings and without even telling them, so that she could have one more moment with him. All by herself and undiluted. And now here he was, coming upstairs to greet her. She reached for the light switch.

Flowers. In the corner. Strange orange spikes she'd never seen before, and palms. The antique table in the middle of the room, which still bore carvings of their names—the table that had been a dumping place over the years for toys, shopping bags, sunglasses, lotion, empty bottles, hats, even knobbles of chewing gum on the underside—was so clear and polished it shone like gold water. "Daddy?"

In the far corner, a man appeared in the doorway that should have held her father. Not slow, not white-haired, not big-bellied and tall, none of those things, but young, broad-shouldered and muscular, low-built. His shirt was vibrantly colored, and he carried two filled bin bags. Seeing her at the door, he began to shout: *"Cosa fai? Esci! Vai fuori da casa mia!"*

Susan stared at the scene ahead of her, everything about it wrong and unfamiliar. The spiky flowers, the polished table, the stranger already taking things away, and shouting at her to get out of his house. The pain she had kept in check, tucked under her ribs, smothered with practical things, smashed open. She felt it flooding her chest, rising into her throat, inchoate, undeniable. Her body began to shake. "No, no, no," she said, because it was all coming apart, she could feel it. "No, no, no."

The last thing she saw was his hand reaching out. Thick fur on his fingers.

8

A Rose in the Wallpaper

Goose woke in a soft sweet bed. He smelled fried bacon, saw a pretty wall crowded with roses, a ribbon of sunshine between curtains, and realized where he was. He'd been walking. He'd walked a really long way, just over twenty miles, but now it was early Sunday morning and he was in Watford. The worst was over. Then, with a lurch, he remembered. His father was dead. The worst was only beginning. He tried to move his head and felt a neon flash of pain.

After the call from Susan—had that been only yesterday?—Goose had stood for a long time in the studio. Strange that at the moment his world yawned open and split in two he had found himself incapable of doing a single thing. He was aware of a sensation like all the air slipping out of him, bit by bit, and knowing even as it went that he could do nothing to stop it. It was the heaviest feeling he'd ever had.

Only how could his father have drowned? It made no sense. Vic was the best swimmer. He'd taught all of them by throwing them into the lake. Even Iris. Goose could see him now at the end of the garden, staring out over the water after his early-morning swim, a towel around his waist, droplets snaking from his great shoulders that were dark from the sun, his hair stuck to his neck in wet spikes. There was always a look of admiration on Vic's face after his first swim of the day, as if he and the water respected the greatness in one another. He loved that lake. He knew it. The currents, the drops, the danger spots. The lake would never drown him.

Goose had spoken to each of his sisters after the news, but there were too many things to say and nothing came close. In the end he'd rung Harry. "Hey, son," Harry said. Goose pictured him—short, overweight and bald on the top of his head, but his hair kinked in a boyish curl where he grew it long at the back, and a Play-Doh-y face that set into wrinkles when he smiled. "How's the old bastard? When's he going to give me that big new painting?"

"Harry, Vic is dead. He was found in the lake. He drowned, Harry. He drowned."

A pause. Two little cut-out expulsions of air. "Sorry, son. I don't understand. What did you say? Vic's drowned? How could he drown?"

"We don't know, Harry. We don't know."

Goose had thought he would feel better once he'd given Harry the news, unburdened somehow, released, but he didn't. He felt the opposite. More trapped inside. And he hadn't even considered what it might be like for Harry hearing that his oldest friend, the man he'd drunk and argued with for years, was gone. Harry said, "Son, would you excuse me?" He must have laid the phone on a table and Goose heard a strange muffled noise in the background that was like a lion roaring inside a blanket. After that his wife had come to the phone.

"Gustav, dear," she said. Shirley Lucas was the only person who used his proper name, which always made him uncomfortable, as if someone else should reply. "I am afraid Harry needs a moment alone. This news has come as a terrible shock. Tell me. Are you all right? Can I do anything?"

He'd lied and said there was a lot to sort at the studio. After that he'd rung Susan and said sorry, but he couldn't make any more of those calls. He couldn't inflict that much pain on another human being. Then he went to the kitchenette and got the vodka and made a plate of crackers with cheese, the exact way his father liked. He sat cross-legged on the floor and ate to stop his mouth sobbing. He drank the vodka neat and smoked a spliff. The phone was ringing again but there was no way he was going to pick it up. The walls of the studio seemed to be leaning in on him.

After the drink, Goose felt strangely sober, as if the alcohol had acted as a deep-cleansing agent and brought a strange new clarity. Maybe you could lose your father and drink the best part of a bottle of vodka and everything would work out fine. He locked the studio, and began to walk. He didn't even know where he was going, though everything looked strangely different, as if someone had taken all the roads and rearranged them in the wrong order. He got as far as Trafalgar Square, where a group of foreign young men were sitting on top of the lions, drinking beers, their bodies all shiny with the sun. "Come up here! Come with us!" they shouted. They helped him up, grabbing his arms as he scrambled with his feet, and he sat with them, feeling that if he could stay here with those young men he would survive. "You come with us! You come!" they shouted as they leaped off the lions, one by one. Suddenly Goose felt free and immortal. It must be the drink. He leaped just like the young men but landed flat on his face. He felt a sting, a punch, flowering through his nose, though strangely it didn't hurt. If anything, he seemed to have no nose whatsoever. He wondered what it was about this day that everything that should hurt didn't appear to hurt at all.

By the time Goose got up, the young men had disappeared. He touched his face and was shocked that his hand came away covered with blood. He was shocked, too, at how red it was. He tried to stem the flow with a painting rag, but then he touched the bone and it gave a soft crunch that didn't sound right. So he kept walking with the rag in front of his face, though people swerved when they saw him, and actually it had begun to hurt so much it was as if his body was one enormous nose.

He followed Edgware Road up to Maida Vale. Dusk fell and at last it got cooler. He was hungry and needed more vodka but there was no way he could go back to the studio—it was as if the telephone call from Susan was still waiting for him. So he kept walking in the opposite direction, putting his feet to the pavement again, again, again. He reached Stanmore, Bushey, saw a sign for Watford and realized that that was where he had been heading from the start. Strange how your body could know a thing before your head.

"Gustav?" It was Shirley Lucas who found him, sitting outside their house. He looked up, forgetting that his face must resemble a piece of raw liver. She gasped. "What on earth happened? How did you get here?"

Even though she was so much smaller, she took his arm and helped him through their front door as if she were taking him into a hospital.

"Mrs. Lucas," he said, with sudden solemnity. "I do believe I might be drunk."

"Yes," she said. "I think you are."

"Do I need to take off my shoes?"

"No, Gustav. I think your shoes are the least of our problems."

She led him through the saloon doors into the kitchen, where she lowered him onto a stool, explaining that Harry had gone to say a prayer for Vic but he'd be home soon. Goose hadn't known that Harry believed in God.

She bathed his nose and he saw with shame the blood in the water. "Keep still," she murmured, "that's right, that's right," as if she was saying she was sorry for everything he had gone through but more with her hands and the cloth. Her hair had been a brilliant red when Goose and his sisters were children, but now it was cut into a white bob that made her face look sharper and a little ugly. She got out disinfectant and said it might sting, then wrapped frozen peas in a towel. "I hope that nose isn't broken. It's going to look a real fright in the morning." She'd never been one to mince her words. He'd always liked that about her.

"I've not said this to anyone, not even Harry, but I didn't like the lake. I know your father loved it, and you all did, too, but whenever we came to visit, I felt a need to get away. You were such excellent swimmers. You could spend the whole day in that water. It looked way too deep to me."

She was right about the lake. From the edge of the garden, the rock fell sharply downward. There was nowhere to stand. As their father always told them, the island was basically a mountain in a lake and they were living on the very top of it. Briefly he had a picture in his head of Shirley in her rubber ring and a white swimming cap with plastic daisies. "Jump! Jump, Mrs. Lucas!" they'd be shouting, but she never could. He wondered why she and Harry had stopped coming so suddenly. Everyone had made fun of her because she couldn't swim, but he'd liked it when she was around.

"I'm sorry," she said. "I shouldn't talk to you like this. It's shock. We think we're so clever. But when push comes to shove, we have to say things about a hundred times just to get it into our heads that they're true."

She fetched him a clean towel for the shower, along with a pair of Harry's jogging trousers and an ironed T-shirt. The clothes weren't big enough but they smelled of fabric conditioner and good people.

"Do you want Harry to call your sisters?" she said. "Tell them you're safe?"

Weeks later, it struck him as strange that she hadn't offered to do it herself. The phone was right there on the kitchen counter. All she had to do was dial their numbers. But he told her it was okay. He wasn't ready to let them know he'd walked all the way to Watford. Netta, for one, would think he was heading back for the loony bin.

When Harry came home, he had a strange smile on his face until Goose realized he was crying. "Son," he said. "What the hell happened?" Goose allowed Harry to pull him close, feeling his arms strong around him and closing everything else away. He was bent right over and his face was mashed into Harry's shoulder, but there was no way he was going to break free. Harry wept and wept and Goose thought what a piece of shit he must be that he had barely cried once. All he seemed to feel was a kind of stunned emptiness. After that, Shirley made a TV dinner with grilled sandwiches and tomatoes cut into frill shapes that they ate on their laps. They watched some program in which everyone seemed to be in sequined outfits and feathers. Goose wondered if he could live here forever. It wasn't as if they had children.

Out of the blue he remembered his sisters dressing him up when he was a boy in a nightie and putting makeup on him that they'd taken from the au pair's bathroom. "Look at Goose!" they crooned, as he tried on lipstick, blusher, a pair of high heels. "Look at Goose!" He'd seen the recognition on their faces of his happiness, which only compounded it, magnified it, so that he'd become excited to show his father too. And when Vic finally came back from the studio, Goose had allowed Susan to push him forward. He had seen the briefest smile lighten his father's face until it had dawned on him that this was his son. "Get that stuff off," he said coldly. "Look at the state of you."

There was no more play-fighting after that. Sometimes Goose would say, "Hit me, Daddy!" and throw a light punch to his arm, but Vic shrugged him off. If only Goose could have been the kind of son his father wanted.

It was midnight when Shirley showed him up to the spare room and called, "Good night, Gustav!" When he'd woken, he looked at the sunlight at the windows and felt happy by mistake. Now he blinked hard, trying not to think about his father drowning, trying to keep himself safe inside this little room with sunshine and rose wallpaper, but it was no use. He could picture it as if it was happening to him, the lake closing over his head, the panic as the current wrapped itself around him and dragged him with muscular force toward the bottom, twisting him around, so that he couldn't tell anymore which was up and which was down. Goose was trying not to shout, wondering how soon he could reasonably get hold of weed in the middle of Watford on a Sunday morning, but now the roses in the wallpaper were coming to life, their tight pink buds yanked outward, exposing bloodred stamens that snapped into heads with teeth in them, their stems coiling into screaming tendrils that flew toward his neck—

A knock at the door. "Son?" It was Harry in a dressing gown. He held out a phone, and Shirley stood behind him, her hands not quite on his shoulder. "It's a message from Netta. She's been trying to find you everywhere. You need to get to Orta, son. I'm afraid there's more bad news."

9

You Drowned

There was no will. At least, nobody could find one. And if there was no valid will, then according to the rules of intestacy all of Vic's personal property would go to his wife. She would also inherit the first £322,000 of his estate, along with half of what was remaining, the other half to be divided four ways between the siblings. That meant not only his apartment, but also the studio and Villa Carlotta. All to be shared with a young woman their father had only just married. Netta had finally got through to her father's solicitor on a golf course late on Saturday afternoon. "I'm sorry," he'd said. "I tried to warn him, but you know what he was like. Your father could stomach most things but he had an allergy to paperwork. I'm afraid this leaves you and your siblings in a very delicate position. Are you sure he didn't leave any kind of secret will? Not even a note with his name at the bottom? Because if I were you, Netta, I'd start searching. And I don't mean nicely."

First things first. She had tracked down his bank manager, who was able to confirm, even though she knew he shouldn't, that Vic had not deposited a will with the bank. Netta had gone straight to Vic's flat and broken in with the help of Robert and a locksmith friend. She'd paused long enough to register that the place looked entirely different, not the pigsty she'd expected. In fact she'd never seen it so tidy. After that she'd turned it upside down—tidiness had never been her strong point—while Robert searched more methodically.

As she feared, there had been no sign of a will. Robert discovered some unopened bank statements at the back of a drawer but they were from the previous year, before Vic had met Bella-Mae, and the payments consisted solely of direct debits to his children, as well as checks to his favorite restaurant, an art supplier and the off-license. Then she and Robert had gone to the studio and turned that upside down as well, but once again found nothing. Not even her brother. To top it all, Susan had now disappeared off the face of the planet and stopped answering her phone. And not a word from Iris. They went back to Netta's, where Robert opened wine and cooked, though she had no memory of either. She left voice messages for her siblings and Harry. Then Robert held her while she lay on the sofa in the dark. "Don't turn on the lights," she'd said. She wasn't ready to see the world without Vic in it.

That night Netta had dreamed her father found her crying. "What's wrong, Antoinetta darling?" he asked. "What happened?"

"You drowned," she sobbed. "You drowned."

His face went pale. He touched his hands and face as if to check he still had them. "I drowned? How could I drown? That's the maddest thing I ever heard."

She would have the same dream on and off all summer. Vic came to her and asked what was wrong, and she'd have to break it to him that he had died. Years later she would hear that it was often like this for the newly dead, that they would come back to the people they loved, trying to understand what was different. Vic would ask for all the details of how he died, and when. They talked about his drowning as if it had happened to someone else. But it was always the same. He could never believe that he was actually dead. "I'm such a good swimmer," he'd say, genuinely at a loss. "How could I drown?" Having to break it to him was like making it happen over and over again.

What she never told him, because she couldn't tell anyone, was that when Susan had given her the news she'd felt anger. A kind of rage that he could abandon her. And after that she'd felt something else she couldn't tell anyone, not even Robert. Because this was worse. She'd felt put out. As petty as that. Like being a child, except that Netta had never really been one. And the reason she'd felt so put out was because Susan had told her the news, when by rights it should have been the other way around. But after that, the grief had let loose and it was like being felled. None of the other stuff mattered.

On Sunday morning, Netta woke on the sofa with a killer hangover and a duvet that Robert must have laid on top of her before he'd gone home. Her mobile was on the coffee table, beside the acetaminophen and a pint glass of water with a Post-it note stuck to the top: *Here is your phone. Here are your keys. Here is water. R xx*

10

In It Now

By Sunday lunchtime, Iris was in an executive lounge at Heathrow airport. Netta had picked her up in a cab, having organized last-minute flights and fast-track security. Iris wasn't sure what she had packed in her rucksack beyond flip-flops and an old green dress. Netta had gathered every Sunday newspaper she could lay her hands on and was now on her third complimentary glass of wine, while Iris nursed a fizzy orange.

"You did what?" Netta was saying. "Iris? You did what?" Two trammeled lines ran the length of her face that Iris had not seen before, as if her cheeks had been dug into with a spoon. "Please say that to me again, Iris. What did you do?"

Iris sat very still. She'd just dropped another bombshell. Compared to the other bombshells falling on her siblings left, right and center over the last twenty-four hours, this one had seemed relatively minor, which was why she'd thought it best to be brave and tell Netta. Now she wasn't sure. She had discovered she had plenty to say in her new job at the cheese counter, but faced with Netta, she was tongue-knotted and a child again. "I mean, when did you do this?" said Netta. "How?"

"I'm trying to explain, Netta. I'm just not doing it terribly well. It's because Daddy's dead. Everything in my head is kind of jangled up."

Iris had left work the moment she got the news about Vic. Afterward she'd rung Netta and Goose in floods. Both had asked if she wanted to meet up and she'd said yes to them, then done her own thing and rushed back to her flat. There might be a heat wave outside but she'd closed the windows. Drawn the curtains. Double-bolted the front door. She wanted to pull the place around her like a blanket.

Already messages had started coming through on her phone. *So sorry for your loss. He was a great man. Call me, Iris.* She couldn't understand: she'd only just been told her father was dead and already people wanted her to get over it. She had turned off her phone, lain on the bed and howled. Because it was her father who'd always protected her. Who worried if she wasn't sleeping properly or getting enough to eat. It was her father who'd had several of her boyfriends followed in her early twenties, suspecting they were trouble, when Iris couldn't see that. It was him, too, who'd said when she was a child that she brought him luck and pulled her so close when he was phoning in a bet that she could hear the wild thump of his heart. And yet he had drowned, the man she knew to be invincible. It was like a vicious uprooting that yanked her from everything she knew—not just her childhood but also the future. Without Vic, who knew what danger she might be in? If she kept her curtains closed, if she checked the fish-eye peephole at the door over and over, then maybe she could stay safe, but everything was becoming unfamiliar, even her body, as if her legs and arms belonged to someone else. So when she'd finally turned on her phone on Sunday morning and found all the new messages she'd missed, ending with two from Netta—*Ring me now!* then *For fucksake why don't you have a proper mobile, like any normal person?*—it had taken every last bit of her strength to call back. She had barely finished dialing the number before her sister began assaulting her with information.

"Susan is in Orta!" Netta had shouted. Full volume. "Can you believe it? I've just found out from Warwick! She left yesterday afternoon! He was trying not to tell me, but he's always been a hopeless liar. And guess what?" Iris had no clue. Fortunately this was only a figure of speech. Netta had no intention of waiting for Iris to guess her next sentence. "Bella-Mae has disappeared! Completely vanished! There was just this man in the house on the lake! Some complete fucking stranger with bin bags! He was trying to empty it! And can you believe she's already announced his death?"

"Susan has?"

"Bella-Mae! On Twitter. *Twitter!* And you know what else is weird? That's the first and only tweet she's ever done. If it weren't for all the hashtags, no one would have seen it. Harry says it's even in some of the Sunday papers."

This had been so much to take in that Iris's head had stalled, in danger of overload. When it came back, she heard Netta talking about flights. "Goose will catch us up, but you know how he is about planes. I've canceled my diary for the next few days. I'm picking you up in a cab in half an hour." Iris had packed in minutes and put on a sweater even though the rest of the world seemed to be in T-shirts. Then she stepped out of her front door into whatever she had been hiding from, so that it could finally begin to take place.

In a few hours they would be in Milan, where Netta had booked another car to take them to the lake. It had turned out—after another phone call—that Susan was now in conversation with the stranger from the villa, who was in fact Bella-Mae's cousin and not stealing things but fetching her some clean clothes. And where was Bella-Mae in all this? Flat out in her cousin's hotel, drugged up to the eyeballs. Now that Iris understood the full extent of the chaos around her, she was embarrassed by her brief brush with what might have looked like insanity, though there remained the problem of how to tell Netta what she undoubtedly should have told her weeks ago, without causing her sister to burst into flames. Her head felt swimmy.

"I saw him," she said, "just before Daddy went to Lake Orta with Bella-Mae. I saw him."

"You did what?" Netta said all over again.

"I went to the flat. He texted me on the off chance."

"Saying what?"

"How was I? That kind of thing."

This wasn't fully true, and Iris picked at a wool bobble on her sweater as she said it. In fact, Iris had rushed over to Vic's flat the moment she'd seen his message. *Are you free, Little Fish?* She'd cycled there so fast she was overtaking double-decker buses.

"This was back in early May? After Daddy saw Goose at the studio? But before he left for Orta?"

"Yes."

"I can't believe it. I can't believe you met Bella-Mae and never told us. What other secrets are you hiding?"

"None. I don't have any. And I didn't meet Bella-Mae. I only saw Daddy."

"Why? Where was she?"

"Asleep. She was asleep."

"Asleep? In the middle of the day? What does she even do?"

"Daddy said she was exhausted."

Netta rolled her eyes. Iris couldn't tell if she was angry with Iris, or angry with Bella-Mae, or Susan for being in Orta, or Goose for having a semibreakdown, though the likelihood was that she was angry with the entire package. "But I don't understand. Why didn't you tell us? Why didn't you say all this before?"

"I tried, Net. I tried to tell you, but you wouldn't listen. And then he left with her anyway and got married and we found out they'd changed the locks. None of what I'd seen mattered anymore. I felt rejected. We all did. As if he'd been playing me for a fool—"

"So how was he?" interrupted Netta. This was one of the reasons it was so difficult to tell her anything.

"I don't know. Very thin. Kind of quiet. He seemed scared of waking Bella-Mae. He told me I'd better take off my shoes."

She had noticed his weight loss straightaway. Maybe it was the light in the room but, for the first time, it didn't look so good anymore. Some of the natural color had left his face, and when he hugged her, he felt like pure bone inside his shirt, so it was possible to imagine a little empty space between the sleeve and his body. Her eyes had gone darting over the flat, hunting for clues.

"And?" said Netta.

"I've never seen it so tidy. It was immaculate."

"It still is," said Netta. "Or, at least, it was until I broke in. It isn't quite so immaculate now."

Vic had always been a tidal wave. Wherever he went, he made a mess, and most of it he dumped on the floor. But there were none of the usual half-finished food trays to trip over that day, no paint-encrusted clothes, no empty bottles or broken glass. Not even when Susan cleaned did it look like this. A vase of spiky flowers that might have been harvested from another planet stood on a table in the hall, and Iris saw more when she followed her father to the sitting room, both now speaking in whispers so as not to disturb Bella-Mae, but even the carpets seemed softer, her feet sinking into the thick pile. Apart from a teapot on the drying rack in the kitchen, and a packet of dried leaves, everything was cleared away. The trees of Regent's Park formed a perfect frieze outside the windows.

"Did he seem ill?"

"Apart from how thin he'd got, no. And he wasn't worried about that. The opposite. He kept telling me how good he felt now that he'd lost more weight. He was happy, he said. But he missed us."

Netta shook her head, disagreeing with their father even though he wasn't there. "Not that much. He chose not to speak to us. He married Bella-Mae without so much as a phone call. I don't think he missed us one bit."

Iris went quiet again. She was remembering the way he had looked at her that afternoon in a tender, troubled way. He'd shifted his gaze to the few familiar things he had managed not to break over the years. A pink papier-mâché elephant Susan had made at school that miraculously stood with only three legs. An old swimming proficiency certificate of Iris's, still in its clip-on frame—it was just about the only qualification she'd ever got. She wondered if those things had always been in the flat, but hidden by his chaos, or whether he had unearthed them and put them where he could keep looking at them. Even his voice seemed less certain, as if the majority of it had been cut away and he was afraid to use the little he had left.

"Daddy?" she'd said. "Are you okay?"

He shot a look toward the bedroom door where Bella-Mae was sleeping. Then he covered his heart with his hand and whispered, "I'm in it now." It was so quiet she barely heard.

"That's what he said?" repeated Netta. "I'm in it now?"

"I think so."

"You think so?"

"I mean that's what it sounded like."

"What was he talking about?"

"I don't know."

"You didn't ask?"

"No, Net. I let it go."

The truth was she hadn't wanted things to be difficult for her father. If he was upset, she didn't want to make it worse. Iris always felt there was an invisible ring of fencing around her, just as there were invisible fences around other people, and she didn't like to climb over them. It wasn't that she didn't care: She just didn't want to expose people to more pain by asking questions it might be difficult to answer. Besides, if people did the same in reverse, if they ventured inside her invisible fencing, there was the very real possibility they would either hurt her or need more than she had to offer. It was easy for Netta. She said whatever came into her head, then walked off, unscathed. Iris felt she was more a bath-cube sort of person, fizzing into nothing. If she didn't hold on to the little she had, she might lose everything.

Netta leaned forward. An objection, an argument, was already forming behind her eyes, going into a crouch along her spine. There was something about her face that was never at ease. Instinctively Iris shrank back a little. "Iris?" Netta said, her voice low but urgent. "Did anything else strike you as wrong in the flat?"

"No, Net. Like I said, I thought it looked beautiful. The only thing I noticed was the teapot. And I don't even know why I'm thinking of it, except that he never used to drink tea before. It was one of those little painted teapots. There was a smell too."

"You mean oil paint? Turps?"

"No. Neither of those things. Kind of sweet but bitter."

"This is all too strange."

"The smell?"

"Everything. Us flying out. Goose at Harry's. Suz already by the lake. I'm surprised Warwick let her do it." Everyone knew there was no love lost between him and Netta. *Historic Warwick*, Netta called him, and not even behind his back.

Iris nodded. Netta was right. It was too strange. On the way to the lounge they had squeezed past holidaymakers with their wheelie suitcases, queuing for all-day breakfasts and beers. The whole thing felt like one gigantic mistake. As if she and Netta knew something terrible that no one else had yet discovered. She didn't know how she would ever fit back into the normal world.

But Netta was still talking. All the fury she had previously reserved for Vic had now regrouped itself into a single full-blown attack on Bella-Mae. "If Daddy was ill, she should never have made him go to the lake. I bet she was nagging him and nagging him and, in the end, he gave in. He had no choice. She wanted to get him as far away from us as possible so we wouldn't be able to stop the wedding. She wanted to drive a wedge between him and us, and we fell straight into her trap." She drained her glass: her red nail polish was so chipped it looked as if she had bitten off the nubs of her fingers. "I should have got a bottle. It's much easier by the bottle." She waved to a server to say she'd like the same again.

Iris said, "Actually, there is one more thing. About that day I saw him."

"Yes?"

"As soon as I left Daddy, his neighbor—Mrs. Lott, you remember?—opened her front door. I got the impression she was waiting. You know what a gossip she is. Daddy never liked her. But she said there was something I ought to know. She'd been hearing strange noises. She didn't know what to make of them."

"Like what?"

"She said it sounded like sobbing. In the middle of the night, she said."

"Daddy?"

"She didn't know. I told her I'd go back in a few days, but obviously they left for Italy and then we found out they'd got married, and everything changed." Now that she'd begun to come clean, Iris couldn't do it fast enough. The more she confessed, the worse it looked. Iris avoided the news as much as she could—it seeped inside her and stayed there until she couldn't think of anything else—but she had seen footage of an avalanche once, the land collapsing on itself and becoming not solid but water, people screaming as it unfolded toward them, and she felt the same panic now. The same sense of everything falling in. "I feel so guilty, Net. I feel guilty I went to see him in secret. I feel guilty I didn't tell you what he said. I feel guilty about Mrs. Lott. I feel guilty about how thin he'd got. And I should never have stayed quiet. I should have followed them to the lake. It's my fault. Everything. It's my fault he drowned. When he began texting us, I was the one who said to ignore him, remember? It was literally a few days before he died. How could I have done that? It's all because of me. Everything. Even Mummy's death. It's all my fault."

At last Netta interrupted, though she seemed to take her time. "Of course that's not true. Mummy had a tumor. You were a baby. Unless you were blow-piping her with cancerous darts from your cot, you really can't blame yourself. But what the hell did Daddy mean when he said he was in it now? What was he trying to tell you?"

Iris would feel the cold for the rest of the summer. Everyone in Europe was wearing as little as possible, even a shoulder strap felt too much, and then there was Iris, always in her cardigan, her shoulder blades sticking through like a wire hanger. She couldn't eat. She couldn't sleep either, at least not for any decent length of time. To surrender to sleep would take her further from her father, a kind of betrayal, or at least an admission that life had moved on, so she lay most of the night with her eyes wide open, keeping vigil for she didn't know what. With her father gone, everything seemed to be in a state of flux. The only meaningful thing was the lake: a powerful current had dragged him away and now seemed to be pulling her in the same direction. She would get thin as a reed, bags under her eyes like pouches. She couldn't forgive herself for failing to ask her father what he'd meant that day. It was a question she would ask on and off for years, long after the split from Netta and Susan. What did you mean, Daddy? What were you telling me?

One day Iris will have two daughters whom she will love more than she thought she could love anyone. But she will never forget the way Vic looked at her the last time she saw him, like a man who'd lost his train of thought and emptied himself into blankness, while Bella-Mae slept soundly on the other side of the door.

11

Cousin Laszlo

Questions, questions, so many questions: her head was on fire. Anger came to Netta as naturally as breathing, but even she had not been prepared for this wretched, roaring rage. How could it be that one night her father was sending texts and a few days later he was gone forever, his life no more than a few lines in some Sunday tabloids? And that was only the first question. Did anyone see him go into the lake? Who found his body? What did they do to resuscitate him? Was he taking pills? Medicine? Was he drunk? What had he eaten in the last forty-eight hours? For all the time she'd spent on the phone to the police, Netta might as well not have bothered. No one could tell her anything about her father beyond the fact that he had drowned. Would there be a criminal investigation? An autopsy? No: the police considered his death a tragedy, but had found no signs of foul play—a local doctor had gone straight to the scene and confirmed there was nothing suspicious. "Nothing suspicious?" she'd shouted right back. "What—a man marries a woman he barely knows and drowns less than a month later in a lake he actually does know, really well, like the back of his hand?"

The *commissario* was polite. He didn't say it outright but he implied Vic's age was the issue. *"È una tragedia, ma ogni anno se ne verificano di questo tipo."* It was a tragedy but, sadly, there were accidents like this every year. People underestimated the power of the lake, simply because it was one of the smallest. There were strange crevices down there, springs and currents. It might be the height of summer, but the water could be fatal.

And now Netta was finally in Orta with Iris. The painted façades of Piazza Motta—those delicate greens and pinks and sandy yellows, the rickety shutters, the frescos on the walls—were lit by quivering reflections of light from the water. Here were the restaurants and bars with their vast white parasols, the horse-chestnut trees. Sailing boats crossed the lake, as perfect as folded napkins. The boatmen dressed as naval officers, in their white shirts and caps, were packing up to go home. It was the same as ever. And yet she looked at all she knew and felt she had never seen it before.

Since it was too late for the passenger boat, they took a private water taxi to the island. Iris was nearing total dehydration from having cried the whole flight, and also in danger of passing out from all the wool she was still wearing. Netta wafted her with her hat and stared at the lake. The lowering sun cast a bright white strip ahead of them, with further sparks popping and snapping, each one overlapping the next in dizzying succession. Netta knew that Iris was watching the lake too. She didn't have to look at her. They were both scanning it for their father.

"His body was in the reeds," said Iris. "Isn't that horrible?" The island was ahead, the little handful of buildings and trees caught in the beautiful evening light. On the far side of the water stood Pella, the waterfront village where Vic had been found. "How could Daddy drown, Net? He was the best swimmer."

Iris reached for Netta's hand, and Netta tried her best to squeeze it. She said, "I don't know. But I'm going to find out."

"I wish we could stay on this boat forever. I wish the next bit could not happen. We're orphans now."

They kept staring at the water until they passed a cormorant perched atop a yellow buoy. It stayed watching them, its black feathers winking in the sunshine. "Do you think that might be Daddy?" said Iris.

"I think it's a cormorant, darling," said Netta.

When someone dies, even the air changes shape. Susan must have been waiting just the other side of the door. They'd barely rung the bell and there she was, pulling it wide open. Her eyes were bright as stars, and she wore her old brown caftan. For the briefest of moments, Netta didn't know her. She seemed bigger. More powerful somehow. As if this was her house now.

"Thank God you're here!" cried Susan.

Then Netta was tidal-flooded with love because, with Vic gone, all they had was one another, and she hugged Susan hard, claiming her back. She could feel her sister's heart going *I am alive! I am alive!* against hers. "Well, this is shit," she said.

"I can't believe it's happening. I keep expecting to see him. Is it really in the papers?"

"A few."

"Maybe if I read them I'll believe it."

"I don't think so. It just makes everything weirder."

Susan turned to Iris now with her rucksack on her back, so big that by rights Netta thought it should have been the other way around, the rucksack carrying Iris, and said, "Sweetheart! Oh, sweetheart!" Iris bent her head to have it stroked, as if she were a little pony, and Susan caught her in her arms. "Look at you both!" she said. "You're so thin! How come you two lose weight when you're sad while I just pile it on?"

"I don't see how that can be true. He only died yesterday, Suz."

Netta took in the frescos on the wall of the hallway, the dragon breathing out butterflies that the little boy tried to catch in his net. The double doors to the music room were open, and beyond the windows, the trees in the garden were a deep green, the lake all blue and diamonds. And yet the villa seemed empty.

"Where's Daddy?" said Iris. "Is he upstairs?" Her face was as pale as salt. Even her mouth was pale.

"No. Apparently the police took his body straight to the morgue."

"What about Bella-Mae?"

"She isn't here either."

"It's all different. It even smells different."

"I know."

Since they were children, the villa had been the same. The same ornate furniture that had been left by the famous harpist, most of it chipped or broken over the years, the same tattered old silk curtains and threadbare rugs, with their father's sketches and unsold paintings hanging on the walls. You could try as hard as you liked to keep the place clean but there was no stopping the mildew, the flaking plaster, the scuffs and stains on the floors that had probably been there since the seventeenth century. But now everywhere they turned, there had been some adjustment—an old broken lamp and ashtray removed from a side table so that you could see the delicate mother-of-pearl inlay in the wood, or chairs arranged in a circle in the music room, as if a small group of neat people had just left. The mosaic floor tiles shone beneath a river of polish. There were no black spots on the walls. No map of mold on the ceiling. The sisters took their bags up the wide flight of stairs that led from the entrance hall, with ornate ironwork balustrades and the stone steps so ancient they hollowed at the center, and at each room they paused without going in, as if the villa had become an exhibition home overnight with taped-off sections and all the furniture with little signs saying they were not allowed to touch. At Vic's bedroom, they opened the door a fraction. It was dark, not one breath of air.

"I can't go in there," said Iris. "I'm not ready."

"Me neither," said Susan. "Francesca called round this afternoon. When she went into the room, she cried and cried. I could hear her from down the garden."

They took the narrower set of steps that led toward the top: the two rooms on the second floor they'd shared as children—Netta and Susan in one set of single beds, Iris and Goose in the other. They checked the green bathroom installed back in the fifties with a showerhead the size of a postage stamp. ("Wash in the lake," their father would shout, when Netta complained, with reason, that the shower was so ineffective she might as well spit on her hand and use that instead.) Here was a pile of gray towels folded one on top of another, and a set of minimalist soap dispensers. Gone were all the half-empty bottles of shampoo and after-sun cream, and everything else no one had thrown out for years. On the next floor, they looked at the single rooms with lake views that Netta and Susan had moved into when they were older—though Iris could never sleep alone and always slipped into one of her siblings' beds the moment they turned out the light—but these, too, had been cleared of all the junk and clutter so that you could see the clean beauty of what was left. The beds were made up with fresh sheets, and draped with tasteful linen throws. The top two floors had never been for the family. They were reserved for au pairs and guests, like Harry and Shirley Lucas, while the garret was accessed by a ladder and was their father's domain. All summer the smell of turps would fill the house, like a toxic cloud. You could hear him singing up there when the work was good, rubbing his hands because he was happy. But you also heard when it went wrong. ("You bastard! You idiot! Fuck shit fuck shit! Where the hell is the turps?") If he was drunk, it was worse. Things got broken and smashed. It was best to keep out of the way.

Susan had made up the two beds in the room she'd once shared with Netta, and put a mattress in the middle for Iris. Netta took in the carved wooden bedheads, the little oval mirror with its gold frame in a pattern of oak leaves. All the magazine pages they'd Blu-Tacked to the walls as teenagers were gone. Only the painted frescos remained: five bluebirds eating out of the hand of San Giulio. Then Susan said, "God, I need a drink," and Netta said, "Now you're talking my language," and they went all the way down to the kitchen. Their feet were so fast their flip-flops echoed, as if they were beating the silence out of the house and reclaiming it for the living.

"I've made supper. Just something light," Susan called over her shoulder, though she never cooked anything light, not even an egg, and everywhere smelled of garlic and basil.

The kitchen was another vast room with an ancient range at one end, a sea of old green majolica tiles above the sink and copper pans on the walls, with a high ceiling that would once have been used for hanging game. On the opposite side, a pair of French windows stood wide open, leading directly to the terrazzo, then the sloping garden with its beautiful trees, the glasshouse and the lake. The sky had turned the palest blue, like a piece of gauze, and the last of the daylight lay in quills on the grass.

"Help yourselves, help yourselves!" sang Susan. "You must be starving!"

Not only was Susan incapable of cooking anything light, she was also incapable of catering for anything smaller than a family of many generations. She had set the table with candles, the best plates and crystal glasses. There were dishes of salami and cheese to eat while they were waiting, with olives, salted grissini and anchovies swimming in olive oil. Only Susan could lose her father and do all that. But first Netta needed alcohol.

"What's happened to Daddy's painting?" she said, en route to the fridge.

It had been hanging here since she was a teenager—*My Sweet Guardian Angel*—in which a woman wearing a pair of dressing-up-box wings and nothing else sat smoking a cigarette and drinking red wine. It was the first in a series of angel paintings Vic had tried one summer and never reproduced, and it had always bothered Netta, not simply because she had to look at it every morning as she ate her breakfast, but also because it made such poor sense as a narrative. This was aside from the whole fact that Netta had met the model several times after her father dropped her, and held her hand as she sobbed over another bottle of red, her mouth dark as a blackberry, saying her life was nothing, it was nothing, without Vic.

Susan said, "Daddy didn't want to see it anymore. That's what Laszlo told me."

Netta pulled out a bottle of sparkling Alta Langa. It was a good one. "Laszlo? Who's Laszlo?"

"Bella-Mae's cousin." All of a sudden Susan's voice had acquired more air. It was loud and bouncy. More like a public announcement. "They've been close since they were children. They didn't have siblings like us, only one another. Apparently she never got on with her parents. She left home as soon as she could and lost all touch with them. But she's always stayed close to her cousin. Anyway, he was very helpful. Once we'd sorted out who we both were, he couldn't do enough to help. It turns out he was the one who spoke to me on the phone in Clarks. So, in a funny way, we kind of met before we met." Somewhere along the line Susan had gone very red—her skin was like a signpost in that respect—though possibly it was the effort with which she had begun to whisk. The words came as fast as the whisking, as if she needed one in order to accomplish the other. "I know I should have told you before. Please don't be upset, Netta. He only wants to introduce himself."

As if on cue, a man in his mid-thirties stepped through the French windows that led to the terrazzo. Three improbable thoughts crossed Netta's mind. The first was that he was Elvis Presley, the second that he was brightly colored and confusingly short for Elvis, the third that he must be very superstitious. A host of silver amulets were caught in the hairs on his neck, warding off bad spirits from at least five civilizations.

It was Iris who had the grace to get up. But that was Iris for you. She went to this man, this Laszlo, and offered her hand, but he sidestepped the handshake and embraced her. She broke free and gave what looked like a curtsy. "It's nice to meet you, Laszlo," she said. The politeness in her voice was painful.

"My condolences. I am sorry for this most terrible time. I am sorry your father die." His accent was thick and, while Netta had to admit that his English was more fluent than her Italian, he had clearly not learned beyond the present tense.

"Thank you."

Laszlo made a prayer shape of his hands and gave a bow. Perhaps it was Iris's curtsy that had set him off. "My cousin sends her condolences. She apologize for not being here to welcome you. Please. Allow me."

It was not Iris he was now addressing. It was Netta. Before she could stop him, he had eased the bottle from her hand, pulled out the cork with an explosive flourish and was pouring her a glass. The sparkling Alta Langa popped on her tongue, like buttery sherbet. She got that first hit. The delicious sensation of being lifted into the air while everything else fell away. She didn't always get it anymore but this was right on the money.

"Laszlo bought it for us," said Susan.

Netta looked at the glass in her hand. She didn't want his gift, but then again she did, so there you go. She drank it.

"Please tell us what you know about Daddy," said Iris. "Please tell us what happened."

Laszlo stepped to the middle of the kitchen and paused, checking he had their full attention. He was a knee-jigger: the man could not stand still. Netta didn't want him there, she really didn't, yet he knew what she wanted to know, and for once she had no choice. She had to listen. "Your father, he swim early every morning. He like to swim before he begin to paint. Afterward he drink tea in the garden with my cousin. It is her favorite time of day. The lake so still, your father so happy. They have everything to live for."

All motion seemed to have left the room. The last light hitting the cut glass on the table, the lapping of the lake, even the sweet smell of basil and garlic. It all seemed to become very faint and insubstantial and there was only Laszlo's voice, creeping through the stillness, like a horrible enchantment. Or was it the story he was telling? Somehow bringing their father to life in the present tense, even as he described the events that had led to his death?

"The morning he die, your father goes out swimming very early. My cousin has headache. Here." He touched his head.

"We know what a headache is," said Netta.

"He tells her he will be quick and she goes back to bed. It is nine when she wakes. She thinks your father he is painting now, and sleeps some more. At eleven she gets visit from police. A boatman find him in the reeds across the water in Pella. He knows straightaway it is your father."

"How does he know?"

"He drink with him sometimes."

Netta nodded. Most people of a drinking age had drunk with her father. In fact, many people not of a drinking age had drunk with him as well. "Who was the boatman?"

"I don't know. I find out his name for you."

"No need. I can find out myself. What happened next?"

"People pull him out of water. But he is already dead. They call police."

"Was he still breathing?"

"No. They wish they find him before, but boatman does not see him at first because of mist."

"Mist? What mist?" Netta experienced a dropping away inside, like missing a step. No one had mentioned mist, not even the police. She looked to Susan, but either she hadn't heard or this was too much to take in, like pouring more water into a glass that's already full. She and Iris clutched hold of one another. They looked ransacked.

"There is thick mist that morning. Everything disappears."

"And Bella-Mae didn't worry? She didn't raise the alarm?"

"As I say to you before, she sleeps. But she feels terrible now. She blames herself."

"If the mist was that bad, there wouldn't be anything she could do. But even if she didn't know that, Daddy did. He would never swim if there was a mist. It was the only rule he ever stuck to. He could smell them coming. He used to warn us about mists all the time."

Suddenly Iris interrupted. "Oh, I can't bear this. I can't bear it. I can't believe we never answered his texts." She tucked into Susan as she wept.

"We have to eat," Susan said at last. "We have to eat because otherwise this is too much. It's too painful."

Netta's appetite was better than she'd expected. On the whole, she ate in order to drink, but this was more like fueling a vast hole inside her, though strangely nothing seemed to have a taste. Iris said, "I'm too sad to eat," so Susan spooned the smallest portions onto her plate and tore off a piece of bread, and in the end Iris managed a few slow bites, though she barely touched her wine. Laszlo sat at the head of the table, lifting his plate to his mouth and filling it with greedy forkfuls, talking about their father and Bella-Mae, how in love they were, what a perfect couple, do you know they never argue, they only laugh, this is tragedy for my cousin, twenty-seven and her life is over, until Netta refilled her wineglass and stood.

"Netta?" called Susan.

"Going upstairs," she called back. She didn't want to hear any more and it felt good to snub Laszlo. In fact, it felt essential. She wanted her sisters, and her brother, of course, but no one else. Besides, this was the closest she could come to snubbing Bella-Mae.

Where could it be? Where? Netta went straight to the garret, but Bella-Mae had already cleared it of everything that had once belonged to Vic. His easel was gone, his jars of paintbrushes, bottles of turps, fresh canvases. She hadn't left so much as a pencil stub. Instead she'd positioned a single chair in the middle of the room, and left the windows wide open to let in fresh air. From there, Netta flew straight down to his bedroom and this time she didn't wait, polite and childlike, at the door. She kicked it open and marched in. She disrupted the stillness like a bad weather front, pulling out drawers, finding receipts and invoices, old gambling slips, even a birthday card made by Iris when she was little, but there was nothing there either. No sealed envelope, let alone a signed will. It was only the sight of her father's Ray-Bans, half open beside the bed, that stopped her. She stood very still, waiting for the grief to strike, like waiting for the pain when you've stubbed your foot and everything goes numb.

But still she couldn't cry, like Iris. Netta even tried to force it. Instead her body gave a low animal sound she didn't recognize. Maybe she'd been grieving for so long she couldn't do it anymore. She told Robert sometimes that she had no idea when the feeling had begun, or whether there was a day it had not been with her. This dull and spreading sense of loss that seemed to lie deep down at the bottom of everything.

A memory. One of those that hits you in a flash, fully formed. After her mother died, waking each morning and wondering if the universe had righted itself while she was asleep. If she and Susan went down to the kitchen, would their mother be at the stove, her hair in its cartwheel, her apron criss-crossed at the back, making porridge and scrambled eggs? Flying downstairs, pursued by Susan, and finding nothing but a sink of unwashed plates. A feeling like a door that has been left open when it shouldn't. She would look at Susan and Susan would look back and the look said, Still dead. It was no wonder Netta had taken things into her own hands. Otherwise it was the end of safety, and after that there was only chaos. Netta became an adult the day her mother died.

What did you mean, Daddy, she thought, when you told Iris you were in it now? Clearly you were talking about Bella-Mae. But why, then, would you come here and marry her? Did she force you? And please tell me you made another will. Anything will do. Just a scribble on the back of a receipt. You were stubborn and difficult, but you were canny and I know you wouldn't forget us. I know you would never do that.

She checked his clothes in the wardrobe. They were arranged so neatly there was a space between each hanger. She went through the pockets. She searched under the bed. She threw off the pillows, pulled back the sheets, groped beneath the mattress. Still no sign of a will.

It was fully dark now. She'd forgotten how fast night came to the lake, even in the middle of summer. She went to the window and opened the shutters. A round summer moon balanced on the tips of the trees, like a soft peach. There was the resiny smell of heat. The stillness of the water. Across the other side, the tiny lights of Orta streaking into the lake. A brief moment of calm for Netta, like being held very close.

Her sisters' voices came from downstairs, light and fluttery, dancing around Laszlo's as they called good night from the terrazzo. She watched him move through the darkened garden toward the water's edge. Her sisters were in the kitchen, but Netta kept watching. Because Laszlo had not gone to his boat. Instead he'd wheeled around on himself and was creeping back up through the garden, caught only by the palest flow of light from the villa. He stood beside the camellia tree and lit a cigarette as he gazed up. From her hiding place, Netta kept looking down. The watcher being watched. She thought of everything he'd said. About the mist while their father swam. Bella-Mae sleeping. Netta didn't trust him an inch. Vic would never have gone into the lake if there had been a mist. It was way too dangerous. So why had he done it that morning? What had made him change his mind?

She thought of the texts he'd sent in the middle of the night: *Where are you?*; *Hot hot hot!*; *So hot here!*; *I've seen the light!*; *It's all making sense!*; *What's happened?*; *What are you playing at?*; *Where the hell are you?* Suppose she'd been wrong and it wasn't his painting he was talking about?

"Netta, you couldn't know your father was going to drown," Robert had said only yesterday, as she tore through Vic's apartment. "You can't blame yourself."

But that wasn't true. When Vic reached out, did a part of her know—an unconscious part—that he was trying to warn her he was in danger? Had the confusion she'd felt before he died been the result of some kind of strange connection with him? One that she alone felt? Because she was the eldest, and knew things about Vic the other three couldn't?

Laszlo pitched his cigarette toward the trees, then slipped into the shadows. She heard, without being able to see, his boat leave the island. The sound of the engine growing fainter and fainter as it carried him across the water. Further dots of light were springing up over the mainland, and the lake held their reflection, like a blue-black quilt running with silver thread.

She would figure out what had happened to Vic, though she already knew in her gut that Bella-Mae was at the heart of it. This time she wouldn't prevaricate or flounder. She would stop at nothing. And there would be something Bella-Mae had left. Some mistake, some tiny clue. There was always a tiny clue and it would be here if it was anywhere. All she had to do was keep hunting.

For an isolated moment, a breeze swept through the room. Papers lifted from the floor, the shutters swayed. The lake gave a shimmer, then went still again. Beneath that sewn-up surface, something alive and present.

12

Private Fantasy

Many years ago, Warwick had said to Susan, "Do you have any private fantasies?" It was midafternoon and they were in bed. She was twenty-one and they'd had sex a few times, and while she wouldn't go so far as to say it had been a disappointment, it had been careful and also considerably quicker than she had been led to believe sex should be, and they also did it with the curtains closed, even though it was a beautiful day outside. "You can put your clothes on that chair," he'd told her the first time. She'd meant him to quote her some poetry, she'd meant at the very least to be French-kissed, but faced with a man already in his socks and underpants—there was something about a man with no trousers that she realized, just at the wrong moment, was hilarious—she undressed swiftly and got into bed.

By this time, Netta had left university and was about to do her pupilage. She had told Susan a lot about sex: in the end, she had set about losing her virginity with the same determination she'd previously applied to passing exams and sent Susan a copy of *The Joy of Sex*, which Susan read from cover to cover, though she was put off by the pictures. (If only the man didn't have that creepy beard.) But the point was, while Netta had slept with quite a few students and even two postgrad lecturers, she'd never had sex with a GP from just down the road. A forty-two-year-old man left by his wife and with two little twin sons whom the whole neighborhood had seen shouting and kicking as he tried his best to bribe them into the car on weekends. And thinking all this, a bold sensual impulse had fizzed right through Susan. It was like being one enormous sherbet fountain. So that afternoon she'd said to Warwick in his bed, yes. She did have fantasies. Would he like to hear?

"Very much," he said. He reached for her hand.

She told him how she imagined sometimes she was at a men's private dining club. She and other women were naked and serving food, and the male diners took the food and rubbed it over the women's bodies and licked it off. She even imagined how it would be to lie on the table and have them smear the food between her legs. Some of the women were wearing little ribbons, she said, instead of knickers, but the men were fully dressed with suits and ties and shoes, and some looked like Burt Reynolds, but not all of them because that would be weird. All of this she had spoken to a glass light fitting above her head that looked exactly the same as an upside-down jelly mold. There was something intoxicating about opening up this space in which she might be desired in that way, the lack of acknowledgment that she was even a person. Having told him her fantasy, she felt bold, desirable and incredibly powerful. Not even Netta would say a thing like that. Her whole body was flushed with the heat of it, between her legs abuzz with feeling.

A silence. A silence so broad and bright you could have taken giant strides through the middle. His hand remained around hers but somehow no longer holding it.

At last he said slowly, "Goodness. I was thinking more of hobbies."

The room froze. Even the jelly-mold light fitting above her head seemed to ice over. She wanted time to reverse. Or, more specifically, not to exist as a concept in the first place. She wanted the words to backflip inside her mouth, unspoken and unthought, or even to say this wasn't her fantasy: she was just telling him Netta's. But her mouth had given up the ghost. "Hobbies?" she repeated, in a tight little voice, the approximate size of a cockle.

"Yes," he said. "For instance . . ." though he went silent for a moment or two and seemed unable to think of any. "For instance, I would have liked to be a concert pianist."

"A concert pianist?"

"Yes."

Now it was her turn to say, "Goodness."

"But I wasn't talented enough."

She couldn't tell if he was being serious. She couldn't tell if they were really having this conversation, and not the adult-rated one she had begun. But it appeared they were having this conversation, because he said, "It's my hands, you see. My hands are too big. I kept hitting two notes instead of one. I had to stop."

Suddenly all she could see was a vision of herself arse-naked on a tablecloth, covered with HP sauce and sundry gourmet snacks, while Warwick played the piano beneath a jelly-mold light fitting.

"Me, too," she said.

He gave a sigh of gratitude, as if they had been way out at sea but now found themselves on what appeared to be a small driftwood platform. "You wanted to be a concert pianist?"

"Not exactly. I would have liked to play the recorder. But Iris got there first."

"I'm sorry to hear that. Did you never learn?"

"No. I never did."

"Does she still?"

"Who?"

"Iris."

"Oh, I see. Yes. She does. I don't think she has any grades or anything, but, yes, she still plays. I don't actually think I'm very musical. Maybe I'll be a chef one day. I like to cook. I have a job writing on a cookery page. Not exactly writing it, more like making coffee for the people who write it. But one day I hope to be a TV chef, like Lesley Waters on cable TV. Do you know her?" Warwick didn't. He didn't have cable TV. He watched the news and *Panorama* on BBC1. "I love Lesley Waters. She can cook anything. My problem is that Goose only likes Pot Noodle and Iris doesn't eat food that is red or green, and Netta is always on a diet from her *Vogue* book. Normally we end up with freezer meals in the microwave. Laura—she's our au pair—loves the microwave. We don't really need an au pair, but every time we ask her to leave, she comes back. So we still have her."

This was far more monologue than the situation required, but Susan was a talker and would have said anything so long as it didn't have the words "knickers" or "Burt Reynolds" in it, though she wished to high heaven she could stop going on about food. She didn't know what she had said—surely it wasn't the detail about Laura and her microwave—but at this point Warwick placed his mouth on top of hers and kissed her.

They had sex because that was what they were there for and not to have sex would have been like boiling the kettle and failing to make a hot drink, but it was polite and quick. It was the kind of sex she imagined amateur pianists might have, as opposed to women in ribbon knickers.

Do not continue seeing this man, she thought, as she rushed home and found the key—not exactly difficult: someone had left it in the front door. She ran straight up to the bathroom, where she showered in hot water for so long she emptied the tank. Do not see that man again, she told herself, as she dried with every towel she could find. "Do not do it," she said out loud, as she got back in the shower, even though the water was stone cold by now and Goose was on the other side of the door, asking politely if he might use the bathroom. For weeks it went on. Susan couldn't get clean enough. She couldn't tamp down the shame. She felt it coil, wire-thin, down her spine, felt it spark and flash inside her when Iris left her recorder out, or even when she left the house and walked past Warwick's, wearing Netta's old French beret as a disguise. And yet six months later, she did it. The very thing Susan knew she must not do she went ahead and did. She bumped into him at the garage shop when she was stocking up on bread, gin and cigarettes. He asked how she was in his gentle, old-fashioned way that nevertheless made her want to scream, and she said she was just doing a little late-night family shopping. He smiled. "You're such a good person, Susan. I enjoyed our afternoons together. It would be nice to see you again."

The sight of him gave her a tight shrinking feeling inside. Even her skin crawled with difficulty. He knew the worst, most shameful part of her and the only way to put things right was to kill off the Susan he had met in bed that day, and make an ally of him now with a more respectable version in the garage. She must befriend Warwick and his monstrous twin sons. She agreed to meet up with them at the park the following Sunday and took a fridge cake she adapted from a Lesley Waters recipe. She took them a leftover lettuce for their rabbits. "They do not have rabbits," said Warwick. Susan was briefly thrown. She thought all normal children had rabbits, for the very reason that she had never had them. (Too much trouble, Vic always said. In the end, Netta presented Vic with a homemade booklet, "Ten Good Reasons We Need a Pet," fully illustrated by the other three, though Iris's pictures were more like tin cans with tails.)

So Susan got the twins a rabbit as a present, and also a wooden hutch for it to live in because obviously rabbits needed one of those as well. She and Warwick had a few dates at the cinema and he took her to a pizza restaurant on weekends with the boys—the boys refused to eat pizza. Another mystery. Susan thought all normal children liked pizza. There was more sex, but always in the afternoon and always with the curtains drawn, and when he asked, a few months on, if she would consider doing him the honor of . . . she said yes. Didn't even let him get to the end of the sentence. "Yes," she said. "I will marry you." And the following year she did, with the full works, even though Netta presented a million reasons why it was a bad idea. She wore a dress so sticky-out she sent things flying as she passed—she felt like a large and lumbering animal trapped in a space that was way too small—with her father roaring drunk before they even opened the front door to get into the pony-trap holding up traffic outside. Her siblings were dressed in spring-themed yellow, with Warwick's boys furious in knickerbockers and page hats. Moments before they walked into the church, Netta pulled off her wire crown and took Susan to one side, followed closely by Iris and Goose: it was like being assaulted by a trio of giant-sized Easter chicks. "You know you don't have to do this?" hissed Netta. "You're twenty-two. You barely know him. You have your whole life ahead of you."

"Please don't get married," said Iris.

"We could run away right now," said Goose. "Netta's worked it out, Suzie. There's still time."

Netta's hair was sticking out in a triangle because of the speed with which she had whipped off her crown, and teenage Iris looked anemic and shipwrecked inside her dress—was she not eating again?—while Goose was so trussed up in his morning suit and yellow tie it verged on cruelty. But they were right. They could go. There was still time. Susan could lift the hem of her ridiculous meringue gown and shout, "Bet you can't beat me!" They would race from the church, Susan's runway-length train looped over her arm, all the way to a plane, then a car, and finally Lake Orta, where they would swim every day in the blue water and lie beneath the trees eating melon. Only that would never last. Netta would leave, just as she'd left for university, and this time it would be for good: there would be no filling the hole she left behind. On the other hand, there was a ready-made place for Susan in Warwick's life. He was reliable and kind, his house was unloved, and he had no idea how to cope with those twins. Besides, look at her. She was wearing the dress. Getting married was the one thing Netta had not yet done. And if Susan did not do it first, Netta would do it soon enough, only she would marry someone handsomer than Warwick and more entertaining; she would do it with a recklessness and style that Susan lacked, and their father would adore her husband in exact proportion to the amount he disliked Warwick, and that would be one more painful thing Susan would have to pretend was not there. So she grabbed Netta's hand that day outside the church and squeezed a little too hard. "Run away?" she said. "And what exactly do you suggest I do after that? Live the rest of my life like a nun? I'm getting *married*."

Susan took Warwick's surname, even though Netta said that was out-of-date and sexist. She wouldn't even go double-barrel. She gave up her job on the cookery page. She threw away *The Joy of Sex*. She jettisoned her old life without a second thought. She wanted to be small and safe and domesticated. She wanted to clean out rabbit hutches for the rest of her life and make wholesome dinners. The twins would never love her—she could see it in their eyes; Susan would never be a patch on their mother, even though she was so chaotic their weekend bags were either nonexistent or filled with unwashed clothes. Yet all this would be bearable because Susan and Warwick would have children of their own, three, four, five, six of them, and they would be a little pack, just as she'd once been with her siblings, only this time Susan would be at the center, loving them with hot meals and pressed laundry, like a human Aga.

Her own children had not happened (No one's fault! Just one of those things!), but it had been a full life and she'd been happy. By and large she would say she'd been happy. Love wasn't the sweeping-you-sideways feeling you saw in films. It was more like getting on the slow train and arriving with lots of stations in between. She'd learned the compromises, the omissions that made a relationship work and which had eluded Netta. She'd found stability and companionship, where Goose and Iris had not. And while it was harder now that Warwick was retired—she had not expected him to want only to stay at home, or even to be happy with doing so little—and while it was also true that, for some time now, she'd felt a kind of heaviness in her soul, a bleakness that brought with it shapeless desires, brief imaginary glimpses of other lives she might be living, she never told anyone. Besides, Susan would have done anything to be severed from the shameful part of her that had lain in Warwick's bed that sunny afternoon when she was twenty-one and asked to be treated like a human dinner plate.

The kind of woman, in fact, her father loved to paint.

"Susan?"

She looked up. Early-morning light flooded the room. Netta's newspapers were all over the kitchen table and even though there were only a few brief references to Vic's death, she'd been sobbing as she read them. There at the French windows was Laszlo. Her heart began to spin, like a child gone mad at the playground. She hadn't heard him come up the garden. Hadn't even heard him dock his hired boat. He wore reflective sunglasses and a yellow Hawaiian shirt covered with parrots and palm trees. It was the kind of shirt that would make Warwick look as if he was going to a fancy-dress party, though the last time they'd attended one, he went as Lawrence of Arabia in one of her caftans and she'd overheard someone say how brave he was to cross-dress.

Behind Laszlo the sun rose with that kind of full-blown pink that makes everything look on fire. You could imagine the whole mainland ablaze, and for a moment she did. Sunlight caught two windows on the opposite side of the water and flashed, their light hitting the lake like a pair of bright comet tails. It felt all wrong to think this, but it was a beautiful morning.

He said, "I'm interrupting?"

"Of course not."

In trying to look at Laszlo, she was met with a reflection of herself in each of the lenses of his sunglasses, as if he had two Susans for eyes. It was making her dizzy. "Come in, come in," she said, though technically he already had and the invitation was a mere formality. Her hand flew to her hair, flattening it nicely back into shape. "I'm afraid I'm the only one awake."

"It is you I come to see."

"Me?"

"Yes, Susan. How you sleep?"

Why was it that everything he said came out sounding as if it was a secret code for something else? She replied—in her most neutral voice—that it had been a bad night because her sister Iris had cried for most of it, and her other sister Netta couldn't stop asking questions no one could answer. She didn't mention that in the end Iris had crawled the length of Susan's mattress to lie next to her, while Netta slipped in the other side, and they had stayed like that, three sticky hot sisters, because even sleeping in separate beds felt like being too far apart. Meanwhile Laszlo fixed her with a gaze, or at least his bi-Susan sunglasses, as if he was seeing not her face or even her caftan, but X-raying right through to the soft folds of her flesh, and she wished she was wearing something red underneath and more lacy until it occurred to her that she didn't own that kind of underwear and she had not had those kind of thoughts for a very long time and, anyway, she was married and her father had just died, turning her world upside down. All this in the chaotic space of one moment.

"Coffee?" she said.

"I like this very much."

She moved around the kitchen, but more as if she were performing the part of a woman making coffee than effectively being one. She boiled hot water, ground beans and spooned them into the cafetière, and these simple things seemed complicated in ways they never had before.

Because Something. Had. Happened. Only yesterday. Face-to-face with Laszlo in the hall, while he shouted at her to get out of his house, Susan had done something she could only describe as sideways. She didn't shout back. She didn't ask who the hell he was and what he thought he was doing in her father's house with two bin bags. She fell. Not a Victorian swoon, but close. Possibly a self-launch in his direction, as if she were giving up everything her life had been until that moment and throwing herself on his mercy. Appalled, he rushed forward to support her, apologizing profusely while he held her, or so it felt, within his arms and told her—at least this was how it sounded—that she was all right, she was all right, he would never let her go. She couldn't remember ever having sobbed like that and she couldn't remember ever having held on to another person like that. Laszlo's voice was so deep it sent tremors shooting up and down her spine, like being buzzed from somewhere beneath her feet. "It is all right," he was still saying. "It is all right." Her head was against his chest and her tears had made a mess of the bright patterns on his shirt. And while it wasn't all right, nothing close to it, she breathed in the sharp spice of his cologne and listened to the steady repetition of his words and began to believe him.

That was not all. Afterward, Something Else Happened. Once they had broken free and cleared up the whole complicated business of who they were, he had become so chivalrous he might as well have been sitting on top of a horse. He had only shouted that the villa was his, he explained, because he was afraid she was a day-tripper and had come wandering in. Was there any way he might help Susan—with provisions, perhaps? He took her to the nearest supermarket in a boat he'd hired. Susan loved shopping for food; she always felt nothing terrible could happen when she was in a supermarket. And being in the cool aisles, talking to this stranger about cheese and olive oil, when her father was only just dead and she'd barely slept and her face was inside out with crying, had felt both bold and the most honest thing she'd ever done. Besides, there was a kind of crazy freedom in speaking intimately to a man who didn't fully understand. She felt she could tell him anything and it wouldn't matter. "It was you I spoke to," she said. "Wasn't it? On the phone? About Daddy?"

"It is me," he said, his face so close she couldn't fully see it anymore. And knowing he was the person who'd told her Vic was dead had been another thing that bound her to him as if with reams of tape.

She'd been aware she should ring Netta to tell her she was in Orta—and also, of course, while she was on the subject of phone calls, her husband—yet Laszlo was still at her side, pushing her trolley, the hairs on his arms so thick they caught themselves in matted twills, little patches of black fur even on the backs of his fingers, so repulsive it actually canceled out its repulsiveness and became thrilling, and for once she hadn't called any of her siblings. She sent the most cursory of texts to Warwick, explaining that Bella-Mae had disappeared and a stranger was trying to empty the house. After all, this was true, or it had been true for a matter of seconds, and was infinitely easier to explain than what had gone on to happen afterward—she'd had no idea Warwick would later regale the whole story to Netta. When she finally spoke to Netta and cleared up the question of who Laszlo was—i.e., not an intruder—and Netta explained that she and Iris were getting the first available flight, it was only polite to invite him and Bella-Mae for dinner. After all, her father might be only just dead but people needed to eat and Susan needed to cook for them. Bella-Mae had sent her apologies via Laszlo, but urged him to stay. Then Francesca had come to call, and he had remained at Susan's side while the housekeeper wept and they both comforted her—as if somehow he and Susan had skipped the process of getting to know each other and transformed into a couple.

And he was here again, and they were alone again, and it dawned on Susan that she had got up early and done her hair, hoping to see him ahead of her sisters. Waiting for him, in fact.

"How is your cousin today?" she said.

"She is like your sister. She cries all night. But now she takes more pills, she sleeps." He produced a card from the pocket of his shorts and placed it on the table. "She invite you to meet her. For tea at our hotel this afternoon. Hotel Navarro is plain, not like Villa Carlotta, but I hope you come. My cousin is a wonderful person. She love your father with all of her heart."

"And is she comfortable at the Hotel Navarro? She doesn't want to be here in the villa?"

"The villa is your home. It is different for my cousin. She does not want to set foot here ever again. Too many sad memories."

Susan took the postcard. The picture was of the hotel lobby. It gave nothing away. The message on the back was short, the handwriting a careful print. *I would like to give you tea at three o'clock. Yours sincerely Bella-Mae.* It struck Susan as professional.

She rinsed last night's dishes under the hot tap. "It's strange," she said. "We know so little about your cousin. Practically nothing. We never met her."

Laszlo nodded. He had taken up a tea towel and was now drying: his sunglasses had become lightly steamed. She passed him a teapot she had not seen before, a pretty thing with blue flowers, and he dried that too. "My cousin worry about this. She say to your father they do not need to marry in a hurry. But he want to marry now. He want to marry in Orta."

"I see," she said, though frankly she did not. Everything was pretty murky.

"My cousin understand his children must be suspicious. Especially your sister. I feel her anger last night."

"You mustn't mind Netta. She is a lawyer. Litigation. She's so clever I don't understand half of what she does."

"Yes, this I know. Your father tell my cousin all about her." He laughed as if this was funny and so did Susan, though she would never normally laugh at Netta. Suddenly she had a great deal of new information to process. Was it really Vic who had pressured Bella-Mae into the wedding and not the other way round? Laszlo thanked her for the coffee, saying some words that her Italian was too slow to follow as he cast his sunglasses up and down the kitchen. "*Dov'è? Dov'è? Mio cugino ha lasciato qualcosa qui.* There is something my cousin leave here. *Ti dispiace se lo cerco?* You mind? I look?"

"*Figurati.*"

"*Grazie.*"

"*Prego.*"

"She need it badly."

He had begun to slide open the drawers beneath the old table with an ease that suggested this wasn't the first time. "Can I help?" she asked, already imagining all the places they might search together, but too late because whatever he was looking for he had located among the teaspoons and slipped inside his pocket. It seemed to be an envelope. Or was it a paper bag? The movement was so nimble she didn't fully see. But also she wasn't fully looking. Not quite.

"And now I must leave," he said. "You need to be alone at such sad time."

"Yes," she said, remembering that indeed this was a desperate time. The worst.

"*Arrivederci, Susan.*"

"*Arrivederci, Laszlo.*"

She accompanied him to the French windows, only somehow she kept going, moving with him across the terrazzo, down through the lovely trees toward the water, talking all the while, talking, talking about heaven only knew what—but as they went, she felt the closeness of his body to hers, and she could not be sure but his strong arm seemed to dangle on purpose at his side, and her arm also seemed to dangle on purpose beside hers, and they were so close, his strong arm and hers, that her own was like a white lamp, emitting sparks of electricity. The sky had turned from watermelon pink to watercolor blue and the early-morning air was lovely—the softest breeze had kicked up from the south, sending little ripples all across the lake. Had it been only yesterday she had fallen into his arms and howled?

"Susan, you are a very nice person," he said, as they reached the water's edge. He asked if she knew the story of San Giulio and the dragon on the island. Even though she knew it very well, and there were frescos all over the villa illustrating it just in case she forgot, Susan smiled and said she didn't. So Laszlo told her about the priest Giulio who came centuries ago to rid the island of the serpents and the dragon that had lived there at the time, sailing in a boat made of his own coat because fishermen were too scared to take him. He told her all this and she did her very best not to see herself reflected in his sunglasses as he then told her how the serpents and dragon had sweetly left the island without much of a struggle and the priest had built a church here instead. "And this is how island get its name. Isola San Giulio!"

"Wonderful!" she said, sounding like a day-tripper and not a woman who'd been coming here since she was eleven and had heard her father tell these stories a million times if she'd heard them once. "How wonderful. You must tell me more about the island some time."

"Yes, Susan. I like this very much."

With that, he hopped into his boat, watching her, she was sure of it, all the time he switched on the engine and moved away, watching her even as she rushed back through the garden, feeling guilty even though she'd done nothing, as if what had passed between them was so deeply intimate and unspoken he had somehow seen right through her caftan and found not the underwear she was ashamed of, but Burt Reynolds, the jelly-mold light fitting, and her husband wanting to be a concert pianist, while she lay waiting, legs akimbo, on the bed.

Netta was already in the kitchen, pitching her phone here, there and everywhere. Her hair was still semi-caught in yesterday's top knot, and she'd clearly forgotten to wash because her eyes were black pansies. "Why the fuck is there still no decent signal in this house?" she said, followed by, "Good morning, darling. Have you found it?"

"What, Net?"

"The will, Suz. Have you found the will?"

Susan had forgotten how intense Netta could be first thing. Every summer she would wake up three hours later than everyone else but with a mind that seemed to be operating at least five hours ahead. Susan poured her a black coffee and kissed her. "Good morning, love. And not yet."

"We have to find it."

"We're going to. Is Iris okay?"

"She's crying in the shower."

"At least Goose is on his way. She'll be better when he's here. Are you okay?"

"I'm terrible." Netta pulled a packet of superstrength acetaminophen out of her bag and dry-swallowed three. She said, "Guess what, Susan?"

"I don't know, Net."

"Last night I looked for the will in Daddy's room. This morning I've covered the whole villa. I've looked for the new painting as well. There's no sign of them. I can't even find his mobile. I found *My Sweet Guardian Angel* in the music room—God knows what it was doing in there—but that's all."

"Maybe Daddy was taking a break." Susan's mind wasn't fully with Netta. It was still partly in the garden saying goodbye to Laszlo. "Maybe he put the new painting in a cupboard."

"When did Daddy ever take a break from a painting?" Netta's voice wavered, and just as quickly she regained control. "Besides, he was working on it. That's what her cousin told us last night. He said it twice. Right here in the kitchen. He said Daddy was painting every day. But it's not here. And we know it's a huge canvas. That's not the sort of thing you put in a cupboard, even if Daddy ever put things in cupboards, which he never did. So where are the paints? The rags? It doesn't even smell of turps. Bella-Mae's cleared everything out. What's going on?"

"I don't know. But I'm in shock. We all are. We're a bit frightened. None of us has really slept. It's important to think calmly and not go rushing into things." Susan put the postcard from Bella-Mae beside Netta's cup, then propped it up in a more appealing fashion. Netta took her coffee without looking: the card bellyflopped straight over.

"Was that him again? The Toad?"

"Are we talking about Bella-Mae's cousin now? Because he wants to help. He came to deliver this invitation from Bella-Mae. It's an olive branch, Net—"

But Netta had no time for olive branches. She was at the full height of her Netta-ness. She was talking about a mist, she was talking about the will. She was even saying something about Mrs. Lott in London. It was impossible to keep up. Then she said, "I thought he was her friend."

"Who?"

"Laszlo. When he called you about Daddy in the shoe shop, he told you he was Bella-Mae's friend."

"Did he? I don't remember."

"Well, I do. That's what you said to me. So why would he say that he was her friend when he's her cousin? Unless he isn't her cousin."

"I don't know. Maybe it was a mistake. Maybe he got his words mixed up. Maybe I got the words mixed up. It was the worst moment of my life. I don't know why you're doing this."

"I'm doing it because we shouldn't be fooled. And how come he got here so fast? After Daddy died? How come he was already with her when she called you, Susan?"

"Maybe he was visiting. Does it matter?"

"Of course it matters. This is the scene of a crime. We probably shouldn't even be here. We could be walking over evidence—"

"This isn't the scene of a crime, Netta. Daddy drowned. It was an accident."

"We don't know that. We don't know anything. There was a mist. That's what the Toad said. Why would Daddy go swimming if a mist was coming? I didn't want to say this in the night because Iris is so all over the shop, but I'm going to the police today to insist on an autopsy. They can't just leave it there. And the results of an autopsy can take weeks."

Susan nodded. She hadn't thought about an autopsy. It hadn't occurred to her. Yet again, Netta was streets ahead. But her mind had also flown to the word "weeks" and balanced there like a bird on a twig. "Well, of course I could stay," she began, but Netta interrupted.

"The villa's different, Susan. Nothing feels the same."

"I know Bella-Mae made some changes, but God knows the place needed updating. Besides, the new painting will be somewhere. Daddy wouldn't be stupid—"

"She took it before we got here. They took it. Her and the Toad. And Daddy's passport, his phone. Where are they, Susan? I wouldn't mind betting they were trying to take all the pictures, except you got here first and interrupted them. That's why *My Sweet Guardian Angel* was up in the music room. The only thing I've found are Daddy's sunglasses."

Susan knew she ought to tell her sister what Laszlo had said about Vic being the one who'd forced the wedding, but the thought kept sliding away, and every time she almost caught it, Netta pounced on something else and threw her offtrack. Besides, more than anything, now she'd heard about them, Susan was desperate to see her father's sunglasses. To smell them, even. Meanwhile Netta was talking about contacting every notary on Lake Orta: if there was no will in the house, it could easily be somewhere else. After that she was going to get the name of the boatman who'd discovered Vic's body, and find the painting. And Netta was right, of course. There was so much to think about that was terrible. Unthinkable, in fact. It was all new territory. Identifying him at the undertaker's, choosing the coffin. All the paperwork to take his body home, as well as organizing the funeral in London. Not to mention Goose arriving in Milan on the coach in a few hours because he didn't like flying. Really there was so much to think about when a person died; the one thing there was no time for was the fact they were dead. And yet somehow in the middle of all this, a soft flame had burst alight. Low in her belly, where no one could see. Just like the first time she'd found out she was pregnant, and she sat with the test in her hand, loving her body in a whole different way because it had this new life inside it.

"You've gone red," said Netta.

"Too hot," said Susan.

She turned away, but Netta pulled her close. She smelled of last night's wine, today's coffee and yesterday's Chanel No 5. "Susan? Promise me one thing?"

"What, Net?"

"Don't die before me. I'm serious. I'll kill you if you go first."

13

Tea with Bella-Mae

Midmorning, and Europe was a furnace. Anyone with any sense was either in a dark room with the air-conditioning full blast, or making their way to the lake. It was perfect down there. The only breeze in Italy played across the water, whipping it up in little white ruffles, or ready to spring around a corner where one narrow alleyway met in a dog tail with another. Parasols were pitched up and down the shoreline, with families underneath. Picnic baskets and coolers, fold-up furniture and ball games. For once the *gelaterie*, terrace cafés and lakeside restaurants were packed and noisy, waiters squeezing between tables with trays of *aperitivi* above their heads. Day-trippers sunbathed on the jetties, or used them to leap into the water. Others were rowing out in paddle-boats. Everyone was letting go. Everyone was part of the lake: when the passenger boat passed, spray tossing its bows, the ripples blooming as far as the shoreline, it wasn't only children who ran to jump the waves. A fine silk-white radiance gleamed as far as you could see and the sun-bleached sky was a dome. The water was a delicious sparkling blue and in the middle was the island, exquisite in its stillness.

Netta, Susan and Iris put on sunglasses, flip-flops and hats. While they took the boat to Orta, then made their way up to the *carabinieri* at the other side of the town, Goose, too, was traveling, though not across water, and not with the smallest hope of a natural breeze. He was coming to Milan by coach from London.

On the way to the bus station the previous morning—he'd gone first with Harry to Vic's studio so that Goose could pack a few things while Harry dealt with calls and the press—Shirley had turned to Goose in her car. She'd warned him to be careful. "Remember Bella-Mae is young. She won't understand the way you do things as a family."

"Mrs. Lucas," he'd said, "she married my father. If she can put up with him, she could put up with anyone. My sisters and I will seem like a walk in the park."

Shirley had made a compressed shape with her mouth as if it were a freezer bag and she was zipping words inside. "Your sisters always get what they want," was all she said. "I don't think you realize that."

She had hugged him in her difficult way and he thought again about those summers at the lake where she got teased because she couldn't swim. He put his arms around her and said, "Bye, Mrs. Lucas. You're the best."

She bristled and pulled away. "Let me know you're safely there," she said.

The two coaches from London to Paris, then Paris to Milan were airless and boiling. Goose had borrowed a black jacket that was large on Harry and the opposite on Goose, but since it was a good one, he didn't want to spoil it by folding it, so he had no choice but to wear it. He needed the jacket because he felt the whole situation in Orta required more than his regular shorts and T-shirt, though he was still wearing flip-flops because the idea of putting his feet in shoes in this heat was like burying them. "Son, are you sure you're up to this?" Harry had said, after the early morning call from Netta. "You're sure you don't need me to come with you?"

Frankly, Goose was not sure he was up to anything. For his whole life, his thoughts and feelings had been directed around his father. Now his father was gone and they had nowhere to go except downward: it was like the days after his breakdown when it almost killed him just to climb a flight of stairs. But that wasn't what he'd told Harry. "It's time to be the man now," he'd said, doing his best to sound like Vic. Except his face was a complete mess. There was terrible bruising and swelling under both eyes and Shirley had put Elastoplast across his nose, which made it look like a joke one. Being a passenger on a bus, where all he had to do was sit still, was the only thing he felt he might manage. She'd given him some heavy-duty painkillers for the journey, with a picnic, and he'd offered the food to a young man next to him, who said he hadn't eaten the whole day, then ate the lot, so that in the end Goose hadn't eaten the whole day either. Neither had he managed to sleep, though he was spaced out on the painkillers. When the bus finally arrived in Milan, it was Monday lunchtime. Traveling toward the dead, it turned out, was not like traveling at all. Because how could you move toward someone who was not there? It was a no-win kind of journey, where the end point was not a gain but a subtraction. A nothing that opened out into more and more nothing.

Milan bus station was heaving. You opened your mouth and got the thick taste of exhaust fumes and heat. A woman pushed past with two children, one in each arm, as if running from a fire. And then, joy, oh, joy, Goose saw Susan. Then double, triple joy, he saw a short woman who wore a black dress, plus an enormous hat, and realized it was Netta, with Iris beside her, calling, "Goose! Goose!" His heart unfolded with love. For one moment, time sidestepped and he was back at the day they had come to collect him from the hospital—Susan wrapping him in blankets, Netta furious with the police, Iris wiping tears and saying, "Why did you do that, Goose? Why didn't you call us?" He waved and began walking toward them.

"Oh, Goose," they said, crowding him all at once. "What on earth did you do to your face?"

"Did you get in a fight?" said Netta.

"And your hair?" said Iris. "Where has it gone?"

"Did someone fight you *for your hair*?" said Netta.

"I had it cut."

She looked gobsmacked. "You mean you paid someone to do that to you?"

Finally they laughed and Susan said, "Oh, God. This is so much better. We'll be okay now we're together."

Then Iris stroked his head, and said how soft it was, as she snuggled her face against the weave of his jacket, breathing in the smell. "We're going for tea with Bella-Mae," she whispered. "She's actually real. Can you believe that?"

In the car, Susan played "Fix You" on repeat from her Coldplay CD and they cried. She apologized that there was no time to get to the villa before the appointment with Bella-Mae, though Netta said why should they worry about being late? After that, they filled Goose in on everything that had happened since their father's death, which struck him as considerable since it had been only forty-eight hours. But then again, they'd always been that way: turn your back on them for five minutes as teenagers and they'd have made the whole villa into an impromptu private party, with Netta fixing cocktails from everything she could find in the drinks cupboard, Susan raiding the fridge to make canapés, and Iris lighting a hundred candles through the garden. Now Susan explained how she'd rushed to the lake and met Bella-Mae's cousin, who had been incredibly helpful, but how she'd also found the villa so different—everything cleared away and spotless.

"It even smells different," said Iris, coiled into a corner of the backseat. It always surprised him how small she could make herself.

"Turps?"

"Something else. I don't know what. Kind of sweet but bitter. His flat was the same."

She told the story about Vic saying he was in it now and Mrs. Lott hearing him cry at night. Netta shoved her face between the two front seats. "I mean, what the hell was that about?"

"It does seem strange."

"And Daddy would never swim in a mist. Would he?"

"Of course not. It was his only rule."

"That's what I said."

Netta turned forward again and went on to explain about a missing painting and no will. He'd been dead only two days, she said, and Bella-Mae had cleared him out. From this angle, she was basically a fast-talking hat.

"But the painting will be somewhere," said Susan, catching his eye in the rearview mirror. "There are only so many places you can look. You can't lose a painting. Can you, Goose?"

"I don't see how. Especially not that size. So what's it like with Bella-Mae?"

He might as well have opened a box of frogs. His sisters still hadn't met her but they couldn't say enough about their father's widow and none of it good, though it struck him the only thing they could really add to the modicum of information already assembled was that she seemed to be a very tidy person, and personally he didn't see how that could be such a bad thing. "But at least she doesn't want the villa," said Netta. "At least we know that."

"That's right," said Susan. "Her cousin Laszlo told me. She doesn't want to set foot in it ever again."

"Not that we were inviting her," said Netta.

"Too right," said Iris, for once in her life surprisingly spiteful.

As for the *carabinieri*, there had been a development. Netta had been amazing, Iris said. "She was on fire," added Susan. She had as good as demanded an autopsy. She'd even threatened to involve the press. The *commissario* still believed there was nothing suspicious about Vic's death but he wanted to rule out any possibilities of alcohol or drug misuse. The autopsy would happen immediately: he was hopeful the results would come within the next few weeks. Not only that, she'd also got the name of the boatman who'd found Vic.

"Limoncello!" she told Goose.

"The guy we knew as kids?"

"Exactly. Apparently he's disappeared. No one knows where he is."

"But Netta will find him," said Iris.

It was only when Netta had asked the *commissario* when she should identify Vic's body that she'd met her first obstacle: he'd told her there was no need because Bella-Mae had already done that. Netta wagged her head, fuming from the front seat. "You see, this is what I mean, Goose. They're amateurs. She shouldn't be identifying his body. She's a prime suspect."

"A suspect?" He couldn't help feeling this was another fantasy on Netta's part.

"Okay. She could be. At this stage you can't rule out anyone. That's why I'm staying here until we get the results of the autopsy. The police will fuck it up otherwise. I don't care how long it takes. I'm going to be up there every day, hounding them. They'll have to manage without me at work for a few weeks. Daddy would want me here, so I'm staying."

There was a pause while everyone took in what she'd just told them. Goose had assumed they would be on Lake Orta for a matter of days. He guessed everyone thought that. But one by one they rushed to agree with Netta: Vic would expect them to stay. They, too, were keepers of his flame. Susan said it wasn't as if Warwick couldn't manage without her for a while. Then Iris said, "Yes, I'll do the same," even though Susan said, "But what about your new job? I thought you were happy?"

"Who needs to sell cheese? Netta's right. It would be wrong to go home without Daddy. I'll hand in my notice."

Goose noticed something new, a fervor in his sisters' voices that registered vaguely as a plea, as if they were desperate not to be left out. Or afraid of what might happen if they went away. As if they might lose something vital, which was strange because surely the loss had already happened.

"What about you, Goose? What will you do?"

"Yes. I'll stay."

It wasn't as if he had anything else to do. Harry was looking after the studio now. The only place to be was here with his sisters.

As for the funeral, they were already onto that. Susan had put out some feelers. Vic would want the whole works, she said. A big church in London. Definitely not cremation. They would arrange for his body to be flown home after the autopsy.

"He'd want Westminster Abbey if we could get it," said Netta. "And none of this bullshit about everyone in happy colors. It's got to be full mourning."

"There might even be interest in a retrospective of his work. It wouldn't surprise me."

Then Netta flapped her hand for everyone to be quiet because she'd just got through to another *notaio* on her phone. They went dead still, straining to hear. "Nothing," she said afterward. "Nobody knows a thing about a new will."

All these half pieces of information were in danger of flooding Goose's head. Bella-Mae, the police, the missing painting, the missing will and now staying in Orta for the autopsy as well. Once again, he had the sense of being in some sort of overlap, as if he were both present and also floating in the middle of absolutely nothing. It seemed to come at him in waves. He would think he was in control, that he understood his father was dead. Then he would think of something else his father would never do, or even that there would have to be a funeral, and he was at sea again.

Susan was the best driver in the family—which wasn't saying as much as it might because Netta was disqualified and neither Goose nor Iris had passed their test. Goose had been in love with his driving instructor and only did the lessons to keep sitting next to him, while Iris had failed several times, the last because she did an emergency stop in a panic when they'd barely left the test center. Nevertheless it took Susan several goes to park Warwick's SUV. It was like maneuvering a freezer chest. Everyone ducked to give her maximum visibility, while Goose peered over his shoulder to call, "Yes, I think you're almost there. You've got it, Susan. Stop. I mean actually stop. Whoa. Whoa. We're touching the car behind."

From there, they walked the narrow cobbled streets where the sun couldn't reach toward the Hotel Navarro. Netta went ahead in her big hat that had gone saggy with the heat. Susan rushed a little behind, her caftan so long it almost touched the ground, pausing every now and then to check her hair in shop windows as she passed, while Goose followed with Iris, arm in arm. "The thing is," Netta was shouting back at them, "not to be hoodwinked by Bella-Mae. We have to stay solid. All we need to know is whether or not Daddy made a will and where he put his last painting. Of course she'll probably be lying, so we've got to be careful how we question her. Leave it to me. I can do the talking. I'm used to this kind of thing. I do this kind of thing in my sleep. After that we never have to see her again. It's not as if we want to be friends."

The street opened into another small square and suddenly the sun was all over Goose again, a solid weight on his shoulders. Day-trippers browsed slowly through clothes that a shop owner had put on racks outside her store. Others sat fanning themselves in the shade. It was so hot, his flip-flops seemed to have grown gummy. He had no idea how Netta kept going. He was boiling inside Harry's jacket.

They were still a good way from the hotel when a woman flew out of a bar to embrace them. "*Che tragedia!*" she cried. It was the same when they passed the next trattoria. Three men this time. They embraced Goose first, as if he were now the man of the family, though by rights he felt it should be Netta, and then another bar owner brought out a tray of grappa and a big group stood silently in the full sun, wiping their eyes as they drank to Vic. "Is this normal?" he asked Netta.

She nodded. "It's been like this all day. No one can believe he's dead."

Farther on, they passed the sign to the Sacro Monte di San Francesco, a beautiful hill of trees, where the views over the lake were spectacular and twenty little chapels were dedicated to the life of St. Francis of Assisi. Iris, as a child, had loved going up there.

"Remember how we went to see the statues every summer?" she said.

"I always found that place spooky," said Netta.

"We could go one day, if you like, Iris," said Susan. "We could say a prayer."

"I didn't know you were into that kind of thing, Suz."

"I'm not. But I've lost my father, Net. I'm clutching at straws."

"Remember how we used to talk about normal things?" said Iris. "Like *gelato* and finding the swan?"

The Hotel Navarro stood above the town with a swimming pool overlooking the lake. A dark-haired, muscular man in shades was waiting for them beneath a line of flagpoles—the flags all hanging like rags—and waved as they approached. It struck Goose that if he was trying to become the man of the family he could do worse than model himself on this one. Confident, exuding authority, his hair set in a quiff, and dressed in a Hawaiian shirt. The kind of man who jumped off statues of lions without breaking his nose. The kind who, as a boy, would have lain in wait for Goose and kicked the living shit out of him on his way back from school.

Susan called, "*Buongiorno, Laszlo!*"

"*Buongiorno, signora!*"

Goose turned to Netta. "That's Bella-Mae's Italian cousin?"

She rolled her eyes. "So he says. It's not even an Italian name."

"Of course they're cousins!" said Susan, with a laugh. She had put on pink lipstick somewhere between here and the car, and the effort broke Goose's heart ever so slightly. "You've got him all wrong, Netta. He's a sweetheart." She waved at Laszlo to show they were not discussing him, in a way that made it perfectly clear they were discussing him.

"As you can see," said Netta to Goose—she was talking through the side of her mouth, "the cousin is brightly colored. You could shut him in a dark room and still find him."

"*Buongiorno! Buongiorno!*" Laszlo greeted each of the sisters with a flamboyant embrace and kisses to both cheeks, though Netta balked within his arms and turned stiff as a post. When he saw Goose, he recoiled. Briefly Goose had forgotten how terrible he looked, what with the hair and now the nose.

"I actually paid for this haircut!" he said.

Laszlo gave a grin that had no life in it and patted his shoulder—there was something about his dark eyes that was simultaneously warm and cold. Then he called to the sisters, all charm, "*Seguitemi!* Follow me, *signore!* This way, please. This way!"

The hotel had seen better times. Back in the early eighties, it had been thought of as the only clean building on the lake, but the décor was still uniformly brown, and beginning to peel, like the papery skin of an onion. At least it had air-conditioning. In fact, the air was so cool Goose wished he could get a cup and drink it. He heard children shrieking by the pool, the splash of water, and waiters clearing the dining room: life happening on another level. Laszlo apologized and said his cousin was too tired to come down but would serve tea in her room. The police had only just left.

"The police were here?" said Netta, whipping off her hat. Beneath it, her hair was stuck to her scalp in a circular ridge. "Why? What did they want?"

"They ask a few simple questions. About your father's health before he die. Bella-Mae tell them he is very happy. He is very well. The police say they do not trouble her again. Though she is very distressed to learn about autopsy. The doctor tell her there is no need for autopsy. She do not understand why police change their mind."

He led the way up a flight of stairs, then another, another, the linoleum a pale gray, the windows smudged with heat. The farther they went, the more neglected the hotel became. The blades of an overhead fan cut the air above their heads, making a churning noise. Laszlo stopped at a room with an uneaten sandwich on a tray outside. He knocked twice, then used a key to let them in. Goose glanced at Iris. "You okay?" he mouthed and she said, "I don't know. You?"

It was empty. Bella-Mae's room was small and modest with twin beds, a low red plastic sofa at the far end and a coffee table set for tea with patisserie boxes. It made Goose really sad, just to look at it. Everything was so functional. And it was a squeeze for two people, almost impossible for six. From the window he could see straight down over the lake, with the island in the middle. He could even make out Villa Carlotta. It looked like a cartoon little house pasted onto a blue background with cutout hills and mountains in the distance.

"Bella-Mae?" said Laszlo.

With a spark of shock, Goose realized that all the time he'd been staring at the window, she'd been in front of him. Backlit by the sunlight behind her, she'd been completely in shadow; she already had him in her gaze. She stepped forward.

And this is where life really happens, he thought later. In that small gap between what you know and what you don't. There was no time to recall the different versions they'd had of her since they first heard her name in the noodle bar, because here she was, not a person they'd imagined or talked about but independent and real. She was skinny and small, but not an Iris kind of skinny where the person seems to have grown all upward and never sideways. She was lean in a way that seemed compact and very strong, though her feet were bare and she wore a shabby bathrobe with Hotel Navarro sewn below the neckline. Her black hair was thicker and longer than he'd imagined and hung so close to her eyes he felt the need to push it out of the way just to help her see. There was the gap between her front teeth that Vic had been so crazy about. But it was her youth that most surprised him. Goose had somehow forgotten—despite all the talk about her being only twenty-seven—that she was actually twenty-seven. He had forgotten how young that was. On her wedding finger she wore a thick gold band.

"My cousin, Bella-Mae!" announced Laszlo, as if he had conjured her out of thin air and was slightly surprised it had worked.

And maybe slightly surprised she was his cousin, too, because, as hard as Goose looked, there was no obvious family resemblance. Netta was right. The only thing they had in common was the hair.

She paused a moment, embarrassed and awkward. Then: "Oh, you're all so beautiful," she said in a rush. "Vic showed me your photos, but that's never the same. Now let me see if I get this right? You're Susan? You're Antoinetta? And you're Iris with the lovely gold bob. Goose, I'm so glad you got here. I know you hate flying. But what happened? What did you do to yourself? Don't you need arnica for your face?" Her voice, surprisingly high, came out in a rush, too fast for anyone to reply. "I know. I look terrible," she said. She had a Kleenex in each hand, rolled up like pink mice. "I meant to change before you got here, but I conked out. The doctor gave me these killer sleeping pills. Honestly, it's a miracle I can still talk. Well, here we all are. Oh, God, can you believe it?" She knotted the tie on her dressing gown. "Can you believe this is real?"

Netta stepped forward to shake hands, but Bella-Mae had different ideas and was already pitching herself at Susan, pulling her so close she almost took her off her feet. Then she did the same to Iris, who had to bend every bit of her to make it work, before grabbing Netta. Finally, Bella-Mae turned to Goose. Her pale mouth gave a twist before she threw her arms around him and he did his best to hold her. Because she was crying now, but really quietly. He felt her clinging to his body, and smelled an earthiness that was so powerful he couldn't tell if it was nice or unpleasant. "I'm sorry," she whispered. "You look exactly like Vic."

She broke free to fetch a box of Kleenex. "You can take a seat," she said. "You don't have to stand on ceremony. There are cakes as well. I know you guys love sugar." She seemed to laugh a little but it was a strange sound, awkward, as if she didn't know how.

The thing was, unless you perched on a bed, there was nowhere to go in that tiny room apart from the very low plastic sofa. Obediently the siblings stood in a line, all four together, then dropped simultaneously, landing as one. Somehow, they'd managed to do it in order, Netta at one end, Iris at the other, though Netta's end seemed to have a dip in it, rendering her lopsided. The plastic was the kind that sticks to the backs of your legs and sucks when you move.

No sooner had they sat than there was silence. Goose was used to silence but this was not a good one. They were all waiting for Netta. That was the thing. They were waiting for her to take control, as she'd promised, but Netta was not taking control of anything. She was seriously caught up in trying to find a seating position in which her right buttock balanced with her left.

"Oh dear, you got the bad end," said Bella-Mae, with the faintest smile. Then a more general "How do you guys find the heat?"

They said yes, they liked it, which was obviously not true, but they were doing their best to make conversation. Except the one person who might have kept this whole thing afloat was dead, which took them straight into another silence.

Bella-Mae asked how they found the villa. Was it clean?

Susan said they'd found it spotless.

"I made a few new adjustments while I was there. Tidied up a bit. Got rid of some old stuff."

They all thanked her, except possibly Netta.

"Orta is so beautiful. And the lake too. The lake is the best place in the whole world. But Laszlo had never heard of it. Had you, Laszlo?"

"It is Italy's secret!" he said, beaming full-on at Susan, who laughed and went pinker than her lipstick.

Bella-Mae knelt beside the teapot and arranged the cups into a circle. She opened the box of cakes. They were iced in bright colors with little jellied sweets on top, like children's party food. "Tea?"

"My cousin make it herself," said Laszlo. "It is very refreshing."

She batted the air. Her fingers were so small that the wedding ring was enormous on her. "I just brew up flowers," she said. "It's no big deal."

She poured the first cup and, being the eldest, Netta reached out to take it, but Bella-Mae clearly didn't understand the rules of simple etiquette and passed it instead to Iris, so that Netta's hands were left midair. With a bow, Laszlo passed a cup to Susan, who laughed and blushed again, followed by one for Goose. Netta reached for her own but got beached on her bit of sofa, and had to be dislodged with an upward movement from the other three. They drank the tea in tiny sips. It was pale, smelled sweet. If Goose had to say what it tasted of, he would have said a lightly boiled Tic Tac, but nicer than you'd think. Certainly not the dishwater his father had drunk that day in the studio. And thinking of the last time he'd seen him, Goose experienced that seasick sensation again of nothing adding up.

"Cake?" Bella-Mae asked. "I know you don't eat red or green food, Iris, but this one is pink so I guess it won't kill you. Goose? You must be starving." She passed him a plate piled high. "How about you, Antoinetta? What color for you?"

"I don't mind. And by the way, no one calls me Antoinetta."

"We all call her Netta," said Susan helpfully.

"Of course. I forgot. Vic told me how funny you were about your name." Bella-Mae burst into peals of laughter. Then she stopped suddenly and her face went slack. She played with the tie on her dressing gown. "You know I had to identify his body? They bring you to the room where he's lying. You hear the slide of the tray. The metal rollers, the wheels. I saw him and I said no. I said they must have the wrong guy. They asked me to look again, and I almost couldn't. But then I did and I saw that it really was him. He just didn't look like Vic. He looked kind of empty. I don't think I'll ever forget the way he looked." She wiped her eyes with the back of her hand. "How are the cakes?"

The cakes? To be honest, they were surprisingly tasteless for food that was so brightly colored. They were even on the stale side. But Goose was so hungry he would have eaten the cardboard box—and, anyway, cakes were the last thing on his mind. Cakes were a difficult prop in a bewildering scene that no one seemed to have rehearsed. Besides, he was lost in trying to picture his father on a tray with metal rollers.

"I don't have a sweet tooth," said Bella-Mae. "But you know what Vic was like. He would have eaten ice cream all day. Except he couldn't because of his health and everything."

"His health?" interrupted Netta, sharp as a slap. "Why? Was he ill?"

"You can't go eating ice cream all day at his age. You'll have a heart attack. The police didn't see it. They kept asking me questions. Like why did he swim that day? Had he been drinking? I told them Vic wasn't drinking anymore. He was teetotal, same as me. He wasn't taking drugs or medicine either. I know I should have stopped him going into the lake, but I had no idea about the mist. How could I? And you know what he was like. Try stopping Vic when he wanted to do something. But the police said there'll be an autopsy now. Can you believe that?"

"It's a formality," said Netta.

"We're staying until the results," said Susan.

"All of you?" Bella-Mae blinked, surprised. "Why would you do that?"

"Daddy would want it," said Netta.

"But the doctor told me there's no need for an autopsy. Vic died because he got lost in the mist. He would have been fine if he'd stayed in bed. They don't need an autopsy to tell you that. Anyway, hasn't Vic been through enough?" Her eyes glassed with tears that were suddenly pouring down her face. Laszlo passed her the box of Kleenex and she worked her way through them like blades of grass. It was terrible sitting there, the four of them watching this young woman they had only just met, as she cried in the most intensely private way.

Netta took a breath to explain, but said nothing. She'd been shamed into silence. Then Goose experienced a sharp jolt to his left arm and realized it was Susan's elbow, cuing him to take over.

He asked Bella-Mae what she did. He meant it as a general starting point before they moved on to the subjects of the will and the painting. It wasn't meant to be the Spanish Inquisition.

But: "What do I do?" she asked, looking suddenly thrown. Yes, he said gently—did she study, did she work, what did she like?—but she flushed and stammered. "I can't talk about work. I can't even think about it. I don't know how I'll ever work again."

Laszlo refilled everyone's cup. The tea had got fiercer. More like liquefied Extra Strong Mints than Tic Tacs. "My cousin is humble. She is very gifted artist."

"So you're a painter?" piped up Iris, but so quietly Bella-Mae failed to hear and she had to say it again. "You're a painter, like Daddy?"

Bella-Mae stroked both sides of her long hair and said kind of yes, kind of no. You could kind of call her an artist, but not like Vic. "I'm more abstract, aren't I?" she said to Laszlo. "I like to see things in a different way. I kind of pull them apart to put them back together." Goose nodded politely and so did his sisters, though he was hard pushed to imagine what type of art that was. It was only years later that he would begin to understand.

"And how did you meet our father?"

"How did we meet?" Just at the point where Bella-Mae might have enlightened them, she appeared to know next to nothing. She turned to Laszlo again.

"You meet online, remember," he said, and Bella-Mae laughed and said that was right, they met online: everything in her head was a blur because of the pills.

"It was one of those chat rooms. You know? For people who can't sleep? It just seems so long ago. Like another lifetime. So much has happened since then. I had no idea it would end like this."

From here, the conversation continued in stops and stutters. She told them she didn't really like to talk about herself. Really her main interest was other people. She'd never been close to her parents, not like they were to Vic. She spent so much time alone as a child that art and TV were the only things that kept her company. The sole person she got on with in her family was Laszlo, and he wasn't strictly her cousin, but her third on her mother's side: as kids they'd been set up as pen friends and kept in touch ever since. Then she'd left home at sixteen to travel and taken all kinds of work so that she could continue her art. She squatted in flats and stayed on sofas of people she barely knew. She lived for a while in a commune. But it was only when she met Vic that she fell in love for the first time. She knew there was the age gap and everything, but it was as if they were the same person. Or not so much the same as two halves that fitted perfectly. He had believed she could do things even when she couldn't. Like swimming, for instance. She knew they were all brilliant swimmers, but when she first came to Orta, she didn't even dare to jump in the water. "I was worse than Shirley Lucas," she said, with a laugh. " 'Vic,' I said, 'if you throw me in the lake, like Iris, I will actually kill you.' " A puzzled look crossed her face. "Not that I killed him," she said, laughing nervously. Then she reached for another tissue. "Oh God, oh God. There was so much we were going to do. It's like waking up and realizing everything was a dream, except if this is the real world, I don't want it. And now the news about the autopsy. It's too much. It's way too much."

Her face crumpled and collapsed on itself, and suddenly she was bellowing out great big sobs, as if she was far too young for this kind of pain. She heaved herself to her feet and moved to the window, looking down over the lake in her grubby dressing gown and with her back to them. Laszlo closed the lids on the patisserie cartons. It was a cue to leave and the siblings stood, apart from Netta, who was still seriously embedded in the lopsided sofa and struggling to hoist herself upward.

Before anyone could ask Bella-Mae the vital questions they had come to ask, she said in a low voice that she was tired and knew they would understand. She needed to sleep again—it was the pills—and her headache was back. She would be leaving Lake Orta the next day. She wouldn't be going back to the villa. Without Vic, there was nothing there for her. She was thinking of traveling, she had no idea where. The police had told her they had no further questions.

It was only as they shook hands to say goodbye—none of the spontaneity with which she'd greeted them—that she said flatly, "It was nice to meet you guys at last. I hope I didn't upset you. If you want me, you can get in touch with my cousin here at the hotel. He's got some things to sort so he's staying for a few more days. Laszlo?"

He went to the wardrobe and retrieved a plastic bag.

"Here," she said. "The police took Vic's passport, but I hid his phone. Do what you like with it. I guess in the end we all have to find our own way of moving on."

There are moments when the present comes at you out of nowhere: the past falls away, and the future doesn't seem to be in the mix yet, so you are left in a strange new place that is like nowhere at all. At least, this was how it felt to Goose as he walked from the Hotel Navarro with his sisters. They might be none the wiser about the will or the painting, but their guesses about Bella-Mae had been so wide of the mark it was laughable. Of course she wasn't drugging their father. Of course she wasn't a rapacious sex-driven grifter, and she wasn't going to take Harry's job either and become Vic's dealer. She wasn't any of the things they'd been imagining because she was twenty-seven. She was an ordinary young woman, just starting out, and now she'd lost the only man she'd ever loved. But maybe that was the way it went. We think we understand one another, he thought. We think we know the truth about people, yet we make mistakes over and over because all we have is our own lens, our own particular way of seeing things. He began to laugh.

"What's funny?" said Susan.

"I don't know. Everything. I mean, it isn't remotely funny. But it kind of is. We got her so wrong."

"You're right." Susan began to laugh, too, and so did Iris. Once they'd started, they couldn't stop. "We thought she was a porn star!"

Even Netta, who was up ahead, carrying the bag from Laszlo, came back. "That sofa! I thought I'd be stuck in it forever. And what is she? Whatever was Daddy talking about? They met in a chat room for insomniacs!"

They held on to one another in the middle of the path as they laughed. The moment they stopped, one of them would start up again and that was it. It passed between them like a bolt of electricity and they were howling again. It was relief more than anything.

Without Vic, life had briefly seemed tipped in the balance. For forty-eight hours, anything had felt possible, even homelessness. But Goose was sure that if he could stay like this, holding his sisters, but tighter, if they could try to love one another a little more, to look after and protect one another a little better, they would survive, just as they'd survived the death of their mother. They would find the things that were missing and, while they waited for the results of the autopsy, Goose would make some repairs to the villa that he should have done years ago. If he and his sisters stuck together, like they always did, they would be all right. He was sure of it.

Why, then, when he closed his eyes that night, were they back? The strange images that had come to him ever since he was a boy and so frightened him? The strange tendrils, the floating fruit, the splitting seed heads? This feeling of things opening out that he didn't understand. A half-glimpsed world blossoming right there in the dark.

"You okay, Goose?" whispered Iris, from the bed she was still sharing with Susan.

"A nightmare."

"Want to talk?"

"It's okay. Try to sleep."

He turned over on the mattress. Shut his eyes tight. But he couldn't shake the feeling that they were wrong about Bella-Mae. That it was not over with her. Far from it. That something was just beginning.

14

Child's Play

Vic had always refused to paint his children. "Draw me, Daddy! Draw me!" Susan used to say, but he never did. If you were lucky, he might sketch a circle, then put some legs on it and, hey presto, it was a pony, but on the whole he said he wasn't a performing clown. His art was a serious business, reserved for the studio. Then, when Iris was six, he announced he'd had an idea for a new picture. This was going to be a child, so obviously he would need a model: they would go to the studio to be photographed and afterward there would be a special tea at Claridge's. "Just one model?" said Netta.

"Just one," he said.

"Yes. I can do that," she said, straight off. "I'll be the model."

Vic laughed and said she was way too smart to sit still long enough to be a model.

"I could be the model," said Susan. "I'm not nearly as smart as Netta."

Vic laughed even more and rocked her in both arms, then said no because she would never stop talking. Even though Goose didn't actually offer, Vic said he wasn't looking for a boy. So that left Iris. "And Iris can sit still as a mouse," Vic said. "She can be my model."

Iris didn't know she could sit still as a mouse until her father told the others, but now that she knew, she became assiduous in her motionlessness. For once, she had something Goose and her sisters didn't and, because of that, her father was going to paint her. She was going to his studio, where she had never been before, and the others weren't going, not even Netta. Every time she thought of it, she felt a secret happiness, as if she had pocketed an everlasting sweet that she could suck a little more goodness from whenever she needed to. It created a tacit rivalry, a sense of superiority she had not known before, an emotion consequently revolutionary in itself. She even noticed her siblings watching her in a different way, as if they had spotted her for the first time.

But then a new Spanish au pair moved in, and Vic was photographing her all the time, even when she was doing ordinary things, like washing her tights. ("He is obsessed," said Netta.) He seemed to forget all about his new painting of a child. As a gentle but silent reminder, Iris sat so still at mealtimes her fork barely traveled the distance from her plate to her mouth. She walked so carefully up the stairs that the others had to push past to get to the bathroom. Sometimes it took her such a long time to get out of the house, descending each step as if with a whole column of books on her head, that the others would be screaming at her to hurry before they died of boredom.

And suddenly the Spanish au pair was gone and Vic said to her one morning, "Little Fish, how do you fancy coming to the studio today? It's time to start that new painting."

She could barely hide her elation. She felt glittery, singled out. She sensed Netta's eyes boring holes in her, as she (very slowly) got up from the breakfast table and went to fetch her coat and hat.

Only it turned out that the coat and hat were not necessary. Neither were her dress, socks or shoes. At the studio, Vic told her to take off her clothes down to her pants, then sit on that blanket over there and play with the bucket and spade.

Iris did not know what to do with what she felt. On the one hand, this was her father, the man who towered over everything else and protected her—and since she had been motherless almost since birth, the one grown-up she had in the whole world. He had selected her to do something incredibly important. Something that Netta and Susan would have given their right arm for. On the other hand, Iris never took off her clothes unless she was getting into the bath and even then she hid in a towel the moment she got out. Netta was the one who ran around the house, beautiful and naked and thirteen, with cherries for bosoms and a pocket of black fuzz between her legs. Netta was the one who never looked at anyone else, convinced they were all busy looking at her.

"Little Fish?" said Vic as if he could read the doubt in her mind. "All you need to do is sit on the floor and pretend you're making sandcastles. It's easy."

But it wasn't. And the fact he couldn't see that made the feeling even more subversive, as if she were betraying the very person she most wanted to please. She took off her clothes, folding them really carefully as if he might change his mind the longer she took, but her father was busy fixing up his tripod and some lights. The silence in the studio was vast and frightening, not at all like home. And actually, there was something about the photographs on the walls of ladies without their clothes that did not seem good either. Of course she wanted her father to look at her, she wanted to be the one he painted and she wanted to please him, but if only she could do it without being present. "Are you ready?" he called, his face not even his face but masked behind a camera.

Iris did everything her father asked her that day. She sat on the blanket just as he said, and she felt him looking at her just as she wanted, but not in a way she understood, more like being watched by someone she didn't know, and she said to herself that she was not Iris, she was not sitting on a blanket. She was nothing, she was floating, she was not in her legs and not in her stomach, she was a thing, not even called Iris, but still as a mouse, a little mouse who lived in a hole with her sisters and brother, and was safe as safe because there weren't even things like cats to be afraid of, there was only cheese, while the camera went *chop chop chop*, taking photographs, and her father—who was not really her father but just a flashing eye and voice that sounded like her father's—said, "Very good. Very good." He sang her a funny song about a yellow submarine that made her laugh, but only briefly because she mustn't twitch so much as a finger or an eyebrow.

"How was the tea?" Netta asked, as soon as they got home. They were waiting, their faces pressed like moon children's to the window. "What did you have?"

Iris said nothing. She didn't even take off her coat and hat. She slept in both that night.

"Poor Little Fish," said her father. "She wasn't hungry. Too much excitement. We had to leave and get a cab."

The painting was called *Child's Play*. Vic always said it was one of his best, and there was a time it was everywhere. A little girl, all blond curls, sitting in a sandcastle, while her father stood behind, hands on hips, as if holding back the sea. It captured innocence. Summer holidays on an English beach. A time that was gone. For a few years it was so popular it even outsold the Athena poster of the young woman with a tennis racket. And yet if Iris thought too deeply about the day she was a model for her father, she was lost in a feeling of confusion, a cycle of thinking that nothing was safe, nothing was good, and it was somehow her fault. She made up rules like not eating food that was red or green—though she couldn't remember anymore why that was a rule, and she only stuck to it because she was so worried about what might happen if she stopped. When she started having panic attacks in her mid-teens, Warwick got her a puffer, though he said it wasn't asthma and was nothing to worry about. She kept secrets about herself, because if she didn't she felt so irrelevant she might as well not exist. But whatever she did, it always came back to the same place—she would always be that little girl from her father's painting.

It was already a week since Vic's death. A week of looking up at the garret window, and finding an empty space. Calling his mobile, just to hear his voice on the answer message. Scrolling through those texts he'd sent in the middle of the night and feeling torn up with guilt for not replying. Looking for anything to explain why he had decided to swim in the lake when a mist was on its way. Slogging with Netta in the full heat up to the *carabinieri* to check if there was news and asking if anyone had seen Limoncello the boatman. Or walking into the kitchen, saying, "Daddy?" followed by that punch to the gut of realizing he was gone. Neighbors and locals dropped by to offer their condolences and express their shock. In the garden, camellia petals were dark red pools on the grass, the hostas were in full flower and the wisteria was heavy with purple blooms.

There had been more obituaries in the press, one calling Vic a "painter for the people," another describing him as a self-made phenomenon. There were daily tweets and emails from fans: a woman who'd run into her burning house to rescue a signed print; a man who'd fallen so in love with the woman in *Serenade* his girlfriend had worn the same red dress for their wedding. Harry told them he took new inquiries at the studio every day. There had also been a tentative conversation with a major gallery, though he couldn't say yet which one. ("I told you!" said Susan. "Didn't I tell you that would happen?") "Obviously I don't want to sound opportunistic," he said, "but Vic's last painting is going to attract a lot of attention. It would be more than good if you could find it."

He was right. Except there was no sign of it. Iris and Goose had looked everywhere and, short of taking up the floorboards, there were only so many places you could look for a work of art, especially a massive one. They didn't even know what they were looking for, though Iris told the others she might have an idea.

"Oh?" said Goose. They were out on the terrazzo, finishing dinner. The white flowers of the oleander glowed through the dark. The moon's reflection gently washed up and down on the water.

"Daddy said to me that he really wished he could paint the lake. He just didn't think he was good enough. But I reckon that's what he was doing this time. No people or anything. Maybe at night, like this. That's why he wouldn't talk to us about it. He didn't want to jinx it."

"You know what I think?" said Susan. "I think it's a picture of us."

"But he never painted us," said Netta. "Only Iris."

Susan smiled and put her face in her hands, looking dreamy. Her eyes were sequins, catching the light from the house. "Think about it. It makes total sense. He never painted us as children, so his final masterpiece is the four of us, but as adults, like we are now. And he said no photographs this time, remember? He was painting from life. Well, who did he know better than us?"

"I reckon it's a full nude portrait of Bella-Mae," said Netta. "And that's why she's taken it. What do you think, Goose?"

"I think all three of you could be right." The swellings on his face had gone down but the bruises were still there, yellowy and green, and even though his hair was beginning to grow back it was doing so in odd ways, more like scraps. "But I'll tell you one thing. I'd love to see any of those paintings."

They fell quiet. Iris pictured her father at the bottom of the garden with his easel. Maybe he'd painted the lake at night with the lights streaming into the water and the stars as big as flowers. Then Netta staggered to her feet. "What the fuck are we doing? Waiting for things to happen? First thing tomorrow, I'm going to see the Toad in his creepy hotel. I'm going to find out what the hell is going on."

But actually Susan woke early and got there first.

She came back a few hours later, dazzled, off-balance, unable to settle. Yes, she'd seen Laszlo. He understood how distressing it was for the family to be left in the dark about the will and the painting. He would ask his cousin what she knew.

What she didn't share with the others, not even Netta—she couldn't—was that Laszlo had been drinking when she found him. "Suzanne!" he bellowed, the moment he saw her. She froze, unsure whether to make her excuses and leave, but he was already moving toward her. Nine in the morning, and she could smell alcohol coming off him in waves. He reached for her waist, and there it was again, the jolt between their bodies, every time they came close. He introduced her to a group of men she'd never met before, all of them clammy and too loud, like him. She felt stranger than she'd felt in a long time, repulsed and yet excited. They'd been up to something when she arrived. Poker? Drugs? Her head was spinning. None of them looked as if they'd slept. His hand was still on her waist, hot and heavy, rubbing at the folds of her caftan. Pinching her flesh, ever so slightly.

She had looked at him, his bloodshot eyes, those dark eyebrows like hoods, his quiff that had begun to break apart, the way he grinned at her with wet lips as if he was considering how she might taste, and she wanted him to know everything. She wanted to take off her rhinestone flip-flops, her wedding ring, her caftan. She wanted to tell him about her failed life, her marriage, the fact that she and Warwick lived like two very old friends who no longer had sex. Or how she had once been full of plans to be a TV chef like Lesley Waters, then a mother. She wanted him to know every intimate, vulnerable thing about her. To slough it all off and lay it at his feet and be nothing, or everything, she had no idea which: her body was filled with a kind of ecstatic confusion at the thought of existing only as he chose to perceive her. She ended up drinking a glass of wine that she did not want, laughing with him and the men when they laughed, but not fully understanding what they said, even when Laszlo parted the hair from her ear and whispered that they were agreeing she was a very attractive woman: "*Bellissima.*" Susan was no fool. Her Italian wasn't fluent but she knew that word. And no one had used it. "*Molto* sexy." His mouth in her ear seemed to radiate heat. She felt half senseless with need.

Afterward she had bought mints, plus a cheap body spray. She'd called Warwick as she lurched toward the boat. She asked how he was and if he had remembered to water the pot plants.

"That's it?" Netta said. She kept staring at Susan as if waiting for the real one to step out and reveal herself. "That's all Laszlo said? That he would ask Bella-Mae what she knew? How long did you stay? You've been gone ages."

"I stayed five minutes. After that I got caught up with people in town. You know how it is. Who wants lunch?"

They all took the ferry to Pella to see the reeds where Vic's body had been found by Limoncello the boatman and threw flowers. Afterward they went straight to the undertaker to choose a coffin, ready for when the results of the autopsy came through: it was obvious Bella-Mae was too young to have any view on that kind of thing. Besides, as far as they knew she'd already left. They flipped helplessly through a huge catalogue of laminated pages with photographs of the alternative caskets and the full range of things you could add, everything from handles in basic plastic to top-of-the-range brass, and each item individually priced with a little sticker in the top corner. Then Netta said, "I wonder if they do an ice-cream sundae," and that was it. Out of nowhere, and after all that sobbing, they were laughing like drains.

The next day, Iris watched in amazement as a speedboat approached the villa across the water—a speck that had been caught in midday sunlight and then became more and more substantial. "It's Bella-Mae and her cousin Laszlo! They're coming to the villa!"

"But I thought she'd left Orta?" Netta shouted back, dashing for towels because they'd been swimming to cool down and no one was fully dressed. "What the hell is she playing at?"

Laszlo moored his boat at the bottom of the garden and helped Bella-Mae out. She greeted them beneath the trees, kissing them formally cheek to cheek. "Goose, Susan, Antoinetta, Iris." Gone was the awkwardness, the shabby hotel dressing gown. The siblings might be in flip-flops and damp kimonos, wet hair dripping down their backs, but everything about Bella-Mae was dry, minimalist and professional. She was in a fitted black skirt and jacket with sunglasses that covered the part of her face that wasn't already covered by her hair, and red lipstick. On her feet, she wore a pair of low elegant slingbacks ending in a point. She could have walked straight from a Vic Kemp painting.

She handed them another bouquet of spiked flowers. "You guys were all so sweet to me the other day," she said, though she seemed to avoid directing this at Netta. "I didn't think you'd show up." Her voice had got harder. A twinge of American that Iris had missed the first time. "This is so weird, right?" she said to Laszlo. "Being here again?"

Iris watched her siblings do their best to go into entertainment mode, even Netta. They might be utterly in the dark as to why Bella-Mae was back at the villa, and indeed who she'd come as, but they were their father's children: they knew how to throw a party.

In a rush, Netta asked everyone what they wanted in terms of drinks.

"I don't," said Bella-Mae, holding up her neat little hand like a stop sign. "Only water for me."

Goose ran round the garden fetching more chairs and setting a table under the trees, while Iris, who didn't know what to do, followed him, unsure how specifically she might be useful, but not wanting to be left alone with Bella-Mae and Laszlo either. Susan whipped to the kitchen and fetched cushions, plus an additional parasol that she wrenched up so fast she almost skewered Goose, who was leaning forward at the same moment to offer a hand. Netta came out with bottles of Campari and soda, while Susan brought plates of tiny canapés she had somehow put together in a flash.

"Lemons!" yelped Netta. "Where are the lemons?"

Goose dashed into the glasshouse and returned with an armful, the leaves still on them.

"Laszlo? Bella-Mae? *Bruschette? Tarallini?*" Bella-Mae was not the only one who seemed different: suddenly Susan was talking with a funny Italian accent.

Laszlo helped himself to so many he needed both hands, while Bella-Mae studied them as if inspecting them for rat poison, then shook her head. "I heard you came to the hotel yesterday, Susan. You had some questions for me? I'd had a bad night. I was asleep. But I have a few things I want to share with you today."

As she listened to Bella-Mae, Iris became aware of a conflict within herself. Ever since they'd arrived at the villa, Susan had been in the kitchen nonstop because there was no dishwasher and the range was almost medieval, and when she wasn't doing that, she was helping Harry track down buyers of Vic's paintings in preparation for the possible big exhibition. Meanwhile Netta was on the trail of new leads every hour and Goose had bought paint and Polyfilla to begin repairs to the villa. Iris had no idea how to keep up. Most of the time she felt as if she had begun to climb a ladder, only to discover there were no rungs beneath her feet. For instance, she'd found herself that morning in the music room, staring at harps, with no recollection of having gone in there to stare at harps in the first place. Yet surely she wasn't wrong about this: surely Bella-Mae had said she was leaving Orta. That she didn't want to upset the family? But from the moment she began to talk, it became clear that neither of these was true.

"Vic didn't make a new will," Bella-Mae said. "I know you've been looking, but there isn't one. So my lawyer's dealing with that now. And I've heard from the undertaker you put down a deposit on a coffin."

Susan stammered, "We thought you'd left. We would never have done it without you if we'd known you were still here."

"I was surprised when they told me, but I kind of understood. The fact is, after I met you, I changed my mind about leaving Orta. I decided to lie low for a few days instead and work things out. And one of the things I've decided is that I want Vic to be cremated. Imagine burying a man like him in a coffin. It would be worse than boxing up a wild bear. He would literally be howling from under the ground." (Iris bit her lip. She couldn't stand the thought of her father howling from under the ground, or even the poor bear in a box.) "Worse still, imagine giving him a church service. Vic didn't believe in God. It was why we had a civil wedding. And we all know what he was like about the press—he hated them. The last thing he'd want would be for them to get wind of this. So this morning I had my own meeting with the undertaker. I arranged for him to be cremated as soon as we have the results of the autopsy. As for the ceremony, I want it to be small. A private gathering here in the garden. We can all dress in normal clothes because he'd hate us to be in black. We'll scatter his ashes over the water, then go our separate ways. It's what Vic would have wanted. Don't you agree?" That question was another thing that was confusing. She wasn't asking their opinion. She was telling them what was going to happen.

Iris thought of the beautiful coffin the siblings had chosen to take him home. Limed oak with brass hinges and a pillow because she couldn't bear the idea of him without one.

"No big funeral?" repeated Susan.

"No," said Netta. "I don't think you've understood. We've come to Orta to take our father's body home after the autopsy."

"I know this might be difficult for you. There's nothing to stop you having a memorial or whatever when you're back in London. But as his wife, I have decided that his final resting place will be beside the lake. He isn't going back to London in a coffin. He's staying here. And I will stay too. Same as you. I'm going to stay here until we get the results of the autopsy."

All of this fell into Iris's stomach like a stone falling to the bottom of a well. She looked at her siblings and their faces seemed so blank and confused. There was a long silence, at the end of which Susan whispered, "More *tartine*?" Nobody replied.

"You're staying here?" said Goose. Somehow he smiled and managed to look enthusiastic.

"Do you mean here in the villa?" said Susan. "With us?"

Bella-Mae laughed. "I can't exactly stay at the Hotel Navarro. You saw that place. It's a dump. Vic would have a fit if he knew I was there. Besides. This is where I live now."

Iris began pulling at the little sticking-out bone of her wrist. For a while, it felt like the only movement in the whole garden. She knew Bella-Mae was right. It was just that she hadn't expected her to stand up like this to her siblings. It gave her a strange new electrifying feeling that she couldn't make sense of. Besides, she was still under the distinct impression Bella-Mae didn't want to set foot inside the villa ever again. They all were.

It was Netta who came right out and said what was on her mind. "Okay. So what have you done with Daddy's painting?" She served it straight. No preamble.

"I'm sorry?"

"He came here to finish it. It was going to be his big new piece. Six months ago it was all he could talk about. He said he was going in a whole new direction. So where is it?"

"I don't understand. Are you cross-examining me?" Bella-Mae laughed, but there was something obstructive in her voice. "I don't know anything about a new direction. The only thing Vic talked about was destroying his old pictures. It was everything I could do to stop him."

"Destroying them?" Susan's hand flew to her throat. "Why would he do that?"

"We'd barely got here and he started taking them down. He kept saying they were from the past, and he didn't want to be that artist anymore. I hid *My Sweet Guardian Angel* in the music room because that was the one he seemed to hate most. To be honest, I was terrified he was going to do something awful, like set a match to it."

Out of nowhere, she began to cry. But this was nothing like the Hotel Navarro. Iris thought this was possibly the neatest grief she'd ever seen. More like someone in a film. "I'm sorry," Bella-Mae said. She blew her nose delicately, as if it were a flower. "I can't believe I'm a widow now."

"We understand," said Susan. "Of course we do." She was crying, too, but properly crying, her face all splotchy.

Clearly Netta was not feeling any of this. She had no intention of crying and no intention of being silenced just because there had been a significant change in Bella-Mae's marital status. "Of course there's a painting. Even your cousin mentioned it. He told us Daddy was working on it here every day."

Sheer panic crossed Bella-Mae's face. "I don't understand." She turned to Laszlo. "*Perché gliel'hai detto?* Why did you tell them that?" Her Italian didn't trip off the tongue but it was a darn sight better than Iris's.

"I mean nothing," he said, in a rush. "I make mistake. I think he is painting because he is artist."

While they were still floundering, Netta made her next move, but from a new angle. She was in full attack. It was terrifying and wonderful, both at the same time. You had to be grateful you weren't on the receiving end. "And why did you clear out my father's studio?"

"His studio?"

"Yes. In the garret."

"I didn't."

"You clearly did. Everything's gone."

"I don't know how. I didn't touch it."

"Oh, so you're telling me his paints magically jumped out of the window by themselves?"

"But he wasn't painting in Orta. I already said that."

"This is what I don't understand, Bella-Mae. My father boxed up all his paints at home. Didn't he, Goose? To begin his new work."

Goose swung his head low, mortified to be dragged into all this. "Well, yes. He did. I mean, that's what he told me."

"So why would he do that if he wasn't going to work on the picture he told us, many times, that he was going to paint?"

If Bella-Mae had been thrown by this unexpected twist in the conversation, she now recovered. Her smile came back. An immaculate red bow beneath her sunglasses.

"Look, I'm afraid Laszlo misinformed you about the painting. Okay, I admit Vic mentioned it once before we came out here, but talking is very different from doing. If you don't mind me saying, we'd just got married. He had other things on his mind when we were in Italy. Vic didn't bring his paints to Orta. He didn't lift a brush. You can ask me as many times as you like, but there is no last painting."

Iris could not bear the sudden vulnerability on her siblings' faces. She looked at Netta, Susan and Goose. They were all stunned.

"No painting?" whispered Goose. "He didn't do it?"

"No," said Netta, but her voice took a wobble. "That can't be true. It was going to be his best yet. His masterpiece. He sent us texts—"

This time Bella-Mae openly laughed. "His masterpiece? Did Vic really tell you that? But you know what artists are like. We get an idea and it's beautiful in our heads, it's the best thing we've ever done, and then we start to work on it and find that we've killed it. Anyway, it normally happens the other way round?" She posed this as a question, though it was another of her confusing sentences that turned out to be a statement. "We do the work, then other people decide whether or not it's a masterpiece. And generally not in our own lifetime. Well, at least we've got that out of the way. Now, if you'll excuse me, I'm going up to my room. It's these pills. I need to sleep the whole time. Laszlo?"

She reached out her arms and he helped her to her feet. As he led her to the villa, Iris couldn't be sure but she thought she saw Bella-Mae rest her head against his arm and Laszlo lifting his hand and touching her hair, ever so softly.

~

Bella-Mae was barely out of earshot and, in the garden, the mood shifted all over again. It was like little explosions here, there and everywhere, each one more powerful than the last, because everyone was doing their best to keep their voice down, including Netta, who was mainly asking, What the fuck? Why had Bella-Mae appointed her own lawyer? Was she getting ready to claim the villa? Had Laszlo honestly not mentioned to Susan that she was still in Orta?

"No, Netta!" loud-whispered Susan. "He said he would give her my message. I assumed that meant she was gone!"

But Netta had on her I'm-not-listening face. Who did Bella-Mae think she was, telling them what Vic would want for his funeral? There was no way she was leaving him here for some hippie-dippy knit-your-own-knickers, noncelebration celebration, whatever the hell that was. "Over my dead body. Literally. You'll have to bury two of us." As for Vic not wanting any attention from the press, that was clearly bollocks. The man couldn't walk into a restaurant without expecting everyone to look up. And in terms of his painting, she didn't believe one word Bella-Mae had said. "She was in the cab, wasn't she, Goose? When he came to fetch his stuff?"

"She was. I saw her as they drove away. She looked back. I'm sure of it."

"Then of course she knew about the painting. It's bullshit. He would have been talking about it nonstop. And you saw how guilty Laszlo looked just now. They're lying. Both of them. And if they're lying about that, they're lying about the will too."

Briefly they heard raucous laughter from inside the villa, then silence again. "Whatever can those two be doing?" said Susan. There was a kind of stricken panic in her eyes. "And why would Daddy have wanted to destroy his paintings?" She moved close to Netta and clutched her arm. "Look, I'm your sister. I'll always side with you. That's a given. But maybe we have to be a bit more open."

"Open?"

"She's young. She's never been part of a family like ours. But she saved *My Sweet Guardian Angel*, remember? You thought she was trying to steal it, and it turns out she was doing the opposite. Maybe we shouldn't have gone and chosen the coffin. Maybe we shouldn't have insisted on the autopsy without at least mentioning it to her first. The last thing we want is to drive her away."

"Susan, I'm hardly driving her away. She has appointed a lawyer. She's upstairs in Daddy's room with her cousin. They couldn't be more present if they were camping on the roof. Don't be so quick to trust either of them. One minute he's saying there is a painting, the next he's denying it."

"Laszlo made a mistake! He said so! Goodness, Netta! Just because you're perfect, it doesn't mean the rest of us can keep up with you!" She laughed to take the sting out of what she'd said, and looked to Iris and Goose, urging them to laugh with her, but she could laugh as much as she liked because for once she was openly disagreeing with Netta, and the sting was there. "This is real life, Netta! You can't treat everything as if it were a courtroom drama. Don't you think, Goose?"

Goose wiped his hands through the little of his hair that had grown back, saying he was sorry, even though at this point no one was blaming him. "Let's not get upset," he said gently. "It's too hot. And we've all had another shock. Who wants a drink? Susan, let me wash up. You haven't sat down all morning."

But Susan said she liked washing up. At least it kept her head in order. And Netta said, why did everyone always talk as if a drink would calm things? (Though it seemed to Iris that a drink was the one thing that did calm Netta, like taking a heavy-duty syringe to a horse.) Then the two of them went up the garden, arm in arm, leaving Goose and Iris behind, with the old feeling that somehow the party had moved on without them.

"They're like this," he told her. "In a few minutes they'll be roaring with laughter from the kitchen and we'll be running up to find out what the joke is."

"I don't know, Goose. I don't see how they'll be laughing about this. Netta is furious." She glanced up at her father's room: Bella-Mae briefly appeared at the window to close the shutters. "Do you really think she's moving back?"

"It looks like it. But even if she is, I don't see how we can stop her. It's her home too. And if there's no will, half the house will be hers anyway."

"And do you think it's true about Daddy's painting?"

"I don't know. It seems strange that he told us he was coming out here to finish, then gave up."

They were interrupted by a glass smashing in the kitchen and Netta shouting, "Oh, fucksake! I'm sorry!" followed by Susan singing, "It's okay! I've got this!"

Goose said, "We'd better go and see if we can help. Coming?"

"In a minute. You go on without me."

Iris checked her pocket and slipped down to the end of the garden. The water was all glittering glass, the sky spooled blue in every direction. She could make out the big white umbrellas across the water on Piazza Motta, the passenger boats pulling out from the jetty, one after another. If only she knew what she thought, but she didn't. It was like that day in her father's studio when she'd made herself become nothing: when Iris was with her siblings, she seemed to disappear. Netta was already marching up and down the terrazzo, barking at Vic's solicitor on her phone, and Susan was clearing the table as she listened to her music, while Goose was helping them, fetching Netta a Campari, then following Susan with a tea towel. Once again, they had taken all the available roles and left nothing much for Iris. She took tiny gasps, trying to calm herself, but even the air felt like something the other three had got to first.

She slipped her phone from her pocket and double-checked they weren't watching. Then she squinted against the sun and wrote: *i wish u wer here. i mis u.* She waited a whole minute for a reply. Then she texted a "*?*," followed by another.

At last there was an answer: *I know. I think of you all the time. I wish I was with you. Shall I call later? It's a bit tricky right now.* She replied that it was okay, she was only sad because of her father. *i no youandme cn never b 2gehter.*

"Mind if I sit here?"

It was Bella-Mae. She was right behind her. Iris hadn't even heard her come down the garden. She'd changed out of her smart suit into an old painting T-shirt of Vic's. It could have covered several of her. It struck Iris that this was the third time she'd seen Bella-Mae and, so far, she'd looked like three different people.

"Your father told me you were the quiet one," said Bella-Mae.

The messages were still displayed on Iris's phone. Bella-Mae was blatantly staring at them. Iris was not a blusher like Susan—years of secrecy had put paid to that—but she felt it now. "Oh, this? This is nothing."

"It doesn't look like nothing."

"It's for a friend. I'm dyslexic. No one realized until I left school. My spelling is awful."

Bella-Mae looked at her curiously, her head to one side. "Funny."

Iris wasn't sure how this could be funny. Of all the things it might be, funny seemed at the bottom of the pile. But Bella-Mae was still staring at the phone, waiting for Iris to explain, and unless she kept repeating that she was writing to a friend, which was clearly insane, she had no idea what to say next.

Bella-Mae spread her towel on the grass. She sat at Iris's feet, staring over the water. Her bare legs were nut brown and beautiful. "Well, don't let me get in your way. You send your text. It looked pretty important to me. Or why don't you just call them?"

"We prefer messages."

"Cute," she said, as if Iris was from a period drama set in the nineteenth century. She kept looking at the lake, her hair thick around her face. "When I was twelve, I decided to stop talking. No one knew what to do with me. The one person I spoke to was Laszlo, and that was only because I wrote to him. Then I began to see there was a kind of power in not talking. People don't know what to do with silence. Vic was different. I could say anything to Vic, and it would be okay. It was like he'd done everything, so nothing shocked him. And he was still a really nice fuck. I don't know if you knew that, but he was."

"No. I didn't." Iris wanted to smile but honestly couldn't. She was too shocked. Sex was not something she ever spoke about, not even with her siblings. She had tried once with Susan, who had shut her down immediately.

"Sex isn't everything," she'd said.

Besides, she couldn't tell if Bella-Mae was confiding in her or having fun. She was beginning to sense with Bella-Mae that it could go both ways.

"He was this great big ball of energy. Even at his age. He had far more energy than me. And he was just kind. Mad and kind. You know? He was the kindest man I'll ever meet. I only had to say I liked something and he'd be on the phone, getting it delivered. 'Vic, you can't keep buying me stuff,' I'd say. 'You know I don't need stuff. You are all I need.' But he wouldn't hear of it. He wanted me to have everything. Or I'd walk in the room and he'd hug me like he hadn't seen me for a hundred years. No one in my life held me like Vic did. 'Let's go dancing,' he'd say. It could be the middle of the night but we'd jump in a cab and find a club in Soho, and there he would be, the oldest person by about fifty years, doing his crazy old-man dancing. I've never met anyone who loved life as much as Vic."

Bella-Mae kept watching the light on the water for so long that it began to move in flickering patterns all over her skin, as if she and the lake were enjoying some kind of private communion. "I know your siblings don't trust me. I know they think I've stolen his painting. But I haven't. Why would I do that? There's no painting to steal. And I didn't kill him either, just in case you think that too."

"I don't," Iris said, though yet again she had no real idea what she thought. Her head had gone buzzy and blank.

Bella-Mae produced a bottle of oil and poured some into the palm of a hand. She worked it up and down her legs. "Want some?"

"I'm okay."

"Suit yourself. Have you sent your message?"

"Not yet." She lingered, biting her lip. She felt her pulse quicken in a mixture of fear and dread and exhilaration. She said, "It's not a friend. It's my lover."

If she had expected Bella-Mae to fall over backward, she was wrong. Bella-Mae kept massaging her skin. She didn't as much as look up. So Iris dared to say more, like playing Grandmother's Footsteps, one small move at a time, growing more reckless with each one. "No one knows, though. Not even my siblings. It's been going on for four years and they still don't know. They assume I'm single. They always have." Bella-Mae closely studied her own calves. Iris took one more step. "It would kill them if they knew I'd kept a secret from them. Literally kill them. They think they know everything about me, you see. We keep saying it's over. Me and my lover, that is. But it's like, even when we say we're going to stop, we still can't."

At last Bella-Mae looked up. Or at least her sunglasses did. "Cool," she said slowly, and she put down her bottle of sun oil. It was exactly then, in the tiniest way, that something began to shift for Iris. She realized how much she wanted to have some kind of closeness with Bella-Mae. It was the nearest she could get now to having her father, but it was also the one thing her siblings hadn't yet claimed. And maybe Bella-Mae had thought the same, because suddenly she pushed her hair back from her face and spoke animatedly. "It's like chemistry. Yeah? It's like you put two things together and they go bang." She made a ball of her hands and then sprang them apart, vigorously fluttering her very small fingers like a shower of explosive dust.

"Yes! That's exactly it."

"That's how it was for me and Vic. We went bang right from the start. You could have blindfolded us and we would still have found each other. It's a miracle, when you think about it. How on earth, on this vast planet of eight billion human beings, do two people who are destined for each other manage to meet?"

"I know!" said Iris. "I know!"

"Well, your secret's safe with me. I'm not going to tell your siblings. Though if you ask me, it's up to you what you do with your sex life."

Iris nodded vigorously, wanting to share more. But Bella-Mae lay back on her towel and went very still. Actually she seemed to fall asleep, though there remained on her face the smallest smile.

"Iris!" called Susan and Netta, from the house. "Iris, darling! Where are you?"

But she didn't answer. She didn't go running to them. Bella-Mae was right. She had a life of her own.

Shards of light glittered on the lake, twisting and snapping, until they became one blinding mass. A yacht cut through the middle with bright green sails. She thought of her father, touching his heart the last time she saw him, telling her he was in it now. Was it the same for Iris? Was she in something with Bella-Mae too? And was it a good thing, whatever it was, or was it dangerous? Could it be both at once? Her breath went in, out, in, out. Lighter and lighter. She thought of how Bella-Mae had stood up to her siblings in the garden and felt the same flicker of excitement she'd experienced before.

The water beside her swayed gently up and down against the edge of the garden, listing one way, then back toward another. Pulling north, never south.

"Are you still there?" said Bella-Mae, briefly stirring.

"Yes."

"I think I was right. Don't you?"

"I do. I need to show my siblings who I really am."

Bella-Mae batted the air with her hand as if she were knocking out a fly. "Oh, I don't mean about that. It's up to you what you do about your family. I mean about the villa."

"The villa?" Even though Iris was standing in bright sunlight, a new shadow seemed to fall on her.

"It's so beautiful. So peaceful. I reckon I could live here forever."

15

Seeing for Yourself

To find the cause of death, you had to look for the smallest anomaly. The tiniest thing that was not right. "Autopsy" came from the Greek word meaning "to see for yourself," and that was what you did. You examined every part of the body until you were satisfied you knew what had caused the heart to take its final beat. You opened the skull to remove the brain. You made two incisions from either side of the ears to the collarbone, another all the way down to the pelvis. You pulled back the skin, exposing everything beneath. Then you cut through the ribs, cleared the fluid, lifted out the organs, cleaned the cavity. It was a methodical process, beautiful in its way, scalpel parting muscle and tissue, rib shears cutting bone. You looked for signs of blockage and scarring in the heart, water on the lungs, poison in the stomach, clots in the blood and tumors. You examined the skin for bruising or needle marks. And if you were unclear about anything, you took further samples to be checked in Toxicology. Then you replaced all you had removed and sewed up the body to be returned to the family—for whom it was not simply a body, not a riddle to be solved, not even a complicated pattern of organs and muscle inside skin and bone, but something else. Love at a rupture.

Netta woke every morning telling herself this would be the day she got to the truth about Vic's death. She must approach the whole thing like an autopsy, leaving nothing to chance. Then she lost the next sixteen hours trying and failing, an exhausting flux of emotions raging inside her, until she crashed into bed. Even there, her head didn't let up. Enough alcohol inside her to floor all three of her siblings, and yet her mind kept churning like a generator. If anything, she was drinking more than before, and she still couldn't get fucking drunk.

"No one admires your ferocity more than me," Vic's solicitor told her on the phone. "But you do understand, Netta, that there will come a point soon where we have to concede there is no will. Either this goes on for years and years, and you contest, or you accept his wife inherits. And at least this means Vic didn't cut you off completely. The fact that he died intestate may work in your favor. Look on the bright side."

But the bright side was not somewhere Netta was in the habit of looking. That was much more Susan's domain. Neither was she used to being beaten.

Bella-Mae was now installed in the master bedroom of the very same villa she had never wanted to set foot in ever again. If Netta wanted to visit her father's things, she had to knock on the door and wait to see whether or not Bella-Mae answered, though seeing her clothes in his wardrobe was enough to make her feel violent. Half of them were brand-new with the tags still on, the kind of things you'd wear to go nightclubbing, though since the day she'd arrived in her little black suit, Netta had never seen her in more than a plain swimsuit or an old painting shirt of Vic's. She slept odd hours and didn't always come down for meals. She brewed a tea that stank to high heaven even with the doors and windows wide open. Sometimes Netta heard her in stitches of laughter with Laszlo, but then she could spend hours alone in Vic's garret room or lying in the garden. On the whole, Netta did her best to avoid her, and remained just as suspicious of her, if not more so, but Bella-Mae was perfectly civil. To the point where Netta wondered if she was being deliberately obtuse.

"Let me help you," said Bella-Mae, catching Netta in the glasshouse. The top windows were all open but the smell in there was hot and filled with sweetness. Bella-Mae plucked a fresh lemon from one of the lower branches and offered it. "Here." It was waxy and bright yellow. You could have stuck a straw in it and got lemonade.

"I'm looking for a phone signal," said Netta.

"Oh," said Bella-Mae. "I see." She stood very still, with one foot balanced on the other and her hands still bearing the lemon. Then she said, "You and me didn't get off to a good start. But you have to understand, I'm not here to challenge you."

It struck Netta as an odd word to choose. "Don't worry. I don't feel challenged by you." She smiled to suggest this was a nice thing to say, but Bella-Mae frowned.

"The thing is, we have a lot in common. You and me."

"You and I? How so?"

"We're both only children."

"But I'm not an only child. I have siblings."

"Yeah, but you are the one who knows what it's like to be the only child. Then Susan came and stole that from you."

"I was very happy to have a sister. I always wanted a sister. I don't remember my life without her."

"Is that why you never had kids?"

"Kids?"

"Babies?" said Bella-Mae, enunciating clearly. "Because you didn't want to share any more of your life?"

"I didn't have kids because I had my career to think about."

"Cos it strikes me as weird that none of you has kids."

"We were too busy looking after our father."

Netta had no idea how this could be funny—she wasn't intending to entertain Bella-Mae—but the young woman gave a wild laugh. "Yeah, that's true all right."

Netta was ready to leave, but Bella-Mae was still standing in the way of the door. Short of manhandling her, she had no way of getting past. And Bella-Mae had clearly not finished establishing common ground between them. "We're both widows as well. We're both grieving. We know what that's like."

"To be widows?"

"To lose the man we love. I don't think I'll ever get over it."

Netta experienced a strange shrinking away inside her. It was five years since Philip's death. Her policy was to block it out. It had been very successful. "I was divorced when my ex died. We weren't together."

"Yeah. I did know that. You must of loved him once, though. If you married him."

Netta balked at her grammar and also the sentiment. "I got over it."

"Is that why you didn't go to his funeral? Vic told me about that. Goose went, right? So did Susan? But not you?"

"I didn't go to Philip's funeral because it didn't feel right."

Bella-Mae nodded. "Yeah. I see that. It still seems really sad, though." Then at last she took her lemon and went to find Laszlo.

Laszlo: another thorn in Netta's side. Or rather Laszlo and Susan. Even though Netta had no choice but to concede Bella-Mae's right to return to Villa Carlotta, she didn't see why she had to bring her Technicolor cousin with her. At Susan's suggestion—she hadn't even talked it through with Netta, just announced it over dinner—he was now sleeping in the top guest room that had once been used by au pairs. ("It seems crazy," she'd said, "us here in the great big villa and Laszlo having to come backward and forward every day from that awful hotel." Iris had agreed. "Completely crazy," she'd said.) Now his bright shirts were slung over the beautiful wrought-iron balcony outside his window, like multicolored flags. Netta had only to walk into the kitchen and there he would be with Susan, the pair of them laughing until the moment they saw Netta, at which point they would fall into complete silence, like two people switched off at the mains.

"You seem to like one another," Netta had said, in her lightest possible voice.

To which Susan had replied, in an even lighter one, "We're just getting along! We're just being polite!"

"He watches you."

"When does he watch me?"

"All the time. As if he could eat you alive."

"Of course he doesn't watch me! Don't be silly, Netta."

But Netta was not being silly. She had seen the way Susan went pink the moment Laszlo entered the room. The way he made a beeline straight for her and flagrantly ogled the curves of her body. Since Vic's death, Netta knew she looked progressively worse and worse. She had, in effect, become another version of her father, dressing in whatever she found on the floor, even when it belonged to someone else. But Susan was the opposite. She straightened her hair every morning and put on a clean caftan. Netta would come down, a hangover so substantial it was like a thing on top of her head, and there was Susan, brewing coffee and making lists for the day, asking how you liked your eggs, even if you all liked them in different ways. Walk into the bathroom and she'd lined up your skin products in order of size, refreshed your towels. And now that there were six mouths to feed instead of four, her meals had become more excessive. Lunch plates were barely cleared away and she'd be marinating seafood skewers for the evening barbecue, or soaking gelatin for a panna cotta. If their father hadn't recently died, Netta would say she was having the time of her life. That Susan was lying to Netta and expecting Netta to believe her lie made Netta feel not just blocked out but also underestimated. And because Susan had always been her ally, and Netta had no one else—not quite like Susan—the rejection hurt, like tiny pieces of glass inside her skin.

She had never pretended to be a fan of Warwick, but she found herself thinking of him as you might about a solid piece of Edwardian furniture that is always in the way until you take it out of the room and discover you miss it.

"How is your husband, by the way?"

"My husband?"

"Yes. The man you live with at home. You do recall that you have one?" (All this said in the sunniest voice.)

"Oh, Netta! That's so funny."

"Is everything okay? Is he okay?"

"Of course he's okay."

"The twins?"

"The twins are okay too. I've never known you to worry about them before."

"I'm not worrying about them now. I'm wondering why you haven't mentioned them recently. I'm wondering why Warwick isn't here."

"You know how Warwick is with the sun. I'm not sure he'll come out this summer. Is there any news on the autopsy?"

"No, Susan. You know there isn't. Stop changing the subject."

"Listen, I know you don't see eye to eye with Bella-Mae. But what can we do? She has every right to be here."

"So you're giving up on the villa? Is that what you're saying? You're going to lie down and hand over everything you love to Bella-Mae? She was napping on sofas before she met Daddy. Now she's inheriting a vast fortune."

"I don't want to argue with you, Netta."

"I'm not arguing with you, Susan."

"Of course I'm not giving up on the villa. I'm just saying that the situation is complicated. Daddy decided to marry Bella-Mae and now we have to deal with the consequences. Isn't it better if we do our best to get along with her? And if she wants her cousin here, too, that's only fair. She's grieving, the same as us."

"But she isn't. That's just it. She isn't grieving. She isn't even sad. She's lying on a sun lounger at the bottom of our garden. She's been there most of the day. In that time, I've been to Orta and back to check for news. You've made another meal, which Bella-Mae devoured before she went to sunbathe again. Short of dying, she could not look more relaxed. I've never seen such a fully rested insomniac. And what about her art? I thought when artists were suffering, they took refuge in their work. Van Gogh may have taken it to extremes, but I haven't seen her pick up so much as a paintbrush, let alone hack off her ear."

"I don't think we can criticize Bella-Mae just because she has two ears."

At this point, Laszlo breezed into the kitchen, wearing a shirt that illustrated major tourist destinations of the world, but so colorful they were borderline high-vis, and Netta thought how wrong she was. Laszlo was exactly what he seemed. It was just that Susan had abandoned all her powers of observation. Only how could that be? She and her sister would normally have been in fits of laughter about a man like him. Not just his terrible dress sense and coiffed hair but his pure white Nike socks and slip-on moccasins. His ghastly schmoozy conversation, all of which was still confined to the present tense. He asked if Susan needed anything in Orta because he was popping over in his boat to do a few errands, and Susan began blushing so hard a bib of pink sat in her cleavage, while Netta said she was too hot, in case anyone was interested, which they were clearly weren't because Laszlo was now walking out of the French windows pursued by Susan, saying on second thought she might come, too, and offering some excuse about onions, leaving Netta high and dry, but also with the distinct impression that two conversations had just been had by her and Susan, one with words and another unspoken, and the one that had been true was the one without words.

It bothered her that Susan had found a place for herself in which she was independent of Netta. It seemed to have come to her so easily.

Netta tried to shift the closeness she'd had with Susan to Iris, like switching your account from the bank to the post office. As a child, she'd always longed for her youngest sister to be old enough to have a real conversation and had consequently never really told her anything complex. In Netta's eyes, Iris wasn't old enough to have a proper relationship. "Are you devastated?" Iris had asked after Philip Hanrahan's death, and there was something in her sympathy that felt vulnerable, as if being kind to other people could only end up with Iris getting hurt. Except here was the thing. Iris, Little Iris about whom Netta knew everything, that's how transparent she was, was also causing confusion. Netta asked if she fancied going for a drink in Orta. She suggested going together to the Sacro Monte to light candles. But Iris did not fall over with gratitude. She politely declined.

"Maybe another time," she said. "I'm busy with Bella-Mae right now. Have you read *The Second Sex*?"

"When I was twelve."

"Isn't Simone de Beauvoir awesome? Bella-Mae's lent me the book. Oh my God, I had no idea."

Netta watched the two of them at a distance and there her sister was, speaking animatedly as if suddenly she had a million things to say. It had never occurred to her to give Iris a book. Frankly, it had barely occurred to her that she could read.

Only last night Iris had told Netta, "I think we should discuss Bella-Mae's ideas for the funeral. I know it's not what you had in mind, but we should listen. It's her right to tell us. And Daddy did love the lake more than anywhere else. I feel she's right, too, about his painting. They'd just got married. Why would he be working?" Then Goose had chipped in and said, "I guess it is a possibility, Netta."

They might as well have slapped her. She couldn't believe the two of them were siding with Bella-Mae instead of her. A slip of a thing who'd married Vic quick as a thunderclap, and now seemed to think she should have the last word on absolutely everything. As if Vic Kemp was her specialist subject and she had all the answers.

"I don't know what's going on," she said to Robert on the phone. "Everything is weird. Everyone is being weird."

And he said, "You've lost your father. Of course it's weird. It's all up in the air."

Except Netta did not want to be up in the air. She wanted to be down on solid ground. She wanted to be running ahead with Susan at her side, or maybe ever so slightly behind, Goose and Iris bringing up the rear.

"Why don't you come home, Netta? I know you're waiting for news of the autopsy. But you could do that from London."

For the first time in years, she felt snappy with him. Except it wasn't Robert. It was the situation. Deep down, Netta wasn't convinced anymore about the existence of the will or the painting. And Vic's solicitor was right. She was running out of time. She could even see that Bella-Mae's idea of cremating Vic in Orta might not be so terrible. Yet to admit that to the others was a dangerous surrendering of her position. If she conceded they might be right, where did that put her? And if she thought about leaving the other three by the lake and going home, she was overcome with a feeling of panic, of losing the ground beneath her feet, as if somehow, now that Vic was dead, she might lose her place in the family too. She thought about the phone call when Susan had broken the news, and there seemed to be a direct line between that moment and everything that followed. As if, right from that phone call, Susan had been trying to steal Netta's place, just like Bella-Mae said.

So, she took the boat every day to Orta, where the pastel-colored façades shone in the light and the lakeside restaurants were filled with day-trippers. She did that pig of a walk up past the church in the spanking-hot sunshine like vengeance on two legs, her flip-flops whacking the undersides of her feet, her dress so stuck to her back it might as well have been skin, and from there she trudged all the way up to the railway station to visit the *carabinieri* building that stood opposite, though now he had only to see her face and the *commissario* made a bolt for the back room. She questioned Francesca the housekeeper, and the local official who had married her father and Bella-Mae. ("They seemed so happy," both said.) She asked if anyone had seen Limoncello or remembered anything unusual about Vic before he died.

Afterward she took herself for an *aperitivo* in the little station bar, then another in Piazza Motta, followed by another, because what the hell? She was dealing not simply with the loss of her father, but also her siblings turning into complete strangers. At night she lay on the single bed that she'd slept on as a twelve-year-old, now watching Susan stroke Iris's back, and Goose stare so solemnly up at the ceiling he seemed to be reading it, and she made a promise to herself not to blow this. Even if they were behaving in ways that infuriated her, her siblings were all she had, and she really must not hate them. Because, actually, this felt like a hole that was right inside her, and if she didn't have her father and she didn't have her siblings, she had no idea how to fill it. She wanted them back.

It was with this resolve that Netta put on her hat and set off to take the boat yet again to the mainland. But for once she wasn't going to the *carabinieri* and she wasn't in search of another *notaio*. She was going to prove to the others that she was right about Bella-Mae and her so-called cousin, and they were wrong.

"Where you off to, Net?" called Goose.

"Limoncello has got in touch. He's agreed to meet up. You okay? You look terrible."

"I've been playing cards with Laszlo. He's fleeced me."

"Want to come to Orta?"

"Yes," he said. "Most definitely."

The boatman crossed himself. "God save me. I was the one who found your father in the lake. *Le porgo le mie più sentite condoglianze.* I saw him go in too. He was caught in the reeds, his body facing down. I guess the current must have dragged him. I will never forget that morning."

They were in a bar down an alleyway, a few streets up from the lake. Like everyone else in Orta, the owner had embraced Netta and Goose the moment she saw them. She had brought wine and plates of cold meat and said they must eat. *Hai bisogno di mangiare.* You need to eat.

Goose sat with his sister opposite Limoncello. The boatman had apologized as soon as they met: It was grief that had kept him away from the lake. That and the shock of discovering Vic's body. Goose remembered how he used to follow them when they were children, like a scrappy dark-haired shadow, wanting to play. It was terrible how much older than them he seemed now. His hair was combed in thin strands across the dark egg of his head, while his skin was tough and burned from all those years on the lake. When Netta poured him wine, he downed it in one. His hands shook around the glass. It was one of those private things that people like to keep hidden about themselves and it pained Goose that Limoncello couldn't.

"I tried to pull your father onto the boat, but he was too heavy. In the end, I had to get out. The water was up to my waist. I began shouting for help and then a few people came to join me. I don't remember who. Someone was telling me to take his arms, someone else was saying, 'No, take his legs.' It was chaos." He stopped to wipe tears but they ran down his face like water on leather.

"So there we were, all of us in the water with your father. Then someone shouted, 'Lift!' and we lifted and turned his body toward ours and suddenly there he was, right in my arms, looking up at me. But his eyes, I will never forget his eyes. They were so empty. This great man

I've known since I was a boy. We carried him out of the reeds and laid him on the jetty. Someone tried to give him mouth-to-mouth resuscitation and we waited and waited in silence. But it was no good. It was over. It was over long before I found him. I stayed with him until the police came with the doctor. I even stayed after they took him away. I did not want to let that great man go." Netta lifted the bottle as if the wine was a question mark and he nodded and said, "*Grazie.*"

"Of course, I knew your father well. We all did. He was always buying us drinks. Even when I was a kid, he bought us drinks. *Limoncello!* I remember this so well! The first time he bought me *limoncello* I was ten. I had never had a drink before and afterward I was sick as a dog. Everyone called me Limoncello after that. If I was on the boat in the early morning, he would stand in the garden before his swim. He would shout, 'Another beautiful day, Limoncello! Here we are, the most beautiful place on earth! And only you and I out here to see it!'

"It was your father who taught me English. And when my daughter was born, he gave me a check because we couldn't afford a pram. He always asked after her, every summer. But this year he did not seem himself. He was too thin. We all guessed it was because of his new wife. And *la signora* is a beautiful woman. Very mysterious. But being so thin did not suit your father. He seemed to me like *leone in gabbia.*"

Netta shook her head, not understanding. Limoncello mimed a lion, and she looked at Goose and laughed, just briefly, but then he mimed being trapped in what looked like a cage and Goose put his face in his hands and said, "Oh jeez."

"Did he seem different in any other way?"

"He didn't come drinking with us, like the old days. If he left the villa, it was always with her. I saw them a few times in the town, but when he stopped to say hello, she would seem impatient and he made his apologies. He didn't take his walk around the island anymore, and I asked for him several times at the trattoria but they said he had not been there all summer. Only once I saw him alone.

"He was in Piazza Motta. He was buying *gelato*. 'Don't tell *la signora*,' he said. I laughed and so did he, but he didn't sound as if he was joking. Then he sat by the water on the farthest bench from the jetty, down by the old derelict hotel, and ate it so fast you'd think he hadn't eaten for days. 'You won't tell on me, Limoncello?' he said again. 'You won't tell *la signora*?' And I said of course not. 'You're only eating *gelato*,' I said."

Netta leaned forward, her whole body on the chase, but Goose found he could only listen with his eyes half closed, as if that might somehow lessen the pain. "Can you remember anything else about the day he drowned?" Netta said. "How did he seem when he got into the water?"

"I was out on the boat, but that morning he didn't notice me. I waved, but he didn't see. He just looked over his shoulder and then jumped in very quickly. As if he were frightened."

"Frightened? Why would he be frightened?"

"I don't know."

"Do the police know this?"

"I told them. They didn't seem to think it made any difference."

"Well, the police are useless. They don't lift a finger. Would you say my father was drunk that morning?"

"Drunk? No. He was not drunk once this summer. I swear on my daughter's life."

"But what about the mist? How could you see him if there was a mist?"

"There was no mist at that point. Not at six when your father got into the water. The mist came in very quickly, about fifteen minutes later. I know because I only just got home in time. Of course, I assumed your father was out of the water by then." He bowed his head. "It keeps coming back to me. The way your father looked up at me in my arms with his empty face. I close my eyes at night and it's all I see." He shook a cigarette from the packet and put it into his mouth, but his hands were trembling so much that he couldn't get the lighter to strike up.

In the end, Goose leaned forward. "Here, let me," he said. And he did. He cupped his hands around the flame to do it for him.

Netta said, "What do you know about Bella-Mae's cousin? Laszlo?"

At the mention of Laszlo, Limoncello paused, unsure how to continue. "I know your father was generous to him. I know he is the cousin of his wife. But Vic was generous to everyone. There is something about that man I don't trust. I hear he is everywhere in Orta these days. Shaking hands, making friends. But I don't believe he thinks of anyone except himself."

He said no more. He didn't have to. To finish, they drank shots of sweet syrupy *limoncello* and toasted Vic. "You have to understand. He was a father to me. I only wish I had stopped him the day the mists came. It is a sorrow I will carry in my heart for the rest of my life."

It's not only themselves that the dead take away. They take a part of us, too: when living, they are inside us, and without them we carry a vacant space. After saying goodbye to Limoncello, Goose walked beside Netta in silence, huffing as if to speak but at a loss for something to say. The shock of Vic's death hadn't lessened. If anything, it was becoming more acute, stinging a little more every day.

"I don't know where to go," he said to her at last. "It's like wherever I walk isn't where I want to be. It's never the right place."

"I know what you mean." For once, she seemed just as lost as he was.

They went up to the Baroque church at the top of the Via Bersani, and he asked if they should light candles. It was dark inside and deliciously cool. They sat for a while staring up at all those gilt statues, waiting for a woman to finish praying, until Netta whispered, "I'm sorry. This isn't working for me," and he followed her out into the sun.

They cut back alongside the lake to avoid the day-trippers, and when they got to Piazza Motta, he went over to the gelateria and came back with two ice-cream cones, one for each of them. "I want to eat gelato like Daddy did that day," he said.

"Oh, me, too," said Netta. "You're so right."

They sat on the same bench by the derelict hotel where Limoncello had described seeing Vic a few weeks ago and ate the ice cream just as he must have done, looking out toward the island. It was midafternoon and the lake was crawling with tiny waves. It was the cleanest blue imaginable.

"Boy, oh boy, oh boy. That was too sad. I hadn't thought what it would be like for Limoncello, finding the body like that. The poor man was drunk, Netta. He could barely light a cigarette, he was that drunk."

"I know."

"And you know why he's drunk? You know why he's called Limoncello? Because our father gave him alcohol. He thinks the world of him, yet he got him drunk as a kid and now he's addicted. What do we do with that? It cracks me up inside."

He felt Netta's hand fumbling for his. Squeezing it. "I think you must be the kindest man in the whole world. If you weren't my brother, I'd ask you to marry me. Why do I only fall in love with men who can't love me back?"

"I don't know." His head was filled with a memory of Philip Hanrahan, laughing as he ate a tray of fish-and-chips. It was strangely comforting. "Maybe you're afraid."

"Of love?"

"Maybe we all are."

"Or maybe I'm just a fuckup. There is that possibility too. Do you ever have unspeakable thoughts?"

"All the time." He was having them right now.

"Tell me."

It made him laugh, how jagged she could be, even when she was alone with him and at her most vulnerable. "No, Netta."

"Do you think Bella-Mae killed Daddy?"

"Do I think she killed him?" He turned to her, assuming she was still semi-joking, but her jaw was set rigid, her eyes very bright. "Is this your unspeakable thought?"

"Yes."

"No. I don't think that. Do you?"

"Limoncello told us that Daddy was frightened of her. He couldn't even sit here enjoying an ice cream because he was so worried about her finding out. He got into the water the day he drowned and looked over his shoulder to check she wasn't coming after him."

"He only said he looked back. Limoncello didn't say she was coming after him."

Netta wafted her hand, impatient. "Okay. Explain her changing the locks to the flat in London. Or Mrs. Lott saying she heard him cry. Was Bella-Mae starving him? Keeping him prisoner? He was practically a skeleton by the time he died."

"Jeez, Netta. Is this what you think?"

She did a goofy smile and pointed at herself. "Welcome to my head."

"What else do you think?"

"Has Bella-Mae stolen his last painting? Was she stopping Daddy texting us when they got here? Is that why he had to do it in the middle of the night? And who the hell is Laszlo? Limoncello doesn't like him any more than I do. Is he really her lover?"

Goose sat for a moment, trying to work it all out. He wasn't like Netta, who thought things and said them at the same moment. For him, it was more a question of waiting to understand. Since Bella-Mae and her cousin had moved back to the villa there was definitely a new energy, a kind of tension. His sisters had become scratchy with one another, quick to take offense. Only that morning Susan had told Iris she wasn't eating enough, and Iris had snapped back that she wasn't a baby. She didn't need to be waited on hand and foot. "And why do we never talk about big things?" she'd said. "Like politics." Though when Netta quizzed her as to which particular item of current affairs she would like to discuss, Iris had immediately shrunk back down and looked at Bella-Mae, who merely drank her tea. After that Goose had started sanding some splintered woodwork in the hallway, prepping it ready to paint, just to keep out of the way. He noticed Bella-Mae sometimes watching his sisters when they weren't looking, her eyes narrowed, as if she were studying them both close up and also from a distance. It didn't strike him as hostile, though neither did it seem especially kind. It was more as if she was trying to work out how they were put together, like intricate pieces of a machine. As for her being Laszlo's lover, he often heard them laughing together, and talking fast in Italian, but if Laszlo was interested in anyone right now, it seemed to be Susan. Goose couldn't help agreeing with Netta about not trusting him, though. When Laszlo played poker, he was quick to lay down the first bet and reluctant to show his hand.

He thought about Vic's final visit to the studio and how Bella-Mae had chosen to wait outside in the cab: there had been something hidden about her, right from the start. At least Vic had never made her his dealer. It would have blown things sky-high.

"I don't know, Netta. Maybe it's me. Maybe I see things too simply. But even if you're right, even if she stole the painting and stopped him texting, even if Laszlo is her lover, it still doesn't mean she killed him. You know something? When Susan told me he was dead, I couldn't move. It was like I'd been shut down. Then I drank the best part of a bottle of vodka and went on a bender. But when I told Harry, you should have heard him. He was howling. Straight off, just like that. And Limoncello, he was the same. My point is, we all do the same thing in different ways. And just because something looks strange to us from the outside, or suspicious, it doesn't mean it is. It only means we can't see the whole picture."

She nodded, but he could tell she wasn't buying it. "You're right, of course. You're a sweet, good person. But I'm not. I've been in litigation too long. I still think Bella-Mae killed him. Or, rather, I don't think she didn't. Was she poisoning him? Drugging him? The autopsy will tell us. Unless, of course, she was fucking with his mind. For me, the jury is very definitely out. We shouldn't trust a word she says."

16

Caftan Days

"I don't have a problem with your sister," said Bella-Mae. "I just don't see why she's so angry with my cousin. It's not his fault Vic died. And, actually, Laszlo's the sweetest guy you'll ever meet. I know he's a bit schmoozy but he isn't hurting anyone. And Vic was the same, right? A complete charmer."

They were in the kitchen. Bella-Mae wasn't helping Susan in any obvious way. She might have spent every spare minute cleaning when Vic was alive, but now her focus seemed to be elsewhere. Out in the garden, light flaked between the trees, glittering and abundant. The stray cat was stretched on the terrazzo like a piece of old carpet and Iris lay beside him, her head in a book, while the lake was as blue as the sky, the hills beyond rising under a carpet of green.

Bella-Mae was right. Netta's rage filled the air like smoke. She made no effort to hide her suspicions about Laszlo, or Bella-Mae, and it was getting embarrassing. Only that morning she'd cross-examined them about how exactly they could be cousins. And the villa was strewn with her things. They were everywhere, as if she had exploded in different pieces on every floor. "Who's taken my sunglasses?" she'd yell, storming up and down.

"Netta? Are you for real?" Susan would say. "You're wearing them."

And yet while she might be incapable of seeing what was literally on the end of her nose, she also watched Susan like a hawk. Nothing slipped past her.

"Don't get me wrong," said Bella-Mae. "I like Netta. She's so smart she's kind of crazy. I just wonder if the tension's getting too much. I guess that's why she drinks. Vic told me about that."

She reached for some yellowpepper slices that Susan had been preparing for Iris and ate them. "But Laszlo is one of the most caring guys I've ever known. Honestly, if he likes you, he'll do anything. His family was really poor and he knows what it's like to struggle. When I was eighteen, I was completely broke. I thought I was going to end up on the streets. It was Laszlo who came to my rescue. He sent me cash, gave me the address of a friend with a sofa. I've always owed him for that. Just don't play cards with him. He's a terrible cheat."

Susan had not played cards with Laszlo. But she would. Despite the warning from his distant relation, she'd do anything, if he asked. And yet what did he want from her? She had no idea. They hadn't full-on embraced since that first day and they certainly hadn't kissed. They hadn't even spoken about anything that amounted to very much. On the whole, he took her on his boat to do her shopping and told her convoluted stories about the history of the lake, half of which she knew better than he did. She listened to every word, trying to decode what was going on between them, and barely able to disguise the high-voltage thrill she felt at just being in the same space. He could have read the phone book and she'd have been on her knees. But sometimes he stopped talking and stared hard at her, just looking, looking, looking, until she was shaking so much she had to turn away and pretend she was admiring the Italian scenery. He didn't need to embrace or kiss her because his eyes were a crowd on her, and they touched whichever part of her they chose.

Even the way he said her name, *Suzaaaan*, drawing out the last syllable as if it were an exotic piece of fruit he was peeling bit by bit, threw her inside out. She was supposed to be tracking down Vic's paintings, but her head wasn't in it. All she could think about was Laszlo.

"So Bella-Mae's moved her cousin in with you as well?" Warwick would say on the phone. "That's the last thing you need, Susan. I hope you're managing to get a rest." And she would tell him she was taking a rest, she was managing, and all the while she was talking to her husband, she was screaming inside with how slow he was, how considerate. Rest? She'd been doing it for years. Living in cruise control. What she wanted was this, whatever it was. This knife edge. And yet surely Laszlo would leave Orta any day. He disappeared in his boat for increasingly long periods of time. The thought of him going for good made her half mad.

"Can I be honest with you, Suz?" said Bella-Mae. "No hard feelings?"

"Of course. It's what Daddy would want."

"Why do you wear those things?" Her tone was reflective, as though she had been troubled by this question for a long time and had been considering many counterarguments before she voiced it. "Why do you wear clothes that don't suit you?"

It took Susan a moment to steady herself. "I always wear caftans in the heat. They hide a multitude of sins." She laughed, but Bella-Mae didn't. She looked genuinely appalled. Almost offended.

"Suz, why as a woman would you talk like that about yourself? What could possibly be sinful about your body?"

This wasn't said in any way that suggested Bella-Mae intended to wound Susan, or further unbalance her, yet it did both those things. "Oh, I hate my body. I've got a mother's body and I'm not even a mother." Susan tried to laugh, making a joke of herself, but it wouldn't come.

"Suz?" said Bella-Mae. She stopped crunching raw vegetables and moved closer. "You're not upset?"

"It's okay."

Bella-Mae fetched her a chair, pushed the French windows together so that Iris wouldn't overhear. "Sit down for once," she said.

It all came out. Suddenly and just like that. In the strangest way it was like talking to Laszlo. Telling him the things about herself that she wanted him to know to establish a bond between them that she understood. It was the heat as well, of course, and the grieving. Everything seemed so close to the surface you might as well not have skin. But it was also the way Bella-Mae had led her to the chair, then slipped her hands beneath Susan's collar and begun massaging her neck and shoulders, deeper and deeper.

She told Bella-Mae about her old ambition to be a TV chef. How as a child she'd make scrambled eggs and imagine the lights on her as she spoke to the camera. How she'd abandoned all that to get married. The excitement she'd felt when she did a pregnancy test and the little blue window filled, the sense of fulfillment, of being a part of something beautiful at last. She talked about the cramps and bleeding that always followed. Six weeks, eight weeks, ten. She'd never got as far as sixteen.

She and Warwick had gone through all kinds of tests. They'd tried IVF. None of it worked, though she'd thought that, he being a GP, this was one thing he could organize. But in the end he'd taken her out to dinner and held her hand. "Susan, I don't know that I can bear to see you go through any more of this. Why don't we accept life as it is? At least we have the twins."

Except she didn't have the twins. The twins hated her.

"How could they hate you?" said Bella-Mae. Her fingers had worked along from Susan's shoulders. They were rubbing and easing the muscles around her scapula.

Now Susan told her about all those years of looking after the twins on weekends. The carefully prepared food they refused to eat. "They only seem to like McDonald's," Warwick would say, embarrassed. "Their mother isn't a cook, you see." Every summer Susan drove them miles in hot traffic to Fun World and Water World, Otter World, World of Mirrors. Who knew there were so many Worlds with only one type of thing inside them? Sometimes the boys wouldn't even get out of the car. She painted their rooms in their favorite colors; she bought a Manchester City Football Club duvet set for Chester, a Superman one for Preston. ("Does that family only name themselves after market towns?" said Netta.) Nothing Susan did was right: Chester switched to Arsenal; Preston woke up screaming because he was having Superman nightmares. From behind the sofa they fired pretend bullets at her from their little plastic guns. "It's just a phase," Warwick used to tell her, "while they adjust."

"It wasn't a phase," said Susan. "It went on for twelve years."

"Where was your husband?"

"He was often on call. Besides, I wanted to be a stepmother. I wanted to prove I could at least be that."

But did it get any easier when they were teenagers, faces cratered with acne and hair so greasy you could slide things off it? No, they stayed in their rooms all weekend on their Gameboys, which should have been a blessing, except that they were supposed to have just sixty minutes on them and she lived in fear of what they would say when they went back home: their mother didn't have a thing about general cleanliness, or indeed about what her children should eat, but she did have a very big one about electronic devices. They took summer holidays in Orta, which the twins hated from the moment they crawled out of the car. First, they weren't strong swimmers and Vic kept hurling them into the water ("Don't you just love him?" said Netta), and second, they were so blond they had only to look at the sun to get second-degree burns. All her life Susan had trusted that the one thing she could be was a wife and mother. Everyone thought that. ("If Netta had children, she would leave them at the airport," Vic announced once. "But Susan is a natural.") A natural, yes. Born to be a mother, just like Martha. Yet her body had failed to read the memo.

"But you have a beautiful body," Bella-Mae said, pushing hard at the skin above Susan's bra. "You've got tits as well. Gorgeous tits. You shouldn't hide them. Laszlo says you're the sexiest woman he's ever met."

If she experienced a thrill inside, Susan did her best not to show it. "Why would he say that? I'm a middle-aged woman."

"He says it because he means it. He finds you very desirable, Susan. To be honest, that's the only reason he's still here."

Was it Susan who came up with the next thought? Or was it Bella-Mae? Whoever said it, they were in Vic's old room a few minutes later.

~~~

It was the first day Susan had been there since he had died. Netta came up here all the time: she treated it like a holy site. But for Susan it was still possible to walk past the room and pretend her father was inside it, so she kept away.

Bella-Mae opened the door. The room was so dark it was hard to see. Unlike Vic, who'd always slept with the windows wide open, it seemed Bella-Mae kept the shutters tightly closed so that the smell of her, that sharp, unwashed smell, was even more intense. She switched on some very bright lamps and told Susan to stand in the light where she could see her.

From the wardrobe, Bella-Mae pulled out dress after dress. They were all things that Vic had bought her, she said. Most of them still had the price tag or were wrapped in plastic. They were highly colored, tight-fitting. Not the kind of thing Susan had seen her wear. Not the kind of thing Susan would wear either. In fact, not the kind of thing she could get over her head because, look at her, she was twice the size of Bella-Mae. The young woman held each one up in front of Susan, one eye half closed, assessing how they would look on her, moving up close, then back into the shadows, as if Susan were a work of art she was in the process of creating and she wasn't sure what to add next. It was like being seen in very clear focus through the wrong end of a telescope, not as a person or, at least, only a physical one. Laszlo looked at her in the same way.

At last she passed Susan a purply-blue print dress with a sequin shine to the fabric. "Try this," she said. "Don't worry about the size. It's supposed to be tight. And you'll need to take off your bra and pants. Otherwise their lines will spoil it."

Eventually Susan got the dress on. Bella-Mae took a step back, once again staring at Susan without passing comment.

"I know," said Susan. "I look terrible." Suddenly the glare from the lamps felt very hot.

"You're wrong. It suits you. Look."
~~~

Bella-Mae led her to the mirror. She scooped Susan's hair on top of her head and said she should wear it pinned up, with her neck bare and exposed. "You shouldn't straighten it anymore," she said.

Clearly the dress was for a woman half Susan's age, yet there was something about how tight it was, how low-cut, the way it stuck to her body like a thin shimmery skin that made her feel she was gazing at a Susan she had not seen before. Brazen and defiant. She'd never dressed like this, not even as a teenager. Vic, who had been so negligent in most areas of parenthood, and had also, let's face it, painted women wearing little more than a suspender belt, had been draconian when it came to what his daughters could put on for a night out. But Susan was sexy in this dress. She was in her father's room—the inner sanctum—and she was also showing off her body under bright lights. She felt the alteration like a pressure in her pelvic bone, around which the rest of her had been rearranged.

It was *aperitivo* time. As she came downstairs, Goose and Netta were arriving at the front door, and Iris had come up from the garden. Netta looked troubled and fractious—Susan could tell something was wrong just by the pinch of her shoulders—while Goose was sighing, as if bad news was a weight and he was carrying it in both arms.

But Susan didn't want more bad news. She had been living with it too long—all those years of failed pregnancies, not to mention the recent events of the summer. She wanted to enjoy this new version of herself, sensual and womanly. It was for this reason that when Netta said, "Suz? We need to talk," and clicked her fingers at her to follow, Susan stopped partway down the stairs and waited until her sister clocked her. "Not now, Netta. I'm about to serve drinks."

"Oh my God!" cried Iris. "Suz! You look amazing!"

She saw Goose pause—a slow emerging expression on his face of gentle bafflement. And she saw, too, the shift in Netta. A look of hurt, a kind of wonder tinged with fury. But Susan stood her ground. It was like pushing things for once to the very edge to see what happened next.

"What have you got on?" said Netta.

"It's just a dress," Susan said. But it wasn't just a dress. She couldn't deny the elation she felt. Her caftan days were over.

Netta came up to her later in the kitchen when Susan was putting the final touches to dinner. Everyone else was out on the terrazzo with their second round of drinks and Susan very much wanted to be with them: she had seen the way Laszlo's eyes widened the moment he arrived back at the villa, the furtive grin he had shared with Bella-Mae, that tiny lick of his lips. Netta picked up a knife and began chopping an onion that had no need to be chopped.

She announced in a dramatic way that she had something very serious to say, if Susan could focus for one moment on the fact that their father was dead and not the fiasco going on in the garden. Her voice was breathy, strangely off-kilter. She described a private meeting with Limoncello, and some terrible things he'd said about Bella-Mae. But Susan was only half listening. Laszlo had begun telling a story and Iris was laughing wildly. She felt a spike of jealousy. She wanted to know what he was saying.

"Did you hear me, Suz?" repeated Netta. "Limoncello said Daddy was terrified of her."

"Oh, Netta. He's a drunk. Limoncello was always a drunk. Of course he didn't see Daddy get into the water that day. I doubt he could see past the end of his boat." She took the onions away from Netta, and also the knife.

"Limoncello said we shouldn't trust Laszlo either. He's a con, Susan."

"Sorry, what?" Iris had laughed again from the terrazzo and Susan rushed to the French windows to look.

"Susan! You're making a fool of yourself."

Susan froze. She said quietly, "You think I'm taking over. That's what this is about. But I have to do this. I have to cook for everyone. If I don't, I'll sink like a stone."

From the garden, Goose called, "Need any help?" and Susan waved back and said, "Just coming!"

Netta said, "I'm glad you cook, Suz. I hate cooking. If it was left up to me, everyone would starve. But I'm not talking about our catering arrangements. I'm talking about murder."

"Murder?" Susan laughed. "Don't be absurd."

"I'm not the one who's being absurd. Look at that dress. What have you come as? You look like a porno mermaid."

"It's because you drink," said Susan, turning suddenly. "You drink too much."

"I beg your pardon?"

"I'm only saying what the others think. Even Daddy thought that."

"Oh," said Netta. "You know what Daddy thought now? Then maybe you can explain where his last painting has gone? Or what he did with his will? Since you know everything."

Susan exploded. All of a sudden, and just like that. She went from calmly smiling at her sister to barely controlled fury in 0.5 seconds. "You do this! You always do this!"

"What do I do?"

"You twist things! You take the words out of my mouth and twist them, then throw them right back at me! Just because you're the cleverest."

"This isn't me being clever. This is me trying to warn you."

"And you never remember my birthday. You never send me a card on the right day. In fact, I suspect Robert sends your cards anyway. It doesn't look like your handwriting. I mean he tries to make it like yours, but I know it isn't."

"Hang on. What are we discussing, Susan? Is it Laszlo or my drinking problem or your birthday card?"

Susan had no idea why she had mentioned the birthday cards, just as she had no idea why she'd brought up the drinking. She would never have normally confronted Netta. But now that she'd done it, it was impossible to undo. It was like something brought in by the stray cat, not quite alive and not fully dead, and not entirely with its skin on either. Susan had started something and, for once, she was not prepared to back down.

"Okay, you want this conversation, Netta? You really want to know? My problem is you. I've had enough."

"I see."

"What do you mean, you see? You don't see. How can you possibly see? So long as you're the top of everything, so long as you're the first, that's all you want. It's like the beauty pageant."

"What beauty pageant?"

"Oh my God. You don't remember. You, swanning about with the tiara, while I had to follow you everywhere in the runner-up sash. And I've been wearing it my whole life. Everything I had, you had to have first. I am always, always the runner-up."

It was strange how Netta didn't seem offended by what Susan had said. She went quiet for a moment, as if she thought it was okay and something of a relief for her sister to come clean about her problems with her. It struck Susan as strange that at the exact moment she had attacked Netta she also felt a flowering of tenderness for her. Together they had faced almost everything.

She pulled at her dress. Felt the bold nakedness of her body inside it. "Netta, you were the one who told us to leave Daddy alone when he met Bella-Mae. Don't get in touch with him, you said. The affair will blow itself out. If it hadn't been for you, he would never have come here without us. He would never have married Bella-Mae, though, frankly, I think she's a perfectly sweet girl, even if she's a bit unusual. But you've never listened to the rest of us. And now we're here and for once I feel like I have a place, and all you want is to take it away from me. I don't believe Limoncello. I don't believe Bella-Mae is a bad person, and I don't think Laszlo is either. And now, if you don't mind, I'm going to serve dinner. I'm going to serve normal dinner to normal people, who are not murderers or whatever else you're imagining. Just normal people, grieving, and waiting for the results of an autopsy that you insisted on in the first place. You think I'm behaving like a fool? Why don't you look at yourself?"

The meal was tense. Susan sat at one end of the table, Netta at the other. Every time Susan asked with forced politeness what she would like to eat, Netta replied with equally forced politeness that she wasn't hungry and filled her wineglass to the top. Iris, sensing the friction between them, kept saying how delicious everything was, until Netta lashed out at her, too, and said, "Well, why don't you eat it, then?" Goose was back and forth from the kitchen fetching more water, more wine, more focaccia, saying how lovely it was to be together, while Laszlo—sitting with his chair tucked right up close to Susan's—held forth with some endless story about a man he'd met who was so wealthy he bought a house that he stayed in only once every year, on the way to another of his houses that he stayed in only twice a year. Susan gripped her napkin to her mouth and laughed and laughed.

All this Bella-Mae watched in silence, her face caught in a curious smile, like someone who's suddenly switched TV channels and found a program that is unexpectedly entertaining.

The following day, Netta and Susan treated each other with a new wariness. They avoided being alone together. If they spoke, it was only in front of the others, and they did their best to remain polite. On the whole, it felt safer to stay apart, though for Netta this was accompanied by a strange longing, missing Susan even as she said tersely, "Morning, darling," and moved away. She was shocked by the way Susan had spoken to her. Well, I see, she thought. This is how it is, is it? She wanted to get back in there and fight some more, see what else Susan had to throw at her, but she also wanted to apologize. Or, rather, she wanted Susan to apologize first, so that she could apologize afterward. But that didn't happen either. Instead, she felt wronged by Susan, and from there the anger grew: each moment of silence that passed between them seemed to calcify and become more impossible to undo. "Fuck it," she said, and stormed into the bedroom they shared. She scooped as many of her things as she could off the floor and headed up the stairs, though she dropped half of them as she went.

"Are you going home?" said Bella-Mae, drifting on bare feet down from the garret and meeting Netta halfway. She was wearing a caftan.

"No. I'm moving back into my old room."

"There's a hole here." Bella-Mae pointed at the wall. She slipped her finger into the plaster, releasing a shower of dust and tiny stones. "See?"

"It's always been there."

"Yeah, but I think it's got worse. Should we get Francesca to fix it?"

"Ask Goose. He's good at that stuff."

Netta didn't eat with the others that night. She took a bottle of red up to her room, and when she'd drunk it, she fetched another. It's all about survival, she thought, lying alone for the first time since she'd arrived at the villa, and trying not to hear the others laughing down on the terrazzo. We're like birds in a nest. We want to love our siblings, yet we need to boot them out. I want to be with them, but I can't. I want to leave them, and I can't do that either. All this will wear me down until I'm nothing but bone. Pure old bone.

She understood that she was in shock. She got that. She also understood that further down the line a lot more shock was coming, and with it more pain. She was going to have to think in a radically different way. She just couldn't see yet what that was going to be.

17

The Division of Parts

Bella-Mae announced that she would like each of the siblings to choose whatever they wanted to take from the villa. If she inherited Vic's stuff, she would only want a few bits and pieces. Besides, she didn't believe in possessions as a concept. She thought you should only have what came to you of its own free will. "So, you guys might as well talk about how you split things and begin to pack them. It's not as if you have much else to do."

Netta pointed out that she had plenty to do. But Susan said she thought it was an incredibly generous suggestion and why didn't she get some stickers while she and Laszlo did the day's shopping? She came back with red stickers for Netta, blue for Susan, yellow for Goose, pink for Iris. Bella-Mae picked out a couple of green ones.

"I still don't see why we need stickers," Netta said. Not to Susan, because she still wasn't talking to her. More to the air in general.

"We need stickers so that we can each say what we would like. It will save argument." Though already this was becoming another argument.

"Isn't this a little preemptive?" Netta said to Goose, but he blew out the longest stream of air.

"No," said Susan, also to Goose. "This is practical. Bella-Mae has invited each of us to take what we would like from the villa. It seems sensible to begin talking in a civilized way about splitting things fairly. That way, when it happens, no one will get hurt. There will be no cause for resentment."

"Suppose it turns out you all want the same thing?" said Bella-Mae. "That could be tricky."

"There is a code," said Susan.

"Where is the code?" said Netta.

"I am about to tell you the code," said Susan, a little tersely now but still smiling.

The code would be numbers. You would grade each item according to how much you wanted it. If you really wanted it, it would be a number one. If you felt pretty easy and didn't honestly mind if someone else got it, it would be a four. Obviously two and three came between those. If they found that more than one person had put a number-one sticker on something, they would discuss how many other number ones each person had and work it out from there. It was a system one of her friends from book club had used, Susan said. "And do you know what? It worked like a dream."

At first everyone was reluctant to use their stickers, except Susan because it was her system, and then Bella-Mae, who placed her green ones on a few items, and all of them with a number one. "If I don't feel passionately about something, what's the point in asking for it?" she said. She went up to the garret.

Susan's stickers mainly went on things from the kitchen, and some furniture that might look nice at home. Goose and Iris drifted up and down the house, putting stickers on things and taking them off again, unsure whether something should be a two or a three, and therefore defeated at the first hurdle. They spoke in whispers. Out of the blue, living together in the villa had become like walking on eggshells.

"The thing is, I don't want to take something that anyone else wants," said Iris. "And, anyway, it seems wrong to take things out of the villa. I mean, are we really saying this is our last summer here? Do you want this china dog, by the way?"

"It seems like the kind of thing you would want."

"But Susan has already put a three on it."

"That means she's easy if she doesn't get it. And I don't think we're definitely saying this is our last summer here. But we don't know what's going to happen next. I guess Bella-Mae is thinking ahead."

"What about a harp?"

"I don't know what I'd do with it. I don't know where I'm going to live."

"At least there are ten of them, though. None of us would have to argue. It's bad enough between Susan and Netta already. I think I'll put a sticker on a harp. Coming?"

They went to the music room. "I always loved that mirror," she said, pointing at the Venetian mirror above the fireplace, embellished with glass flowers.

"So why don't you put a sticker on it?"

"Is this kind of like going antiques shopping? Except it's in our own house? And, anyway, happiness is not to be found in material things." She placed a sticker on the mirror, and another on a harp. "I'll say the mirror is a number four."

"Meaning you don't mind if you don't get it?"

"Meaning I don't want to argue. You haven't put stickers on anything."

Goose put a sticker on a harp. He also put one on a table lamp. "It's a shame you can't put stickers on the frescos," he said. "Those are the things I love the most."

"What about wineglasses? Do you have any?"

"Not really. They generally get broken."

"Then let's get wineglasses. There are loads in the kitchen. We could both take some and we wouldn't have to fight."

But the kitchen was covered with blue stickers. Susan had landed on it like a swarm of locusts. "What is it about stickers," said Iris, "that you only realize you want something when someone else has already put a sticker on it?"

"There's a tureen. No one's claimed that yet."

"I don't want a tureen."

"Teaspoons?"

"Are we seriously splitting up teaspoons? All I want are some wineglasses. Why does Susan need the whole lot?"

"Put some of your stickers on the wineglasses so that Susan knows you'd like them too. What number are her stickers?"

"Ones!" said Iris. "They are all number ones! How can she put number ones on all the wineglasses? There must be at least thirty. Doesn't she have any wineglasses at home? Fine. I'll have the carafe. But I'm definitely going to put a number one on the mirror in the music room. And I'm taking another harp as well."

Throughout all this, Netta remained in the garden, checking her work emails with several Bacardi and Cokes to make them more interesting. After a few hours, there were stickers of every color except red in all the rooms.

"Where are Netta's stickers?" said Susan brightly, over lunch.

"I'm not doing any."

"But if you don't do your stickers, how can we know what you want?"

"I want this fiasco to be over," said Netta. "Put a sticker on that."

18

Artist

"Do you ever have dreams?" a therapist once asked Goose. She was softly spoken and wore a charm bracelet that jingled every time she moved her hand. That was the problem, really. She was so nice and tinkly it seemed abusive to inflict all his trouble on her.

"No," he said. "I don't."

"You don't have them or you don't remember them?"

"I don't have them."

"Shall we talk some more about that?"

"Could we maybe not?"

At the end of the session, he'd told her he was sorry but he didn't think he should come to therapy anymore. "Why? I thought we were getting somewhere," she'd said. She was right, although it surprised him she could see it: He generally said almost nothing for the entire fifty minutes, answering her questions as briefly and politely as possible, but he had begun to take comfort in the silence between them. He had grasped that silence wasn't about nothing: It might be about waiting. And he knew that to find what he needed to say, there was a whole lot of waiting to get through first. But he'd also realized with her question that he was unwilling to go further. That somewhere in his head he had successfully hidden a thing so monstrous that the only way to survive would be to remain as far away from it as he could. And that was why he had not continued with therapy when it was the one thing that might have helped him.

She'd been spot-on about his dreams. As a boy, he'd had nightmares all the time. Not simply the ones about exploding fruit and seed heads, but full-on massacres. He killed his father, his sisters. He walked into assembly and discovered he'd killed the whole school. It was never intentional. He didn't go in with a gun or anything. It was more that he stared in horror at all the dead people around him and realized that—because he seemed to be the only one upright and still breathing—he must have been responsible. He'd wake sobbing. What kind of child dreamed about killing people? It was just as well he'd kept quiet in therapy.

"Goose," Philip Hanrahan said to him, another time, "gentle Goose. Tell me. How did you miss out on the chance to become hot-tempered and difficult?"

"I guess Netta used that one up," Goose said. Philip had looked at him from the driving seat and laughed. Goose had laughed, too, then blushed because he saw how pleasurable it was to make a man like Philip Hanrahan laugh. But also because he suddenly thought Philip might be the one person big enough to bear all the bad stuff.

And now here he was, a grown man, and nothing seemed to have changed: He had the same terrible suspicion that, despite himself, he'd caused the death of Vic. Only it wasn't by fighting him, as he'd dreamed as a boy, but by doing nothing. A better son would have saved his father.

Goose had been filling a long crack in the music room, taking care to avoid a fresco of a tree filled with birds, but then the sun had hit the room full-on. He was playing cards to cool down when Bella-Mae came and stood watching from behind her very thick long hair. In the end, he asked politely if she was looking for Iris and she said no, she was looking for him. "I found another crack in the wall upstairs," she said. "I thought you should take a look. What are you doing?"

"I'm playing Patience. You want a go?"

"Fuck, no."

She was wearing Vic's painting jacket, but it was so big on her the sleeves hung right down over her hands. He had an awful feeling she might not be wearing anything underneath.

"You and Iris put stickers on the harps," she observed. "I didn't know you could play the harp."

"We can't."

"Crazy to ask for them, then." She pulled her small fingers across the strings. It made a noise that was strangely jarring for something so elegant. "Your big sisters are falling out."

"It's a difficult time."

"You know what I think? I think there isn't enough love to go around, so they're fighting for every scrap."

He nodded. She had a way of saying things, getting to the heart of them, just when you least expected it. She came and sat opposite him at the card table. "You're called Goose, right?"

It was an odd question because she knew he was. She'd been calling him Goose ever since they met. He smiled though, and said yes.

"Like a duck?"

"No. Not really a duck. Geese aren't ducks. Some migrate from as far as Canada." He had no idea why he was giving her a lesson in how to tell a duck from a goose. He sounded defensive and also patronizing. "Goose is a nickname. My real name is Gustav."

"Gus-tav?" She repeated the name as if it were two separate and solid items. He hadn't heard it spoken like that since the day Shirley Lucas had rescued him outside her house in Watford. Already that seemed so long ago.

"Yes," he said. "But no one calls me that."

"Why not?"

"I couldn't say my name when I was a kid and my father thought it was funny so he imitated me. The nickname stuck."

Bella-Mae said, "Huh." She yawned. "You like men, right?"

He said yes. He liked men. He liked women as well, just in a different way. "Jesus." She rolled her eyes. "Do any of you ever say what's going on in your head?"

He smiled. Despite her difference, he had to admit there was something about her he liked. Perhaps it was the intensity with which she listened. She was like Philip in that respect, only more on the back foot.

"I was in love with my sister's husband."

"Historic Warwick?"

Her eyes widened and he laughed. "I like Warwick. He gets bad press from Netta but, actually, he's a very good man. But no. I fell in love with Netta's husband. Philip Hanrahan."

"Did Netta know?"

"No."

"Did he?"

It was only now she asked this question that he found the answer. "Yes, I think he did. He never said anything about it, though." He remembered how hard he'd cried at Philip's funeral, overtaken by a backwash of grief that shocked him.

"You know what you are?"

"What am I?"

"An artist."

The shock was considerable. He'd been expecting a word like gay. Nancy boy, even. Faggot. A poofter. The kind of things he'd got called at school. But not this. He began to stammer and spoke a tumble of words, all at once. "I'm not. Daddy was the artist. He had only to think up a title and he could see the whole painting. He could do it in a day . . . But art is not good for my head, you see. I had a breakdown. Daddy saved me."

"Daddy, Daddy, Daddy," she said. "You're all the same. Vic could be an arse. You know that?"

"You don't understand. It was really bad. I was seeing things. In my head. All kinds of weird shit. I walked. I walked miles until in the end I got arrested. They sectioned me. I put my family through it. But he took me in. He gave me the bedsit and the work. If it wasn't for him, I don't know where I'd be."

She leaned so close across the table that she knocked his cards out of their piles. He could see the tendons in her neck as she jabbed her finger at him. "Artist, artist, artist," she said, practically poking him. "But you think that's easy? You think being an artist means you give up and go crying to Daddy when it goes wrong?"

"I tried once. I had to destroy every single painting."

"Yeah, I heard about that. You know what I thought when Vic told me that story? I thought, Only a true artist will destroy his own work. No one else would have the guts. And you don't stop being an artist just because you tell everyone you're shit. I knew you were an artist the first time I saw you. That day we came to the studio and I waited in the cab? I looked back as we drove off, and it was the way you were standing, all kind of sad, sad, sad, and open. It was like you had no layers of skin."

"Yes," said Goose. "I remember that day." To his shame, his eyes began to sting.

"It's obvious, just looking at you. The way you stare at things. Like you're making shapes out of thin air. Or the way you see beauty where other people don't. But you know your problem? You're scared. That's your fucking problem. You close up. You won't let it happen. You need to commit, not arse around feeling sorry for yourself. See this?" She tapped the gap between her front teeth. "I got this because I jumped out of a window when I was a kid."

It seemed unlikely that you could get a gap like that from knocking out a tooth, but he let it pass. "Why did you jump?" he said.

She gave a laugh that was closer to a hoot. "I wanted to shake things up. Otherwise you might as well be a block of wood. Wake up! Wake up!" She snapped her fingers so close to his face he blinked. "Stop being such a scaredy-cat, Goose," she said, which struck him as a bit of a mixed metaphor. "You got your fingers burnt when you were twenty-four. So what? Life sucks." She shrugged her shoulders as if she was bored now, and got up. "Don't forget that hole in the wall."

Later Goose was out on the terrazzo, smoking a spliff, when he noticed Bella-Mae down by the lake. She was still in his father's painting jacket, but then she went on all fours, waddling across the grass, pausing every now and then to stretch out her arms and give them a shake, as if they were wings. It seemed she was pretending to be a great big fat goose, and it was making her laugh. She stepped out of the jacket—Jesus, he'd been right, she was wearing nothing underneath. Her body was beautiful, slender and muscled, like a young man's, with deep pockets of hair beneath her arms and between her legs. She leaped with a huge crazy star jump into the lake, screaming wildly, and he remembered her saying Vic had taught her. Then she swam so smoothly she appeared not to break the surface of the water.

Watching her, Goose experienced something strange. As if it weren't Bella-Mae he was seeing but himself. As if this young woman had held up the mirror to what he was, then performed some kind of magic trick where she jumped right through the middle and disappeared, leaving a space for an alternative Goose, who might be free like her.

He threw what was left of his weed into the lake and got back to work on the house.

At twenty-four, Goose had done exactly what Bella-Mae had suggested. He had given everything to his art and secretly produced a series of still-life pictures of apples in watercolor, the paper of identical and almost square format, the subtle differences coming from the play of light and aging of the fruit. The work was obsessive. If he wasn't physically in front of those apples, he was thinking about them. He even dreamed apples. He painted studies of the fruit over and over, bearing witness to its daily change, the way the skin finally wrinkled, bruised and decayed. He studied those apples for so long he didn't see them as apples anymore. They were *life.* Each with a story of its own. In the end he had found his own way of playing with perspective, moving it up and down, left and right, so that when you looked at the apples from the front, you might also get a sense of seeing above and behind them. He experimented with color to suggest textures, and even smell.

When he finally showed them to his flatmates, they were astonished. "You did this? You did this?" they said. They looked at him as if he had doubled in size.

It had taken all Goose's courage to tell Vic about his pictures, but after the reaction of his friends he craved his father's approval too. Vic had never actively discouraged his son from painting, but he was derogatory about art college, which was why Goose had gone straight from school to his job at the theatre company. Yet the minute he heard about Goose's watercolors, Vic was full of wild ideas. He was talking about a gallery, a champagne reception. "Don't you need to take a look at them first?" Goose said. "I don't know. They could be shit."

Vic was adamant. He would see his son's paintings, like everyone else, when they were in the gallery.

Then Goose had hung them that day and realized his catastrophic mistake. No one painted apples, at least not like that. They were too realistic, too bound in the present. Watercolors were for cowards. You might as well make a fruit salad.

After his breakdown, Vic had done everything to support Goose. He explained a career in art was not for the fainthearted. You had to be single-minded. You had to be tough. "You don't have the stamina for it," his father said. "You can't handle failure." To begin with, Susan had worried that working for Vic might be a bad idea, but Netta argued that at least Goose was safe at the studio. And, actually, he found that helping his father with his work, while avoiding art himself, had been a way of keeping close to it and simultaneously hiding. Like weaning himself off without going cold turkey.

"No more loony stuff," Vic said. "You hear me, kid? And no more talk about weird shit in your head."

It was Philip Hanrahan who had come closest to understanding how complicated Goose's feelings were about art. Before they met, Goose had already fallen in love many times and always at a distance: His secret passions had no regard for looks or availability and regularly left him heartbroken. And one of the men he loved both immediately and from a distance was Philip Hanrahan.

Goose got along with Philip—everyone did—because he was larger than life and irrepressibly happy. A few weeks before his marriage to Netta, he'd told Goose he had to do a work presentation in Scarborough and wondered if Goose might like to come as his assistant. The drive was long but seemed to take no time. Philip told stories that went on and on; one story seemed to evolve into another. In Scarborough, Philip had found a restaurant he'd read about in *Time Out*, only it was under new management and they'd ended up on the pier instead, drinking beers and eating fish-and-chips. "Well, this is a first!" said Philip, and it had made equals of them, because even though Goose had never been successful like Philip—Philip could speak four languages—he had definitely eaten a lot of fast food. Before they turned in for the night, they went for a last nightcap along the front and Philip asked all about his breakdown. It was the first time Goose had been able to speak about it and it dawned on him that it was because he was happy now. "Did something happen that day in the gallery?" Philip said. "To make you turn your back on your own art?"

Goose had paused. He'd experienced a dark awareness that something had happened, something so dangerous and wrong he didn't want to know what it was. "No," he'd said. "I just went apeshit. My family was amazing."

"Hm," Philip had said quietly. "Hm. I see."

Goose went up to the Sacro Monte with Iris. He needed to get away from the villa for a while and she wanted to visit the statues in the chapels, just as she'd loved to do as a child. Goose agreed with Netta about the Sacro Monte. He'd always found something slightly spooky about the life-sized statues that told stories from the life of St. Francis, but Iris lit candles for Vic and the views were giant-sized. You could see right over the lake and the island to the hills and mountains beyond.

"You all right?" he said. She was staring at a statue of the saint with a lamb, but her face was pinned into a frown.

"No," she said. "I used to love this place, and now it seems—I don't know—like it can't reach me. Like, since Daddy died, I don't know who I am."

They walked down to the square to buy more bread for dinner. She took off her flip-flops and stuck her feet into the lake. The water was so clear he could see the pale V across the top of her toes from the rubber strap of her shoes. They each had those marks now. Like family tattoos, after all.

He took two smooth white pebbles and rolled them in his palm. He said, "I know what you mean, Iris, about not knowing who you are without Daddy. I don't know who I am either. We've lived charmed lives, all of us, because of him. And yet we don't know how to be anything. We don't even know how to be ordinary. We don't have the tools. It's as if we expect greatness because our father was great. But we are not. It's no wonder Bella-Mae hates us."

"She doesn't hate us. Why would she? I think she likes us."

"Okay. Maybe that's too strong a word. But I sense she wants to shake things up."

A look of fear crossed Iris's face. "Why?" she said slowly. "Why would Bella-Mae want to break things up? How could she even do that?" She shook her head. "I'm sorry, Goose, but you've got her wrong. She's not like that. She's just a very strong person. Personally, I feel inspired by her."

Two ducks were coming toward the shoreline. The water fanned into a V behind them. Iris took a piece of bread from her pocket that she tore into crumbs, then held out in the flat of her hand. He watched as the ducks came right up close to eat them. She smiled and so did he. He was grateful to the ducks for eating out of Iris's hand.

"This is nice," she said.

"What is?"

"You and me. Doing small things."

Susan was waiting at the door of the villa. Her face had tanned over the last few weeks into a beautiful golden glow, but now it looked pale again. She'd been crying. "Where have you two been? We've been searching everywhere." Netta came behind her, fists clenched, her jaw paralyzed with fury.

Instinctively Goose put his arm around Iris and drew her close. "Suz?" he said. "Netta? What now?"

The results of the autopsy had come through.

19

Allergic Reaction

The sun was a blowtorch. Day-trippers found places to sprawl under the big leafy horse chestnuts, staking out the smallest slivers of shade. The whole square seemed cut open with light. At a café overlooking the lake, Netta ordered another vermouth. She'd phoned Robert and told him the results of the autopsy, and for the first time, she heard him sigh. "Inconclusive?"

"It means the pathologist doesn't know. It means there's something suspicious. They want to do more specific tests. They'll be looking for signs of poison. I told you Bella-Mae was at the heart of this." He yawned down the line. "I'm sorry, Robert. Am I keeping you up?"

"Of course not. It was a late night. I'm listening to you, Netta."

She felt wounded. She couldn't help it. And she was buggered if she was going to be nice. "You sound just like Philip used to," she said. Then she hung up.

She was beginning to wonder why, when you lost someone you loved, you started missing all the other people you'd loved. As if grief was a hole and, once it was there, any dead person could come along and jump into it too.

Since being in Orta, Netta had begun to miss her mother with an intensity that appalled her. She'd found herself thinking about the day her mother had taken her to buy school shoes. Round at the toe and with a buckle. Probably the only sensible pair of shoes she'd ever owned. She thought of the afternoon tea afterward and realized that the reason it had been special was because her mother had allowed her to order whatever she liked, for once. She remembered creeping into her mother's room in the last few days of her life and the revulsion she'd felt, which she understood now was terror. After Martha's death, Netta would sometimes tell herself that her mother wasn't gone for good but had simply moved to a different part of the country. She'd invent an alternative life for Martha with a new house, new friends, a new haircut. (Though no new children. She never gave her those.) The fantasy would end with her mother turning up to take Netta home. "What are you thinking, Net-Net?" Susan used to ask. And for once Netta wouldn't share her secret game, because if she did Susan would want to play, too, and if Susan played, it wouldn't work anymore: they would both have to go back with her mother. But she found herself, at the age of forty, wishing all over again that Martha would appear out of nowhere and put out her hand and say in her no-nonsense way, "Okay. That's enough now. It's time to take you home."

Her mother wasn't the only person Netta found herself missing. Since the results of the autopsy, she'd begun to remember Philip Hanrahan. It shocked her that she hadn't thought twice about not attending his funeral. It shocked her that she could have been so sure back then.

"Oh, it was a beautiful service, Netta," Susan had told her afterward. "The church was packed. Honestly, Goose was a wreck. Lots of people asked after you."

"Huh," she'd said. She'd changed the subject.

She had met many people in the brief time she'd been married to Philip and she'd dropped them like hot potatoes the moment she'd got divorced. She didn't need them feeling sorry for her. Yet she and Philip had been married for three years, and even if he'd been in love with Robert the whole time, three years wasn't nothing. She and Philip had made a house together and gone to parties and each slept on their own side of the bed, and all those things that married couples do. Not only that, when he had taken her hand and said, "Darling Netta, I'm afraid there's something I need to tell you," he had cried, that great big man—Jesus, she thought, he was overweight. He had cried because he knew how much he was going to hurt her by ending it. "I do love you," he'd said. "I loved you from the beginning. But I can't love you the way I love Robert."

And what had she said? "Fuck you, Philip Hanrahan," and speed-dialed a lawyer. But when you say "fuck you" to a person you love, she saw this now as she finished her *aperitivo* and waved for another, you are not simply saying it to them: you are laying waste to your own love too. And not acknowledging what you love is a form of self-sabotage.

After two more glasses, Netta moved on. She was unsteady on her feet and too hot, but she didn't go back to the villa. Now that there was this new development with the autopsy, the tension had become unbearable. It had taken a certain amount of nerve, waiting for the first set of results. But waiting for the second was worse, like clinging to a buoyancy aid. Netta insisted the results proved Bella-Mae was guilty, while Susan said that was ridiculous. If the police suspected Bella-Mae, they would arrest her. Besides, how many murderers stayed on at the scene of the crime? Iris agreed with Susan, even if she did it more subtly. As for Goose, he was doing his best to fix things in the villa that were obviously irreparably broken. Bella-Mae had become quieter, more watchful and withdrawn. She spent long periods in Vic's garret.

Netta tramped up and down the little alleyways and streets of Orta, sweat coursing down her sides. She stood at the exact spot where she had stood with her father when she was twelve. She passed the little fountain where she and Susan had practiced smoking, watched wide-eyed by Goose and Iris. She passed the bar where Philip Hanrahan had once told her he loved Orta so much he would like to eat it.

And then she came to a small art supplies shop she had never seen before.

Netta might have been a stranger to the new shop, but clearly the owner noticed her likeness to Vic the moment she stepped inside. She came rushing to the door and gripped her hand. *"Che tragedia! Che cosa ter-*

ribile!" How sorry she was, she kept saying, and how was the family? Was it true that the results of the autopsy had been inconclusive? And yet she'd had the pleasure of meeting Signor Kemp only that summer. He'd come into the shop and admired the stock she had on display and asked if he could make an order.

Netta was nicely on the way to full-on smashed, but she sobered up as if she'd been drenched with a bucket of ice-cold water. "I beg your pardon?"

"He wanted some paints," the owner said again, with an apologetic smile. "I didn't have those colors in stock, so he said he would come back."

"You're saying my father ordered paints before he died?"

"Sì, signora. Sì."

"Do you still have them?"

"Sì, certo!"

The woman reached under the counter and pulled out three tubes of oil color, held together with a rubber band. "He said he needed them to finish his new piece of work."

It was everything Netta could do to remain upright. It was here in front of her—those three little tubes of oil paint—the proof that her father had been working before he died. She felt a kind of rushing pressure in her head, like being sucked backward. "Are you okay?" the woman asked.

"Let me get this clear. My father ordered new paints?"

"Yes, but I didn't have those colors in stock, so, you see, I had to order them. He laughed and told me he would have to be patient for once. He would wait."

"When was this?"

"Not long ago at all. A few weeks before he died."

Netta picked up the little tubes of color. She rolled them in her hand. More than anything that she'd held of her father's since he died, more than his mobile or the clothes in his wardrobe that still smelled of him, these brought him closest. "Signora? How did my father seem to you when you saw him? Would you say he looked unwell?"

"Obviously I had never met him before. If he was ill, he didn't say it to me. I overheard people saying he'd lost a lot of weight. But they put it down to his wedding. Would you like a glass of water? Something stronger? You are very pale."

Netta shook her head. "Did my father tell you anything about his new painting? Is it possible, do you think, he wasn't working on it? That he abandoned it? Threw it away?"

The assistant laughed. "Signora, he was covered with paint. He said he was painting. I don't see why he would lie. But he was an artist. It's bad luck to talk about your current piece of work. All he told me was that it was his masterpiece. He was very excited."

Netta couldn't tell if it was joy she felt or fear. The two seemed strangely related. All along, her siblings had thought that what they didn't believe couldn't exist. But here at last was the proof she had been searching for: The unthinkable was true and she had been right about Bella-Mae all along. She had found what she needed. And she felt incredibly alive.

What Netta did next, she would regret for many years. If only she'd stopped at this point, phoned Robert—better still, if she'd gone home—everyone might have been saved a great deal more pain. But she didn't. She had the bit between her teeth. Months later, when she told the story of her split from her siblings, Netta would highlight this particular day as the turning point, the pivotal moment beyond which there was no going back. "You're quiet," Robert would sometimes say. "You missing them?" He wouldn't even have to say their names.

"Never go back," she would tell him, sounding exactly like her father. "Never apologize." Every birthday she would dread arriving home and discovering that Robert had arranged a surprise party with all the people she'd offended or lost during her drinking years—and, let's face it, you could have filled a church hall with them. But he took her at her word, and never did.

Besides, her sisters weren't in the same country. That summer had divided each of them from their old lives so irreparably it was like being two different selves. There could be no reconciliation now.

It was that last hour of twilight, when the sun has gone but the sky is still softly, airily blue, stretched naked above you. The lake was in stillness: you looked down at the water and found the moon, the first bright stars. Yet the day's heat remained in the garden, stuck beneath the trees: Netta was so hot she could barely lift a fork. And Susan had gone to town. Literally. While Netta had been visiting the art shop, then drinking heavily as she decided what to do, Laszlo and Susan had sailed off in his little boat to a market at Omegna, at the other end of the lake, and come back with enough food to feed every day-tripper on the island. There was so much you could barely find the tablecloth. At the end of the garden, he barbecued gamberi and tender pieces of squid, which attracted every biting insect this side of Milan, while Susan made her own recipe for garlic dressing, plus vegetables, diced, sliced or grated into some kind of exotic cold dish, with a special potato salad for Iris because the pink of the prawns, the green of the endive, and the red tomatoes were all going to be a major problem. Susan had pinned up her hair and put on a lipgloss that made her mouth look like a piece of fruit about to explode. Sitting at the head of the table in a tight white dress that showed off both her figure and her tan, little candles bowing up and down all around her, she looked dazzling. Queen Susan, with Iris and Goose as her prince and princess siblings, while Netta scowled behind a wine bottle, like the bad fairy no one had wanted to invite. Besides, she had three tubes of oil paint burning a father-sized hole in her pocket.

"Remember how Daddy would go to buy something in a shop?" Susan said. "And if he couldn't get served, he'd wave it above his head and shout, 'I am walking out! I have not paid! I am walking out!' until someone ran to serve him?"

"Oh, God, I wanted to die when he did that!" said Iris.

"Or what about the time he got so drunk he delivered a painting and it was still so wet half of it was down his dressing gown? Remember that, Goose?"

"Of course I do, Suz. I had to get him into a cab and take him back to the studio. He was furious. He had to do the whole thing all over again."

The stories went on and on. Bella-Mae laughed as Goose and Iris began joining in, telling her and Laszlo all the crazy things Vic had done when they were children. Sticking a broken crown back into his mouth with superglue because he had such a fear of doctors and dentists, or going to do the week's shopping and coming back only with chocolate biscuits. Or what about Microwave Laura, the au pair who could make an entire Sunday lunch in ten minutes flat and none of it edible. "She almost set fire to Iris once," said Susan, and Iris said it was true. Laura had gone to light a candle and dropped it on Iris by mistake. You might have thought she'd be scarred for life, she said. At least afraid of candles. But she wasn't. She really loved them.

"Tea?" said Bella-Mae, and she poured it for everyone from her special flowery pot.

Netta remembered those stories, of course she did. They were her childhood. But they were private property. Not show-and-tell. And there was nothing remotely funny about them. She was beginning to wonder if they'd shared the same parent. She took more wine and gave a sarcastic smile, until Susan glanced at her and said brightly, "Oh! Okay, Netta!" in a way that made it clear she knew something was wrong but wasn't going to give it any traction. Meanwhile Iris was so busy waving her fork in the air and talking about *The Second Sex* that she seemed to be the only person capable of losing weight during the course of a two-hour meal. And then there was Goose who said, every time there was a lull, "Well, this is good, isn't it? It's lovely to be together."

Susan told Bella-Mae that her tea was delicious. She said it was so delicious she wanted the recipe.

"Verbena to aid digestion, plus a little mint, and vervain to help us sleep. There's a touch of licorice as well. I'm glad you like it."

Susan said it was the best tea she'd ever tasted. So did Iris. So did Goose.

"Is this the same tea you gave Daddy?" said Netta. "Or was that a different kind of poison?"

It was as if she had cut a hole out of the air and thrown a stick of dynamite inside it. Such was the shock that no one moved. It was only Bella-Mae who turned toward Netta. She pushed back her hair from her face and looked at her strangely. "I'm sorry. What are you talking about now?"

"I'm talking about the autopsy. That's what I'm talking about."

"You think I poisoned your father?"

Immediately Susan rushed in to smooth things over. She was clearly trying to turn the evening back from a potential war zone into a suburban dinner party. "Who would like more to eat? Your plate is empty, Bella-Mae. What can I get you? Another prawn? Can I pass more tomatoes?"

But what Netta had said was still between them. It might as well have pulled up its own chair. Iris said suddenly and with a laugh, as if she had surprised herself: "You know what? I think I might try some tomato. I mean, it's only tomato. What harm can it do me?"

Everyone watched in wonder, or was it complete confusion, while Iris lifted the smallest slice onto her plate and began to eat. She chewed very slowly, far more than any normal tomato required, then took a long gulp of tea, and chewed a little more, blinking with the effort. She closed her eyes and lifted her chin high, swallowing it.

"Oh, Iris!" said Susan. "You did it! You ate red food!"

After that, it was obvious that Iris was going to try a little bite of everything red she could see on the table, followed by a little bite of everything green, while everyone laughed and congratulated her, and put forward more and more things to experiment with, as if she had become a performing seal who ate only green or red things. It was hideous.

Netta reached for the wine again. She said, "Susan, what is all this? I mean what the fuck is going on?"

"Netta?" said Susan, still on her brightest hostess setting. "What's wrong with you?"

"What is wrong with me?" Netta paused, partly for dramatic effect but also because she had no idea where to start. She could not believe that her own family was doing this. That she had set off an explosion and now they were running about, heads down, trying to sweep up the damage and put everything back together. She was clenched like a fist. "Bella-Mae is not here because she misses Daddy. The autopsy proved he did not die of natural causes. She is not telling us the truth. And this time I have evidence. I have solid evidence."

A fresh silence fell over the candlelit garden, another terrible one. Even Susan seemed at a loss. Methodically she began to stack the empty plates. Iris poured more water, drinking in furtive sips. Goose stretched back his head as if he were looking to the heavens for divine intervention.

Netta pulled out the three tubes of paint. She laid them in the middle of the table in the space that Susan had only just cleared. "Daddy was working before he died. He ordered more colors at the end of June to finish his picture. Bella-Mae has been lying to us all along. She's lying about everything."

Iris reached for the tubes of paint, but couldn't pick them up. Goose stared, freshly wounded. Susan took a breath that came and went without a sound.

Briefly Bella-Mae touched her mouth. She seemed as shocked as the others. "No," she said. "No, Netta. You've got this wrong."

Laszlo watched Netta with such hatred she knew she was seeing right through him.

And then she had a thick, slow feeling of things not being real. Of being in a place that was full of dark and sludge. She was aware that she had got what she wanted, that she was at the top of things and had proved herself right, but somehow in the process she had grown monster feet and claws. She reached for her glass, but missed. Wine went everywhere. Susan threw a napkin over it.

"Netta," she warned, "don't you think you've had enough?"

Yes, she'd had more than enough, but there was more to say and Netta had to get it all talked out of her. So, while the others watched in horror, she plowed on. Further into the monster mire and the sludge. She reminded everyone, just in case they had forgotten, that Bella-Mae had hidden their father's phone from the police. "She was keeping it for us," said Susan.

Netta spoke over her. "That is hiding the evidence, Susan. It's a criminal offense." She reminded them that when Goose had asked how Bella-Mae had met Vic, she couldn't remember. And where were her paints, where were her sketchbooks? Where was there any sign that she was an artist, like she said? "You were the one, Susan, who thought she was taking Daddy away from us. You were the one who said we should get a private detective."

"You said this?" said Laszlo, now turning on Susan.

"Netta, you're drunk," said Susan. Her face was ablaze. "You have a problem. I'm telling you right now. You have a real problem."

Of course she was drunk. Of course she had a problem. Her whole life: That was the problem. Drinking with her father at the age of twelve, just so she could be more like him than the others. Pushing boundaries all the time, just to stay ahead. Cutting herself at university because she missed Vic so much she didn't know how else to get on top of the pain, her thighs still flecked with silver darts that she covered with a sarong every summer so that he would never see. Sleeping with men who could drink like her, and waking in the morning without a clue who they were. Married three whole years to someone who was never going to love her in the way she wanted, then in love with the man he'd rightly chosen over her. What else could she do with her life but throw her own private party? She could function at work and sometimes the alcohol improved her performance, but recently it had begun to seem bigger than she was. She sensed the alcohol was winning. And now here she was, this monster at her sister's table, ripping everything open, and the only way to live with it would be to start drinking again in the morning. "Have you forgotten Daddy's texts before he died?"

"What texts?" said Bella-Mae. "What texts?"

"Netta, no," said Susan.

"Have you forgotten what he told Iris? Have you forgotten 'I'm in it now'?"

"I'm in it now?" repeated Bella-Mae. "Why would Vic say that?"

"Netta, don't," said Susan.

But then a terrible new thought hit Netta, and this was a lightning bolt. "She was there. She was *there*, in the noodle bar, right at the beginning. She was spying on us. She was there at the Singing Wok."

It wasn't Susan who came back at Netta. It wasn't even Bella-Mae or Laszlo. It was Iris. She began to cough, as if something had gone down the wrong way, but she couldn't stop, she couldn't stop coughing, and suddenly she was starting to hyperventilate. Drawing up short breaths that had nothing to them. "Help," she stuttered. "Help." She was ashen, her skin slick with sweat. "Help. Help."

"Okay, Iris," said Goose. "Relax, Iris. It's okay."

He tried to pat her back, but she was trembling all over. "Goose. I can't. Feel. My hands. My heart. It's going berserk."

"Her puffer!" said Susan. "Where is it?"

Iris stood and bent over the table. "At home! At home!" She was wheezing as if the little air she could get was suffocating her.

Suddenly everything was confusion. Everyone was on their feet. The tomatoes, Netta was yelling. Iris must be allergic. But Susan was yelling back that she wasn't. You couldn't be allergic to a tomato. Yes, you could, Netta shouted. Some people were allergic, especially if they hadn't eaten the things for thirty-plus years. Iris was having some kind of anaphylactic reaction and all because everyone had been feeding her fucking tomatoes.

Goose moved between them, trying to calm things down. "This is a panic attack. She's having a panic attack. She always gets them."

Susan said, "Someone get a paper bag! Calm down. Just calm down, Iris! You're okay!" But the person who sounded not at all calm or okay was Susan.

Meanwhile, Laszlo ran to the kitchen and came back with plastic bags. "Are you trying to kill her too?" roared Netta.

"Come on, Iris," said Goose. "Breathe now. Breathe."

Iris backed toward her chair to sit, but it knocked to one side and instead she fell to the ground, hitting the corner of the table with the side of her head. Then a cut bloomed above her left eye and suddenly there was blood all over her sweet dolly face, and she stopped moving.

Susan screamed. Netta staggered. Goose lumbered inside and came back with a toilet roll.

It was Bella-Mae who took control. She rushed to Iris's side. Somehow in the panic she had been forgotten. She knelt beside her and pulled off her cardigan. "Breathe! Breathe! Breathe!" she said. "Come on, Iris! Breathe!" But Iris had gone so still she barely seemed alive. "Goose!" Bella-Mae said. "Carry your sister inside. Susan, I need ice. Laszlo, fetch a blanket."

Within moments, Goose was carrying Iris's limp body into the villa, while Susan and Laszlo rushed after him for blankets and ice.

Bella-Mae turned to Netta and said quietly, "You think that's the way to get rid of me?" She reached for the oil paints and took them into her hands, staring at them long and hard. Then she, too, left the scene, taking the paints with her, not in a demented panic, like the others, but altogether more heavily and calm.

Briefly everything was stillness, except for the lapping of the water in the dark.

Netta stared at the chaos. The abandoned table. The fallen-over chairs. The candles burning up and down the garden, like tiny eyes jumping. The trees swinging to the left and right. She was so drunk she had to squint to find her way to the house. Twice she fell. "Oh, Antoinetta Kemp," she heard her mother say. "What in heaven's name have you just done?"

20

Falling, Falling into the Abyss

Long past midnight, and Susan couldn't sleep. She was too wired. It was the stillest night. Iris was upstairs, stable now and being looked after by Bella-Mae, with Goose as her assistant. Netta had crashed out in her old room. Susan and Laszlo had cleared up and washed up, and now they sat at the table on the terrazzo, waiting for more news. Susan talked and talked. The windows were wide open. Anyone could hear. Yet Laszlo fixed her with his impenetrable dark eyes and it was like falling into the abyss. She had no idea what to do but talk.

The words came falling out of her. Oh, not just about her wedding, the wedding that Netta did her best to cancel at the last minute, or those many years of marriage, looking after the twins every weekend and wanting her own child. She talked about being Netta's sister, always the runner-up. Wearing the clothes that Netta had worn first. Echoing what her sister had just said, and running ever so slightly behind. Nothing Susan could do was remarkable because Netta had always done it first and, chances were, she'd also done it better. All her life Netta had been a wall between Susan and the rest of the world.

She felt as if she were waking from a dream. A dream in which you went along and went along and, whatever you did, you weren't changing anything. You were just doing what you did, because that was what you'd always done. You'd always come second.

Laszlo's bare knee was almost touching hers. She felt a bolt of pleasure, low in her pelvic bone.

He said, "You are right about your sister. She drinks too much. She has problem. What she say to my cousin is cruel. Just because your father buy those paints, it does not mean he is painting. My cousin tells me over and over that he does not paint in Orta and I believe her. She loves your father like no one else. Your sister is jealous because she is drunk lady."

It was incredible to hear him speak about Netta like that; intoxicating, too, as delicious and forbidden as anything Susan had ever done. Hearing him confirm the thoughts in her head was like closing another door between her and Netta. Her life before Laszlo seemed to belong to a different woman.

After the autopsy, they would leave here. She would follow him wherever he wanted to go. Even if there was no will, she would inherit something. They would travel: Laszlo's childhood had been poor and she would make up for everything he'd missed. They would book hotel suites in Paris and have sex all afternoon with the curtains wide open, and afterward they would eat oysters and shellfish and all those things Warwick couldn't eat because they didn't agree with him. There was only one question that kept her back.

From the house came the sound of a door closing, a tap running.

"Do you think Iris will be okay?" she said.

He nodded, moved his knee even closer to hers. "My cousin look after her now."

"I've never seen her so bad. She's had panic attacks before. But I thought she had died tonight. I really thought she had died."

He reached for her hand and she gave it to him. He moved his finger over her knuckles and then he lifted it to his mouth and kissed it. She was shaking.

"Laszlo," she said.

"Suzanne," he said.

"You came to the villa the morning after my sisters arrived. It was just you and me in the kitchen. You said you were looking for something. Was it . . ." she had to look away ". . . was it my father's will? I won't tell the others. But I have to know."

There was a silence that felt longer than it was. Even the lake seemed to stop moving. "Oh, Suzanne," he said, his voice erupting right through her. "You think I steal from you? I never do this. That day in kitchen, I take envelope for my cousin. It contain wedding certificate. This is all."

He pulled her face toward his and pushed his mouth on hers. It was thick and delicious, like sucking a melon. Or being sucked by one. Technically she couldn't tell where his mouth stopped and hers started. Except there was one more thing she had to know. She pulled away.

"What now?" he said. "You still want talking?"

"Why did you tell me you were Bella-Mae's friend? And not her cousin?"

At this he laughed. "Because I am her friend! She has no other friend in the world but me!"

Never mind Netta and her proof, her evidence. This was all Susan needed. She and Laszlo were kissing, big time. They were lips and tongues and teeth like two melons taking bites out of each other. Already his hand had made its swift passage to her bare stomach—she breathed in, flattening it—then it was on her ribs and, hey presto, it had moved with wondrous dexterity inside her bra. His leg was between hers, and now she was tugging at his shirt, and she could feel, oh, she could feel his erection, and her bra was undone and he was yanking at her sleeve and he was pushing her to the ground—they were on the ground, the chairs had somehow disappeared—they were rolling on the ground, his hands between her legs, and yet only a fraction of a second ago they were in her bra, which was, she now realized, not on her at all, but a thing abandoned on the also-abandoned chair, both of them very much left behind in the past tense, and he was unzipping his shorts, and pushing himself inside her.

Her love for Warwick was a piece of cement that had once held everything together, yet she did not want to be held together. She wanted to break into a million pieces. If this was the abyss, she wanted it. Her siblings were in the house, and Iris had just had a terrifying fit, and this was so dangerous it was all wrong, and yet she wanted it, but already he was pulling away.

"Don't stop," she said.

"No," he told her.

"Yes," she said. Angry now.

He rolled off, struggling to zip his shorts. There, in the space behind him, a whole new scene had set itself up that had not been there before. Goose was at the French windows, a look on his face of utter confusion. He was holding a tea-towel in one hand and the ice-cube tray in the other. "Bella-Mae sent me down," he said, beginning to stammer. "She sent me down here for more ice."

The following day, Goose said nothing to Susan about what he had seen. She knew he wouldn't do anything to hurt her. She was certain he wouldn't tell Netta or Iris. But she could sense that it was a weight on his shoulders: he had seen something that made him worried for her and afraid, and he didn't know how to hold this one together, or even deal with the potential sadness except by heaping it upon himself. When he moved his things out of the bedroom they all shared to give Iris more space, it was a relief. At least it took away the awkwardness.

Besides, Susan's head was too full to stay for any period of time with her siblings. Now as she passed Laszlo on the stairs, taking Iris a glass of iced water, he pressed her against the wall and groped her freely, just as he'd done in the garden, then laughed and moved on. If he helped her into his boat, he kept his hand firmly around her arm. "I want you," he mouthed to her, as she passed him a cup of coffee, with Netta just outside on her phone.

Susan no longer cared. She, too, moved her things out of the room she'd shared with Iris. The desire she felt for Laszlo rose up and flowed through her, a river wild and rapid and overwhelming. There are moments in life when a great softness is coupled with a great hardness.

And nothing would have persuaded her to give up Laszlo. Not even her siblings.

He could treat her how he liked: she would still come.

They had installed Iris upstairs like a little sick empress, everyone waiting on her hand and foot, making a fuss as if she'd survived a plane crash and dragged herself through a snake-infested jungle, instead of having a panic attack and crashing her head by mistake on a very sharp corner of the table. Since her collapse, her siblings barely allowed Iris to leave the bedroom. She only had to call for water and they were running up the stairs with a thermometer as well. If she tried to get up, they worried so much she went back to bed. The cut on her forehead could probably have done with a stitch or two, but Iris insisted she didn't want any more fuss. Instead it was held together with plasters and a dressing that either Susan or Netta would come and change every few hours.

Iris discovered she liked having a room of her own. Sometimes in the dark she heard her siblings whisper, "Is she okay?," "Is she too hot?," "No, she feels cooler now," and stayed very still with her eyes closed. It drove her half mad, but at least it gave her space to think. She would find Goose sitting on the end of her bed, staring at thin air as if he were drawing shapes with an invisible pencil. He'd bring a flower from the garden that was perfect for the color and shape of the vase. Or one of her sisters would keep her company and end up listing all the complaints she had about the other. But on the whole, it was Bella-Mae whose visits she waited for.

They talked about Gloria Steinem, Germaine Greer, Patti Smith. They talked about the patriarchy, the climate, pollution, free will, the need for rebellion. It was like trying on different shoes, just as Iris had done as a child, except this was inside her mind. Iris sometimes felt pushed by Bella-Mae, provoked, even looked down on, but at other times Bella-Mae was full of enthusiasm for Iris's ideas, nodding her head and waving her hands, shouting, "Yes! Yes! Yes!"

Bella-Mae told Iris about her art. How she wanted to experiment with something she'd never done before, something so big people wouldn't be able to ignore it. She didn't care if people didn't like it, that wasn't the point of art. She wanted to be true to her vision. Because if you weren't true to your voice, she said, you might as well not have one. And Iris said yes, she thought the same, except even as she said it she didn't know if her voice was hers or someone else's. Then Bella-Mae would pour another cup of her tea and Iris would close her eyes because her head was ready to implode with all the new ideas bursting inside it, and she'd wake again to find one of her sisters back at her bedside, complaining about the other:

"Can you believe what Susan is wearing?"

"When will Netta stop going on about the painting?"

Iris began to see how intricately bound her sisters still were. Even now they weren't speaking to each other, it had oxygen: it was a kind of speaking. She understood, too, that she had briefly hoped she might benefit from their falling-out and somehow win herself a place in the center of the family, but that had been naïve. The only reason they could be so kind to her, and indulge her as they did, was because she was at the bottom of the line, where she posed no threat. She was a prize to be fought over, but not a real person.

They'd seen her collapse simply as yet further confirmation that she couldn't be relied on as a fully grown adult. No matter what she tried to do, they would always expect it to amount to very little, and that was the reason, she thought now, that she had spent her adult life doing useless jobs, like selling cheese. Because they expected nothing else.

But surely there had to be another way of becoming seen and heard that didn't involve lying in a bedroom with the shutters closed.

Bella-Mae was playing cat's cradle with string looped between her hands when she said, "I want to tell you something I haven't told anyone, not even Laszlo. A few days before he died, Vic saw you in the garden."

There was a tiny electric moment. Iris eased away from her and said, "What do you mean, he saw me?"

"We were sitting on the terrazzo. Vic looked down at the water and he pointed. He said, 'Here comes Iris.' He thought you had just got here."

"Was he drunk?"

"No. I told you already, Iris. He'd stopped all that. The fact is . . ." here she paused and twisted her wedding ring ". . . Vic changed in the last few days of his life. It was like he was experiencing things in a new way. And that time in the garden, he saw you clear as day. He thought you had come out here to see him."

"But now I feel awful."

"Why?"

"Because I stayed at home."

"It doesn't matter. He wanted you to be here and so he saw you."

Iris weighed the words for a moment or two. She said, "Was he happy to see me?"

"Oh, he was really happy."

"What about my—" She broke off, unable to say it, or too ashamed, but Bella-Mae knew exactly what she was thinking, and answered.

"No. He didn't see the others. He didn't see Netta or Susan or Goose before he died. He only saw you."

Iris had been searching for the key to change, and now she had it. Even if it was only in his imagination, her father had seen her. He hadn't seen her siblings. He had needed her, just as he'd needed her once to be his model. He had always found something in her that her siblings couldn't see. She had a whole life about which they knew nothing. If she didn't tell them soon, they would go back to London and everything would be the same. She would be living alone and stroking other people's cats and going to Susan's for Sunday lunch because they all thought she didn't eat enough, and missing texts from Netta that demanded why the fuck she didn't have a proper phone like any normal person.

She was on the edge of something and she didn't know what it was except that it was like the avalanche she had seen once on the television. She didn't know how, or when, but as soon as she could, she was going to put herself right in the center.

21

A Quiet Calm

As soon as Harry heard about Iris's collapse, he said he was coming straight to Orta. "What the hell is going on out there?" he said. "Why did no one tell me?"

The four siblings were established in their separate bedrooms. They scanned the water every day, awaiting further news about the autopsy, but the *commissario* didn't turn up in his boat. Mealtimes were no longer something they shared, but took separately. Footsteps outside the villa sounded enormous, as if they were bringing bad news.

However, when Harry announced that he was coming, there was a general feeling that, with him at the villa, things might settle again: the old order would be restored. Susan and Goose made up a bed; Iris came down to the garden, where she cut flowers for his room before she went to lie down again. They drove to the airport to fetch him, Goose in the front with Susan, Netta and Iris in the back. "There really is no need for you to do this," Susan told them. "Laszlo said he would come with me." But Iris insisted she had something important to tell them in the car, and Netta said that if Iris was going, she was too. Which obviously left Goose with no option. Anyway, he'd missed Harry. He was more than happy to go and meet him.

"Are you listening to me?" Iris said halfway to the airport, but Susan put on her Coldplay CD and Iris was drowned out.

When Harry walked through the Arrivals gate, he stretched out his arms and embraced all four of them. "Kids," he said. "What a mess. Tell me everything. Netta darling, take off that hat—I can't see you under there. Susan, what have you done? You look radiant. Iris, how are you, little one? Goose, come here, son. Come here. Right then, kids. Let's sort out this chaos."

At first it really seemed they had been right about Harry's arrival. He took the room beside Laszlo's that he and Shirley used to occupy every summer. In no time, Laszlo's shirts were taken down from the balcony. They ate as a family again with Harry at the top of the table and Netta at the other end, Iris on some cushions under a parasol. Laszlo was relegated to a side position beside his cousin. When he began one of his endless stories that only Susan found so hilarious, Harry interrupted, asking everyone what they thought about the heat wave. With Harry, Bella-Mae was nothing but polite. She answered his questions without guile. He, in turn, was charming.

"Tell me what kind of art you do, Bella-Mae."

"That depends, Harry. How do you define art?"

"Well, in Vic's case, it was paintings. But I don't think I have seen your work anywhere."

"I'm in a process of change. My main work has been more like installations."

"Netta, darling, try the Barolo. Isn't it good? What kind of installations?"

"Kind of experimental."

"All art is experimental."

"Vic's wasn't."

Harry laughed. "Describe your last piece of work to us."

She pushed back her hair, leaned forward, her eyes suddenly very bright. "I rented a warehouse. I filled it with tiny pieces of glass. When people walked over it, it crunched beneath their feet and broke into more pieces. I called it *Icarus Is a Woman*. Not many people came, but that's not what art is about. It's about pushing things to the edge."

For the rest of the meal, Bella-Mae went quiet again. When Harry suggested a round of cards, she excused herself and said she needed an early night. Netta fetched more wine and was on such good form she won almost every game.

Harry agreed with her that the painting had to be in Orta somewhere. He did not believe that Vic would have given up on something he'd felt so passionately about, even if he'd just got married. The next day, he and Netta went back to the art supplies shop to question the owner further about what she'd said that day; he met Limoncello; he visited every *notaio*, and arranged a meeting with the *commissario*.

"Susan," he said. "Let's start thinking seriously about this major exhibition of your father's work. I want you to talk me through everything Vic left here. Every sketch, every painting."

"Yes, Harry."

"By the way, darling, beautiful dinner, as always. You could have been a TV chef. And, Goose?"

"Yes, Harry?"

"The outside of the house is looking like it needs some love, son. Why don't we pick up some yellow and pink emulsion?"

It wasn't that the differences were forgotten now that Harry was there, and everyone was reunited. Netta and Susan remained frosty, especially when Harry wasn't looking. They still sent Iris to rest upstairs. But an even keel had been reestablished. Harry was a steadying influence, just as he had once been for Vic's art. There were even moments when a soft breeze picked up over the lake and swept through the garden. Somehow this, too, seemed to be to do with Harry.

And then came the piece in the *New Yorker*.

It was the most damning article Goose had ever read. The writer compared looking at a Vic Kemp painting to eating a Cadbury Creme Egg. "Basically it rots your head and makes you feel sick." Not only that, most of his work was a bad copy of someone else's. If art had one shared quality, she went on, it was that it offered an individual response to the world. It was not commercial and neither was it safe. It should provoke thought and break boundaries. It should not sit somewhere back in the 1970s when men wore creepy driving gloves and wolf-whistled at women from building sites. In her view there was more sexual excitement in a packet of crisps, and it would be a sad day for Britain if any galleries chose to hang a Vic Kemp. It was basically showing off by a not-very-good amateur, who would have been better served doing painting by numbers. "Remember the emperor who had no clothes?" she wrote. "Well, here we go again. It's all a fake."

The effect was immediate. There were tweets and messages all over social media, with his work reimagined as painting by numbers. There were endless jokes about Cadbury Kemp Eggs.

Goose read it all and felt his world toppling over. He wanted to be able to get on with the business of mourning his father, yet new things kept getting in the way. And although he wanted to dismiss what the journalist said, he knew deep down that she was right about one thing at least: Vic would have done anything to be thought of as a great artist, and if that meant plagiarism, he would do it. Goose had seen him lining up his easel alongside a reproduction of someone else's painting and copying it, line by line, shape by shape. Once again he thought of the day he'd put on the nightie and it dawned on him that his father's problem hadn't been that Goose was dressed as a girl but that he had dared to steal the limelight. Nothing mattered more to Vic than to remain center stage. He would do anything to get there, even if it meant stealing from another artist.

"The *New Yorker*," complained Iris. "I mean why couldn't it have been a paper no one reads?" She said she'd only just started reading the news and now she had to give up again.

"Well, I guess that's it with the major gallery," said Susan. And she was right. Politely it was made clear that Vic's inclusion in an exhibition was no longer on the cards.

But it was Netta in whom Goose noticed the biggest shift. She gave up talking about the last painting. She stopped charging here, there and everywhere, a woman possessed. Instead she'd sit by the lake, burning furiously under her hat, with a bottle of wine.

"At least we know he loved us," Goose said, crouching beside her. "Every family has its own way of doing things."

"Goose," she said sadly. "For once in your life, can you stop trying to make this okay?"

22

I Need to Tell the Truth

It was Harry's idea. His treat, he said, before he went home to try to limit the damage caused by the *New Yorker* piece. They would take the passenger boat to the Venus restaurant in Orta and have one of those blow-out lunches Vic had always loved. "And you know what else we're going to take a break from? All this shit in the media. The autopsy as well. Just for one afternoon we're not going to talk about any of that. We're going to eat and drink, and celebrate the old bastard. All of us together. Like he would have wanted."

By the time everyone collected in the garden for pre-lunch drinks, it was clear they were excited and happy about Harry's plan and had each made some kind of effort. Susan had gone to the hairdresser for a blow-dry and come back with her face fully made up, her hair in ringlets. She matched a belt with a low-cut tight turquoise dress and looked to die for. Netta wore one of her old Donna Karan numbers, but this time she'd ironed it and put on red lipstick, so that for once in its life her hat was the most elegant thing in the world. Goose combed what he could of his hair and wore the black jacket he'd borrowed from Harry. It was Iris's first big family meal since her collapse and she ventured downstairs in a bottle-green dress that gave her pale skin a beautiful luminous glow, like early evening on the lake. Harry wore a light suit and a tie.

("You handsome devil," said Netta.) Even Laszlo had put on a jacket. ("Oh!" Netta said. "It's beige! You own something beige! Who knew?")

But it was the sight of Bella-Mae that gave everyone the biggest surprise. She came down in a sleek red dress and high-heeled shoes, her thick hair tied so hard back from her face she looked as if she was smiling all the time. It should have been obvious from the start that if the day belonged to anyone it would be her. There was a shimmering quality inside her stillness. A sense that something was about to happen.

It was there, too, that sense of release, in the weather. The evening before, a canopy of dark cloud had moved in from the mountains and heavy rain had come overnight, the first in months, falling for hours on the gardens and rooftops, the dusty streets, the loggias and windows. They'd woken to a landscape freshly revived, a dripping calm, the pines giving out a juicy scent of resin, the colors sharp and clear as if wiped with a cloth. There was that melty breeze again, soft and lovely. It sent little wavelets running up and down the lake that twinkled as the sunlight bounced on them. People were back in paddleboats and kayaks. Teenagers stretched out on the jetties, arm in arm, and families gathered beneath their parasols. The strongest swimmers made their way as far out as the buoys, while children ran in and out of the shallows. A hazed stillness hung over the distance, but down there it was perfect.

"Iris, do you have cream on?" said Susan. "And where is your hat?"

"I don't need a hat."

"Take mine, darling," said Netta.

"I like the sun. If I didn't like the sun, I would stay in England."

But Netta ignored her and insisted on walking with an umbrella practically on top of Iris's head, as if she and the sun were in some kind of personal competition for her sister, which Netta, of course, was hell-bent on winning.

At the restaurant, waiters led the party to a large table set for them beside the lake. Harry sat at the head with Bella-Mae smiling at the opposite end, and he ordered the best of everything. The best bottles of Alta Langa, the best Barolo, all the house specialities from the menu. "Keep them coming!" he said.

Everything about the afternoon was right. The gentle breeze, the sparkling lake, the starch white of the tablecloth, the day-trippers coming off the boats, their faces full of excitement. The painted buildings shone in their soft blues and pinks and yellows. Restaurants and cafés were full again, and beneath the Palazzotto two buskers had set up with a flute and violin. The waiters brought dish after dish. *Fassona* tartare, tiny fried anchovies, stuffed squid, lightly seared prawns, potato gnocchi with cuttlefish stew, dishes of *agnolotti* stuffed with smoked fish, and ravioli with beef. There were baskets of fresh focaccia, fresh trout from the lake baked in garlic and oil.

"Iris, eat some of the risotto," said Susan. "And don't touch the tomatoes." She moved them to the other side of the table, as if they couldn't be trusted not to leap into Iris's mouth all by themselves.

"You know you're in the sun, darling?" said Netta. "I'll speak to the waiters." She got them to move some more parasols, putting Iris so completely in shadow she asked if anyone had a torch so that she could see her food.

But all this was said lightly. The tension had gone. Harry kept ordering more sparkling wine, more red, and topping up glasses. Once again, all the old stories came out about Vic, so many that he seemed to be back among them, full of life. Then Susan turned to Netta and told her how nice she looked in her dress, and Netta smiled, if a little awkwardly, and said, "Oh, this old thing, I guess it scrubs up." But the ice had been broken between them. By the time the waiters brought out desserts and plates of fruit and cheese, Susan was calling, "More Barolo for my sister, please," while Netta was telling everyone that the only reason they'd survived the summer was because Susan had spent every waking minute in the kitchen.

"She could have been a TV chef," she told the waiters. "Like Lesley Waters."

At five o'clock, the restaurant began to empty, but no one at the big table by the water had any intention of going home. They ordered more bottles, and Iris went to the tobacconist for cigarettes. She sat in the sun beside Goose.

"You okay?" he whispered. Because suddenly there was something about her face that seemed tight and anxious. He hadn't seen her with cigarettes for years. "Are you having another panic attack?"

"No," she said. "And before you ask, yes, I am wearing sun cream. And, no, I don't need a hat." She pulled the cellophane from the cigarettes and screwed it into a tight ball that sprang outward the moment she dropped it onto the table. "To tell the truth, I feel really good. After all the chaos since Daddy died, and that awful piece in the *New Yorker*, it seems different today. It's like everything's going to be good again." He saw the spark in her eyes, two little pink dots on her cheeks, and realized that what he had taken to be anxiety was something else. Excitement. "Remember how you and I learned to smoke right here in this square? Watching Susan and Netta?"

"I do," he said. "They gave us pencils to practice on."

"Netta was always telling me off because she said I looked like I was spitting out flies."

While Iris smoked, he watched his eldest sisters across the table and he could picture them at the same time as young teenagers, only a few feet away, Netta cupping her hands around the flame so that Susan's cigarette would light. He saw them showing him and Iris how you inhaled, then blew it out, as if you intended to extinguish a tray of candles. "They're amazing, those two," he said. "I'm glad they're back together."

Iris nodded, but then she said, "Sometimes I think I've been hidden behind them my whole life."

For some reason, he noticed the light around her at that moment, and he would always remember it. It had turned beautiful, as if someone had poured it over the lake and the land, this golden bright light that came running down the buildings behind her, so that they were more defined than before. More yellow, more blue, more pink. It had the same effect on Iris and her green dress, as if she, too, were shining from the inside.

She kept smoking. She inhaled fast, blew out, inhaled again, more like she was pecking it. She still didn't seem much of a smoker. Perhaps she sensed him thinking that, because she shook her head and said a little sharply, "I'm not a kid anymore, you know. I'm an adult. Just like Netta and Susan."

The plates were cleared. His sisters changed seats. Laszlo was now sitting with Susan, his arm curved around the back of her chair, and they were talking so intimately that her head was touching his. Netta was laughing with two of the waiters: she looked the most relaxed she'd been all summer. By now Harry was ordering more wine for Limoncello, who had appeared in the square and been beckoned over by Netta. Waiters also brought out bottles of whisky and grappa, courtesy of the management. It was only Bella-Mae who seemed alone. She sat with her vast sunglasses on, perfectly still, her face smiling, though once Goose caught her attention and she lifted her glass of water as if to toast him.

Harry took to his feet and clanked his glass with the side of a knife. He could barely stand. "To Vic," he called.

Everyone raised a glass. In fact, Netta raised two, one in each hand, and both full. "To Vic," they all shouted. By now several passersby and the waiters had come over to listen. There was in effect a second group around the one at the table, and Harry called for drinks for them too.

"Vic," he said, "you could be an arse." ("Hear, hear," said Netta. More laughter.) "But you were my best friend. You were a force of nature. I don't care what that bloody journo says, you were an artist. You didn't paint for hoi polloi like her. You painted stories for real people who thought art was above them. That's what your work was about. There is not one day of my life when I will not miss you."

He'd begun to slur his words, and the more he spoke about Vic, the more emotional he became.

"He didn't care that he'd never been to art college. He had a rough childhood and he learned the kind of things you don't get taught at school, like how to survive. And even if his art was a hobby to start with, he was a great. A true great. You know why? Because he had the common touch. People could look at one of his paintings and see a romantic world where they might have that kind of love. And isn't that what we all want in the end? Don't we all want love?"

There was general agreement. "*Amore!*" someone from the crowd shouted. People laughed, though a few were wiping their eyes, and then there was the silence that follows a speech, like that, when no one quite knows how to carry the conversation back to the ordinary. Susan went to Harry and hung her arms around his neck as she planted a kiss on his cheek. "Thank you, Harry," she said. "That was beautiful." Somehow more drinks had arrived. They just seemed to be turning up of their own accord. Everyone had reached the next stage of drunkenness that feels like being fully sober.

Briefly Goose remembered the Christmas his father had forgotten, when Harry and Mrs. Lucas had saved the day with a whole readymade version in the back of their car. He thought of the beautiful tree and how he had lain beneath it with his belly so full of lunch he'd had to elongate his legs to make space for it. And from there, he thought of Mrs. Lucas again. How she'd bathed his nose and driven him to the coach station. Iris was right. This was the first day since Vic's death that seemed to hold some kind of hope and possibility for the future.

Already the sun was going down. Across the lake long ribbons of cloud floated above the western horizon, and the mountains rolled to meet it. A wash of pale pink seeped upward from the lower margin of the sky and rimmed the clouds with fire. Above them, the clear blue shaded to lavender.

Iris shoved back her chair and took to her feet. "*Amore!*" she called. "*Amore!*"

Goose clapped for silence because Harry was helping himself and Limoncello to the last of a bottle.

"*Amore!*" she said.

Finally you could hear the water lick the shore. You could hear the smallest ripple. For once, everything was stillness. Everything was about Iris. And her face was radiant with the thrill of it.

Her heart was beating like a hundred birds rising inside her, yet at the same time she felt calm. Incredibly calm. And tall, too, as tall as houses. She was tall. She might be the youngest, but she was the tallest Kemp sister. She was full of the future and the undefined rebellion that was about to happen.

"I am in love. I am in love. And the man I love, he loves me too. He's a good man. He's such a good man. I love everything about him. I love the way he speaks. I love the way he walks. He comes into the room and my world lights up. I know it might be a surprise, but I won't keep the secret anymore. I want you all to know. I want to tell you everything."

There was laughter, even applause. Iris saw Susan turn to Netta and smile, with a kind of intrigued wonder. "Well, well. Little Iris has a lover!" and Netta said, "Well, well, well."

Iris kept talking. Some of the words were coming out in a muddle because she was very drunk, and she was definitely repeating herself, but she didn't care: she felt like someone who's discovered karaoke for the first time and won't let go of the microphone. "I'm going to tell you the whole story. Right from the beginning. Because it started four years ago."

Netta laughed. "Four years ago! You dark horse!"

Iris was enjoying this more and more. She was even using theatrical gaps to build suspense. "He was walking me back to my flat one night and then he looked at me and I looked at him and, honest to God, it was like . . . it was like . . . it had been there all the time . . . this thing between us, except we couldn't *see* it. We tried to stop, but we couldn't. It was like it was bigger than us."

"Tell us more, Iris!" shouted Laszlo. Meanwhile Harry was on his feet again. He was swaying. He was talking about *il conto*.

"It's complicated . . . I know it's complicated. But life is complicated . . . You don't choose where you fall in love. It just happens . . . It's like chemistry. It's like when you put two things together and they go bang." She smacked her hands together and made fluttery movements with her fingers, like stardust falling. "And then what can you do? We tried to stop. We really did. We tried to avoid one another . . . we stopped calling. We stopped going to the same places. He even talked about going abroad for a while, just to try to get over me. But it's love. It's love. When you're in love, what can you do? It's a miracle, when you think about it."

She raised her glass to Susan, who blushed a little and laughed.

"We don't make plans. We can't. We know we can't be together, but that doesn't mean we're not in love. I love him, everyone. I love him. I love him. I even love his wife." Now she lifted her glass again, and this time it was to Harry.

All of a sudden, Susan was not laughing. She was standing and blinking at Iris as if she were indeed seeing her for the very first time and was appalled by what she'd found. She said, in a low voice, "Iris?" while Netta also rose to her feet, saying, "Iris? Hang on. What are you saying? Is Harry . . . is Harry your *lover*?"

At the other end of the table, Harry said, "Iris, please." He looked ill.

Netta put a hand to her mouth. "No," she said. "No."

"No," echoed Susan. "No, no, Iris. Not Harry. Not Harry, Iris. You're making this up."

"Four years?" Netta was saying. "You've kept this secret for four years? I mean, what the hell?"

There was a moment of suspense such as when a wave sucks back from the shore, rolling everything with it, before a fresh wave rolls up and peaks and crashes forward, bringing chaos. Iris glanced toward Bella-Mae, hoping for some kind of support, though Bella-Mae's smile had subtly changed as if only her face was keeping it in place. Her sisters were crowding in on her and Iris felt herself cower, but she wasn't going to back down. "You think you're the only ones who can fall in love? You think I'm still a baby?"

"But Harry's an uncle," said Netta, only she was beginning to shout. "He was making a speech about Daddy two minutes ago. They were best friends. They drank together. They did everything together. Fuck, Iris. What are you playing at?"

"Iris, please," said Harry again. "Let's all calm down. Let's stop this."

"You can't be sleeping with Harry, Iris. You can't do that. What about Shirley? She's his wife. I mean, what the fuck?"

All the conviction Iris had felt, all the joy, was spilling right out of her. It was for this reason she didn't see Susan until it was too late. Her sister's face was suddenly possessed, on fire with the most intense fury. She stepped closer to touch Iris's hair, and for the smallest moment Iris smiled, thinking Susan had come to her rescue, but then Susan slapped the side of her head so hard Iris felt the shock of it ram right through her jawbone. Her ears rang. "How dare you?" Susan cried. "How dare you?" The combination of the blow and all that alcohol sent Iris stumbling sideways, but this time she steadied herself on the table and didn't fall to the ground.

Netta turned on Harry and screamed at him to leave. She screamed at him to pack his bags and get out of her villa because he was the lowest piece of stinking shit and she never wanted to see him again.

"Your villa?" echoed Iris. She was holding her cheek. "When exactly did it become yours? It's just as much mine as yours. But this is how it goes with you two. You treat life as if it belongs to you, and all I get is the scraps."

From this point, it seemed to Goose that everything peripheral disappeared—the table, the waiters, even the lake—and all he could see was the three women he loved more than anyone. Somehow they'd moved so close they were almost gripping one another. Everything they said came in overlaps: he had never heard their voices sound so similar. At the same time, the distance between them was unfathomable. He could run around them in circles, bind them with rope, but they'd still tear free. There was nothing he could do to stop this.

"You always had to have more, Iris. You always had to have more than the rest of us."

"It started right back with the painting," said Susan.

"The painting? The painting had nothing to do with it. Daddy painted me because I was the only one who could keep still."

"How do you think it was for us? How do you think we felt, having to look at that painting of you every day?"

"Why has it always got to be about the painting?" yelled Iris. "I don't even like that painting."

"It was the same with the keys. Why were you the only one who had a spare set of keys to his flat?"

"Because I lived around the corner, Susan! You live in Tunbridge Wells!"

But Susan's fury had grown so mammoth it was spilling over the edges. Clearly, venting it on Iris was not enough. She turned on Netta. "This is your fault!"

Netta reeled, but quickly retaliated. "Mine? How is it mine?"

"If it wasn't for you, insisting on the autopsy, and sending everyone to look for the will and the painting, we'd all be home by now. But you went on and on and on. It was all you could think about. It's killing us. I swear it's killing us. It's all your fault. You forced us into this. But this is what you always do. You push and push and push, because everything has to be your way. You've ruined everything."

"My fault? How could this possibly be my fault? I'm not the one who's spent the summer chasing Elvis Presley. If it wasn't for me, the whole thing would have been a fiasco. You would have given everything away by now, because your mind is on one thing and one thing only, and it happens to be inside that man's trousers. You were unstoppable. You had to take over. Just like you took over Daddy's life. You practically smothered him. If it hadn't been for you, he might have grown into a proper old man, but you catered to his every whim so that he was no better than a child. I used to think Mummy was to blame, but of course it wasn't Mummy. It was you. Everything he ever asked for, you gave him, and why? Because you were so desperate to be his favorite."

By now they were screaming. Grievances and wounds that had always been unsayable, that were so painful it was best not even to think them, had found their voice, but alongside them were other things, a rivalry so primeval it was hard to tell if his sisters were being serious. It was Netta's fault Vic had turned his back on them. It was Susan's fault he had died. It was, God help them, Iris's fault they had lost their mother. If she hadn't been born, Martha would still be here now. They were tearing so many pieces off one another, they were down to skin and bone. Netta was groping for her bag, staggering as she tried to work out how to put on her hat. Iris was tugging at her arm, while Netta pushed her away and screamed that it was the end. Then Harry was saying, "Calm down now, girls, let's all calm down," which, as far as Netta was concerned, was like putting a match to a fuse. She called him every name under the sun.

Iris began to sob. "I'm sorry, Netta. I didn't mean to hurt you. I didn't kill Mummy. I didn't. I didn't."

Susan let out a great roar. "What about me? Why aren't you apologizing to me? Why is everything about Netta? It's just greed or something. She can't let me have anything. Ever since Daddy died it's been unbearable. Because in the end all she wants is the crown. She'll fight any of us to get her hands on it."

In the middle of this vortex of ancient hurt, a still and quiet center had been taking shape, one that Goose did not fully notice until, from the other end of the table, came a slow *clap, clap, clap*. Another voice spoke out, part English, part American. "Bravo," said Bella-Mae. "Bravo."

They turned to her. She didn't stand. She didn't honestly need to. All this time, she had watched and watched from behind her sunglasses. They had drunk wine as if it were water while she had drunk water as if it were wine.

She said, "You know why I loved Vic? Not because he was Daddy. Not because his paintings sold all over the world. I loved him because, even as an old man, he could change.

"All his adult life he'd painted those awful pictures of men and women. But when I met him, he didn't want to be that anymore. He wanted to live his own life and swim in the lake.

"So you want some truth? Is that what you're all looking for? Gloves off? Because the truth is staring you in the face. Your father was no saint. Your father was no artist. That was why he told me to burn his last painting."

The air seemed to go *clutter-clutter-clunk*, like a tower of Jenga bricks falling over. "Hang on now," Harry said slowly. "What did you just say?"

Once again, the light changed. The sun, about to sink, threw out one last bright flare over Bella-Mae, so that her red dress was a spill of fire. "I was trying to save you all. Fuck knows why. You're destroying each other anyway. But since this seems to be the end, yes. He made me his dealer before he died and, yes, there's a painting. Only here is the thing that none of you can face. That *New Yorker* journo was right."

23

The Last Painting of Vic Kemp

Here they were. Back at the villa in the music room with the ten harps that no one could play. Everyone queasy and reeling after so much food and even more wine, and twice the sun they should have had, yet atrophied. No one really able to stand for any length of time, but doing it anyway because chairs felt all wrong. Dusk at the opened windows. Beneath the chandeliers, dust motes, like specks of shattered glass. The painted trees on the walls, the colorful birds caught frozen mid-movement, the tension in the room so thick you could have stuck a spoon into it. The rain already forgotten.

Laszlo had gone back to the Hotel Navarro, where he had previously deposited a bin bag in the hotel safe—one of the two bags he had been carrying out that first day when Susan interrupted him, and only one of which contained clothes for Bella-Mae. He'd brought it back to the villa and here it was, placed in the middle of the floor, tied at the top.

The family stood before it in a broken semicircle, Iris close to Harry. He looked as heavy as a carcass, and just as butchered. His tie hung loose, his face was burned. She held her hands clenched like claws, angular inside her beautiful green dress, which had somehow gained a stain the shape of a small island. Susan stood alone, glancing at Laszlo, who watched no one but Bella-Mae. Netta, in her dark glasses, ground her teeth in the silence as if she were chewing tacks. But it was Goose, poor Goose, who reached for a chair and didn't sit. Instead he used it to lean on, like a cart he had pushed halfway up a hill.

He had been thinking about this painting ever since his father first mentioned it. When Bella-Mae first told them it didn't exist, he had mourned its loss like another death. He had talked about it with his sisters, and even though they'd each had different ideas as to what it might be, he'd visualized every single one of them as if he had painted them himself. There was the family portrait Susan had suggested—all four siblings sitting in this very room, staring at their father, and the nighttime picture of the lake that Iris believed in: lights from the hills spilling down in yellowing cones, the water richly colored with purples, blues and greens. Even the stars Goose had seen: starfish of lemon, pink, green and forget-me-not blue. And finally there was the nude portrait of Bella-Mae that Netta had talked about. He'd seen it in his mind's eye as she appeared the day she'd slipped free of his father's jacket, her naked body strongly muscled, almost boyish, her hair falling down her spine, like black treacle.

Still no one spoke. No one moved. All their attention was focused on that bin bag, as if it contained not just the painting, but their father himself.

"You're sure you guys want this?" Bella-Mae said. "Because we can stop it. We can say none of it happened."

Netta snapped, "Of course we want to see. It's our father's last painting. It's our right to see it."

"Then don't say I didn't warn you." Bella-Mae moved toward the bin bag in her heels, which went *pock-pock-pock* across the floor. She crouched and untied the top.

"Wait? The painting's in there?" said Harry.

She shrugged, as if she couldn't be bothered with a reply to him.

Finally she eased out the canvas they had been searching for all these weeks. It was frayed at the edges, loosely rolled and only about a foot at most in diameter. Susan said in a hoarse voice, "No. This can't be right. This can't be his last painting. It was a huge canvas." She was shaking.

"No. This is it. He tried to do a big canvas but he couldn't make it work. He felt too exposed. In the end he cut it up into pieces. This was the smallest. That's why he used this one."

Bella-Mae unrolled the canvas. In the silence Goose heard his heartbeat, his breathing, the gentle lap of the water outside. Despite the heat in the room, the air shivered.

She laid the painting flat on the floor so that they could see it. She rolled the bin bag into a ball and smoothed her dress as she stepped away, allowing the work to speak for itself.

And this was the moment, Goose would realize later, that finally and irrevocably split them apart. Like raising a glass snow globe above her head in which their whole lives were contained, their trust and love and self-respect, and letting it fall to the ground and smash into a thousand pieces.

Goose looked down at his father's last painting. He couldn't speak. He couldn't move.

Netta gave a sob. "Oh my God," she said. She retired to the edge of the room, where she put her hand over her mouth as she paced up and down on a fragment of the floor, as if someone had drawn a chalk line around her beyond which she must not stray and for once she was obeying the rules. She stole occasional glances at the picture, checking it hadn't turned into a masterpiece in the time she'd looked away. She began to make sharp little noises, mewling like a child.

"I don't believe it," said Susan quietly. After the row, she looked hollowed. She groped her hand toward Laszlo, but his arms stayed at his sides. He kept watching Bella-Mae, who sat on a chair, her thick hair almost covering her face, her eyes half closed, not so much watching the scene as seeing beyond it. Above it.

Iris took a few steps forward and stopped, her flip-flops almost touching the canvas. She stared down at it, as if it were a mangled animal she'd just found, her face that same blend of revulsion and pity. "Harry? It's terrible, isn't it?"

He turned to Bella-Mae. "Christ, are you sure about this? Are you really sure this is the painting?"

"Yes. This is his last one."

"What are those even supposed to be? Those ball-shaped things?"

"Apples."

"They're apples?" He shook his head in disbelief. "You mean this is a still life?"

"Yeah."

"A study of apples?"

"That's what Vic told me. I mean, I admit it's kind of hard to tell."

She wasn't lying. It was almost impossible to work out what this was. It was easier for Goose to say what it wasn't. And first off, it was not a nude study of Bella-Mae—not unless she was a line of bright green-and-red ball shapes. It wasn't a loving portrait of his children—not unless they were ball shapes too. It certainly wasn't a landscape: there was no purple-blue water, there were no beautiful stars. This was a still life in oil paints. A study of five things that could possibly be apples on a white cloth. Only when had apples ever looked like this? So irregular and inedible? Such awful colors? One was so big it appeared to be in a different room from the others. Another had something emerging from it, pink and green, that Goose realized, with a twist of revulsion, was a worm. And the background was no better. The cloth had been crudely painted in blocks of solid white with black lines as thick as a marker pen that suggested neither folds nor shadowing. The perspective was lopsided and amateurish, the angles wrong, the colors carelessly applied. Goose had no idea how to criticize his father's work. Neither had his sisters. It was a muscle they had never developed. So he stared and stared, convinced at first that the mistake must be his, that he must be looking at it wrongly, and desperate to find something that might still preserve his idea of his father as an artist. But you could squint, you could stand back, you could go up close like Iris, and there was nothing. No skill, no beauty, no vigorous energy of a true still life. There wasn't even his trademark porn slickness: without half-dressed people, everything that was weak about his work was exposed. Put simply, it was one terrible, terrible painting. At the bottom he'd signed his name with a flourish. *Vic Kemp*.

Goose knelt beside his father's last work and, staring at it, all he could say was "Oh. Oh. Oh." Cold played over his skin like a fever. It was like jumping into the lake and discovering that his father had been lying all along about how deep it was. And then it wasn't like that at all. It was like sinking into the current and being thrown downward head-first.

Because this was not simply a bad still life study. That was something Goose could maybe have come to terms with, once he'd got over the shock. He might even have found a way of explaining it, given enough time. Taken the blame. But this was an exact replica of one of the ten pictures Goose had destroyed when he was twenty-four. His father had even copied Goose's arrangement of fruit: the only real difference was that Vic had done his picture with oil paint. Goose had tried to play with perspective by moving it up and down and left and right so that you appeared to be looking at the apples from simultaneously different viewpoints. For some reason (why?), Vic must have remembered this technique and tried it for himself, but it had not worked for him either. If anything, it was more disastrous. The fruit had become entirely flat. Goose had selected yellows, greens and reds to suggest the youngest apples and their full volume, with russet, oranges and deep greens for those that were older. Vic had done the same, but his colors were thickly applied, one jutting against the other in a way that only exaggerated how unrealistic the choice was. To capture the way light hit the fruit, Goose had made pinpoints and slashes of pale blue, and Vic had copied those, too, but his were ugly splodges landing on the apples like something shat out of an unforgiving sky.

You could call Vic many things. An alcoholic, a womanizer, a cheat. But you couldn't call him an artist. The real wonder was why he hadn't wiped the canvas clean with turps. The work of art that Goose and his sisters had been focused on for all these weeks and months had only ever been beautiful in their imaginations. What Vic had left them to remember him by was a bad copy of his son's destroyed work. What could hold them together now? Nothing. They were looking from one to the other. All those torn-out feelings hanging naked between them. Everything was over.

"That's it," said Netta quietly. "I give up. I don't care about the will. I don't care about the autopsy. I have no idea how to live with this." Without another word, she left. They heard her flip-flops, slow and heavy, all the way up the stairs. It was the only sound in the whole villa. The sound of a woman losing herself, step by step.

Iris put her hands to her mouth and began to sob, but no one went to her. Susan clutched her arms around her own shoulders, as if she wished they were another person.

Goose pressed his head against his hand. He felt spent. Whatever fuel had been keeping them all going until now had finally burned out. Without melodrama, without actual violence of any kind, he wished to be dead; he wished for everything to be gone away. But at the same time he thought this, he knew it wasn't true. He would keep bearing this, because in the end he always did.

Netta was the first to leave. She packed in a panic, throwing what she could find into her bag, but leaving most of it behind. She didn't take her hat. She walked away from the villa without saying goodbye, too stupefied to find her way back to her old life, barely able to see. With the painting, everything she'd been fighting for had fallen away, including the will. Her father, in whom she had believed more than anyone, had proved himself to be no more than a sham, a hoax. If his life amounted to nothing, then so did hers. And while she didn't give a flying fuck about her lost inheritance, what crucified her was that he had not given his children's future a second thought before he died. He had let them go. She called Robert from the passenger boat and, as soon as she heard his voice, all those fighting words she had built her life on abandoned her and she could only make little-girl sobbing noises. "What happened?" he said. "Can you get to the airport?"

She went, "Hn hn hn."

"I'll organize you a ticket for the plane. I'll be there to meet you when you land. All you have to do is get to the airport, Netta."

"Hn hn hn," she said.

She cried about Vic. She cried about Philip Hanrahan and her mother. She cried because a rupture of continental proportions had taken place and she would never see her siblings again. She cried because what had happened to her parents and the man she had once married would happen to her, too: There was no longer anyone between her and the void. And it could come at any time, the end. It could be only five minutes around the corner. Literally at the end of the jetty. She had thought the pain of losing Vic would demolish her, but this was in another league.

At Milan airport, she got to the toilets in time to be violently sick; as a result, it was the first dry flight she'd taken since she was twelve. And even though it was unbearable sometimes and the headaches were excruciating, not to mention the shakes and the drinking dreams, she never touched the stuff again. She went to rehab, attended an addiction clinic, then AA. She almost fell off the wagon several times: any mention of her sisters, or that summer, and she still felt the old instinct, as strong as internal wiring, to slip free of her head and drink, drink, drink. But Robert stuck by her side and she didn't. She never made it to full-blown therapy. ("One step too far," she told him. "How am I supposed to trust someone who never shouts at me?") But she did sign up for online Pilates. ("You win some, lose some," said Robert.)

While Netta began her journey home, Susan was upstairs with Laszlo in his room at the villa. He was holding her shoulders as if she were a toy that couldn't balance by itself, and telling her in his most understanding voice that it was not her, it was him. She was a good person, a sexy woman, she was the most fun he'd ever had, but he had a problem. He had a problem with commitment. He couldn't help it. His mother had never loved him and now he didn't know who to trust. It was better for her if he left now and she went back to her husband. She would get over Laszlo in no time. Probably tomorrow, he said.

And Susan said, "When people say it's me, not you, they generally mean it's you, not them." She felt the tears fill her eyes, like two fishbowls. "And I will not feel better tomorrow. Trust me. This is going to make everything worse." She wanted to add that she'd completely had it with parents who failed their children, but she sensed that wouldn't help.

"You really are such fun, Susan. If I am with any lady it is you."

She struggled a little with his use of tenses, but understood he was still saying goodbye. Her phone began to ring—it was lying on his bed beside his suitcase—and they both saw Warwick's name. "Shouldn't you get that?" he said.

"Are you joking?" she said.

After seeing her father's painting, Susan had gone alone to the end of the garden, convinced Laszlo would come to find her. She had waited and waited in the dark, and the longer she waited, the closer she felt to madness. She'd looked at the tiny lights across the water and briefly wondered why all the stars had dropped out of the sky. Then she'd noticed Laszlo at the window of his room and rushed upstairs. She had never wanted to be subsumed by another person as much as she wanted it at that moment.

His shirts were thrown on the bed. He'd already emptied the drawers. She had a sense that half of him was already in his suitcase, but the other half was still available, floating freely, and if only she could find the right thing to say she could bring him back to her. But after the consumption of such an extraordinary amount of wine, and the cataclysmic explosion that had just happened within her family, stopping Laszlo was like trying to pick up jelly with your bare hands. Everything kept sliding away.

"Susan," he said. He moved free of her so that he could continue to pack. "We both know this is not forever. It is like beautiful accident that happens in beautiful place. It happens because you are sad and because of magic of Orta. But from beginning, we know this has to end."

"No," she said. "It wasn't because I was sad. And, anyway, it isn't the end of the summer! There is plenty of summer still to go!" She had grabbed for her sunny voice but couldn't keep up the exclamation marks for much longer. It was beginning to dawn on her that everything she had borne that day, and indeed the whole summer, had been possible only because of Laszlo. From the beginning, she had pinned her sanity on him. If he went, she would have to face the loss of her father, the falling apart of her life in general, and was terrified she hadn't the strength. "I know this is casual! I want casual! The last thing I need is commitment! But that doesn't mean we have to stop now. We could go somewhere else. Away from my family. Away from all this craziness. We could go to Paris! We could take a suite in a hotel. No strings attached! I tell you what. Why don't we just stop this conversation right now? Why don't we take the boat to Orta? Get an overnight train . . ."

He looked baffled by the speed at which she was going, but not beaten into submission. "You think it is a good idea to go back to Orta? After the row you make with your sisters? Didn't you drink enough already?" He snatched up the last shirt and folded it badly.

"Where will you go?" she said.

"I have friends."

"What friends?"

"My friends have boat."

"What boat?"

"In Greece. They sail between islands. They ask me to go with them."

Then Susan had a brilliant idea. "I could come to Greece! I've never been to Greece! And I love islands. You know how much I love islands. You could teach me all about them."

"No, Susan. This cannot be. I leave, Susan. I leave right now."

"No," she said. "No." She picked up her phone—she didn't know why, it was something to do with her hands—and magically it began to ring. It was Warwick yet again. She threw it down. "No, Laszlo. Don't be like this. Don't go tonight. Go tomorrow, if you have to. Tomorrow I will be fine. But don't do this to me, Laszlo. Don't do this. You can't go now. Stay one more night. I can't be alone."

Suddenly the room was stripped of him, and he was closing the suitcase. Panic swam through her. She must do something. She must make him stop. All she knew was that she was being abandoned by someone who ought to love her. She sprang on him, just as she had fallen on him the very first time they met, only this time she clung to his arm—the same arm that had gripped her so hard—as she pushed him roughly from the door. "No," she shouted. "No. You will not leave me. No. I love you. No."

He looked at her hanging on to his arm and his mouth froze in a kind of disgust. "Don't do this to yourself," he said.

Appalled, ashamed (*I am not this woman*), she let him go. He picked up his suitcase, pausing, she noticed, to check his reflection in the mirror before he left. She seemed to be crying, yet she had no tears. She remained very still as she heard his feet running down the stairs, two at a time. Stop him, she thought. Stop him or your life will be over. But she didn't move. She heard Goose calling, "Laszlo? Are you leaving?" No reply apart from the heavy clunk of the front door.

She turned off the lamps and sat on his bed. She peeled her turquoise dress as far as her midriff and gave up. She unhooked her bra, let her breasts hang free. Then she lay down and curled onto her side. The room was wheeling. She remembered Netta saying once, "Stick your foot out of bed onto the floor, if you're drunk," and then she remembered her singing her entire Donna Summer medley, and, to her surprise and despite all her anger with her sister, it was thinking of this that finally made Susan sob. Her phone began to ring and she scrambled to find it, but it wasn't Laszlo. It was Warwick.

"There you are. I've been so worried. Robert called. He told me about a terrible argument and the painting. What happened, Susan?"

"Warwick, it's been a long day." She was still on her side with the phone to her ear. A weight seemed to lie inside her, like a thick fire blanket, flattening everything, taking all the life out of it.

"Can we talk? I know it's late. I understand you want to rest but I just need to talk to you, Susan." She listened and didn't seem to feel anything. "I know how terrible it's been since your father died. I know I should have done more to support you. I know that our marriage hasn't always . . ." he hesitated, trying to say it ". . . hasn't always been easy."

"Warwick," she said, in a blank voice, almost asleep, "it's over."

There was a silence, during which nothing but the word "over" seemed to exist in the world.

"Over?" he said at last. "Susan? What do you mean?"

"I've been having an affair with Laszlo. You should hate me. I'm leaving you, Warwick. I'm sorry."

That night he did his best to talk her around. It was more than he'd said in years. He apologized for the twins, her miscarriages, the way he'd been since his retirement. She could only keep listening without interjection of any kind, as if her life was a film that had already been made and she was now watching on a cinema screen. It wasn't even a very good film, she thought. It was just a life.

He said, "I remember you with your siblings when you were young. I remember the noise that would come from your house. And when you and I began to see each other, I asked myself how I could give you that happiness. That big bursting life. Have I done that? I don't think I have. So when it comes to forgiveness, it is me who should be asking it of you." His voice broke. "Susan, I am sorry."

It dawned on her that she had got up that morning with no clue that everything was about to arrive at a crisis, just as she'd gone into the shoe shop to buy sandals unaware her father was dead. How could you be such a stranger to your own story? Iris's betrayal might have felt like losing their childhood, but Vic's last painting had stolen far more. Moonlight cast strange shapes on the walls that made the room seem tipped at an angle.

"What do we do now, Susan?"

"I don't know. I guess we stop."

There. It was done. And look how easy it was. To pull apart everything about your life, to cast out the people you loved. Easier than fighting to keep them—all that compromise, all that bargaining. She was so tired and drunk and ransacked. Best to let it go. Her marriage, her sisters, her father. Her old life. Don't even look at them, just put them out with the rubbish. Years later, she would understand how much it must have taken that night for Warwick to be so generous, to let her walk away and leave him behind. He loved her more than anyone. He always would. But it was the thing he had said about her siblings that hurt the longest: *That big bursting life.* All gone.

Goose was clearing the kitchen when he heard the stray cat outside. It was probably waiting for Iris, but she and Harry were locked in an intense whispered conversation in the music room. He took milk out to the terrazzo, but there was no sign of the cat. There was only the intoxicating stillness of the night air, and then he realized the noise he'd heard was coming from Laszlo's window. He went upstairs and knocked. Susan's voice sobbed, "Goose? Is that you?"

He put a blanket over her and sat on the edge of the bed.

"I'm a mess," she cried.

"We all are," he said.

"You know what I always wanted?"

"What, Susan?"

"For Daddy to paint me. I just wanted to know how he saw me. I thought my whole life would make sense if he painted me, and I would finally know who I was."

He fetched a cold flannel—her makeup was like streaky war paint—and as he did, he found himself thinking of Shirley, the night she bathed his nose. She must have known all along about Iris and Harry. Maybe that was why she'd cut her hair so blunt and ugly.

Oh, Mrs. Lucas, he thought.

"Will you hold me until I'm asleep?" said Susan.

He sat with her for the whole night, cradling her head in his lap, first as she cried and then gave in to groans that finally softened until they became unconsciousness. In the strangest way, it felt like holding everything together for the last time. Keeping it all safe for one more night in his hands that had always been too big. But first thing in the morning, Susan got up and showered. He went to the kitchen to make strong coffee, thinking she might have changed her mind about leaving, but fifteen minutes later, she came downstairs with her wheelie suitcase. For once she hadn't used her straighteners. She'd allowed her hair to fall thickly toward her shoulders and she was wearing a smart skirt and blouse. There was something stripped-back about her expression that he'd never seen before. "I'm going now."

"Where, Suz?"

"Paris. Don't ask me why. But I always wanted to, so it's where I'm going. I fucked up two relationships last night. My marriage and my only fling."

"Well, that must be some kind of record."

Briefly she smiled. "Tell me, Goose. Am I a joke?"

"A joke? No, Susan."

"I feel like my whole life's been some kind of pantomime." She paused as if she had more to say about her life, but didn't. He guessed she hadn't worked it out yet. "Well, this is it, then. You don't have to come and wave me off. We can say goodbye here."

But he did. Of course he did.

Iris found a dead bird at the bottom of the garden. She dug a hole in the ground with her fingernails and made a grave that she filled afterward with grass and earth.

Once again, she hadn't slept. She'd heard Laszlo leave the villa the night before, and later she'd heard Susan sobbing in her room. She lay beside Harry and he repeated the things he had told her in the music room. He would leave his wife. He would make everything good, she needn't worry. He would always look after her. Then she heard him sleeping heavily at her shoulder. Strange that now she had the very thing she'd been hoping for, she saw she'd never really wanted it.

Strange, too, how the only thing she now wanted was the very thing she'd decided to be free of.

Being a sister was her habit. Her way of life. It was going to take a long time to disentangle herself from it. She brushed the dirt off her knees and went to make a start.

24

The Father

Goose waved to Susan as she boarded the passenger boat and he watched the whole time it crossed the water. He even waited for it to return, wondering if she might have changed her mind. Maybe she would get as far as the car, or maybe she would get to the Italian border or even to Paris, then see her mistake and rush back. Except he knew she wouldn't.

When he returned to the villa, Harry was waiting for him. There was no sign of Iris or Bella-Mae: the house was very still and quiet. Already Goose could feel the new gaping lack of Susan and Netta, just as he'd felt the absence of Vic when he'd first arrived. It isn't only the dead who leave ghosts behind them.

Harry was dressed for traveling in a lightweight suit and straw hat, without looking convincingly like anyone who had ever traveled much farther than Watford. Goose knew he looked a sight—he'd barely slept, and he had one hell of a hangover, they all did—but Harry seemed worse. His eyes were bloodshot, his face so burned the skin had done something strange and looked set. He said, "I'm waiting for Iris to pack." He took off his hat, nervous, then cleared his throat several times. "But before I leave, son, there's one thing I need to say. Will you hear me out?"

"If you want. Though, quite frankly, I wish I could kill you. It's what my father would have done. So if you don't mind, I'd rather you didn't call me 'son' anymore."

Harry kept his head bowed, looking down at his shoes. It struck Goose that this was the first time he'd seen a pair of lace-ups in weeks. They were so polished they looked straight from the box. Harry still wasn't saying anything, though, so in the end Goose did the decent thing. He put him out of his misery.

"I'm guessing you want to talk about my father's last painting. I'm guessing you want to know if I knew. Well, I didn't. I had no idea what he was going to paint. All he ever said was that it would be a masterpiece. So there we go. The joke was on me."

Harry shook his head. "It's not Vic's art I want to talk about. It's something else entirely. And I don't have much time. So I am going to say it to you straight."

"If this is about Iris, Harry, I don't want to know."

"What has happened between me and Iris is tremendously complicated. But this is about you, Goose. Why did you do it? Why did you destroy your paintings when you were twenty-four? I understand you'd like to kill me, but I've honestly never seen you swat a fly. So why the hell would you do that to your own art?"

Goose froze. He felt unsteady, as if he were ill. The answer was so obvious it was humiliating, especially after everything else they'd been through. "Because my paintings were terrible, Harry."

"But why did you think that, Goose? I understand you and your sisters will never trust me again . . . But on this one thing you have to believe me. I knew almost nothing about art when I started off all those years ago, flogging your father's paintings on a market stall. But those paintings you did for that exhibition? It was the same as the first time I saw Van Gogh's *Sunflowers*. Or even the fucking *Mona Lisa*. It was like I didn't know art could do that until I saw those pictures."

"Stop it, Harry. I don't know why you're dragging this up."

"What happened to you that day at the gallery? You were nervous, yes, practically crapping yourself. But you were excited. Then Vic arrived and I went down to fetch champagne. Fifteen minutes later, we saw smoke in the backyard. What went on in the time I was downstairs?"

Goose shook his head. The air felt too close. He backed away. Hit the corner of the big table with his thigh.

"Vic knew those paintings were something. I could see from the way he stared at them, as if he couldn't understand how you'd applied the paint. 'They're special,' I said to him. 'Aren't they? My God, you must be proud.' He looked at me like he was terrified. I could see it in his eyes. He was so jealous he didn't know what to do with it. But I would have broken free of your father and shown your paintings and sold up my house, if I had to. I like to believe I would have done that. But you never gave me a chance, because you destroyed them. Vic and I never mentioned your pictures again, and he made me a rich man."

Goose wanted a smoke. More than anything, he needed that emptying feeling, like being smudged inch by inch from the inside out. Like lying in bed for hours on end because you're so high you don't know any more what's day and what's night.

"And in the end, look what he did. His last painting, his great masterpiece? He copied you. And you want to know why? Because you're the artist, Goose. All those years he kept you working for him, I believe he was frightened. I know it's wrong to speak ill of the dead and I know he was your father, but you've got to hear this. Vic wanted to be sure you wouldn't paint again. Do you have any idea how wrong that is?"

Goose didn't answer: Susan had suddenly appeared at the top of the stairs. His heart soared. She was back. Or maybe she hadn't really gone. Netta had been the leader from as early as he could remember, but Susan had been the glue that stuck them together. Then he realized his mistake. It was Iris. She had washed her hair and the wetness had made it dark. "Harry, I'm ready to go now," she said.

Harry nodded and took one last look at Goose. The desperation in his eyes was clear. "Just tell me one thing. Was Bella-Mae telling the truth about me as well? Did Vic really make her his dealer?"

It was Goose's moment. His last chance to try to hold everything together and somehow make good the little that was left. But he couldn't do it. It wasn't in him to keep lying. "That's what he told me."

Harry stumbled as if punched. He put his hand to his heart. Then he moved away, passing Iris as he climbed the stairs.

She came down slowly, one step at a time. She wouldn't catch her brother's eye. "Do you hate me?"

"No, Iris. I could never hate you. You're my sister. But Mrs. Lucas?"

"He said they weren't happy." She bit her lip, shifted her weight angrily from one flip-flop to the other. "Anyway. We won't last. Him and me, I mean. He'll go back to his wife. He always does."

"Oh, Iris." He wanted to hug her, but, from the way she stood, all knotted and bony, it was clear she couldn't.

"I'll write to you," she said. "If you like. I know my writing's crap."

"I love your messages."

"Sell the villa. I don't care anymore. I don't want to set foot here ever again—"

"Iris?" he said, interrupting her. "We could follow Netta and Susan. We could go right now. It's not too late."

She flashed him a look that silenced him. And there was a hardness in her voice that reminded him of something inflexible, like a rod of iron: "You think I'm going to beg them for forgiveness? Go on my knees like a child? No, Goose. You're wrong. It's way too late."

So now it was only him and Bella-Mae left at Villa Carlotta, but he couldn't face her, and he guessed she felt the same, because he hadn't seen her since she'd revealed the painting. He opened a beer from the fridge and took it into the garden, but after all that drinking the day before, it made him feel sick and he ended up pouring it away. In the kitchen he washed some dirty plates and dried them, just in case Susan came back, but then he remembered again that, of course, she was never coming back. He went up to the room Iris had been sleeping in. She'd stripped the bed and emptied the cupboards, leaving the doors and drawers wide open, so that the place looked ransacked. "Oh, Iris," he said. "Oh, Iris." Then he went to Netta's room, followed by Susan's. Some of Netta's clothes were left on the floor, and there were empty bottles, but Susan's bed was made and the curtains at the window partly closed, as if she had got it ready for the next person. In their different ways, each of his sisters had left her old self behind.

Goose went back to the garden and lay beside the lake. Here it comes, he thought, here comes the bad stuff, and he wondered if it had been the same for his mother as she lay dying, or his father as he stepped into the water, or Philip Hanrahan in hospital: that sense of an ending. For the first time since his breakdown, Goose felt the depression crawling through his body, inch by inch, taking it over, like a rash on the inside of his skin, closing all the goodness down. Already he was beginning to shake, but this time he made himself stay, waiting for the memory to come, in the same way he had waited in the silence all those years ago with the therapist. Knowing that something monstrous was lurking out there, which he didn't want to see.

"Tell me about it," Susan used to say, after his breakdown, when he was living with her and Warwick. "Explain this so that I can understand. What happened to you in the gallery? Did Daddy say something?"

"Let me get this straight," Philip Hanrahan had said to him, that time in Scarborough. "You never paint? You work in your father's studio, yet you never paint? How does that work for you?" Goose knew he had seen right through him, and maybe that was the reason he had fallen in love.

Curled up now on the grass, he saw himself at the exhibition of his watercolor paintings that night in the gallery when he was twenty-four. As if the narrative he had been telling himself for twelve years had been drawn back, like a curtain, so that he could see what was really there. He saw himself taking each one, unwrapping it carefully, holding it out to Harry, his hands so sweaty and trembling Harry couldn't take it fast enough. Those ten watercolors, all the same size, square in shape, the differences between them lying in the subtle play of light and perspective, the aging of the fruit, the delicate shifts in color. He saw the excitement on Harry's face, the way he moved from one picture to another, jigging backward and forward on the balls of his feet. "They're even better than I thought," Harry was saying. "They're bold. Fuck, they're bold. It's not just the way you've captured the detail. Or the light. Or even the way you've played with perspective. Anyone with talent could do that. It's like for the first time—does this sound crazy?—I know what an apple is. Like they are the most beautiful thing in the world and I never saw it before." He laughed. "I have no idea what you're on, but I can tell you one thing. Your old man is going to be proud."

It was like hearing something Goose had been listening for throughout his life. Like hearing the one sentence that makes sense of everything you've ever thought, or tried to do. Imagine if someone painted your portrait, then showed it to you and you realized, Oh, I see. That's who I am. That's *me*, just as Susan had always wanted. That was how it felt to Goose when Harry spoke about his paintings. As if everything about his twenty-four years of living had become a series of dotted lines that joined up to arrive miraculously at that moment. Then the door to the gallery was opening and there at last was his father.

"What have we here?" he was saying, voice booming. "What have we here?"

Already Harry was clapping Vic on the shoulder and laughing. "This is a big night!" Then he was talking about champagne, and singing as he went down to the basement to open bottles.

Goose waited as his father took up a position in the center of the gallery. He was drunk. Goose could smell it from where he stood. Vic remained in the center, lurching from one painting to the next, saying nothing except a slow "Yup. Yup. Yup," more to himself than anyone else. It went on and on. Goose's heart thudded in his chest, a lonely radar. At last a noise came from Vic that sounded like a sob.

"Daddy?"

It wasn't a sob. It was laughter. Vic made an effort to stop, pulled a straight face, then took another look at the paintings and began howling. "Well, kid, it's a nice effort. But no one paints just apples. Watercolor is for cowards. I mean, this isn't art. It's a fucking fruit salad!"

Panic. A panic like no other. Like falling down a chute with nothing to stop him. How could Goose have got this so wrong? His pictures were a joke. He was a joke. He needed them to go away. He needed them not to exist in the first place. But how could that happen when they were hanging on the walls of a gallery for everyone to see? He thought the shame would kill him. He wanted it all to go away. He wanted a world in which he had never seen an apple or picked up a paintbrush.

He said to his father, "It's only a little show, right? No one will come."

Vic laughed. "Are you kidding? The press have been invited. This is a shit-hot private gallery."

"I don't know what to do. Please. What can I do?"

His father patted his shoulder. Staggered again. "Leave it with me. I'll make a few calls. Pull some strings. You wait here. Just don't do anything stupid while I'm gone." Then he went to find Harry in the basement, leaving in such a rush he forgot to take his lighter fuel and matches.

But being alone with the paintings was even worse. Goose experienced this overwhelming sense of injustice, of having been deceived. He was angry with himself for daring to be an artist, but most of all he was angry with those terrible still life watercolors for allowing him to think they could be anything beyond a farce. He was taking the matches and the lighter fuel. He was pulling the pictures down, almost wrenching them off the walls, dragging them down the fire escape before Vic or Harry could come out and stop him. He kicked his foot through one, smashed the glass on another. He had never hated anything the way he hated those paintings. Then he doused them with the lighter fuel and watched them catch light. By the time Harry found him, it was too late. The damage was done.

He threw out his art materials. He handed in his notice at the theatre. He had crossed an invisible line that had always separated him from despair, though in fact he didn't know the line was there until he stepped over it. He spent the next few weeks in bed. When his sisters rang, he told them he had flu. And when one of his flatmates knocked on the door and said, "Listen, I know times are hard, but do you think you could ask your old man for some rent?" Goose packed his few things and left. He walked and walked and walked. In the end he was staggering along the A40 until the police stopped him: Nowadays he wouldn't have been sectioned, but because he was shouting about how he had to be punished they drove him straight to an acute psychiatric hospital. At night he was kept awake by shouts and sobs. One morning he woke, gasping for breath, and found another patient had him by the throat. As soon as they were allowed, his sisters came to fetch him.

That year, he would walk when he felt up to it. If he was at Susan's, he went out of Tunbridge Wells until he reached the hills, and if he was at Netta's he set off from the British Museum and kept going until he reached the river. He was living in a world of hurt.

Then the visions—the ones of strange flowering fruits and seed heads that had started coming to him after his mother died—started up again, but in earnest. In the end, he decided the only way to avoid dreaming was to avoid sleep altogether. He took cocktails of uppers that rushed through his body at a hundred miles an hour, but those would be followed by downers in which he lost days at a time. He heard the world going on outside his room, he heard his sisters doing their best to get along with their lives—talking to one another on the phone—and had no idea how they did that. It was only when Vic turned up at Susan's one Sunday for lunch and said, "Okay. Enough of this shit. You need to snap out of it," that he agreed to go and live in his father's studio until he was fit to find another job. And the rest, as they say, is history.

Could a father really do that to his son? Had Goose's paintings caused Vic such conflict that the only thing he could do was destroy him? The idea was too atrocious and terrifying. It was too much for Goose to hold in his head. That he, the son who amounted to so little, could also have been the cause of such a wrong thing. That he could be this powerful, and yet not powerful at all. Nothing was what he thought it was. He needed weed. Except he had thrown it into the lake, fooling himself that he was free of it.

The water was a shock of cold. Briefly the dark closed over his head. So this is what it's like, he thought. To drown. But his body was already fighting to save him, his arms clawing the water, his feet kicking upward. He swam so hard the effort tore at his gut. Then he flipped onto his back and floated, his heart hammering inside his chest. The sky was a pure delft blue. A train cut its way through the distant hills. The moon was still up there, pale and see-through, like the gummy leftover of a sticker. He looked at the painted palazzi and Swiss chalets across the hills, the island in front of him, the different shapes of loggias and balconies, the gray monastery at its center.

How could he still love this beautiful place when it had brought him so much pain? And yet he did. He swam back to the garden, then walked up toward the villa to make a list for the day, just like Susan would.

Goose and Bella-Mae stayed on at the villa for almost a full week, though he never saw her. By some tacit agreement, they seemed to have agreed to coexist, while also leaving each other alone. He guessed her pills from the doctor had run out and she was back to not sleeping at night because he often came down in the morning and found something like a chair pushed away, when he was sure he had left it out before he went to bed, or the draining board empty even though he had stacked the washing-up there last thing. He even thought he heard her once or twice in his sleep, moving things around up in the garret. For a few days he felt too unwell to do very much at all, beyond trying to call his sisters, buying the day's food in Orta, and continuing to work on the villa. Then, one morning, he found a leaf she must have left on the kitchen table. It was a beautiful thing, incredibly delicate, all the green removed, so that he sat for a long time studying the intricate lacework of venules reaching out from the midrib, finding himself trying to work out how you could capture such a thing and make sense of it, until he realized that what he was thinking about was basically called art.

He left her a glass of freshly squeezed lemonade before he went to bed, and in the morning the glass was dry and empty on the draining board, but there was a thistle head on the table. That night he made two portions of salad and left one out for her. In the morning the bowl was dry and clean, and on the table he found one apple.

It wasn't exactly the first time he'd seen an apple in twelve years. But it was the first time he'd allowed himself to sit and really look at one again. He stared at the waxy green of the skin, the plump dimple around the stem, he smelled the rosy sweetness of it. And in his mind's eye, he reached for a pencil, trying to discover the exact shape it made in the world.

"Of course there's yellow in it," he said to himself. "But you would need blue. Why did I not see that before? And those little pimples? You'd need to find a way to suggest them, like inverted pinpricks."

Then he turned round and there she was. Same as always, watching from the door. He had no idea how long she'd been there.

"Talking to fresh fruit?" she said. "That's the first sign of madness."

He laughed. It occurred to him that he'd missed her.

Her hair was tied back loosely from her face and she was wearing the old bathrobe she'd had on the first day they'd met, with *Hotel Navarro* sewn just beneath the neckline. There were black smudges on her hands that looked like charcoal. She had another bin bag.

"How have you been, Bella-Mae?"

"So-so. I'm not sleeping very well, but I guess you figured that out. Have you heard from your sisters?"

"No."

She shrugged, as if to say she'd expected as much. She lifted the bag onto the table and began unpacking rubbish that she took to the bin. An empty Tampax box, some loose hair, a water bottle. She could have been an old woman on the street, foraging through bins.

He said, "I guess you think we're pretty insane."

"You're a family. They're all insane. But at least you have one."

"I'm not sure. You saw what happened. I don't think it's looking very good for us now."

"Yeah, well. Your father was the linchpin. When you lose something like that, it's bound to fall apart."

She went to the sink in her bare feet and poured a glass of water that she drank in one go, wiping her mouth afterward with the back of her hand. "What are you going to do?" she said.

"I'll stay here. Until everything is sorted. If that's okay with you?" She nodded. "Then I guess I'll go back to London. What about you?"

"I'm going to the police."

"With new evidence?"

She gave a full-throated laugh. "Seriously, Goose? What new evidence do you think I've got? You still think I killed Vic? Why would I do that? Because he was a shit artist? Because he plagiarized your work? I'm going to the police so that they know where I am when the results of the autopsy come through." She walked out, taking her empty bin bag with her. "I'm off to pack," she said over her shoulder.

Goose was sanding the French windows when she came back. She had changed into the black suit, the one she'd worn the day she came to the villa to announce she was moving back. On her feet was an old pair of flip-flops.

"Susan left them," she said. She laid something flat on the table and told him to join her.

It was Vic's painting. If anything, it was even worse now that Goose was looking at it in the light of day and without his sisters. The crude shapes and colors, the botched play of light. In silence, she went to a drawer and pulled out a box of matches, a tin of lighter fuel. She placed them next to the painting.

"He asked me to destroy it and I said I would, but I never did. It's yours now, Goose. As his dealer, I'm giving it back to you. Whatever you choose to do, I won't ask questions. No one will."

She moved toward him and, to his surprise, she hugged him hard, as if she somehow wanted to get right inside him and embrace whatever was at the heart of him. There it was again. The sharp smell of sweat blended with something else that was very sweet. As she moved away, he noticed the threadbare cuff of her sleeve. Either the suit was old or it was another thing she had picked up that had once belonged to someone else. "The fact is," she said, "we're all born. We're all going to die. So the only interesting question is what we choose to do with the middle."

It turned out to be the last thing she told him. When he went upstairs to find her later, she'd already cleared out her things and left. He hadn't even heard the front door. And she was the one, he thought, who seemed fully absent when she had gone. Not like his sisters, not like his father, all of whom Goose could still see obliquely from the corner of his eye, coming out of a room, or marching up and down on the terrazzo, and whom he would continue to see, if he just allowed himself to believe it, for years and years, like a rustling on the edge of things. Bella-Mae was the one who could extricate all trace of herself as if she had never been there in the first place. As if you had imagined her, or created an image on something that was blank. Her lawyer contacted him about the sale of the villa and informed him that Bella-Mae had no interest in keeping anything from the villa. What the siblings did not want should be sold, and the money split five ways. He gave a contact address in Palermo.

Goose didn't set fire to his father's canvas that day. He could have. The means were there, and also the incentive. He had struck the first match and the flame danced, hungry for the brushstrokes. It might have brought closure to something that had started the night his father took art away from him. An eye for an eye. But Goose had never been like that. Harry was right. The only person he had ever ventured to hurt was himself. Instead he took the canvas out to the garden, as if he were carrying a sick dog. He laid it on the grass and took a tin of exterior emulsion and a thick paintbrush. He covered it, inch by inch, in a layer of opaque yellow. He wasn't blocking the past. He wasn't even taking it away because there was nothing left to take anymore. He painted over the crude colors of the apples, their botched shapes, the splodges of light, the ugliness of the tablecloth. All that envy, thwarted ambition and failure. He laid it all to rest. When it was dry, he rolled it up and slipped it into a bag, ready for when he left. Never mind all Susan's stickers. In the end, it was the only thing of his father's he would take.

25

A Sense of an Ending

The days flowed one into another. Goose stayed on at Villa Carlotta to wait for the results of the autopsy and organize the sale of the house. After the chaotic energy of the summer, it was a strangely blank, empty time. He closed up his sisters' rooms and his father's, though he found a number of things Bella-Mae must have been collecting in a corner of the garret—strange things, like old envelopes, a saucepan lid, empty wine bottles, a few broken paintbrushes, stray buttons, as well as some large-scale sketches of different parts of the female body that he saw were his sisters. Susan's fleshy shoulder. The curl of Iris's bare spine, like a string of pearls. Netta's dark eye before her first few drinks, alert and unblinking. With very little detail, and subtle flicks of the chalk, she had caught them exactly. He boxed them up because they were beautiful (if only Susan could have seen those drawings), but Bella-Mae never sent for them.

He picked the last of the lemons in the glasshouse and gave away his father's clothes. He continued repainting the outside walls and did his best to keep on top of the garden. He arranged for the things his sisters had chosen to be delivered to their home addresses, including the huge mirror and two harps for Iris, all those glasses and the kitchenware for Susan, though as far as he knew both were still abroad. He chose a small carved bookshelf for Netta, so that she would have at least one thing, and he gave the only vaguely modern item in the villa to Francesca as a thank-you. (A cut-glass vase. She loved it.) The rest he sold to a local dealer and split the profit, such as it was, five ways. When an offer was made for the villa at the asking price, it was accepted. He put out milk every day for the stray cat and spoke to the woman in the souvenir shop to ask if she would do the same when he left.

By the time the *commissario* came across the water in his boat, it was mid-September, already more than two months since Vic's death. The camellia petals were gone from the ground, the hostas were over, the bougainvillea was giving up its leaves. There were days of pure sunshine, starting with a golden early morning light spilling over the hills, threads of mist, and ending with a firecracker of a sunset. Now that the school holidays were over, there were fewer day-trippers. It had always been Goose's favorite time.

The *commissario* looked awkward sitting at the kitchen table in his uniform. He placed his cap on his lap and pulled out his notebook, opening it, closing it, opening it again, as if it contained a speech he hadn't yet learned.

"Signore? How much would you like to hear?"

Goose took a deep breath and said, "Everything."

The *commissario* began by telling Goose things about his father he already knew. That he was seventy-six, his eyes were green, he was 6'2" tall with white hair that had once been black, a scar on his left hand.

"It was from an accident with a painting knife," said Goose.

Then the *commissario* told him things that were new to him: his father's weight when he died, the circumference of his head, the length of each limb, and bone. There were no signs of alcohol or drugs or other intoxicants in his blood. Suicide and homicide had been ruled out. "It seems your father died of natural causes. Arrhythmia, a condition of the heart. It causes the heart to beat irregularly and faster than normal."

Goose sat for a few moments, unable to reply. The weight of everything he and his sisters had gone through finally settled on him—the suspicions and denials, the fury, the doubt—though he did not feel heavy. If anything, it was like soft ash blowing through him. At last he said, "How did I not realize that?"

"Arrhythmia tends to affect certain groups, such as older people or those living with heart disease and high blood pressure. But it can be impossible to detect and this is most certainly why it was not spotted in the first autopsy. It can even be missed in a normal checkup. Did your father never complain of problems?"

"No. He never complained about his health at all." But even as he said it, he remembered his father that day in the studio before Christmas, staring as if he was seeing not what was in front of him but something altogether more terrifying. Or even the last time when Goose had found him clutching his chest and short of breath. Had Vic known all along?

"When someone dies by accident," said the *commissario* slowly, "it can feel to those left behind as if an injustice has occurred. As if someone or something must be to blame. It can take many years to accept that this is not the case. That in the end, nothing can be done to change the loss. But you are free now to visit his body at the undertaker's and begin the process to take him home. I expect this will be a relief to you and your sisters. I can only apologize that it has taken so long. If I can help with the paperwork, please let me know. It can be complicated."

"Thank you, but we've changed our minds about the funeral. There will be no ceremony in the UK. We have chosen a simple cremation in Orta. It's what he would have wanted."

At the door, the *commissario* shook Goose's hand and said he'd heard that the villa had been sold. He was sorry the family were leaving after all these years. He placed his cap on his head, and looked up at the sky as if he were expecting rain, though once again it was an exquisite unbroken blue. "Do you know?" he said. "The thing I will miss most?"

"No."

He smiled. "Your sister in her big hat. Every day I look at the door, waiting for her to come and give me a hard time."

"Yes," said Goose. "You and me both."

So, in the end, it was only Goose who went to view his father's body. The chapel where he was laid to rest was dimly lit and cold, with a cloying vinegar smell that must have been chemicals. Soft piped music was playing, Bach (surely not the old Hamlet cigar advert?), and a chair was set beside the coffin—the same coffin that Goose had chosen all those weeks ago with his sisters, but that seemed another lifetime, one that belonged to children. He guessed you were meant to sit on the chair and have some kind of conversation with the body except now that Goose was in the room he wanted nothing more than to get out of it. Besides, he had no idea what you said to a dead body, even if you were its only son. He inched closer. It was the stillness of his father that threw him. At last he could see his vast feet, then the clothes Goose had sent for him to be dressed in, until finally he dared to look at his face. What had he been expecting? Worms? His eyes were closed, his nose seemed thinner. But in fact he looked surprisingly healthy for a dead man. Kinder, in fact. Maybe the myth was right. Maybe there was peace in death, even for a conflicted man like Vic. And then he saw that his father had been made up by the Italian funeral director especially for this visit. He was wearing foundation and rouge on his cheeks, concealer beneath his eyes, a little pink on the lids, a few strokes of mascara.

Goose couldn't help it. He smiled.

And this might be a general truth about the dead, or it might just be what happens when your father is lying in a coffin wearing full make-up, with organ music quietly playing and no obvious sign of an organ, but it was at that moment Goose understood that his father was truly gone.

He stood for a while, wondering if he would cry, or say any final words, but found he didn't do either.

Quite honestly, it was a relief to step back into the sun.

Vic was cremated in Orta and it was just like the story Netta had told them in Kettner's about the family who split their mother's ashes. Goose was the only family member who attended. There were a few local shopkeepers and bartenders, some men he had drunk with over the years. Limoncello was there with a woman Goose guessed must be his wife, and she held his hand throughout the brief service while he wept as if something on which his life depended had been taken away, but the whole thing was over in fewer than fifteen minutes. Afterward the others invited him to join them for a meal, though Goose declined.

In the following days he filled in endless government forms so that he could have the ashes delivered in separate canisters to each of his sisters, and another to the address in Palermo for Bella-Mae. There was no big funeral, no speeches or songs, and no one dressed up for the day in bright happy colors or the more traditional black. Goose took his canister down through the garden—it surprised him how much you got even when it was just a fifth—and twisted the lid to scatter Vic into the lake, though he didn't so much scatter as drop in a claylike clump, and that was another thing Goose hadn't been expecting. In the end, he had to swirl them with a stick, the ashes of the great man who had once stood between Goose and the world. He said a prayer for him and another for his mother, as well as Netta, Susan and Iris. After that he ran out of things to do, so he sat beside the lake and kept his father's ashes company as they began to sink. Briefly he tried to sing, but nothing much came to him except a snatch from the Coldplay album Susan had played all that summer.

He watched each wave as it approached the shore's edge and was pulled back by the drag of the current. It struck him that grief was like the lake. It couldn't be contained. It moved whichever way it chose. Even when that was north, instead of south.

The apartment in London was sold in a day. The studio was put on the market. Vic's estate was divided between Bella-Mae and the siblings. Susan used her inheritance to stay in Paris to do a classic French cookery course and rented a flat in the Latin Quarter. After a few months, she rang Goose and although the conversation was stilted at first—neither knew yet what their common ground might be without the rest of the family—it got easier the next time. She admitted she'd tried to shake her father's ashes over the Seine, but in the end the river seemed too busy so she'd put the canister back into her bag. She was probably just going to keep it, she said. She even found she talked to it from time to time. Meanwhile she and Warwick had agreed to take a break, though they weren't calling it a divorce. He was being very kind, she said.

"He's a kind man," said Goose.

"I know I made a fool of myself with Laszlo and everything. I can't even think about that man now. I know I hurt you as well as Warwick. But something inside me kind of exploded after Daddy died. As if there was no stopping me."

Susan continued to ring Goose from Paris. She never wanted to say any more about that time on Lake Orta, but she could talk a hundred words a minute about what she was learning. In that way, at least, Susan didn't change, and it made him happy just to listen. How to make a roux, a béchamel, a fish stock, reductions, a salad dressing, or fillet a fish. "But you know how to do those things, Suz," he said once. "You cooked all the time for us."

"No, I never learned professionally," she said. "I only taught myself." She described how she would finish each day so exhausted she could barely stand, but she'd stop on the way home to buy the same ingredients so that she could practice what she'd learned that day, again and again. As soon as she completed the classic course, she signed up for Cordon Bleu. Goose asked her about where she lived, trying to picture it. "You know what? I don't really notice it," she said. There was a kind of bafflement in her voice, as if this had only just occurred to her. Later, when she got her first job in a French kitchen, she said she would be working crazy hours, and he supposed that must be true, because for a few years she would mainly call in the middle of the night when he was asleep. He suggested visiting a few times and she always said yes, then failed to give him a date. "Guess what I'm eating right now?" she said once. "A McDonald's. The twins would have loved me, after all."

Goose heard from Iris, too, less frequently as time passed. To begin with she was always sending him postcards in her jumbled-up handwriting. She'd tell him where she and Harry had got to next, and what they were doing. In her hunger for travel, for new places and new people, there was clearly the hope that she would leave behind her ghosts. Goose heard three months later that Shirley Lucas had been taken into hospital and Harry was back to nurse her, so he guessed that in the end Iris had done exactly as she'd said and given up Harry too. She was still traveling, she wrote to Goose, and sometimes she had work, sometimes she didn't. One month she was on the verge of happiness, the next she was on the mend from disaster, and somewhere she switched from male to female lovers, though there, too, nothing seemed certain. She said she liked traveling most of all, the freedom of being between two places. *basicly i will go anywher hwer there isn't woter*, she wrote another time.

The last he heard from her, she was heading for a mountain retreat in Italy where volunteers lived in a commune, observing and recording the lives of wolves and bears. *i may not b able 2 rite agan, she put. its so out of hte way*. And Iris, who had once found it so hard to be true to her word, was true to this one. She stopped writing.

Netta was the only one of his sisters who came back to London. After a health scare—liver failure—she spent a few days in hospital. He visited her every afternoon, and read out her favorite problem pages. The worse the dilemma, the more pleasure it gave her. After that she took a job with a smaller law firm and switched to part-time. He would have loved to believe she was happier, but there was always something missing for Netta. They'd see a film in an art house cinema, or go for a walk along the river. They didn't even need to speak—it felt like catching up, just being together. But if he tried to bring up the subject of their sisters, she flew off the handle. "You want to drive me back to the booze?" she'd ask. You could say it got easier with time, but it never got healed. Too much had happened that summer, and too much time had passed. Susan and Iris grew as women over the years, but something for Netta just stayed small.

As for Shirley Lucas, Goose visited her in a hospice two days before she died. She was asleep in a wheelchair, her head stacked to one side, her hair snowy white, wearing a beautiful cardigan he felt sure she must have knitted for herself. He took her hand until she woke, and it was like holding a bird. She told him, "You were the son I never had, Gustav." He went to the funeral and sat at the back, where he wept as if he had lost his own mother, but he left as soon as it was over. He would never see Harry again.

He asked himself if it was inevitable, if the break between his sisters had been coming for a long time, perhaps as far back as the beginning, when they told themselves they were the Kemps, a little apart from and above everyone else. He thought of Susan wanting Vic to paint her so that she could know who she was, and realized it was pretty much the same for everyone. We're all trying to find out who we are, beyond our parents. In yellow-washing Vic's picture, Goose finally let go of the father they'd all wanted him to be. And in letting go, he discovered it was in him to love the broken man who remained. He remembered little things. The time Vic burned the top of his scalp and walked around with a spare pair of underpants on his head, the leg holes looped over his ears. Or the night he brought home indoor fireworks but got the wrong box and set off a Catherine wheel that almost set fire to the whole kitchen. The way he shouted, "Come on, kids!" and dived headfirst into the water. That great big man who became a silvery fish when he was in the lake.

The lake. He thought often of that, too, its changing light, its magical reflections, its sunset as radiant as a Persian carpet. For a long time he woke missing it terribly. And his sisters, oh, his sisters. He'd see a plate of tomatoes and think, Iris, maybe don't eat those. He'd see a woman in a mad hat and wish she was Netta. He'd walk past an open window, smells of exotic food filling the emptiness, and say, "Oh, Susan. Boy, oh boy, you could cook." There were some things you never got over. No amount of thinking or talking would make them right: The best you could do was find a way to live alongside them. And Goose would have given anything to be back on the lake with his sisters. In the end, we're given so few people to love, and they were his.

He kept Vic's last painting. The rolled-up canvas cracked with time, the yellow coating of paint began to splinter. But he kept it to remind him of the emptiness of a new beginning. A promise of hope that things might change for the better when they appeared to be at their worst. And they did, of course. In time, and in ways he didn't expect, they really did.

26

Mirror Image

But suppose, just suppose, there is another way of telling this story. Like one of those famous mirror-paintings by the Old Masters, where a reflected image at the back of the picture shows another viewpoint, an alternative and more truthful way of looking at things than the story played out in the foreground.

A man in his seventies meets a young woman in an online chat room for insomniacs. He is scared about his work, but also about his heart. He is too frightened to tell anyone or see a doctor, so he barely sleeps. She tells him how she never sleeps either: she was the loneliest child, neglected by her parents, often left with nothing to talk to except a TV—she still slips in and out of accents as if they're clothes—and she's been free-falling ever since. In no time, he's wild about her. He wants to speak all the time. It's the crazy gap between her front teeth, he says, or the way she hides behind her hair when she laughs. It's her ideas about art—he loves that she's so young, she isn't sure about his work. He falls in love because he's at the end of his life and she's at the beginning of hers, and he adores what she has. All that life unlived. He asks if she would like to meet in person and she would: she's desperate to meet this man. When they do, he's everything she knew he would be—so big he blots out the isolation of her childhood. They talk all night and all the next day, and when she goes to his vast apartment in Regent's Park—you could fit her entire bedsit inside his bathroom—they're still talking. She falls asleep and stays that way for a straight eight hours.

From there, things happen very fast. He takes her for lunches and dinners. He showers her with gifts—except his taste is appalling, and she leaves them in their packaging. Let's do this! Let's do that! He wants to try everything: his appetite for adventure is endless. They visit galleries, and she explains how art for her isn't about great masterpieces. It's about breaking boundaries. Making something that can evolve to reflect the changing times. "Yes! Great idea! Art that dissolves with time!" he says, mishearing, though one thing she notices is how twitchy he gets around other artists' work, as if just being in the same space diminishes him. She tries to tell him more about her ideas. How she wants to experiment on a bolder scale, take her work out of the galleries and into public spaces. To discover the point where the ordinary becomes hallowed. Yes, he says, he wants to work on a big scale, too, and they are back to talking about him again. When they can't sleep at night, he hails a cab to Ronnie Scott's or they go dancing. In the morning they close the curtains and crash out. He tries crazy diets to look younger, enrolls at a gym, though with that kind of weight loss at his age you begin to look too thin. She makes herbal tea because she's never drunk caffeine and suddenly that's another thing he's obsessed about. The worse it smells, the healthier he believes it must be. He tells her about a big new picture he couldn't paint—but now that she's with him, he's sure he can do it. He says she is his electricity. His spark. So she stays because he's the first person who needs her, and she stays because she hasn't anywhere else to go. But most of all, she stays because he finds her life wonderful, when before she could make no sense of it.

When she lies on top of him, her hair falls down over them like a curtain and it is as if there is no one else in the world, only her and Vic. She feels lighter, lifted higher than before, but also somehow uneasy, as if she's done something wrong. Because this is happening so fast. And instead of working on her own art, they're talking all the time about his, and when she isn't doing that, she's cleaning the flat because she's never lived in a place so beautiful. Sometimes at night she sobs in frustration out of the window and she doesn't know why, except she's in love and, deep down, she realizes the relationship is going in one direction, and that is nowhere. It might even crush her: with Vic, there's only room for one artist, and it's definitely him. Anyway, what about his kids? "Oh, they'll love you," he says, in his great barreling voice. "Marry me! Marry me! Marry me!" He sings it from the bathroom as he's cleaning his teeth. He writes it on Post-its that he sticks all over himself. She goes to put on her shoes and there is a note in there too. *MARRY ME!*

To ease her mind, he agrees she should meet his children, though the noodle bar is her idea. It's a neutral space and she hopes they might like a place like that—it will be a change from all those stuffy restaurants he loves. But when she arrives, he panics at the last minute and doesn't acknowledge her. She walks past the table and out of the noodle bar, and returns to his flat to pack her few things, but he hurries back before she can leave, and he's beside himself. Oh, God, he's so sorry. He's an old rogue, a terrible person. But he will introduce them, he promises. He will, he will, he will. And they will love her, of course they will. Only every time they make a plan, it's the same story. He comes up with a reason to cancel at the last minute until she can't bear it.

She goes away with her cousin Laszlo, who is on the run after another affair with a married woman. It's the worst kind of holiday. Out of nowhere there's a heat wave. Mid-April, and the beach is packed, and pubs are filled with severely sunburned people drinking beer and eating fried food. Besides, Laszlo is beginning to irritate her. In the space of a day, he's losing money on cards and asking her for a loan, or chatting up more women who are clearly married and, quite frankly, should know better. And even though she needs to think about her work, she can think only of Vic. "You leave him for this?" Laszlo says one night, as they pass a man puking under a streetlamp. "You leave rich man to live like this?" She calls Vic at three a.m.

He picks up on the first ring. "Oh, my darling," he booms. "There you are at last."

She hears his voice and knows her life is a waste of breath without him. All she wants is to spend the rest of her life with this man.

He promises everything. He will change; he won't rush her anymore; she will meet his kids. He insists she will be his dealer now, not Harry. (But why would she be his dealer? She's an artist, same as him.) She moves back into the apartment, though in the end the nearest she comes to meeting his children is by unearthing anything she can find hidden in the flat, even old swimming certificates. She goes with him to the studio to meet Goose, but he leaves her waiting in a cab outside. The only thing she sees of Goose is as they drive away and she takes one glance over her shoulder. There he is, covered in paint. Looking so open and vulnerable, the whole story falls into place. He is the artist. Of course he is. He is the true reason Vic can't work. If anything, it makes her love Vic more. He's just as lost as she is.

Except that he tells her every day how well his work is going. It's all in his head. ("I'm in it now," he keeps saying.) He is so protective of it that he changes the locks to his flat, though in truth she still hasn't seen him pick up a paintbrush. And then, one morning, she wakes to find him packing their bags. "Let's go to the lake! No more wasting time! I will finish my painting by Lake Orta! Oh, you'll love the lake!"

He's right. She falls in love the moment the cab dips off the main road, and there it is, this bowl of blue that seems to change color even as she looks. She's never seen anything like it. He teaches her to swim and at last she can feel it, the joy people talk about when they're in love, the kind of happiness where everything reflects off everything else and becomes even more itself. It's no longer just about Vic. It's Orta, it's the island, it's Villa Carlotta, those beautiful fading frescos, the early-morning water, still as a piece of glass. Vic badgers her and badgers her to marry him, and one night she laughs and gives in. Why not? Why not marry him? Sure, this is not forever, but in the end, what is? She asks her cousin to come over and be a witness, and the wedding takes place a few days later. If she's guilty of anything, it's believing Vic when he insists his children will come around to the idea in good time.

After the wedding, Vic finally starts painting. He tells her how much he hates everything he has done before, but this new work will be different. The ultimate expression of himself as an artist. He's up in the garret for hours. At last there is a space for her to think about her work:

she, too, might be going in a new direction, though she doesn't know yet what that is. She's still waiting.

Every day he's up in the garret, shouting and swearing at his work, trying to get it right. When he finally presents it to her, he bites his nails and paces, waiting for her to pass judgment. She looks at it for a very long time and says nothing.

"You hate it," he says impatiently. "It's shit."

And she says what she knows to be the truth: "I don't hate it, Vic. But I know you do. And what's the point, if it isn't saying what you want to say?"

He asks her to take away the painting and destroy it. "Just get rid of it," he says. "I never want to see it again."

For the last few weeks of his life, there is something so beautiful between them that she believes they are on a whole new plane. The love rushes up inside her as if she might die of pure happiness. Vic says his painting days are over. He chucks out everything from the garret: the oils, the canvases, the turps. He doesn't want them anywhere near him. Instead he puts a chair up there so he can sit and watch the view, just as it is, without trying to impose his will on it and reproduce it in oil. They swim, they make love, she brews her calming tisanes to help him sleep. Though sometimes, these days, she just mixes herbal tea bags and a flower from the garden. It's hardly magic.

"Why did I spend my life working so hard," he says one night, "when I could have lived like this?"

But she's worrying about something else. Occasionally, after a swim, she notices him down in the garden, clutching his heart, though if she asks, he denies it. Sometimes he's short of breath and he's only climbed one flight of stairs. It's all that crazy dieting, and the hours he spends swimming—he's been shedding weight so fast she thinks it comes off him in his sleep. But he won't accept that something may be wrong. Point-blank refuses to see a doctor. So at night she curls into the great suburb of his body and lies with her arms hooked around his back, whispering plans for all the places they will never go, the things they will never see. It doesn't matter anymore that this isn't forever and that her art is on hold, because for now, this is what she wants. This man, this lake, this house, these last days with Vic. Then, very early one morning, he goes down to the water, even though he must know a mist is coming. He dives in.

What is he thinking? That the mist will not happen? Or does he go in, still unchanged and believing he is invincible? What she feels now is that he goes to the lake and smells the beautiful morning, the mist that will come soon, thin tendrils of it already in the air, and glances quickly over his shoulder to make sure she isn't watching, then goes in. Knowing that the freest he will ever be is in the water. Thinking that if his heart hurts a little, never mind. He can swim it off. That day in the lake, Vic finally becomes an old man.

She howls when the police tell her. She howls when she sees his body at the morgue: they have to carry her in and carry her out. She howls so loudly in her cousin's hotel suite that she's moved to another room. She feels as if the whole world has disappeared. She doesn't want to see the villa ever again.

In the end, though, she does. She goes back to claim what is rightfully hers, but also because when she finally meets his children, she senses something going on, but deep underground where words don't reach, in a place that can be captured only as an image. They're so close they still share the same bedroom and yet they're simultaneously beginning to fracture. There is nothing she can do to stop them. Why should she? If anything, she puts her finger inside the cracks just to test how deep they really go. She is an artist, after all: she can't help it. She doesn't love them, she doesn't hate them. She is outside and within. She has put her work on hold to be with their father, but now she's in the middle and reflects back at them what they are.

And what they are is raging. They are falling apart.

PART THREE

Billy Mason

London, 2025

27

Invitations

They fall in love through walking, only not like walking all those years ago in childhood when Netta and Susan took him with Iris in the pram, and other people's homes looked as small and safe as birds' nests. Not like walking when he was twenty-four and all he wanted was to leave himself behind: without art to help him, he couldn't see how to function as a human being. Not even like that summer years ago on Lake Orta when his father died and walking was a kind of hunger, because wherever he went he still felt lost. No, walking with Billy is a different kind of walking. A joining up.

Billy has a book called *Secret London* with guided tours of different parts. Every weekend, Billy tells him where they will go. Islington, St. Martin-in-the-Fields, Vauxhall, Soho, Greenwich. He reads out all the stories behind the buildings they're looking at—and it's like hearing the story inside the story.

"Are you sure you're not bored?" says Billy, often, looking over the top of his book. He has very thick glasses that caused him no end of trouble as a child, though Goose loves them simply because they're Billy's.

Goose laughs, and says, "No. Tell me everything. I want to hear the whole lot."

So Billy does. They can be standing in the middle of a busy pavement, people tutting as they swerve to get past, and there is Billy Mason, wrapped in his scarf, with his googly glasses, his face boyish still although he's middle-aged, telling Goose that this is the spot where there was once a chapel and green fields, probably deer, and this is why it's called Whitechapel. Can you believe it?

And Goose can. Because even though they're surrounded by brick and cement, and the only deer around here is being served in a haute-cuisine burger, Billy has said it is so, and therefore it is. All those stories, Goose thinks, going on behind what we see. These days he can notice a woman push away her untouched cup of coffee, a boy standing alone at the bus stop, even a man yelling at strangers, and it doesn't hurt in the way it once did, as if he is all those people too. Now he feels the urgency of the world in a new, startling way, because it's like seeing it through Billy's eyes, myopic as they are but always optimistic.

Or perhaps it is seeing with the eyes of an artist at last. Both present and letting go.

They stop around lunchtime for a beer and sandwiches. Normally Billy has already decided on the pub, only sometimes it isn't where Billy thought it would be and they end up walking another mile to find it. "Oh God," Billy will say, a huffing profile up ahead. "I'm sorry, Gustav. I'm sorry. It's here somewhere. I'm sure of it." Goose will take a moment to answer, because there, for a moment, he sees Netta in her hat, always up at the front. "Oh, now I've upset you," says Billy, running back. But Goose insists he hasn't. It's only the cold.

It still amazes and thrills him that such a thing can happen. That another man can love Goose in equal proportion to the amount he loves him. He always assumed this kind of happiness was for other people. But it also thrills him that Billy knows where they're going, and has a guidebook, even when their destination is not always where Billy thought it would be and they have to keep walking. It's a kind of faith, a mad faith that things will work out for the best, despite the evidence. And this is also why he falls in love.

How could he have been so afraid?

When he asks Billy to marry him, Billy says, "But I thought you weren't into all that. I thought you had a thing about commitment. I thought you wanted it to stay just like this." Goose says it's true. Despite his success, he is still frightened of commitment and he does love it just like this. He is lying in Billy's arms on a mattress in the middle of the bedroom. There is nowhere else he would like to be. Not even the lake. But he would also like it to be like *that*. Like married.

Billy puts on his glasses to check Goose isn't laughing. Though in fact there is something beautifully bug-like about a buck-naked man with NHS prescription glasses and, for once in his life, Goose does laugh at him. And Billy says, "Yes. I will marry you, Gustav Kemp. Yes."

So now Goose has to meet Billy's friends. They all want to hear about Goose and how he met Billy. It turns out there are many friends: Billy can go for a coffee and within five minutes he's struck up a conversation with the barista and the girl collecting dirty cups. There are dinner parties, lunches, morning coffees, afternoon teas. Goose goes to meet Billy's cousin who lives in Norfolk and his second cousin who moved to Leeds because she's still in love with her ex. There are Billy's aunts and great-aunts and his piano teacher from when he was five; there are old next-door neighbors. Then there are all Billy's godchildren. Billy has pretty much no money, but he lavishes what he has on his godchildren: if Goose had children, he would definitely make a beeline for Billy in terms of godparenting. Billy arranges tickets for the ballet for Goose to meet all ten of them—they're so high up and so far from the stage Goose has vertigo just looking down. ("Tickets in the gods for the godchildren!" says Billy.) The godchildren, who range in age from six to twenty-five, crowd around Goose to kiss him goodbye. They say they're so excited about the wedding. "Will you tell us how you met?" asks one, a very earnest-looking little girl, with extrathick glasses just like Billy's and a mouth crammed with metal, who breaks Goose's heart simply by smiling.

"And what about your family, Goose?" another asks. "We can't wait to meet them too."

Goose nods. Polite. We didn't make it, he wants to say. We tried to drive past the wreck and we didn't survive. But there's a limit to how much truth people really want to hear, especially at the ballet. So the smile is enough, sad though it is. He and his sisters have not been together for many years, not since that summer on Lake Orta.

But the story of how we met, thinks Goose, is much happier. Let me tell you this one! I had finished a painting and I was sitting on my own in a late-night café six months ago to celebrate—yes, that's how shit-hot my life was—when your nephew/godfather/piano pupil/ex-neighbor/old school friend walked in to buy a coffee. He was wearing a coat so large it was the kind of thing most people go to sleep under, and he paid for the drink, then took it outside for someone on the street. I thought, You're the one. I bought him a coffee. And yes, I felt everything as I ran after him. Excitement, fear, shame, hope, desire. I tried to say, "I thought you should have one, too," except I was trembling so hard I dropped the cup. So in effect he lost two coffees that night. The one he gave away and the one I threw down him.

It is decided they will wear matching tweed jackets for the wedding, only Goose's will be moss green and Billy's will be the blue of a song thrush's egg. They will also wear kilts. At first Goose is surprised, because he had no idea Billy was Scottish. If anything, his accent is a bit west, but not as far as Devon, more like Swindon. "I'm not Scottish," Billy says, "but I want to wear a skirt to my wedding."

Goose wants to wear a skirt too.

They are made by a tailor in east London, and when they go for the fitting, they stand side by side in the mirror in their not-quite-finished tweed jackets and their beautiful kilts and begin to laugh. "You look like a giant tree," says Billy, "and I look like a blue weed." Once Billy, who is not only so pale he looks Iris-colored, but also at least a foot shorter than Goose, said he was the kind of boy Goose would have kicked the shit out of at school. But Goose had reassured him. "No. You're wrong. I would have been hiding right behind you."

And then it comes to the guest list. Billy has so many people to invite (so many people to love!) they probably need three weddings. Goose designs the invitations, an exquisite tall green oak in watercolor with the palest blue willow, though secretly he believes that Billy is the oak. He sends them, of course, to his sisters. He kisses the envelopes. He knows they won't come.

"Tell me about them," Billy often says, and Goose says, "I will. I promise. One day I'll tell you the whole story." Except he never does. It's too painful. What he manages are the smallest scraps of information, one at a time, which is in itself hurtful because he would give everything to Billy. So all Billy knows about Goose's past is that he has three sisters, none of whom speak to one another. He knows that Goose was number three in the package and adored numbers one, two and four, that he can still remember Netta and Susan taking turns to push Iris in the pram, while he held on to whichever free hand came his way.

Goose talks about Netta, who could have ruled the world but her demons got in the way, and Susan, who probably needed to be Netta, and Iris, who tried to stay small but grew and grew, only never outward, so that in the end she towered over the other two like a slanting beanpole. He implies that there was a summer years ago when they went to fetch their father's body and everything fell irretrievably apart. He admits it is a long, long time for siblings to stay separate. ("But for so many years?" Billy sometimes repeats. "How could you all let that happen?") But the worst truth is that what felt like an act close to sabotage at the time has slowly, slowly become habit, and even acceptable. Or, rather, Goose believes it has become easier for the four of them to live alongside the divide than deal with the trauma of trying to piece it back together. The risk of more hurt, more humiliation.

Painful to him as it is, this is what his sisters want. At least, that is what he tells himself. We become familiar with what hurts us and refuse to change.

The information he shares with Billy feels like a series of holes that have not gone away but been darned. And as it happens, Billy—who is also an artist, working not in watercolor but textiles—is practically the only man in the twenty-first century who still darns. At night he will sit under a cone of light from the lamp, a sock so close to his eyes he seems to be using it as an extra pair of glasses, one hand holding the wooden mushroom inside the sock, the other with the needle and the yarn—also one foot tucked on top of the other, because when Billy does something with one part of his body the rest of it joins in—creating the warp threads vertically, then weaving the weft threads horizontally. He darns holes so beautifully that Goose finds he prefers the mended bit to the rest of the sock.

Sometimes Billy says, "What I can't believe is that you went wandering off as kids all day and no one stopped you." (Billy is an only child. This is why he makes brothers and sisters of all his friends.) "It makes me so sad to think of the four of you alone like that." Goose has never seen his childhood as sad, or at least no sadder than anyone else's; yet suddenly he knows the acute loneliness of those four children, staring up into other people's houses while their father worked, waiting for the lights to come on, watching other children being given their tea, or being helped into bed and kissed good night. He holds tighter on to Billy and says he loves him, like a pledge, as if to remind both of them that this is something solid, something that will never go away, so long as they both keep tending the flame.

About Vic, Billy is not forgiving and not judgmental either. "He was the father you had to deal with," he says. He has a theory that children choose their parents before they are born. Much as Goose wants to believe Billy, he is not so sure that life can be so neatly made sense of.

"Art will out. If it's there, it will find its way, you can't stop it. The mistake is to think that it's always kind. Vic wanted to be a serious painter and couldn't. He saw it as his salvation and then did whatever he could to make it happen, because deep down he knew he didn't have the talent. Isn't that the real tragedy?"

Goose remembers Bella-Mae, the way she jabbed her finger at him and said, "Artist, artist, artist," as if she were giving him a parking ticket.

For she is there too. She is woven into his thoughts, even after all these years.

Bella-Mae is known for her fragmented sculptures of the female body, in the style of ancient Greek art and installed temporarily in public spaces that are about to be redeveloped. She does not believe in the permanence of art. Her pieces are made of polyester resin and white marble dust, designed to dissolve over time, to disappear inch by inch. Nevertheless they are vast and their weight is unimaginable. (Though Billy tries. It's much like guessing how many sweets are in the jar, but an artist's version.) Lying on one side, or pinned almost upside down, they give the impression of bits of goddess that have dropped out of the sky. A head the size of a boulder, a hand, a half-winged torso. She has been called a fake, a provocateur, and also one of the most significant artists of the twenty-first century. Her work is interpreted by fans as a mirror reflection of the patriarchy, though others see it as a commentary on the state of Europe. (Her critics call it pop art. Trash. Not to mention a hideous waste of money.) Almost nothing is known about Bella-Mae Gonzales's background or private life, and she is absent from all social media. She has never referred to her brief marriage to Vic Kemp, though in the only interview she ever did she mentioned a man "I once loved with all my heart." Goose wonders if she knows about his work. The art world is a small one.

His sisters know. Of course they do. They could not be prouder. "My brother, the artist," they say. Susan has his work on the walls of her restaurant. And yet here is the thing. Over the years, he has always sent them invites for the opening night of his exhibitions and they never make it. *Wonderful!* they will RSVP. *Can't wait! So excited!* Then something crops up and they cancel at the last minute. There are always very good reasons—Iris does not live in the UK, a sous-chef is unwell and Susan has to take their shift, Netta has a new case at work—but really he knows they're frightened of being in the same space as one another. And deeper than this, he senses that the world of art is still too conflicted for them, too complicated and painful, not only because they are the children of the disgraced though mostly forgotten semipornographic artist Vic Kemp, but also because they believed their father for all those years when he insisted art was not good for Goose. It was a kind of collusion, even if it was ignorant. And anyway, what collusion can be truly ignorant? So they missed the opening of his first exhibition in Colchester, where he was heralded by one critic as the new Hockney, the next in Leeds, then in Whitechapel. ("I'm not the new Hockney," he told Billy. "And also, has anyone noticed? I paint flowers." "Don't be so picky," Billy said. "Hockney is a byword in the arts for being British and successful. Show some gratitude.") But Goose does not need to be Hockney or even the best painter, because in the corner of his mind he knows very well what he is: an artist. That is enough. It is what he is, it is what he does. If he does not paint, he is only a fragment of himself.

It began with line drawings. Not the still life pictures that he did when he was twenty-four and his father would later copy. Instead he faced the strange shapes that had filled his head since he was a boy. At long last he got to know them and saw them for what they were, and because he allowed them to present themselves in precise detail—he didn't flinch, he didn't hide—they no longer frightened him. Or, rather, they no longer held the power of the unknown. The rose he'd seen in Shirley Lucas's wallpaper the morning after his father died, the exploding seed heads after his breakdown, the shapes that seemed to twist and roil and explode like fireworks above his head at night as he lay in his father's studio: he beheld them with the eye of a camera and then he painted what he saw with the exactitude of a scientist. And because it was such a long time since he had dared to use a pencil, every line seemed rinsed and fresh; everything was new to him and untouched, full of light and even fragrance. It was as if he was giving shape and color to something that already existed on the paper. These days he uses fine brushes for the intricate detail, watercolor and tempera for the coloration. He has developed a style of his own, incorporating increasingly complex touches to bring details to life.

An *Observer* critic writes:

> They are painted with such skill you begin to believe the petals of the rose are the real thing, not painted at all. It is in fact surrealism in reverse. And just because some of these paintings are witty and amusing, it does not prevent them being beautiful or profound. You look at a Gustav Kemp rose and it appears more real, more itself, than the one in your garden. Even the more disturbing images—I am thinking now of his most recent studies of a dying blossom—leave you with a crystalline sense of wanting to make the most of life. His art knows both beauty and decay, poised in the single moment where light becomes its own shadow. Kemp takes Nature away from the floral and into the psychological. And yet he paints flowers.

The work is slow, painstakingly slow. It takes all he has, every time. Goose is forever missing a deadline. Art for him is the language of loss: to find a picture, he has to abandon many other versions along the way and sometimes he imagines all those failures filling his studio, like ghosts with half faces. It's a process of hoping every morning, despairing every night, then getting up in the morning and daring to hope yet again. (He keeps knocking at the door, just as Bella-Mae said. Billy says this is what he loves about artists. That, despite all their pessimism, they don't give up. They are optimists, after all.)

It feels to Goose as if all his life a great river has been inside him, a river that he glimpsed once or twice, but which on the whole he kept dammed up, so that when it broke out, it was only in strange and frightening flashes. Now it has found its rhythm, its flow. But he hopes that one day the river will carry boats and birds and fish, and all of them will have a little of Billy in them. Billy for blue eyes, Billy for blue sails. They will sweep the past clean.

His sisters have still not met since that summer on Lake Orta, and it is only Goose they ring. They always repeat the same questions, which they try to pass off as casual, but which break his heart because he knows they are not. "So Iris is still traveling?"

"No," he will tell them yet again. "She is living in a commune in the Central Apennines. She's working on a conservation project to save wolves and bears."

"I guess you barely hear from Netta. She was always a workaholic."

"No, she decided to go with a smaller company. She works part-time now. You know this."

"Are Susan and Warwick back together?"

"She says they aren't. But recently they've become close friends again. She's full-on at the restaurant in Paris. And you know Warwick's a grandfather now?"

When he broke the news that Iris had given birth to a little girl, he was convinced Susan at least would jump on the first flight to Italy. Instead she went very quiet, then said, "Oh, okay. I see."

Netta's response was: "She called her Opal? What is she now? Some kind of hippie?"

Yet if he ever says to one of them, "Listen. Why don't you just ring her?" they will sigh defensively as if he's asked for something monstrous, then snap out a reply.

"No," they will say. "No. I don't think so. If she wants to talk to me, she knows where I am."

He warns Billy not to get his hopes up for the wedding. They won't come, at least not all three of them. And painful as this sounds, he would rather not have any of them there than be forced to pick just one. "But it's okay. There will be so many other guests. The truth is, you wouldn't have the chance to meet them properly. It's for the best. It is. It's probably for the best."

Two weeks before the wedding, Billy wakes Goose in the middle of the night. "It's Netta. Gustav, it's Netta. Gustav? Wake up."

What's happened? These are the thoughts that fast-flash through his head as he swims to consciousness. Is she back in hospital? Another lapse? Netta is dead. That's what Billy is saying. Driving. Drunk driving. She was on her own in Italy. One of those dangerous hairpin bends. She must have put her foot on the accelerator instead of the brake. No one else was hurt. Even when Billy says it again, the words don't add up. "She's dead," he says. "I'm so sorry, Gustav. She's dead."

Suddenly Goose is being carried by a high, horrible wind, which has wrenched him free of the world as he knows it. He hears himself say "Oh God" as he stumbles up in the dark. Even his voice seems to belong to another man. He crawls across the floor, but his legs fail him, so small is his strength.

Susan and Iris are on their way to the airport. They're going to bring Netta's body home.

He thought he was free of the past, he thought they were all free of it, but here it is, all over again. You can't lose what happened simply by turning your back on it. He wrestles to put on clothes, as if clothes can equip him to bear this any better. Already pictures are flooding his head, his poor stupid brain trying to process this new information and make sense of it. (We can manage this! We can!) He sees Netta looking at baby photos when they were little, laughing because she said her nose looked like Charles de Gaulle's. He pictures her as the teenager he so adored, marching out of the house, top to toe in black like a Gothic princess, so heavy on her feet she could shake the whole house. He pictures her in her great big hat. He pictures her eating gelato beside the lake, doing that goofy smile and saying, "Welcome to my head." He sees her staggering with drink at the Venus restaurant, yelling at Iris that she will never see her again. He doesn't know how he will paint. He doesn't know how to cross his arms or put on a pair of trainers. Losing his father was one thing. But this is too terrible. It is too cruel a way for everything to end. He doesn't know how he will live with this and stay sane. He doesn't know how he will not kill things.

It's still the middle of the night, but he's left the flat, left Billy. He is a blind man, staggering toward Edgware Road, no longer able to distinguish between what is good in his life and what is bad. He's walking away from everything. Except where is he heading? He can't even go to Watford anymore. That place of safety has gone too. He hits a side street and stumbles down it.

A crowd of people block his path. Men and women are being offered hot food by volunteers. Others are going through boxes of clean clothes and shoes. A hand on his shoulder. "Can I help?" It's a young man, flip-flops on his feet. The kindest face.

"I don't know what I'm doing. I think I need to pray."

The young man nods, as if he was somehow expecting this. "Follow me."

There in a church with orange carpeting, a simple table for an altar where someone has mistakenly left an electric kettle, the light a twitching on-off fluorescent strip above his head, Goose does something he has not done since he was a boy. He goes on his knees. He screws up his eyes, which are pouring tears, and he makes fists of his hands. He prays to God, to Allah, to Whoever, the Sky, the Earth, the ancient deities, whatever is greater than he is, to those candles Iris lit for their father at the Sacro Monte in Orta, to the kind man at the door, to please, please, I beg of you, make this not true. Give my sister back to me.

You think people will wait until you're ready. You think they will act according to your time. But they do things their own way. Life does things its own way. It is too late.

Outside the church, he calls Susan. She picks up immediately. She is sobbing and Iris is sobbing in the background. "Why did we all stop seeing one another? How could we let that happen?" Then Iris comes on the line and there is her voice, lower and harder than it was that summer on the lake, no longer childlike, but a voice that is as much a part of him as his own skin and bone. "Goose, Goose. Remember that last summer we had? What did we do to one another?"

"I'm coming with you," he says. He is already waving his thanks to the kind man. He is trying to hail a cab, and all he can think about is the hole inside him, that darned-over hole, which has torn open again because it was only held together with warp and weft. "Wait for me, Suz. Wait for me, Iris. I'm coming."

Goose wakes to the darkness of the bedroom. He hears the soft breathing of Billy beside him, the way it makes a quiet popping sound as it goes in and out. He sees the clock beside the bed: three fifteen a.m. Nevertheless it still takes awhile to undo the dream and everything he has just been through. Did he find the soup kitchen? Did he go on his knees on the orange carpet? Did he speak to Susan and Iris? Are they traveling together to Italy? No. Is Billy real? Is Goose going to marry him? Yes.

The room is very still. It has that thick middle-of-the-night smell of garlic and sleep. His clothes are over there, folded on the chair, beside Billy's jeans and T-shirt—despite his impeccable artwork, Billy's few possessions have the look of things that have fallen from a great height and exploded on impact. A siren rings. A vixen gives a scream. Even though Goose is certain he's awake now, it takes more time for the dream to fall away. If he closes his eyes, it wants to start rolling again.

He thinks of how he called Susan, spoke to Iris. The relief of knowing the two of them were together after all these years. He curls toward Billy and holds tight to his freckled back and feels the steady boom of his heart, like an engine room. Netta is not dead. Susan and Iris are not traveling to Italy. The world is as it was.

And while his relief is the size of a riddled moon, it means that his sisters are still divided.

Billy stirs. He turns and looks at Goose with his beautiful eyes that startle Goose every time he opens them, like two iridescent blue beetles. He says, "Are you awake? Did you have a dream?'

Goose nods. "A really bad one."

Billy takes him in his arms. He rocks him gently. "Just a dream," he says. "Just a dream." Only even as he says it, Goose goes over it again: losing Netta forever, speaking to his sisters, deciding to return to Italy. It was so real he still can't believe it didn't happen. He can't shake off the feeling that if he hadn't gone down on his knees in his dream and prayed, it might have continued to play out. But the gods blinked. Netta did not die in a car crash. She is alive.

Billy kisses Goose's shoulder. And maybe somehow he knows Goose's dream, too, because he says slowly,

"You need to get your sisters together. They need to be here for our wedding."

28

Wedding Day

Netta says she is sorry but she can come only so long as Susan and Iris don't, and Susan says that if Netta doesn't wish to see her, she certainly doesn't wish to see her either, while Iris says this is triggering for her and, besides, she is already committed to an Extinction Rebellion march, so if she is arrested it will obviously be tricky to get away. But they are unanimous about one thing. They want Goose to be happy. They are overjoyed he's getting married. Susan offers to bake an eight-tier wedding cake, Netta orders ten crates of champagne, while Iris sends a box that contains hundreds of small colored-glass lanterns. (*Oh Goose*, she writes in a postcard. *I fel so dab abot htis*. She still refuses to have a smartphone, and her spelling is both as rushed as always and entirely her own sweet creation.)

"You see?" says Goose. "I told you it wouldn't work. I told you they wouldn't come. It's too hard for them. Too much happened that summer."

Billy writes to all three of them. He is charming but steely. He follows this up with a phone call. Several. He rings them every morning and ends with the same question, "Have you any idea how short life is? I spent my entire childhood wishing I had sisters."

"Family is everything," he says another time. "Even when it falls apart."

His last shot goes: "Goose is fine. He will live. He will keep breathing. So will you. But my gut is screaming with how wrong this is."

They agree to come as long as they are allowed to stay in separate rooms and not speak. "And just because it's your wedding, don't expect me to be nice," adds Netta.

It's a perfect spring day. Not one cloud in the sky. The English countryside has become a vast velvet-green eiderdown, while here in London the leaves on the trees are so new you can see straight through them. The studio is filled with guests and overflows on the square outside—it already constitutes a health-and-safety hazard—with fairy lights wound around anything vaguely static, and garlands made with puffs of pink blossom. Susan's eight-tier wedding cake is a construction of such beauty—iced flowers appearing to fly from one level to the next—it takes center stage in the kitchen, while everywhere you look seems to twinkle with Iris's lanterns as if encrusted with emeralds and sapphires. Out in the back garden, which, let's face it, is really a yard, some of the godchildren are performing as a string quintet and have moved from Bach to a more upbeat jazz medley. A buffet is laid out in a small marquee, which will afterward become the dance floor.

Billy is wearing a blue shirt that seems to be in some sort of collusion with his blue eyes. It is almost indecent, the effect it has.

Goose's sisters arrive late. Susan is first, nerves making her awkward and formal. Her hair is flecked with gray and she has it shoulder-length, allowing the thick curls to come freely. Warwick is at her side, bearing a wrapped gift and dressed like something out of an eighties Moss Bros catalogue.

Goose experiences the moment of shock he always gets these days when he sees them on WhatsApp. Time has played its tune on all their faces. Yet it isn't just that they've grown wrinkles, extra pads of flesh at the jaw. He can see traces of Vic, but someone else, too: Martha. The mother he adored and barely knew. She is there, for instance, in Susan's eyes, and the way she chews, just a little to the left. There's something, too, about the set of her upper lip, the way it seems to soften and disappear when she's anxious, a detail he cannot possibly recall about his mother, yet he looks at Susan now and finds that he does. All these ghosts we carry.

"Warwick and I are not together," she tells Goose, before he can so much as kiss her. "We're seeing how we go." He sees the tremor in her hands and his heart flips all over again. He remembers her final night in the villa and how she sobbed while he held her. "Where are they?" she says in a rush. "Are they here yet? What are they wearing?"

"They're not here, Susan."

"They're not coming?"

"No," he says gently. "They said they would. But you're the first."

She straightens her dress, a floaty one in a colorful chiffon that celebrates her curves without clinging to them. Then she passes him a Tupperware box containing canapés she says she made at the last minute. They're like banquets, in doll's-house size. He has no idea how you would begin to make something so exquisite, unless you had tweezers for fingers. "I'm first?" she says, nodding to herself. "Okay, that's good. That's good. Warwick, come with me."

Iris turns up next, in a glorious kingfisher-blue trouser suit that she's quick to tell him she bought from a charity shop. Next to her is a man the size of a bear with a great big beard to match. He is holding the most perfect child Goose has ever seen in his life—*his niece, Opal!* Hair so yellow it makes an egg yolk look pale!—and she is fast asleep. "Meet Ivan," Iris says, already searching over Goose's shoulder. "Are they here? Where are they? How do they look?" She wears her hair long now, and a pair of wedge heels that increase her height. She leans to adjust a vast balloon-sized shape on her front.

"Iris?" he says. "Iris? Hang on. Are you pregnant again?"

"Yes," she says, matter-of-factly, but also only half listening because she is clearly far more concerned about not meeting her sisters. "Didn't I tell you?"

"No. You very definitely did not tell me you were pregnant again."

"Oh, well, I am. It's why we came back to the UK. It's due next month." She looks like some kind of goddess in her wedge heels. For once, he has to look up to her. "Are they in the kitchen? Where are they? Ivan. Follow me."

Oh, this is the happiest day.

But it's Netta, whose face is a little puffy now after all those years of alcohol, her mouth bracketed by deep lines, it's Netta who reduces him to tears. She's wearing black, same as always, but she has gone off-piste with a fuchsia hat the size of a cartwheel. Robert stands next to her in an ironed polo-neck sweater. Goose hugs him and briefly remembers Philip Hanrahan. The trip to Scarborough.

"I am here, too, you know," she says, a little spikily.

Netta, dearest difficult Netta, oh, how I love you. I brought you back from the dead because I couldn't bear life without you. And you will never know.

"Where are they?" she asks, swiftly followed by, "Are they out the back? In the studio? The kitchen? Because I don't want to see them."

The wedding ceremony seems to be over within moments. Goose is so nervous and happy he doesn't recall saying, "I do."

"I did, though, didn't I?" he asks Billy later.

"You did. Loud and clear."

The party begins. In no time, his sisters have engineered things so that they are as far away from one another as is humanly possible. You have to admire the skill of it. Netta and Robert are in one corner of the studio, her back firmly to the room as she talks with three of the godchildren. Susan is outside in the marquee, rearranging the contents of the buffet table, and telling everyone she meets that she isn't with Warwick, they are just Seeing How They Go, while Iris and Ivan, by far the tallest couple in the building, talk with huge enthusiasm to other people with babies. Billy greets each of them like people he has loved his entire life. He asks if they would come and say hello to one another. Politely, very definitely, they say no. But his sisters do not know Billy. They do not know the love force that is Billy. He asks Netta if she would like an alcohol-free mojito, but explains it might be ten minutes because his cousin from Edinburgh hasn't the faintest clue how to squeeze a lime. "Oh, for fucksake," she says, rolling up her sleeves. "Let me do it."

He does a different version of the same song to Susan, only this time it's about canapés. "Wait. Who's running the kitchen?" she asks, interrupting. "Is it Netta?" As soon as she is reassured it isn't, she is heading in that direction. "Follow me, Warwick."

Meanwhile Billy simply approaches beautiful kingfisher-blue extremely pregnant Iris and says that all the little lanterns seem to have gone out and he wonders if she could light them. "Where are your matches?" she says. "Where are your candles?"

And he says, "Oh. Bottom cupboard. In the kitchen."

Goose watches his sisters heading toward the same room. His heart is pounding. He thinks he might actually be sick. Maybe he'll just go and sit quietly in the marquee with the godchildren until this episode is over, but Billy sends him his big-blue-eyed look that says, You think love costs nothing? You get off this one scot-free? Off you go. Go on after them.

The effect of his sisters being in the same space is like pouring liquid nitrogen on a perishable item and causing it to flash-freeze. Suddenly all those people who were happily chatting around the drinks table discover they have nothing to say. Those who do not leave become very still, so that even though they are technically in the kitchen they might as well not be.

When Susan sees Netta squeezing limes beside the sink, she says tersely, "Oh."

Netta glances up and finds Susan reaching for a tea towel, and says, "Oh" back.

Surely it's already over, and yet it seems to be a matter of pride to both that they will not be the first to leave. That each of them, now they are here, will in effect remain so supremely herself that the other will be driven out of the room. So Netta continues to wring the life out of a sackful of limes, while Susan hitches the tea towel around her waist and says elaborately, "Excuse me, please," as she heads toward the fridge to search for ingredients.

It is Robert who goes to Susan and hugs her and says how nice it is to see her again, while Warwick sidles toward Netta and attempts to greet her, though Netta is, of course, far more difficult to manhandle, partly because of the hat, but mostly because of who she is, and she says something terrible, like "Long time no see. At least we're not dead yet."

Meanwhile Iris swans into the room followed by Ivan, bearing their child, as if her sisters are not there at all, announcing to anyone who is listening (everyone) that she is only looking for matches and candles.

There is an electric moment when his three sisters see one another across the divide of lost years. What can they say? What set of words will heal such a rupture? Then Susan clocks Iris's belly. She picks up a J-cloth to prepare a work surface. And there it is. The telltale sign: her neck, her cheeks, even her arms are swamped with heat. She puts a hand to her mouth; her eyes flash with tears. "Oh, hello, Iris," she says breezily, as if she was speaking to her only yesterday.

Netta looks up. Does the same as Susan, but in reverse. Registers that she is soon to be an aunt for the second time and pales so fast she looks bleached.

"Everyone, this is Ivan," Iris says. "Ivan, this is everyone."

Maybe it's simply the silence, but they appear to speak very loudly.

Ivan tells everyone that he's so happy to meet them at last, even the people who are not directly related to the mother of his child. He has heard so much about them.

"No, you haven't," says Iris, lighting her candles.

"Susan is the same," says Warwick, laughing, but more as if to suggest it would be a good thing to laugh than because he is actually amused. "She often talks about them."

"No, I do not," says Susan. She whisks eggs with a certain amount of violence.

"Oh, Netta, too," says Robert.

"I so don't," mutters Netta. "Fuck off."

Goose keeps guard at the doorway. The tension is exhausting. He folds his arms, straightens his spine, plants his feet firm, at last filling his great big body. His sisters do not try to leave the kitchen. Fractured they may be, but he knows they have never been fainthearted. They continue to do what Billy has asked, as if his existence depends upon it. Ivan continues to weave between them, wondering how he might help. It occurs to Goose that if he hadn't just married Billy, he would fall in love with Ivan on the spot. In fact he would fall in love with Robert and Warwick as well. What good men his sisters have found, despite the troubled, complex one who fathered them.

Fifteen minutes later, Susan, covered with flour, her hair frizzing outward in an electrified nimbus, the tea towel still around her waist, is piling hors d'oeuvres she has knocked up, the tiniest curls of prosciutto, beaten egg and smashed olives on savory crackers the size of your fingernail, with something like a puff of whiteness on the top. Who knew there was prosciutto in the fridge? Who knew about the jars of olives? They taste like tiny pieces of salted cloud on a biscuit base. At the other end of the room Netta and Robert make mojitos—both alcoholic and virgin—at such speed they flow like water, while Warwick heads out into the garden with glasses on a tray, valiantly sweltering in his dickie-bow and velvet suit. "Drinks!" he calls. "Who would care for more drinks?" Everyone would.

Meanwhile Iris, twining her hair through her fingers, looking for all the world as if she has been traveling for years (she has been traveling for years), lights box upon box of tiny candles that flicker in front of her like a million pieces of gold on water. Ivan moves to the sink with sleeping Opal draped over his shoulder and begins to wash fresh glasses, which he dries and delivers to Netta. He fetches a pile of used plates and washes those, too, then takes them to Susan.

"Suzie!" Netta barks, from behind a jug of vodka and lime. "Do we have more ice?"

"How would I know?" snaps Susan.

"Look in the fridge."

"You look in the fridge."

"Iris, look in the fridge."

"I'm busy with candles."

"*Fine.* I'll look in the fridge."

And just like that, they are almost communicating.

What is it that makes Goose leave the house for a moment and head into the square? Is it relief? The love he feels for Billy? His sisters? A need to step outside his happiness so that he can see it for what it is? Or does he simply need a breath of air? It is a little of all of them. He slips out of the front door, past the overspill of guests on the steps and into the sunshine. He opens the gate and finds a bench in a corner. In the warmth of the afternoon, the trees give off a fragrance like mint, a sweetness that adds to the tranquility of the place, which seems—for just this moment—like the only place in the world. He watches the terraced house that is his studio and now his marital home, with all those people he loves inside it.

And he thinks, Do I deserve this? If I care too much, will I lose it? Like I lost everything before? Should I walk before it's too late?

And there he is, even on his wedding day, remembering Bella-Mae. Her thick black hair, her fingers like birthday-cake candles. The smell of her, sweetened and pungent. Her herbal tea.

He tries to imagine a version of the world without her in it. But to find that, there is so much to undo. Nevertheless his head has a go, like a film rolling backward. His sisters will not leave the villa in three separate boats. They will not see the horror that is their father's ultimate piece of work. They will not discover that Iris has been having a four-year on-off affair with Harry. Susan and Warwick will not separate; she will not fall wildly in love with Laszlo. Netta will not become fanatically obsessed by proving Bella-Mae's guilt. But it can't stop there. Once you start, time will have to keep spooling backward, reversing everything that has happened. Because, in truth, so much had already been put in place before he even heard Bella-Mae's name. All those years Goose worshipped his father, alongside his sisters, his breakdown, his spoiled exhibition, the crushes that led nowhere, the bullying at school, his mother's death when he was three. Or even his thirty-third birthday, when he realized he had now lived more years than she had and wondered if everything after this was simply on loan. There is so much he would have to undo, and where do you stop? He would have to keep unraveling the past until he was no more than a speck on the horizon. A broken promise that Vic and Martha made to each other one night as a result of meeting by chance on the number 68 bus.

But it is also true that without Bella-Mae Netta would not have given up the alcohol that was otherwise going to kill her. Susan would not have gone to Paris and worked first in a restaurant, then washing pots in a Michelin-star kitchen, followed by chopping vegetables until they were almost invisible, working her way month by month up through the kitchen, which means she would never have broken free from the lost place that had become her marriage. Iris, who could not stand to be seen for who she was, would never have gone traveling the world until she found her own two feet, and once she had found them, she would not have met Ivan, who is the size of a bear, while ironically living up a mountain and looking for real ones. There would be no Opal.

But most of all, if there had been no Bella-Mae, Goose would have stayed wiping the paint from his father's brushes, disturbed at night by images he couldn't understand, smoking weed to block out the devastating truth that his father was not an artist but a man whom he and his sisters had agreed to revere in an unholy pact, even though he had betrayed his son. He would not have seen that the missing picture existed only in their collective imagination and was worthless in every sense of the word. He would not have taken the canvas from Bella-Mae that day and made the choice not to set it alight but to yellow-wash it and begin again. To make a thing of beauty where there had been only pandemonium. He would not have picked up a pencil and looked at the strange visions of an imperfect world that used to haunt him. Which means he would not have been sitting in an all-night café at three a.m., celebrating the finishing of a new picture all by himself, when a man with a coat the size of a duvet came to buy coffee for a stranger on the street. And it is this thought in the middle of everything else—the thought of never meeting Billy—that is the one for which he would thank Bella-Mae most.

Netta did not die. Time was reversed.

He will never know the whole truth about Bella-Mae. When someone dies or disappears, we can tell stories about only what might have been the case or what might have happened next. And perhaps it is simply a question of control, but it is easier to imagine the very worst than to allow a space in which several things might be true at once.

Goose remembers flip-flops on Lake Orta. The sound they make on the pavement—thin and hollow, that *slap slap, slap slap*: nothing between your foot and the rest of the world except a flimsy piece of rubber. Well, how crazy, he thinks. How batshit crazy to think something so insubstantial could be enough to protect your feet and keep you safe, but in the end how beautiful. How brave. To lose the world as you know it, to live in a time that is suddenly upside down, the old rules gone, and yet to keep going, day after day, when all you have to help you is a little bit of a rubber on the sole of your foot.

And there he is again, back on Lake Orta. The reflected sky and hills held in the stillness of the water, the island floating like a memory in the middle amid tender shades of blue and pink and gold. The smell of honeyed cypress. A flow of petals in the garden. The frescoed walls, the glasshouse filled with lemon trees, the harps that no one could play. That heat wave of a summer.

Billy calls his name from the gate. He stands beside Goose's sisters and waves. Silvered afternoon sunlight slants down on them, the kind that makes each one look like the most radiant and separate incarnation of herself. Netta, who might have ruled the world if it wasn't for her demons, in her great big wedding hat; Susan—already holding the sleeping Opal—the Cordon Bleu chef, whose only problem was that she loved Netta so much she wanted to be the same; while pregnant Little Iris suddenly looks so enormous it occurs to him that she might give birth right there in the square.

Oh, you people, he thinks. For you I will endure anything.

"Gustav!" they call. "It's your wedding day!"

And it is.

29

Work of Art

It stands over thirty feet high, installed for the summer in the center of Hyde Park. You can spot it between the treetops from as far away as Lancaster Gate and the Royal Albert Hall. People say you can even see it from up in the air.

It's a stand-alone piece. Not one of her usual broken female body parts that will disintegrate over time, but an entire body cast in bronze, and for the first time in her career, this is a male one. His posture is in the style of an ancient Greek statue. He stands like Saturn, bare-balls naked, poised for action, in a position that could either be warlike or an invitation to dance, depending on how you look at life. His left arm is stretched forward, the palm wide open, the right raised high above his head, while one leg is bent slightly at the knee, the heel raised from the ground and the toes firmly planted, the muscles of the back leg taut. Close up, each of his feet is the size of a container truck. Cast in a gallery in Stroud, his massive head alone weighs 220,000 pounds.

But it's the body itself that is the wonder. Though made in bronze, each limb, each muscle, each curl of his hair appears to be not flesh and bone but layer upon layer of broken domestic objects. Look closely at his mighty hand stretched above your head, and the fingers are buttons and snapped-off paintbrushes. His muscular arms are really a big hat, a doll's head, feathers, an old menu, empty paint tubes and chipped teacups, the corner of an envelope. Around his torso twine children's shoes, diaper pins, a woman's bra, a pair of Ray-Bans missing a lens, a set of keys, a measuring tape, a mobile phone. His hair is tendrils of photo negatives and newspaper strips. Even the features of his formidable face are—when you look up—made not of eyes and a nose, but a great buildup of things like beads, a broken Rolex, a tin can, a bottle opener shaped like a naked woman, a half-eaten packet of sweets, a cigarillo. Buried in his forearm is an upside-down bottle of turps, a saucepan lid. Down in his calf lies a porn mag. Around his wrist is tattooed a snatch of words: *This is my truth.*

He straddles the earth as if he is either emerging from it or sinking down. It could go either way. Children play beneath him, hauling themselves happily over his giant toes, while adults sit in the empire of a shadow he creates across the grass. From nearby trees, people have already hung little tokens of their own: photographs of a loved one, notes with scribbled half sentences, ribbons, plastic butterflies and flowers, weather-ravaged toys, a baby bootie. And yet despite his magnificent size, there is a sense he is on the cusp of growing too big. One false move and those carefully balanced pieces might slip, until one crack joins another, then another, and in the end he falls to the ground like a shattered pot.

But for now he towers above the world on this beautiful summer evening. Awe-inspiring and unstoppable. The Homemade God.

Acknowledgments

Stephen Sondheim famously compares the writing of a song to the making of a new hat. The artist starts with a blank page. Yet by the end, there is somehow a thing where previously there was not. A hat, in fact.

Many people were kind enough to help me as I struggled to render and wrench this book from nothing. To listen as I tried to work it out, read early drafts (several times over), and offer extensive, thought-provoking notes. It is them I would like to thank most of all. Niamh Cusack, Christabelle Dilks, Damian Dibben, Sarah Edghill, Myra Joyce, Amy Proto, Emily Joyce, as well as my agent Clare Conville, Elizabeth Milne, and my editor's assistant, Katherine Cowdrey.

For advice about things legal, I am grateful to Christopher Stonehill and Lucy Middleton. Thank you, Julie Lyon, for things other, and to John Rodgers, for all your detective advice. Thank you to Gabriel Griffin for inviting me to your home on Lake Orta and answering all my questions over the last few years, to everyone at Casa Fantini, to Andrea Del Duca, and to the woman I do not know who smiled at me early one morning as she set out chairs in Piazza Motta.

Thank you to my editor from the very beginning, Susanna Wadeson, and to my U.S. and Canadian editors, Clio Seraphim and Melanie Tutino. Thank you to the Dial Press team: Leila Tejani, Chelsea Woodward, Madison Dettlinger, Whitney Frick, Avideh Bashirrad, Raaga Rajagopala, Richard Elman, Andy Lefkowitz, and Caroline Cunningham. Thank you to Kate Burton, César Castañeda Gámez, Polly Peraza-Brown, and everyone at Conville & Walsh. Thank you to my children.

Last, but not in the smallest bit least—thank you to my husband, Paul Venables. Who reads every word, including the ones that get cut by me later. Who allows these imaginary people to move in with us and come on walks, and doesn't complain when they pack their (sizeable) suitcases and turn up with us on holiday. Thank you for being my person.

Thank you for helping me make a hat.

ABOUT THE AUTHOR

RACHEL JOYCE is the author of the *Sunday Times* and international bestsellers *The Unlikely Pilgrimage of Harold Fry*, *Perfect*, *The Love Song of Miss Queenie Hennessy*, *Maureen Fry and the Angel of the North*, *The Music Shop*, *Miss Benson's Beetle*, and a collection of interlinked short stories, *A Snow Garden & Other Stories*.

Rachel's books have been translated into thirty-seven languages and have sold millions of copies worldwide. *The Unlikely Pilgrimage of Harold Fry* was short-listed for the Commonwealth Book Prize and longlisted for the Man Booker Prize. The critically acclaimed film of the novel, for which Rachel also wrote the screenplay, was released in 2023. *Miss Benson's Beetle* won the Wilbur Smith Adventure Writing Prize in 2021. Rachel was awarded the Specsavers National Book Awards New Writer of the Year in December 2012 and was short-listed for the UK Author of the Year in 2014. In 2024 she was awarded an honorary doctorate by Kingston University.

Rachel has written over twenty original afternoon plays and adaptations of the classics for BBC Radio 4. She lives with her family near Stroud.

ABOUT THE TYPE

This book was set in Garamond, a typeface originally designed by the Parisian type cutter Claude Garamond (c. 1500–61). This version of Garamond was modeled on a 1592 specimen sheet from the Egenolff-Berner foundry, which was produced from types assumed to have been brought to Frankfurt by the punch cutter Jacques Sabon (c. 1520–80).

Claude Garamond's distinguished romans and italics first appeared in *Opera Ciceronis* in 1543–44. The Garamond types are clear, open, and elegant.